Sharon K. Grosh

Lazarus Rising

Black Rose Writing | Texas

ISBN: 978-1-68433-503-9
PUBLISHED BY BLACK ROSE WRITING
www.blackrosewriting.com

Printed in the United States of America
Suggested Retail Price (SRP) $22.95

Lazarus Rising is printed in Cambria

*As a planet-friendly publisher, Black Rose Writing does its best to eliminate unnecessary waste to reduce paper usage and energy costs, while never compromising the reading experience. As a result, the final word count vs. page count may not meet common expectations.

"Choose a comfortable chair – you'll be on the edge of your seat! Beautifully written, starkly realistic, *Lazarus Rising* will remain with you long after you close the covers."
– Kathie Giorgio, award-winning author of *The Home for Wayward Clocks* and *If You Tame Me.*

"Thought-provoking and terrifying, *Lazurus Rising* carries us through a very real apocalypse, and in doing so. highlights the beautiful ingenuity, strength, and compassion required for humanity rise from the ashes afterward."
– Jeff Konkol, author of *Citadel of the Fallen.*

"What would you do to survive a worldwide apocalypse? Would you even want to, even if you were prepared for one? These are the questions Sharon Grosh explores in her suspense-filled debut novel, *Lazarus Rising.* A story told through the eyes of multiple characters, you will find yourself caught up in the minute-by-minute dangers each of them face, and the difficult choices each makes to stay alive after a single cataclysmic event irrevocably changes the world as we know it. Both a gripping story of human courage and a profound examination of what it means to be human after civilization collapses, this is a novel that demands multiple readings. I can't recommend it enough."
– Steve Searls, author of *My Travels with a Dead Man.*

"What would you do if this was your last day on earth? How would you survive a catastrophic world event? *Lazarus Rising* is an original novel that explores these and many other questions. A large array of complex and fascinating characters take the reader on a journey to explore corporate intrigue and in-fighting, Eastern philosophy, survivalist models, genetic engineering, biodiversity, and many other engrossing concepts. The book contains action-packed scenes, taut with tension and suspense and it also captures the small moments that help give life meaning. More than an apocalyptic novel, this book is about finding love and self-awareness and coping with life's struggles. *Lazarus Rising* is an enthralling and captivating read."
– Alice Benson, author of *A Year in Her Life* and *Her Life is Showing.*

All the characters portrayed are
fictitious and bear no relationship
to any person.

With much gratitude
I dedicate this
book to

John Heresy

who captured my
imagination and held
it for a lifetime.

LAZARUS
RISING

LUMING - 1

Luming remembered the last round of Pat O'Brien's famous Hurricanes. A New Orleans drink with enough rum in them to intoxicate a date whose name you wouldn't remember the next morning. Luming was never lucky that way. He remembered a very blurry trip to the bathroom. His first moment of cold sobriety was the moment he walked into his home, looking around at its beauty and realizing he needed to go to bed to work the next day. He had mortgage payments.

While he opened his eyes with sun rays beating into the room, Luming still tasted tropical flavors swirling in his mouth. He heard ringing. That never happened. It must be a new hangover symptom. Alcohol always interested him. He never experienced a hangover. He now realized head pounding, cotton mouth, and nausea as new phenomena.

Luming started to remember something about grabbing a taxi to the airport, holding Carry-Away Pat O'Brien Hurricanes in plastic glasses and finally dumping them at the curb before entering the airport. He still believed Hurricanes delivered warm tropical island breezes, sliding down your throat, creating generosity toward humanity.

The doorbell ringing continued and not politely. This is good, my ears are not ringing. Luming raised his head and shoulders, looked at the digital clock, 6:30. No one rings the bell this early. It must be an emergency. He threw on his jeans carefully so as not to change the height of his head to the floor too quickly and start his head throbbing again. He walked down the stairs, grabbing the railing in case he miscalculated the steps. He opened the door to Chris, his neighbor and casual friend who lived across the street. A little relieved, he knew that Chris understood, although he never saw Chris drink even a beer.

"Yo, what's up," Luming said in his practiced casual accent.

"I need you," said Chris.

"Come in and have coffee," Luming said. What's the problem?

"No, you do not understand. There isn't much time."

Chris's face looked stressed. "Okay, please come in. I'll get you tea then." Tea might have a more calming effect.

"Let me ask you a question," Chris said, his nose twitching as he stared at Luming.

Luming noticed Chris staring at him but said nothing. "But first, let's have some coffee instead of tea and then we'll talk."

Chris sat down, sighed a little, pulled out his laptop and worked while Luming made coffee. Both men remained quiet.

It irritated Luming. He only wanted to finish his PowerPoint. His head pounded to the typing. Luming asked if he wanted OJ. Chris just stared, looking right past Luming.

Chris then snapped out of his trance and asked, "Okay, so my question to you is, if this was your last day on earth, Luming, what would you do?"

Luming groaned. "You're kidding, you got me out of bed for that! All this time, I imagined you needed some kind of help."

"I do, I do," said Chris, "but you do too. We will be annealed, annihilated, and completely pulverized today."

"Oh, is that all?" Luming dropped into his chair. "I just did that for three days."

Chris sighed. "I understand that this is a strange question, but we're friends and you have to trust me now. If this was your last day on earth, what would you do?"

Luming said without hesitation, "That's easy, rob banks."

"Rob banks? For the money?"

"No, not for the money. For the thrill. What a rush. Walk in with no fear of jail."

"Seriously?" Chris said. He looked at Luming, typed a few words into his computer and then slammed it shut. "I can see you are, and understandably so, not taking me seriously. How about this, I will give you

$100,000 today, transfer it into your account? Does that sound like I mean it now?"

Luming sighed and said, "You are *feng tien*, crazy person. I just told you that money is not important to me."

"No, really, I'm serious," Chris stated slowly, looking into his eyes with an intensity that increased Luming's heartbeat. "I'll have the money transferred in the next ten minutes and you can look at your account and see it clear by the time you get to the bank to pick it up."

"Regardless of what you are cooking up, Chris, I have two critically important meetings today. I've got one where I'm presenting to an executive committee and have to send out my PowerPoint slides before noon. My co-workers are expecting me to change the PowerPoint presentation regarding the Lazarus project. Let's talk after I do that."

Chris bent over, touching his shoes with his hands and said to the floor, "You'd rather spend your last minutes on earth giving a PowerPoint presentation, this coming from the man who wants to rob banks?"

"Right," Luming said, "I get it. One PowerPoint presentation does not a life make. However, I still love my job, my car, my house, and I probably would say, yes, I am working a white-collar job and yes, I will probably die one day, with a laser pointer in my hand. My future is with my company. No, work is not my whole life, but it is a big part of it. I returned from partying and drinking with friends for three days in New Orleans. That has to count for something. I am the first generation in my family to have a job and make lots of money doing it," Luming said slowly, remembering something in his past when the words left his mouth. He knew that his actions already brought shame to his family, even though they did not know what he had been doing for three days.

"Let's go over this once more." Chris still crouched over. He slowly got up, breathing deeply as if breathing was part of his speech. The whole sentence became a big breath in and out, with the words floating out of his mouth hastily. "I'm transferring all the money I have in the world into your account, $100,000 to be clear, to show to you I am serious when I say we will die today. Instead of trying to show you the information that proves this, I will give you this money. That has to mean something."

Luming felt the coffee hit his veins back to the heart, to be re-pumped at a slightly faster rate, raising more than just a few millimeters of mercury and ending with heaviness in his gut. A prickly warmth crept into his hands, forming them into a scooped shape. Hangovers are all different, depending on the alcohol imbibed the evening before. This reaction was completely new to Luming. This was not a hangover. This was something else. The air was warm and slightly moist around him. He looked out to see snow. He got up, put his cup down and rested both hands on his stomach. His synapses sputtered a few more times and then he gave up resisting. It must be this sense of adventure that Chris was presenting to him that was creating tension in his body. Having the balls to rise to the occasion, no matter how ridiculous, was a game he used to play back in China. Risks made him better. He always could face challenging situations. When he came home with his handmade pants torn, bruises on his body and a smile on his face, his mother did not have the heart to yell at him.

Bottom line, he could not disappoint his team because they always counted on him. That was important. Get to work on the damn presentation. Last minute changes were imminent, never satisfied with the last draft.

Why was Chris' proposal stopping him so? One hundred thousand dollars was a ridiculous amount of money, but if Chris was being truthful about transferring all of his assets, that was something he could not ignore. Guessing it was the rum swirling around his head and the lack of food in his body, he continued to consider all the angles except this one. A Chinese heritage did not allow him the freedom he now experienced each day. He did everything that was asked of him. The reward was not being beaten. Individuality was discouraged, but they lived a comfortable existence. Some people disappeared but no one commented on it. Justice came from the knowledge that it would never happen to your family, as everyone did what authorities asked, in hopes of not being fired from your job, exiled from school, or worse, just disappearing. A duplex with a backyard, front porch, and an apple tree was an unbelievable luxury that Luming was starting to take for granted.

Luming got up to pour more coffee and touched Chris on the shoulder and said, "Let's go but save your money. The acquisition meeting is today's priority. I don't know what you have up your sleeve, but I'm in."

"Okay," said Chris, "the bank is not open until nine, so let's get us a decent breakfast on the way."

"I like that idea," moaned Luming as he stood up to experience an elevation change that increased the pounding in his head.

Chris jumped up. "I would love to be proven wrong. Now you must take the following," and he handed Luming a list including a flashlight, backpack, water bottles, aspirin, and various odd things like extra laptop batteries, cell phone connectors and extra electronic devices.

"Aren't we eating?" begged Luming. Chris made a strange face and his look of determination made Luming forget his question. Luming turned and went upstairs to grab his backpack he used for camping. That should satisfy Chris. He threw his laptop in, realizing he could send the changes while they sat over breakfast. Luming stopped and was reminded of the 22 carat jade locket his mother gave him the day he left. He knew the significance of it. She did not have a daughter to pass on the mother line. He always appreciated the meaning of the locket and knew one day, he would pass it on to someone he loved. That stopped him in his tracks. He better call her later on to see how she was doing. He promised to call her when he got back from his trip, but was too hungover. Oh well. Unless Chris was right about the end of the world scenario, he still had plenty of time to contact her.

Chris was already outside when Luming turned to lock the door, looking up at the beautiful apple tree leaning over into the neighbor's yard. It would be sad if his mother never visited.

JANE - 2

Jane woke up to the loud sound of something crashing against the window, probably a bird. She pressed a button, turning on the bright LED light and grabbed her Tool Box sitting next to the bed. The flat blackness coming through her large bedroom window verified that it was very, very early. Birds flew into her window, but that was during the day when they saw the reflection from the woods. She mentally went through a list of explanations, jumped up to turn on the outdoor light, and saw a Barred owl sitting on a tree branch. She adjusted her wings and flew away. Curious, owls never fly into the window. They would never make such a miscalculation.

After her initial reaction, she realized going back to sleep was not an option, feeling the adrenaline rushing through her veins.

"I can start the day. Yes, 4:45 is not too early," she whispered to herself and turned off the alarm. Gentle dialogue toward herself was a change she made a few years ago. Instead of her inside voice testing each activity for fault, she was patient with herself and explored her busy mind with a kinder, detached attitude. Talking to herself mindfully was one suggestion recently made by Dr. Blue, her therapist, to offset the constant flow of ideas passing through her mind non-stop.

Sorting through her meetings for the day, she already knew that two required no preparation. One required downloading the 510k for The Paradise Lost Company. Their operations resided in China. She knew their financials, research activities and patent positions by heart, but at this meeting of executives, someone would ask for a copies. Irrelevant information but so typical of executives.

"You have a complex job and you are constantly seeking solutions which do nothing to quiet your mind," Dr. Blue told her. "Your first step to recovering your life is to become an observer of yourself. Not an easy thing to do. So have a conversation with yourself, as if you are your best friend."

Wise words from a woman she trusted.

Jane got up, started the Keurig, showered, tossed her hair and applied makeup, all in fifteen minutes. She created the perfect blend of Tanzanian, Kicking Horse, and ten percent Hawaiian coffee. Today, she could feel it enter her bloodstream. It was like getting control of a truck sliding sideways down an icy road. With her busy mind, coffee did not wake her up, it slowed her down. It was a simple, pleasurable companion to her day, one of the few. I wonder what Dr. Blue would be asking me right now? She would first say, "besides your addiction to speed, you are addicted to ideas. You need to stop your mind race and start observing what it is about your first cup of coffee that brings you so much pleasure." So, thinking about her first cup of coffee, she caught herself talking to the coffee. She was having a conversation with her coffee. That can't be good. The next thing Dr. Blue would say, observe it and let it go. No judgement. At least I was aware of doing it and not blaming myself for engaging in such mindless behavior. Dr. Blue would call this progress. Good, I'll share this with her today.

Jane slipped into her navy blue suit and pale blue shirt, leaving the top three buttons open, revealing a shadow of cleavage. Thank God for suits. The negotiations she dealt with daily, always tricky and every detail, including what she wore, made a difference. The need to control the meeting required that she create the impression that she was not someone to mess with. The suit was her armor. The concept was dated, but it still gave her the confidence she needed to do well; another "companion" to support her in her day. She liked the concept of naming her morning experience.

Dr. Blue spent a lot of session time worrying about Jane's obsession with what Dr. Blue called a kind of survival neurosis or, more formally, Future Traumatic Stress Disorder. Jane was in therapy to help herself calm down, but she wasn't planning on revealing her private side. One day, she opened the Tool Box to grab a worn-out paper calendar to check for an alternative appointment time, and Dr. Blue made a comment. "Not doing e-calendars, Jane?" Right after she said that, Blue reached over and exposed Jane's charging socket on her Tool Box. The top of the Tool Box fell open and revealed rechargeable batteries of every size and the companion battery chargers, charging cords for iPods, iPads, iPhones, three laptops, and Kindles all organized in custom-sized pockets, carefully nestled in the cover of the kit. She had the smallest laptop and a Blackberry strapped to the sides using Velcro strips, charging from the inside of the case. Dr. Blue, normally a cool cucumber, seemed a little anxious.

"Where are you going with this, 007?" said Dr. Blue. In the past, she told Jane stories about the impact James Bond books had on her in high school. The James Bond series was on a list of books that were restricted. If they caught you reading books like Salinger's Catcher *In The Rye*, or Nabokov's *Lolita* or *Dr. No*, which she and her friends all read, they would suspend you. One decade later, '80s videos opened up pornography to a large male audience, and suddenly James Bond novels were no longer considered risqué. After that, students would download porn on the library computers. The real crime was the accelerating effect of a billion dollar, hardcore, pornography industry resulting in the loss of innocence on society. Dr. Blue was always popping up with long diatribes like that which Jane supported, since it left less time for her own examination. She found old feminist stories interesting and often wondered if anything really changed for women since those times. At least she suspected that men with power still maintained a private sexist attitude toward professional women like herself. To keep her career going, she still had to be man like in corporate America and beat them at each turn. She always exuded confidence, followed by well-documented success.

Remembering that hour with Dr. Blue and her inquiry about the Tool Box reminded Jane that she had to reschedule her next appointment. Maybe Dr. Blue could see her this afternoon after her last meeting? She moved the charged batteries from her home office into the Tool Box and checked each circuit carefully. Green lights told her everything was fully charged. She calculated that these batteries would remain charged for about one month, depending on the environment. Her home generator had five years with the fuel she stored in the back yard and the solar panels would run infinitely if they received 1,000 watts per square meter of energy transmitted by peak hours of sunlight. Of course, a nuclear winter would render solar panels useless. Preserving energy for an anticipated catastrophe was a secret she kept even from Dr. Blue. I wonder what questions she would ask me if she knew that! Dr. Blue went over Jane's background many times, not finding obvious triggers for the strange behavior she knew about. Her parents were not abusive, divorced, alcoholic, obsessively religious, overachievers, unhealthy, or poor. Her mother worked part time as an editor of a women's poetry journal just so she could be there when she got home from school. My childhood was bereft of drama and filled with boredom. So why was she spending hours in therapy?

Jane picked up the Tool Box and lowered it again to make sure that both security latches were fastened and the battery charger was still blinking green. All set. Now just pick out my shoes and I am off, 5:48. Enough time to pick up a breakfast at F&Gs and restock the bottled water supply she stored in her car. My day should begin nicely. The checklist in Jane's head had no problem working overtime, so each nuanced idea would either be deemed appropriate and necessary or saved for later.

"Perhaps a bit robotic," Dr. Blue would say, "but you are showing signs of being fully present in your daily activities." Dr. Blue did not understand the extent of Jane's preparations.

Heels were a necessary evil for day-to-day business. Walking ten miles home to safety in Prada shoes was crazy. She had to design armor that allowed her to survive a catastrophic event. She created a portable, compact uniform designed for survival. The shoes, comprised of high-density nylon and flexible supports, laid on top of her backpack. Imagine being so prepared that one could fling out a $1,200 Prada heel for a $2,500 custom-made shoe for walking in dangerous concrete rubble. The other necessary item in her survival kit was coveralls. Specially made for her slight figure, she designed a brown, non-woven, Dacron-insulated and waterproofed jumpsuit. Brown was a difficult color to create in Dacron, but working with the fabric manufacturers, she identified a biodegradable dye that was added to the final rinse of the process. The manufacturer's lab person she worked with was more than willing to send her ten-yard samples for her evaluation. She looked like a walking piece of shit, but she didn't care. The critically important thing in a catastrophe was to be camouflaged from anyone who might follow her.

Jane unlocked her car with the garage door opening simultaneously. She eased into the Beemer, hiking her skirt so it would not wrinkle, wishing she could put it on when she got to work. She loved this car more than anything. It was twenty-five years old with a stick shift, but it was in great running shape and considered a classic. This car ran on only one circuit board. It was that simple. She had a silver soldering tool and spare components like capacitors and resisters for anything that would eventually break down. From the outside, it looked like a well preserved black BMW, but inside, she had a turbo engine put in for power and the interior contained storage for gas and water and a massive battery capacity to charge her electronics. It was just the way she liked her life, outwardly simple and internally secretive. Her other survival vehicles, more robust, but the Beemer satisfied her daily commute needs.

After stopping at F&G to get her greasy fried egg sandwich to go, she entered the underground parking garage at work. The melted snow was reduced to water, showing tracks from cars that entered the building before her. As she got out of her car, she noticed the usual cars parked tight to the entrance of the building. Every morning there was a black Eldorado, a black Mercedes, and a brand-new-looking red M-5 tucked in the corner behind the last car. Executives, she murmured to herself. The efforts they made to avoid being in contact with unimportant employees. They drove to work early and got into an executive private elevator before untermench, the German word for subhuman, could track them down with questions. Employee interactions could be messy, and it was easier to avoid them all together. At 6:20 AM, the rest of the parking lot was empty, except for a few bluish-gray cars, Camrys or KIAs, parked farthest away from the entrance of this underground parking ramp. These cars, permanent fixtures, showed no watery boot tracks to them. She never saw the owners, but assumed they were the accountants, working all night, earning fewer wages than she did when she started with the company. How can that be? she wondered. The people who were responsible for ensuring each column added up accurately and rolled out daily, sometimes hourly, for critical decision-making, worked so many long hours for so little. It reminded her of Dan, her mentor at work, who kept asking, "Did you really expect it to be fair?"

But fairness was what she believed in. Everyone had an equal chance, taking turns, they favored no one child over the other. Was it better to be treated unfairly to understand how the real world worked? What were executives teaching their children? How to one-up the other guy, how to play golf and make backdoor deals? It was too much to speculate about. It boiled her blood and was disruptive to the goal she set for the day, so she had to set aside these internal conversations and move forward. Someday, there might be a reciprocity. Dr. Blue mentioned Karmic Justice as a departure for things of which she had no power to change. "I wonder what form that would take," she said out loud in a soft voice.

Jane took the elevator to the ninth floor, grabbed a cup of stale coffee and opened her office door. Office doors were scarce. There was a movement to 'cubicalize' all offices, except for the executive suite. Soon she would be sitting in a honeycomb with other people listening to everything she said.

Her office was nice, not too noisy, a good view of the park and far from her boss. No one wanted it, so she took it.

She quickly responded to several emails, sent from China. She needed to connect with Dr. Shin to double-check that everything was going well on his end. Next, she viewed recent Rosebud Motor activities, a Korean company she was tracking, and then moved on to tweak her five-page PowerPoint presentation, adding a few more assumptions regarding the NPV calculation. That done, she completed a few brain teasers and word games to keep her mind sharp for the day. Her male colleagues always made such a big deal about how long and hard they worked on their presentations. Creating the ultimate experience in a PowerPoint presentation was a modern parlor game. A 3D rotating pie chart with embedded algorithms would impress the management reviewing the PowerPoint. Content was important, but they rewarded entertainment. Jane preferred to be succinct and have answers to anything that might come up versus spoon-feeding all the information. This allowed her to spend the rest of the time with her *outside activities*, as Dr. Blue referred to them one day.

She studied the exit routes from her building. Walking the hallway in pitch black, feeling her way toward the Exit sign, would be a challenge. She had various flashlights instantly available, including an app on her phone, but it was still good practice to memorize the filing cabinets, desk configurations and doorways, just in case.

DAN - 3

Dan was having a hard time adjusting to his day off. He sat and looked around the kitchen and thought if he had retired three years ago, he would know exactly what he wanted to do today. He would have a routine. Doing something new just for a day made little sense. The main reason to retire now was his health. To reduce the wear and tear that stressful jobs have on the aging body. He did not need the money nor did he think anyone would care at work if he faded out of the picture. His ego left the building a long time ago, which gave him an immense advantage in the corporate setting. His niche these days was to help one struggling manager, using his years of executive experience as a way of giving back in some meaningful way. Most executives retired to serve on multiple boards for other corporations, writing off travel costs while paid to attend meetings in exotic locations. Executives also consulted, which required a confident attitude, an attribute they never found lacking. Dan didn't want to do to any of these things. Maybe there was something around the corner for him to do.

Dan's intuition used to tell him everything he needed to know until he lost everything he cared about. There were his trips to Asia, lasting three weeks, leaving his wife Laura to take care of their daughter Brenda with no one around that could help her manage. He cared about his family, but he also cared about everyone else. His colleagues in Asia were his highest priority and when they needed something, calling at odd times of night, he was available. Upon reflection, he might have even encouraged that. They were honest, hardworking individuals that he respected. He would do anything to help them deal with their problems. Dan recognized that working for a Fortune 500 company away from headquarters was an anathema. In China, meeting goals was not about your last performance appraisal, it was central to saving face for your family. They tied performance to the family's face, extrapolated to social standing, and had consequences of which Dan could not imagine.

Dan never quite understood until it was too late. In Laura's words, "You care for others more than you care for me." Brenda was ten when someone found Laura more interesting than he did. Coming home to an empty house the same day he was served papers made his trustworthy inner voice scream. Divorce went so quickly, it seemed like it was happening to someone else. He could have tried to save their marriage, instead he was wrapped up in shame. Laura wanted custody of Brenda and he wanted what was best for Brenda. Laura knew what was best for Brenda and he did not want her growing up in a divided home. Later, he realized that it was shame that drove his desire to look normal and move on. He faced it every day at work, where everyone had perfect marriages and stay-at-home wives.

A cooing sound coming from the other room snapped Dan into action. "I hear my granddaughter, who is such a pretty baby." Why Brenda feels comfortable having me take care of Elizabeth, I'll never know, he thought.

"I guess there is something I would rather do than work, if it involves this pretty baby," Dan said. With over six weeks of banked vacation, and a family life long gone, Dan acknowledged that a vacation day was well spent right at home with this amazing, pink-skinned, soft-smelling, cuddly little person. Brenda left for Washington DC early this morning and he was happy to help her out by even taking her to the airport. As he played peek-a-boo with Elizabeth, he stopped to scare her with a funny face that elicited the highest-pitched, squealing notes only audible to dogs. He was sure she knew that today was a play day. No language cards, music instruction or Chinese syllables, just this old guy who loved to make her laugh.

Elizabeth was reaching for her feet when the phone rang.

"Hello," said Dan. It was Jane.

"Hey, Dan. Hope I didn't disturb you."

"No, just taking in the essences of a lovely flower," he said, not sure what he meant, but thought it would throw Jane off enough to laugh.

"Oh, taking care of Elizabeth again," she summarized in a stressed, crisp voice that sounded like a hammer hitting a nail. "I'm sorry, but I'm calling to let you know that I will send my presentation for your review between eleven and twelve o'clock, as we discussed."

"Jane, you don't need me to review anything. You'll be fine. Are you getting nervous about the meeting?" There was a long pause, typical of a conversation with Jane. She processed each question carefully before answering.

"No," was all she said.

Jane and Dan never spoke much about their mentor relationship, but it just seemed to work. Jane was the ultimate street fighter. She was effective, aware of everything around her and rarely off her game. As long as it was a game, Jane managed beautifully. She never worked on anything over five hours before it was needed and many times much less than that. He recently saw her in action during an all-day meeting where she had to present. She had a few slides hitting key points. She led the discussion beautifully, ending with unanimous agreement. During the rest of the meeting, she tracked everything that was said without glancing at distracting emails, briefly adding only what they needed, without the normal grandstanding everyone else seemed to favor. Everyone was used to her by now and realized she had a talent for getting it right, while being odd about her personal interactions. She made a strange comment one day to him that if the world would end as they knew it, what purpose would it serve to be working on PowerPoints the night before a presentation?

"Jane, I'm getting ready to feed my granddaughter whose skin is the texture of a flower petal. She reminds me of that opal that reacts to the environment. For example, since the phone rang, she is now turning darker, and she's shaking her head side to side. Can we make this quick? I'm getting behind in my cooing and cuddling. There is this art form of anticipating her needs before she gets fussy. It won't be long now, before she needs something," said Dan.

"I'm hoping to make this quick. I was reading Rosebud Motor's blog this weekend, that Korean company I told you about. I found some strange activity," said Jane in her softer voice. Dan left a long pause before he spoke.

They spent most mentoring sessions on brainstorming new ideas and sharing personal experiences. Dan knew Jane offended people. Her brain worked overtime and her mouth spoke directly from the brain center. She did not chat as Midwesterners seemed to be so adept at, but she had an ability to draw people into a deeper conversation within minutes of meeting her. It was Dan who spent time with her, showing her ways she could calm down the brain and also find a softer voice in which to speak. The focus on softening the voice helped most people slow everything down and be a more effective listener. A softer voice was more pleasant and created a more inviting experience.

"I didn't know you knew Korean," Dan said. He was trying to recall if it was Mandarin or Cantonese that she spoke.

"No, I don't speak Korean, but I can auto-translate about a hundred words accurately. This morning, there was an even larger increase in volume around the same blog. A sudden fifteen-fold increase. I was seeing the same words used many times, describing disaster. The top words I translated here were 'Catastrophic, Artificial Earthquake and No Peace.' It's a little concerning Dan. I also found that NSA operatives closely studied Rosebud Motors and I don't know the reason yet. Wait, something's come up. I'll call you back," and she hung up as abruptly as she started.

"Yep, that is Jane. A bundle of brainy energy," sighed Dan, eager to get back to Elizabeth. At first, he vehemently disliked mentoring. If he had to mentor someone, he made it clear on the first day that he did not have a lot of time to do this. He would say things like, "Let's make this short. Tell me what you need." At least he held back and did not say, "Get the hell out of my office." It soon became clear to everyone that these meetings weren't working and HR gladly took his name off the list of mentors. He never mentored again until Jane came along. Dan later found out that Jane requested him and he was surprised when this relationship with her developed past the first meeting. HR called one morning, which was very irritating since he was clear that he only accepted afternoon HR conversations, allowing him to make a beeline to the door if needed.

"Well, I'll meet with her once and then decide," he said to the nicest HR woman he knew. "Frankly, most women cannot stand me. I'm sure she has the wrong person." He agreed to meet the next day, and that was when Jane started as Dan's mentee.

Jane walked in that day, slim and toned, wearing a navy blue suit, pale blue shirt open suggestively and tawny legs without nylons, fit into high heels that seemed bound to her feet. Some women can wear heels, but very few can pull it off successfully. Jane wore heels like a gazelle, walking around the building all day with a delicate stomp.

She appeared at the doorway and seemed to more than fill the office without having entered yet. Her presence preceded her with a light citrus aroma, maybe mixed with tarragon or thyme. She was five eight-ish, her head sat on top of her neck and not forward. She seemed relaxed and present with Dan.

"Hi, my name is Mrs. Dalloway," she said with a wink to the literary reference.

Dan got up, offered her a chair. "Mrs. Dalloway is a character in a book written by Virginia Woolf, dated 1925, and the response to your introduction is, My dear, it is good to finally meet again."

"Right," said a beaming Jane. "I knew you'd pass."

"Hmmm, I'm relieved," said Dan, "I never want to fail," he stated with heavy sarcasm.

Reflecting on that day was amusing to Dan. Little did he know he signed up for over two years with Jane. Actually, the relationship was mutually beneficial as Jane helped him out many times. He was now growing a global business with a twenty-four percent topline growth last year and this year, the bottom line was also improving. Jane did not even work for him, but she often provided him with sometimes off-beat, but relevant information that translated to him making great business decisions. She picked him and sometimes he wondered why.

She had quite a few peculiarities. She was obsessed with electronics, most of which he could not help but observe. She carried two black cases, one reminded him of a tackle box, fitted with a shoulder strap that was long enough to cross over her chest and separate her cleavage. Those power blouses she wore had just the right reveal to flaunt some colorful underwear that also carried a faint flower essence. The other case was actually a backpack that she also took everywhere. The backpack alone made it seem like she was preparing for a mountain climb rather than meetings in executive offices. He teased her about it once, hoping for more information, but she came back with a cool banter without more information. That was Jane, artful avoidance of anything that did not fit in her purview.

Not surprising, the executives loved her. She communicated briefly, fielded all questions, and led them right where she wanted them while still letting them feel like it was their idea. Her style was effortless. She never seemed to try hard at anything she did or the stress never showed, which was why their phone call struck him as unusual.

Mentoring meetings with Jane were filled with such content and wisdom that Dan sat back and studied her rather than paying close attention to what she was saying. He used to debate her through a kind of dialogue, trying to trip her up or find a hole in her proposals. But no, she was tight, and with no frills. "She leaves you wanting," confided an executive one time to Dan, "I will always sit up and listen to her."

Dan put down the phone and smiled at Elizabeth and sent her his invisible kisses. She appeared to think the kisses lived inside bubbles she burst with her fat, chubby hands when they floated over her head. Dan could not remember when Brenda was little. The past was a blur. He he only remembered a strong need to support his family and provide for their future. How could he have missed such an important time? Laura would have answered that question instantly. She always had those answers, and he felt helpless when she fired back at him. He did not even recognize himself when she spewed angry accusations at him. Job interviews, decisions and a crazy job filled with unknown expectations from his management were the foreign country he traveled in. Laura had no compassion toward the anguish he felt about his job and growing responsibilities. It filled her with resentment that her job was reduced to taking care of Brenda. Once divorced, Laura left the state and moved away with little contact. Dan was left with his muddling thoughts about guilt and thought Laura and Brenda were probably best without him. He faithfully made childcare and alimony payments on hopes that would bring them back. The last time he saw Laura was at an art demonstration on YouTube, sponsoring a watercolor paint company that she founded. Thankfully, it was Brenda who sought him out, once she turned eighteen. Granted, she was heavy with child and needed support, but they bonded immediately and he skipped the step of fatherhood and became a grandfather instead. His gratitude for having this second chance was never far from these thoughts. He kissed Elizabeth on her neck and made a bubbling sound with his lips that sent her into a lower pitched squeal easy on the ears. "Let's go to the park, little one," said Dan.

He looked outside to see what kind of day it was and saw a white layer of snow on the ground. He then breathed out the word "Damn," when he saw Betty, his neighbor, walking across the street toward his house, carrying several bags and using a cane. She wasn't a bad person, he thought. She was attractive and friendly, but recently, he felt a strong need to do less for others and more for himself. This was his Lizzy-day. He let some time pass until he answered the door with Elizabeth in his arms and swinging her around to get her to fuss a little. Elizabeth just smiled and reached out to Betty when she walked into the house. Dan pulled her back into his chest.

"Well, I see you have the little one today," she said, stating the obvious as most mid-westerners do.

"Yes," he answered, keeping it short and simple.

"Well, I saw your car in the driveway and said to myself, Dan must be home playing with his darling granddaughter again."

"I am," Dan said gruffly, but smiling so she would think it was a joke. He didn't want to hurt her feelings, but he wanted to show to her he was not in a social mood.

Betty asked, "Have you seen the paper this morning? I am curious about a development in plant genomics."

Betty had multiple degrees in various sciences, including Plant Biology, and she was some kind of sensei-teacher for a martial arts group. Apparently, she was unique, being the first woman to qualify for teaching her kind of martial arts. Dan recalled getting lost in their conversation about her background as Betty could be in a one-sided conversation for a long time without a break. Dan did not have the interest nor the time to talk, so he cut her off right away and said, "Yes, that sounds interesting, Betty. Hey, can you come back later? I have to get out before it snows again to pick up some things for Elizabeth. Sorry about that." There, I did it.

"Great," said Betty, "since you are going out, you can give me a lift to my studio on West Nile Street. I twisted my ankle yesterday, and I am supposed to be teaching in half an hour and I don't think I can make it on foot. Sorry, I should have been more clear about my dropping by, but I live alone. It's not always easy to live alone, especially when you need help from someone else. I'm feeling a little agitated today and am slightly overwhelmed with this foot. Hello, teaching Aikido with a bad ankle feels so weird. Hopefully, you can help me out."

Dan felt terrible. "No problem, Betty. We can easily give you a ride."

"Appreciate that, Dan. You've paid your karmic dues for the day. For that, my students will be very grateful to you." Lizzy was interested in Betty's glass bead earrings and necklace with feathers all in various purple or blue hues. Betty leaned over as Lizzy reached for them, pulling away from Dan's chest. "Aren't you the curious one, Lizzy?"

"Okay, I can get us ready," said Dan quietly. She even called Elizabeth by his special name for her, Lizzy. She was something else. As he looked around the house, he decided getting out with Lizzy would not be a bad idea. He moved into action. He changed her diaper, then bottles of milk and juice and everything else went flying into the big baby bag Brenda gave him when she left. Dan compressed an additional stack of diapers in the outer pocket and was ready to go. You can never have too many diapers. Something he learned in the class he took before he started to babysit Elizabeth. A quick look at his badly torn jeans forced him to do a quick change and in twelve minutes, he was ready to escort Miss Betty to her class for a karmic advance, whatever that was.

"It's worth it," he said to himself. He recalled that at ten months, it was good to expose babies to different people, and Betty was different.

Dan drove a simple Ford Explorer that could make it through most snowstorms if needed. It had plenty of room for a baby carrier in the back. The color was racing green, the only homage he had to making his vehicle a little sexy. Dan put Lizzy into her seat and all of Betty's bags on the floor, laying her cane on the far seat. Betty piled in the back seat next to the baby and started entertaining Elizabeth with sounds, hand movements and baby words. Dan was still jealous as Lizzy laughed at Betty. He then sat back, took a big breath and decided he would relax as he realized how bad jealousy made him feel. He never realized that this was not just caretaking but ended up being a constant reminder of his own issues. He should appreciate the fact that Betty was good with Lizzy.

He made a u-turn in the street going east and the morning sun momentarily blinded his eyes. The phone rang, disrupting his concentration in making the turn. It was Jane again. There was an unusual trailing in her voice and she awkwardly asked, "Sorry to cut you off so quickly. What are you doing?"

Jane was not someone to chit chat and Dan asked her if she was okay.

After a long pause, she said, "I am not sure what's going on."

"Is it the Rosebud bloggers?" said Dan. "Maybe you're overthinking it." As Jane's voice was being beamed through the car speaker phone, Dan realized that Betty stopped playing with Lizzy and was listening.

"Dan, I can't explain this. It would sound too weird even for me."

"What's too weird for Jane? Now I'm interested!"

"Something very different is going on," said Jane. "Do you remember my visiting a survival group a year ago to learn about what they were doing? I was following their blogs last evening and recognized the name Lazarus, used several times. Not unusual, Lazarus is a common code name for special projects around here, and I guess it also draws survival groups to using it. Initially, I was curious, but did not have time to pursue it. This morning, I was on a call with our lab guy in China. He was saying due diligence of the seeds we were testing produced plants with growth spurts five times over the medium average in the first two weeks, compared to the last three years. Not only growth spurts, but increases in chlorophyll, root anchorage and leaf size. I was impressed and feeling good about my intuition about this deal. If you recall, the team also called the deal 'Lazarus' to keep the acquisition confidential, even though it is not a public company."

"So, what about the survival group?" said Dan. "Or are you worried we cannot work fast enough to make this acquisition? I'm not sure of your point here, Jane." When stressed, Jane often made several divergent thoughts that she eventually wove together, but Dan wanted to speed it up.

"Yes, it's neither. It's about this call to China. About five minutes into the call, I felt an electrical surge in the line. It was like my earpiece was getting warmer and then I felt an electrical shock. It was brief and so was the warmth, but Chin Lou also felt it and commented on it."

"That's it? I still don't get the connection," said Dan, feeling irritated. "Sorry, but I'm running Betty to Aikido right now. Can we talk later?"

"Aikido?" said Jane, "Aikido. There are only a few places that teach it around town. I became a Sandan when I turned twenty-one and studied under Professor Dun at the U during my last two years of graduate school.

In fact, my minor was in Aikido and mental health." There was a pause and then Jane asked, "Are you with Betty Sapphire?"

"In the flesh," said Betty. "Jane, I think we met at my sangha at the university about six years ago. The terrace overlooking the Japanese Garden on the north side of campus. "

"I recall that very well," said Jane. "The dedication you made for Ing-sensei was an auspicious moment for everyone that attended. Remarkably, the whole community could pay homage to sensei's life and his contributions toward humanity. Well, Betty, it's a small world and everyone worth knowing knows Dan, I guess."

"Yep, I am just starting to realize this about Dan," said Betty from the back seat. "Hope to see you at one of my classes, Jane. I could not help but overhear your conversation about plants growing in China. Sounds like their GMO research has improved. Did you see the article in the paper today about arresting individuals crossing the border with five pounds of GMO seed from Canada?"

Jane paused. "That's very interesting, Betty. We are dealing with that very issue right now. I must check out your class one of these days. Talk to you later, Dan. My Lazarus contact is calling me. What a crazy morning!"

Dan turned off his phone, now realizing all phone calls synced into his speaker. He noticed a quiet moment of silence until...

"Dan, you have such interesting friends," said Betty.

"I was mentoring Jane, but now I'm someone that she bounces ideas off of," stated Dan. "She's definitely an interesting woman and I believe capable of managing a lot of stuff successfully. When I first met her, she was pretty intense and a little abrasive. I said to myself, here's someone who needs to take a break. She was finding meaning in everything she experienced and could not filter herself. Over the two years I've been mentoring her, I learned to stop worrying about her and just be there to listen. Since then, she has changed little, except she seems to be a better listener."

Once Dan parked the SUV, Betty opened the door and two students ran up to help her out of the car. She graciously discouraged any help and moved with considerable agility. Dan admired her perseverance and wondered about her age. She never complained once about her ankle. She waved at the line of students waiting for her outside the studio and waved at Dan. The students bowed and appeared to be saying something which she responded to and returned the gesture with three bows. Dan thought their actions looked interesting. He wondered why he had such a hard time liking Betty. Did she have to talk so much?

Dan turned back to check on Elizabeth who was already asleep. He laughed at his initial reaction to Betty coming over and observed that sometimes an interaction can end too quickly. Oh well, thought Dan, there'll be plenty of time to learn more about Betty. Maybe he could ask her over for dinner sometime.

He left the car running with the heater on while he checked emails with an urgent message from Martha to call Brenda.

"Damn, what is going on?" Dan sighed. Why does this morning seem different? Was it his day off? Wondering what Brenda wanted, he called her and left a message. She was probably in the air by now.

LOIS - 4

It was a nice morning to walk Suri. A light snow fell during the night. The air was fresher than the day before. Snow air, wondered Lois. Is that a thing? She slammed the front door loudly behind her. Maybe that will wake up her brother, Clark, who crashed on her couch at 3:00 AM. She didn't mind too much, but this was definitely becoming a pattern. He had his own inheritance and could afford to buy a nice house.

She noticed another large cobweb she removed two days ago. It was tedious, removing spider webs without killing the spider and transporting them to another location. Each time she moved the spider several blocks away, a new spider started building the next day, in the same spot, completing a full web in forty-eight hours. She would then take pictures of the new web pattern to determine if the pattern was specific to one spider or the environment. Each web design was captured using a 3D camera and mathematically measured using an algorithm she wrote. She hoped to compare the two webs visually and mathematically.

Her brother presented another pattern, but she wisely did not study him because humans were way too complex to draw conclusions that have any merit. She checked the signs of autism but thought he also could have traumatic brain injury, symptoms were similar. Lois often asked her mother about this but she just shrugged it off. "Always, asking me embarrassing questions, Lois. How can you even think I dropped him as a baby?" She worried that he was headed for a difficult life and one which she realized would impact her life. Now that her life was more stable, she might help him.

Lois observed patterns all her life. Once she realized she could use this passion around her PhD thesis, she was committed. Developing special algorithms of non-human life forms was easy, and these arrays were a major emphasis of her graduate work. No two situations were identical, which required a sophisticated approach and clear-cut measurements of whatever she was observing. She burnt out Andy, her programmer, with too many divergent ideas. At least she had the wisdom to hire someone to write programs for her. Now she had to find someone new.

What was it about walking the dog that gave her so many good ideas? Suddenly, Suri stopped. She would bark at any speeding car coming toward them and continued to bark at the car until it was a block away. This morning was no different. Satisfied that she upset the driver, Suri came back to a heeling position by her side, looking smug about her recent conquest. Lois never got used to Suri's game, but she was also proud of her self-actualized activism.

So in anticipation of hopping on the 7:45 bus to the U, Lois moved Suri along, walking fast. Suri followed her tight, without a leash. Both of them mimed the leash, since leash laws became instituted. Suri heeled right next to her left leg and when Lois stopped, Suri would sit. Suri was always very excited about this walking spoof, wagging her tail and looking up at Lois when someone walked toward them. She never sniffed other dogs or jumped on people. Lois was proud of Suri's behavior; Except for her chasing cars speeding toward her, she was perfect.

Suri always exhibited special qualities. One day when Suri was a puppy, she refused to go for a walk. Lois pulled her out the door. She sat and whimpered. Lois looked around and could see nothing wrong. "What's up, Suri?" she said. Suri turned to the door and Lois had to follow. That day, for no other reason than monitoring Suri, Lois stayed home. Suri sat in front of the TV with her head down with that sad Golden Retriever face. Evelyn, her college roommate, came downstairs at 9:12 AM and said, "Lois, turn on the TV," and quickly left. Lois found the remote and turned it on to frantic newscasters barely composed enough to explain how two large buildings, the World Trade Center, had planes sticking out of them. September 11, 2001, was the date that Suri lay in front of the TV all day without moving. She finally went outside at 3:00 PM. Like most people, it took Lois a long time to recover from the events of that day, but she never forgot Suri's odd behavior. She did read a small article on page ten of the paper, three months later, stating, statistically, 15.5% more people stayed home that day. Maybe Lois thought, they also have highly sensitive dogs like Suri. She started playing with these statistics, trying to plot out these patterns, but it quickly became very complex. With her recent successes with algorithms, she needed to revisit that question again.

After completing a Bachelor of Arts in Mandarin and Math by the time she was twenty-one, she was pulling together her PhD thesis, completing classes and teaching. Now after three years of graduate school, she was paid as a TA and just moved into her newly rented house with an option to buy. Clark showed up six weeks ago when she first moved in, looking for a place to sleep. He stayed for two weeks and then disappeared until now. Lois thought he probably found a woman who liked him enough to invite him to live with her, but eventually realized his salient enthusiasm for things he knew nothing about.

Today, Lois had a light schedule and wanted to get into the language lab early. She hated to wait for space, so showing up at 8:00 AM ensured that only a few people would be there.

The students that showed up early were studying Arabic. She liked the sound of Arabic. It was a soft language and was a beautiful contrast from the crisp sounds of Mandarin. It was an old language, almost as old as Mandarin. Cantonese was a young language in comparison. Lois translated the Chinese expression, "Learning is a treasure that will follow its owner everywhere" into three versions,

学习是永远跟随主人的宝物

學習是永遠跟隨主人的寶物

Xuéxí shì yǒngyuǎn gēnsuí zhǔrén de bǎowù].

And in Arabic, she translated," التعلّم هو ثروة سوف تتبع صاحبها في كلّ مكان.

There was something about matching language with the wisdom it held that inspired her to work on the older languages. It was like the written characters held the wisdom. At least those old civilizations used language a lot more to embark on philosophical truths.

As she walked back into the house, she grabbed a brush, took off Suri's collar and brushed through her silky palomino-colored hair. All of Lois's awareness was focused on soothing Suri with the brush. It was a nice reprieve from thinking about her lab, her brother, 9/11 and Suri liked it too. Finally, she was propelled into action. Grabbing her backpack, she headed out the door. Suri, with a running start, ran across the room and put her paws on Clark's chest, resulting in multiple curse words all strung together like 'S', the F-bomb, and J-F-C, all coming out of the mouth of a man who had a remarkable hegemony of language even after sleeping on a couch.

"Yep, I gotta go," shouted Lois. "Clark, please, if you leave this time, let me know where you are. You can easily do this, and I would be thrilled if you did this. Find a place and let me help you move in. Hopefully, you haven't burned up this month's trust money already. It's only October 21st. I'll return around seven and hope you'll have made some progress. I have a lot of writing to do tonight, so no disruptions. Get a job around something you like doing. You are good with kids. Check into being a health care aide. There are some positions at the U you might find interesting. Take care, and bye-bye." He was still sleeping and heard nothing she said.

With a squeeze to Suri's left flank, Lois stepped out the front door and jogged to the bus stop.

MICHAEL - 5

The morning sun came up over the flat horizon filled with prairie grasses. The view from Michael's floor-to-ceiling windows was dramatic, casting a warm, rosy red color on their shimmering white bedspread. Michael noticed the light dusting of snow laying over the top of the grasses, not bending them over. White clouds were emerging from the periphery, moving toward the center of the crimson sunrise, creating a living oil painting. "The day doesn't look like it knows what it's going to be," Michael mused out loud. He sat down in his favorite chair and watched the clouds change shape. The sun was rising with strong rays beaming lower in the horizon, typical of late fall when the sun came up low, but intense. It was as if the sun was passing straight through the windows into his soul. The warm rays encompassed his heart, and he felt his whole body relax.

The warm feeling passed and Michael looked at his watch realizing he might have delayed too long. Taking a pause from his morning routine was not typical for him, and he needed to find the time to make up for that. "Routines are always good," said his mother, speaking to him through his racing mind. He learned organizational skills and project management from her. She managed three boys, a part-time job and his father who complained about everything. Each day, when the boys came home with their backpacks full of books, she had them sit in the kitchen and do their homework right there in front of her. She baked cookies, cakes, or bread. She was not subtle about bribery and found it very effective. Another skill he gained from her.

Her management of Bud, his dad, was her other important task each day. Bud loved to chide the children, embarrassed them by calling them pussies, implying that they were obeying a *woman* rather than a real man. She ignored him and overruled anything he said if it stood in the way of her sons' battle for a better life. Every time Michael sat down to study, he heard her encouraging voice and he could taste her warm oatmeal raisin cookies. Studying the law passed from his mother's determined heart through to his insatiable sweet tooth.

He also knew he wanted more. He wanted even more than what his mother wanted for him. He wanted to be a wealthy lawyer, with power and a family that would propel him to the apex of a corporation. His mother gave him the means, but he had the vision that filled in the gaps to motivate him to being the very best. He was in the top 2% in law school, which required careful, well-crafted approaches to learning and an unscrupulous attitude toward his fellow law students. Each student needed to push back, allowing Michael to advance one more step to being the top student. His antics were subtle, sublime, and secretive. Those were also characteristics that make a good corporate lawyer.

Some days, when he looked out his windows, he would just think the rolling prairie woodlands surrounded by deep woods were worth all the gold in the universe. It was ironic that hard work gave you what you wanted but did not give you the time to enjoy it. Michael found pauses like this coming up more frequently. It must be a sign of aging and his retirement date looming over him. What would it be like to get up and not have a job to go to? That thought snapped Michael into action. "I will not pasture like a racehorse, at least not yet!" Michael said out loud.

Cutting workers over age fifty was a legal issue and handled delicately. Eliminating all of the highest-paid salaries was not legal, but it was an effective way to restore the bottom line. Michael made sure he was part of the committee that carefully crafted guidelines for headcount reduction. The legal ramifications of age discrimination could seriously the company's reputation. He was only fifty eight, but he even felt uncomfortable about removing highly paid professionals. In anticipation of corporate cutbacks, he made sure that they considered him indispensable to anyone who made HR decisions. Job elimination from reorganizing groups was a way to eliminate people in his age bracket. This program alone resulted in significant savings to the bottom line and made room for the promotion of newer employees, improving the retention of millennials.

The legal department of most Fortune 500 companies operated silently and depended on lawyers like Michael to oversee the big picture that kept them out of trouble. His plan was when the time came for him to retire, it would be on his terms. Preferably a scenario where they asked Michael to stay on, maybe begged him to stay one more year, knowing of his talent in saving the company from legal issues.

Michael grabbed his coffee, scrambled out of the chair, looked at the armoire and realized it was navy blue suit day. The navy suit, shirt and tie, neatly hung, on the butler with his socks and shoes, complements of Marcella's attention to detail. The combination of a navy and pale orange tie that contrasted with the perfectly flat-ironed, bright orange shirt was a little loud for his taste, but a good choice for the people that he would meet with. Passing barbs with his clients about his bad taste in clothing usually led someone to come up with the appropriate lawyer joke to add to the frivolity of the room and created the perfect environment of trust and humor.

Lawyer jokes were a great way for a lawyer to insert himself early in the meeting as the center of attention. Michael believed his approach was good and provided a nice release from serious legal work. He wanted to appear like a real guy, so important to the Midwestern culture. His added value was in herding the cats and the dogs and especially the vice-presidents who often stated that no lawyer would run his business. Michael always showed support for their hair-brained ideas until it was necessary for him to trek up to the CEO. It was a delicate dance for him, but if required, he would show how poorly conceived a deal was and have to make specific changes to make it happen. No one could win an argument if one carried the "I am here to protect the company and not take it down with this one deal" torch. Michael's arguments were lock tight and obscure. It was nearly impossible to win an argument against him. Everyone soon recognized that it was best to learn the legal way, create an alliance with Michael and make sure each step met with his approval. Yes, few VPs got past him, but those that did eventually paid for it.

Michael was his best in a meeting behind a closed door. He was always willing to work out a compromise to meet the business' needs, but only if the client was appropriately obsequious and willing to work out the deal his way. Anyone not familiar with deals was his worst enemy. Their ignorance constantly challenged him and caused him a lot of wasted time.

The final cup of coffee finished and his poly-wrapped shirt and tie taken off the hanger, he punched through the sleeves and tucked in the shirt. He looked at his belt, which needed replacing soon. I wonder if I purchased Gucci. If that would that be too much? Gustaf, his trickiest VP, was a well-known Gucci aficionado and would recognize anyone with good taste. Was mimicking him a good thing? Michael carefully cultivated the impression that he was an average guy. It was rare for him to bring up his wealth. His car was average and rarely was anyone invited into his home. Alternatively, Gustaf was unabashedly proud of everything wealth brought him as he parked his new red M5 BMW as close to the door into the building as possible. Maybe a bond would develop, sharing mutual love for Gucci in this desert of bad Midwestern taste. He might make a good choice. He would call Karen, his clothing assistant, to buy him a Gucci belt from Sax's for his next meeting with the VP.

As he finished dressing, he looked out the window at his uninterrupted view. Housing developments and power lines were miles away. The creek winding across his backyard always reminded him of having an independent water source in case of a catastrophic event. This did not come cheap.

Michael's passion for the law and what it could do for him included creating a series of related city council decisions in his district that protected his 34.6 acres. This included preserving the view surrounding his estate and creating 60 acres of dedicated parkland. He and Marcella also made, anonymously, a large donation that ensured that there would be no builders buying land surrounding his home and spoiling the view.

For Marcella, it was never about buying the biggest house in the most prestigious neighborhood. Originally, she had to convince Michael to buy a large track of land, as she loved nature. She said he could create an architecture masterpiece, if he wanted to, which he also did. Marcella was so thrilled at building their home on preserved prairie land that she also did what she could after they wrote the contract to make sure this all happened. She followed each local contractor and development proposal to make sure nothing happened to Michael's deal. It also took up a lot of her personal time, but she loved it. They both wanted to secure their legacy and their children's future.

As Michael prepared the finishing touches of his well-appointed accoutrement, adjusting his cuff links and watch, he had a feeling that his moment of peace had passed. His started reviewing the deals he was working on for the day and one email he needed to write. Running a little behind was not a good way to start, but he had several ways to fix that. Marcella left early, about 4:00 AM, to make rounds before her surgeries. She was off by 3:00 PM and they would not see each other until dinner, 7:30 PM at their favorite restaurant. Once the kids left the house, Marcella decided that since they could afford to eat out, it would be easier to eat out most weeknights. Then they could focus on their time together and the kids could join them whenever it worked out for them. They also would come home to a clean, serene home with a well-appointed kitchen, without messy dishes and pans that needed washing.

He grabbed his suit jacket, picked up his briefcase, and opened up the door to the garage. He unlocked his car door and the garage door opened simultaneously. This recent installation worked well. Jane, who in passing mentioned this, was his source of electronics, but he rarely let on to this as he wanted to share as little information about his private life as he could with her. She was dangerous. He opened the door to the backseat and placed his large leather, hard-sided, monogrammed attaché case into the backseat of the Jeep. She based car selection on making it to work in the depth of winter, so he bought a black jeep, complete with heated seats, steering wheel and an all-wheel drive. It was an understated choice that made him happy and did not draw attention to any appearance of wealth.

The drive in to work at 6:00 AM was pleasant, sans the crazy drivers. Individuals that leave this early were typically seasoned enough to drive in snow without causing accidents. Light classical music played while Michael thought about how his life worked out. How the children were okay, but definitely not perfect. Marcella did not push them, much to Michael's mother's dismay, and always supported what they wanted to do. Michael was not that good at disciplining his kids either. He relied on Marcella to do the right thing. She was a wonderful combination of intelligence, kindness and had beautiful natural waves in her hair that showed a few strands of gray, becoming to her Italian face. She was a natural beauty. He and Marcella found each other while he was studying to pass the bar and she was interning at the hospital, finishing her PhD in cardiology. They formed a partnership, advanced themselves in their respective professions and raised two children, their efforts complemented by many nannies, housekeepers and babysitters. His younger daughter, Kay grossly misinterpreted Marcella's intention that her children be who they were and not live by someone else's expectations. She was bright, perhaps the brightest girl he knew, before she turned into the hormone-raging monster at fifteen. She was in art school now, studying music and writing poetry. Be patient, was all Marcella had to say. His only recourse was to force her to go to a real school, but it was a little late to change the course that Marcella set for their children. He trusted Marcella and was sure it would all work out if she said so. At least their combined incomes allowed them to put away at least two million dollars per child. They allowed Kay and Max to take from their trusts once they turned thirty. If that fund grew as it had been, the trust fund would have doubled by that time. At some point, Marcella thought they should let them know about the trust, but Michael was against that idea. They were good kids and would find their way more easily without knowing about the safety net they secured for them. Michael knew that they might not be important influencers like their parents, but Marcella was happy to see them navigate using their personal instincts rather than prescribed protocols of success.

As Michael drove into the underground garage, he took a deep breath. The rest of his day would embody calculated ease and compassionate facial expressions. He was clear, confident, and willing to strike if required.

His first stop was to pick up a large box of doughnuts, treats for someone's birthday. Yes, it was a pain, but a small price to pay to appear genuine, caring and gracious about whoever's birthday it was. He hated picking out doughnuts, sorting through all the toppings and filling options and randomizing it from last month's selection. Carrying the box up to the office was even a hassle as the sweet smell of gooey fat bombs made him nauseous.

As Michael rounded the corner, he realized it was time for an early teleconference with Japan. He rarely showed up, providing him with the opportunity to emphasize his importance. He never lied about not attending and could always point to several crisis situations he was working on.

This ploy of avoiding meetings was not unexpected. Most teams knew this about him. They'd probably be a little worried if he did show up. He was looking forward to a peaceful morning without barking into a speakerphone. He could always catch up months later, since he rarely knew what they were talking about.

Asian colleagues fell in two camps. One pretended to agree to everything and just did their own thing and the other group would not make a move without his blessing. He could not remember which group had the call this morning. It really made no difference to him as he could deal with either situation later. He was mentoring a new attorney and he might put her on this account to stay close in case he needed to intervene.

As he walked into his office and looked out at the panoramic view, he felt a heavy weight across his chest. What would a day be like if he did not have an office like this to come to? A view fifteen floors up. Yes, a heaviness in his chest was the physical feeling he had whenever he thought about retirement. His job was most of his life and that required him to look around the corner to what was next. Did he ever feel comfortable in his skin at home like he did at work? Everything he did was for the survival of his family and for his advancing legacy that allowed him to control his work destiny. What was his true nature? Without the heavy responsibility of his job, was he kind and caring? These contradicting messages were flying across his brain.

It was over twenty years ago that he learned a good lesson about corporate life. It was a painful time. That moment transcended him from a plebeian attorney into a serpent, rising out of the water, tipping boats, floating and carrying them down into the depths with no chance of survival. Yes, that was a good reminder, and he surprised himself at the time how devious he could be. He would never forget that lesson.

His phone rang and Max was calling. He better answer it. "Max, how are you doing?" He forced an extra chipper attitude. "I'm at work, what's up?"

Max had a computer job at the university and worked from 11 PM to 6 AM. He was going home from work by this time.

"There is an anomaly in our server and I agreed to stay over and help fix it. Just letting you know I must cancel dinner tonight as I will need to catch up on my sleep to be back at work by eleven this evening," said Max.

"That's cool and I hope things are good. Dad loves you, bye.' As Michael hung up the phone, he started to look over his calendar for the day. Kelly always printed it out for him the evening before and flagged anything that was important. She flagged this afternoon's meeting for the Lazarus acquisition meeting, Jane's deal. Lazarus, he thought. Why does everyone call their project Lazarus? The idea that Lazarus rose from the dead after four days had some significance to so many projects that were killed by groups of managers and still survived to become successful projects. It was the good ones that rose from the dead.

Maybe I could talk to the key stakeholders before the meeting. I'll call Kelly to set up several quick meetings for me. I think at least four executives deciding on Lazarus could be persuaded to vote down her proposal.

JANE - 6

Jane hung up the phone with Dr. Shin. As she looked out her office window, she saw geese moving in a long spiral pattern. From her vantage point, nine floors up, it appeared they were flying upwards in two vertical chains, then diving straight down, intertwining the lines and coming back up to complete the cycle. It made her think, double helix! She thought about the Barred Owl this morning, behaving strangely, hitting her window. She must have read a book about animal behavior predicting cataclysmic events. She wished she had the time to record and analyze things like bird patterns. This job was keeping her from her real calling, wasn't it? That was a new idea. I better make sure I connect with Dr. Blue today.

The odd flight pattern of birds, combined with the mass of emails streaming on her computer, and the call from Dr. Shin, definitely formed today's outlook. This was also the day she would get final approval for their deal and Shin just told her on the phone with an oh-by-the-way tone that he contracted with a seed producer three years ago to scale up his genetically modified seeds in Iowa without a license to do it! While they were not the latest genetics that she received, they were close. The seeds in Jane's Tool Box were designed to improve the survival for months or years without sun. The significance of this information on today's meeting was gripping her conscience. Should she disclose this information at the meeting? Was Dr. Shin's action irresponsible or just practical, moving the project forward, saving them years of scaleup. Dr. Shin was an old friend of Dan's and she thought he was trustworthy. If she could work out this deal, it would advance their research by more than a decade. This was that paradigmatic. Catastrophic consequences caused by sneaking in modified seeds in this country were well documented. It was a felony to carry seeds into the country without a license. She knew these kinds of antics were just what legal would look for to kill her deal. So far, the ethics of their proposed partnership was stellar. Why would Shin tell her this now? She needed talk to Dan.

She pulled two heavy envelopes from the Tool Box. The seeds inside these pouches were the future. She then placed one seed pouch in her backpack and one back in the Tool Box. Dr. Shin gave her these seeds. She had assumed that these seeds were the only seeds with these traits outside of China. How could Dr. Shin deceive her like that? She did not have any protection as her having the seeds in the US without a license was just as problematic as someone growing them in Iowa. It was all part of her obsession. People might call her a survivalist, but the survivalists she visited were isolationists. They required a full complement of everything they needed to survive as a group with no outside help. In fact, they planned to use violence against individuals crossing onto their land.

Spending a weekend with the Wyoming group, opened her eyes. Their organized efforts designed to take out intruders were aggressive. This group was militant. Their place was a stronghold that contained an unabashed amount of guns and ammunition; it was almost an excuse to form a military compound. This group was well protected against the unknown or have-nots. Alternatively, Jane built herself a refuge with one shotgun and a handgun. She could handle four people with energy reserves set aside for five years. The advanced seeds she received from Dr. Shin on her trip to China three months ago helped Jane preserve a place in any post-apocalyptic future. She could bring a significant food source with her and help anyone who survived against starvation. Food, shelter, energy and water were basic needs, which, if everything went according to plan, she could provide. She was not willing to kill to protect herself, or was she? That she was processing this level of detail about survival refreshed her need to see Dr. Blue as soon as possible. It was an unhealthy rabbit hole; Dr. Blue often reminded her of this in their sessions.

With five minutes to spare, she did a few personal things online, finding two more places that carried large water storage containers. Finally, she checked her battery chargers in the Tool Box, making sure each one was a hundred percent.

Reviewing her PowerPoint for the meeting, she removed any reference to recent plant results, and she finally relaxed, taking a few sips of cold coffee. This opportunity would sell itself with no mention of plants with accelerated plant growth under unique growing conditions. That information might bring too much positive attention, resulting in skepticism by the M&A group because of overselling, e.g. something that sounded too good to be true. She always wanted to lead a presentation to the more obvious questions, limiting discussions that spiraled down into gray areas where there were no answers.

Hearing something outside her office, she made eye contact with Michael who stopped outside her door and waved through the window, smiling. Oh boy, this is all I need, she thought.

"Come on in," she shouted.

"Hey, just wanted to stop by and let you know I'll be attending your meeting today and I look forward to it. Can I help with your presentation?" asked Michael.

"Oh no, I think I'm fine." Thanks to Dan, she was good at understanding executive double speak and could translate. Michael's offer to help meant he wanted to find out what she was doing. At least she knew enough to navigate carefully around him. He would not make any mistakes and reveal his thoughts, so she better be selective with her information.

"The M&A group reviewed the financials yesterday, which they endorsed, asking only a few clarifying questions. Priya will be at the meeting and she appreciated the heads up you gave her on the recommended risk analysis percent for the NPV. Research and Development are drooling over this as it provides a wide landscape on which they can play, but I think legal will vote it down since the deal does not have a zero risk indicator. Am I right, Michael? Aren't you good at surfacing doubt in meetings like this?" Jane said, surprising herself with this edgy rancor.

"Wow, you're in a mood!" said Michael.

"No, just being realistic. I can't remember a time when you did not sabotage something I did. Now, I expect it. Short of doing nothing, I think we have to move forward with something, otherwise, we do nothing and doing nothing is not an option. Michael, if we did nothing, you would be out of work." Feeling a flush bloom up in her cheeks, she took a breath, smiled and said, "Just kidding. Do you have questions about the deal that I can answer? How does it sound to you? You know that IP coming out of this acquisition will be amazing and we will have exclusive ownership rights for all patents and patent extensions." She beamed, knowing how important that would be to him.

Michael rarely lost his cool, but his face turned pale, almost a pale amber color and then he looked up and said, "You had me going. You know I think you're great. I support you, but I need to know what the issues are before the meeting so I can help you in the best way I can. Acquiring a Chinese company is not trivial. I will have to provide extensive input for the executive committee to approve this."

"Michael, we are in excellent shape. We've had many meetings on this deal. You received a copy of the final executable agreement six days ago and nothing has changed since then. If you had issues with any part of this deal, you would have let the negotiation team know that. We've sent you copies. Am I right?"

"Of course, of course. I'll take one more look, Jane. But please proceed as if you have my approval. Well, I've got to go. The CEO demanded a meeting with me yesterday, and this is the only time I can meet with him. I better run, Jane. Good luck!"

Michael quickly left her office and left the door open. Jane got up to close it and started to relax again. I forgot about him. Yes, the snake is always slithering around. I wonder what's up with him. He hasn't been around much lately or since the last time I presented a deal to this committee. He tried to mess with me that time, but thanks to Dan, I could steer around the traps he laid. Dan makes Michael nervous. Ideally, Dan should be at the meeting. Why is Michael afraid of Dan, she wondered? Dan reversed a final judgment in some magical way, Michael came back and very, very sweetly turned things back to where they were before he dismantled the whole deal. Getting her MBA in M&A and Strategic Analysis did not prepare her for the reality of corporate processes. They taught that logic and analysis led to great business decisions where instead; the reality was you would have self-serving snipers often taking you down before you could get anything done. Now why don't they teach that in school!

Dan is home. I need to call him again, talk to him about Shin and let him know that Michael might cook something up. I wonder if Michael knows Dan's on vacation. It's this kind of paranoid thinking Dr. Blue said gets me in trouble. She added, "Even if it is true, you can't do anything about it. Just move forward in the way that makes sense to you and do not react personally to his attacks. Keep an objective mind." It was so easy to say that. While that comment made her feel helpless, she believed in karmic justice. If he was targeting her solely to make her look bad and allow management to question her judgement, he deserved to have something bad happen to him.

I remember the very first deal I did, fifteen years ago, a pupster, not knowing what I was doing, but faithfully following protocol, Jane thought. I was seeking approval and had my first face-to-face meeting with an executive. I prepared all night for the meeting with key points to review for his approval and entered his office just as Michael was leaving. He acted surprised at seeing me, but quickly nodded and slid away on the grease under his auburn wingtip shoes. Mr. Cleveland, the Vice President of Sustainability, welcomed me in his office, asked a few personal questions about my career and let me go through the whole proposal asking no questions. He got up. He shook my hand and thanked me for being so well prepared. I asked him to sign the agreement. He said he would think about it. Corporate speak for no. I never got past first base. What was the problem with me and why did I suck at this was my initial conclusion until I compared notes to several other business women who helped me understand. "Really? Is it that bad?" I asked. "Are you talking about the glass ceiling?"

The glass ceiling is a reality, according to these women. Men developed the term. They love the image of women suffocating under a glass ceiling, seeing the prize, but not being able to achieve it. Most women who understand the game will walk away, knowing it's just not worth it, thus the shortage of female CEOs in Fortune 500 companies. Life is too short for such soul-sucking activities for what you get in exchange. Most executives know that the means justify the end, and the end is power. Jane's pet theory, generalizing everything she knew in her world, was men want power over others and women want power to be independent.

That first incident with Michael was the beginning of Jane's education in reality. Outwardly, she looked like she was ambitious, but inside, she wanted to find out how far she could be promoted without losing her soul. She excelled in her own way, stayed away from private situations and tried to be as understated as possible. Quietly competent was Dr. Blue's analysis. Initially, she worked hard, too hard, but eventually, she worked smart and did not pay homage to time-wasting activities like creating the most exotic PowerPoint presentation. She got promoted; job opportunities came to her, and she continued to climb the corporate ladder, her soul intact, so far. She developed a reputation of tough competence; except for Michael, no one wanted to mess with her. She found a niche she was good at and she would do it until she received some sign that it was time to quit.

"So this meeting will be an interesting one," she said out loud to no one. Suddenly, another knock on the door disrupted her thoughts. She hollered, "Come on in," as if everyone was deaf around here.

Sheryl poked her head in and said, "How are you doing? Anything I can do for you?"

"No, I should be okay. I was looking at a catalog and need to buy another battery for my laptop. Can you do that for me?"

"Oh, I thought you already had two? You know how hard it was to get approval for the second."

"Yes, but I am traveling to China next week and need to switch batteries on the flight. It's 2008 and planes still don't have outlets. Wait a minute, let's do this. Just go out at lunch for me and pick one up at any electronic store. I'll pay for it out of my personal account and we'll find some way to get reimbursed for it later."

"Okay, that is another approach, Jane. You know I would order one if I could," said Sheryl.

"Here is a hundred dollars and let me know what I owe you. If you could have it here by 2:00 PM, I'll stop by and pick it up. By the way, I'm in the Manatee conference room this afternoon," said Jane.

"I know that, Jane. Good luck today. I know it's an important meeting. You know Kelly, Michael's secretary? She just told me he was asking her to set up fifteen-minute meetings with the executives that are attending your meeting before the meeting! We thought you might want to know that."

Jane smiled. The secretary network was great. She helped her many times. Sheryl was a master at furthering Jane's cause. She was right about Michael's plan to sabotage her deal." Thanks, one more thing, and then I have to leave. Dan's on vacation and never gets my numbers right, so if he calls on my office phone, please transfer him to my mobile."

"Okay, no problem."

Sheryl was a gem. Jane admired her. She was beyond a support person; she had three kids and a husband. But she also was a talented watercolor artist who consistently showed in two local galleries. Once they realized how to work together, they were mutually supportive and understanding. Jane did not need much handholding and Sheryl was an expert at working the system. At least she knew now, with certainty, that groundwork was being planned to sabotage her deal. Stay on task, she said to herself, as if Dr. Blue was guiding her through this difficult situation. Glancing at the clock, Jane needed to get to her next meeting and contact Dr. Blue.

LUMING - 7

The feel of early winter coming on strong, with cold blasts of wind combined with a grayish, wintery white sky overhead, put a damper on Luming's attitude and a wish that they drove, rather than walked. Walking reminded him of his neighborhood's character, houses built in the 20s, all with big screen porches surrounding the front of each house and individual backyards, separated by chain-linked fences. Each block had a refreshing redundancy that Luming never experienced growing up. Each block had an alley, connecting the row of houses from the back and a sidewalk that pulled together the block from the front. Alleys were a necessity for everything that needed delivery into the house, which left sidewalks dedicated to foot travel and a special way of capturing life as it went by. While Luming felt so mismatched with his job and the corporate environment, coming home to this neighborhood always made him feel comfortable, cozy and secure. Owning such a home was beyond what he imagined ever having and if his mother ever saw it, she would faint.

The walk cleared his head and provoked him to think more clearly about what he was doing, walking next to Chris who was transferring money into his bank account to prove it was his last day on earth. That was an odd gesture, one that Luming found different. Chris was unique and Luming suspected he might be an outsider. They developed a friendship in the last year, but all he knew was Chris was a software programmer with a passion for developing apps. He worked out of his home and would disappear for days, then stop by to see Luming to have two beers and he'd pull out a joint from time to time to smoke. He was a cool friend. Job security was important to Luming, so carrying on too long this day with Chris was out of the question, but Chris' out-of-the-box thinking intrigued him. He was interested in making this work. If he stuck to his plan and returned to work by 11:00, it would all work out.

One of Luming's lifelines was their current destination called, "The Breakfast Nook". He could always get a warm meal, served quickly and cheaply. Stanley, the owner and short-order cook, took your order, cooked it and collected your money, cash only. Small businesses like coffee shops, knitting stores, computer repair and even electronic dealers started to occupy these boxy houses in order to survive the latest recession. Stanley, laid off from the Ford plant five years ago, was ahead of the curve. This place worked and was widely popular with anyone who wanted a good breakfast in ten minutes and to be out the door in 20. Stanley always had some helper, like a neighbor kid or college student, and kept his house open from 6 to 11AM.

The sign on the porch door of the house was painted in crisp black lettering. It said, "The Breakfast Nook," and scrawled below it in red script was, "... don't stay too long." Luming loved this. After walking through the porch and the entry door, the aroma of toast made from fresh bread hit you first. Four long wooden tables occupied the living room complete with a bench where anyone could sit and eat, singly or in groups. Chris and Luming headed for the back, where the kitchen was set up with a long bar with fixed rotating stools, mimicking a traditional small-town diner, separating the kitchen from the diners.

They sat down on two empty stools directly in front of the grill. Just the aroma of bread that came out of the oven every twenty minutes that complemented the freshest eggs fried next to thick apple-smoked bacon made any stomach rumble in delight. Stanley scraped his grill continuously, flipping eggs, potatoes, and sausages, creating a pleasant scene for everyone to watch and a nice sound of clattering and clanking that produced steaming plates of good food. The menu was simple and never changed. Number 1 was fried eggs, bacon or sausage, potatoes, toast and coffee and Number 2 was the same option without the meat. Luming enjoyed the rich scent that came from bacon and sausage, but ordered Number 2 because of his friend, Brother, a Tibetan Buddhist priest, suggested that he try vegetarian for a while. As Luming became an insider at The Nook, he discovered that you could get an off-the-menu omelet, but only if you could survive the penetrating stare that Stanley gave you when you asked for it.

Once they were delivered, Chris and Luming dove into their white porcelain plates and did not speak until they were swabbing up the eggs yolks and grease off the plates with toast. Simple, fresh, and fast settled Luming down from this unusual morning.

Chris looked around, "This is living well."

"Yep," Luming said. "America has better breakfasts than any other part of the world." They looked at each other and laughed at the absurdity of their conversation. Luming felt how much it meant to him to share this good meal and connection with a friend.

They sat and Chris turned to look outside and said, "Listen, Luming, this is your last day and you are doing a superb job of dealing with it so far. Kindly help me understand what you want to do after we stop by the bank."

"Yes, I'm sorry, man, but with some coffee and food in my belly, I'm not so sure about your proposal and what it means. Frankly, I would love to indulge you, but I'm not sure what to think and I really gotta be at work by eleven."

"No, no," said Chris. "You gave your word and I have already had the money transferred. I am serious and you will be too, once you realize my proposal is real."

"Not so fast," said Luming. "I did not agree to anything, and especially to receive your money. Why would you send me $100,000? What kind of prank is this?"

"Didn't you say you wanted to rob a bank?" begged Chris.

"That was just a theoretical idea. It sounded like the way a plot would go in a movie, rather than a serious comment," said Luming, bristling at Chris' urging.

"Okay, so just relax, Luming," said Chris. He leaned back on his stool, looking around and grinning from ear to ear. "I know you want to do this. Think about it. What if this was the last day of your life?" Chris said with the emphasis on 'your'. "Is there anything you want to do, before you die?"

Luming looked around to see if anyone was paying attention to what Chris just said, a little too loudly. The scene was frozen in time. The old guy sitting next to him was still and probably deaf. Stanley kept scraping the grill and the rest of the noise of plates and cups clattering kept their conversation under any radar.

Luming knew Chris well enough to know he could be very persistent. But what would the last day look like? He saw his grandfather die of cancer, which was the last time he thought much about death. "Okay, I have an idea. Theoretically, I know how I would like to spend my last day."

Chris swiveled the stool around, his legs flailing in the air until he was facing Luming directly. "Okay, man, what is it? You have my attention."

"Well, I'm interested in people's lives and what they do all day. Being a so-called foreigner, I am fascinated with people. How do they spend their days? I came from a small village with houses packed close together, like a parking lot. Everyone knew what everyone did all the time. People here have a lot of mobility. I also think they do lots of things that are just private. They have so much unabated, uncompromising freedom, I've always wondered what they did with it. They can go anywhere and do anything with no one watching them. If we drove around and followed people in their cars, ones we profile to be interesting, or walk behind people downtown to see where they go, or just stalk people for no reason, we might find something interesting. I guess the idea is simplistic, but it's to just follow people. Maybe we'll get lucky and observe something outrageous, like a crime that we can prevent. Think of it as a cross between a guardian angel and a superhero. I think it would be intriguing and satisfying. How do you know the end is coming, Chris? Do you have a crystal ball?" said Luming, finally warming up to the idea.

Chris shook his head and said, "To be honest, Luming, your idea sounds weird. I enjoyed robbing banks better. Robbing banks shows your commitment that it is the end of the world. This idea does not fire me up." Chris's phone rang, and he picked it up.

"Hi, what a surprise," he said with an animated voice. His face seemed to change as he listened. He locked eyes with Luming, then he looked to the floor. Chris hung up and said, "Something's come up. I have to run but will meet you at your house at 9:30. I'll get a car to pick you up. You can make your decision then. I'll let you know then how I got my information. I'm counting on you, Luming." Chris threw his coat over his shoulder, bolted out the door, and sprinted down the block. Luming, having no choice, paid the bill of eight dollars plus a two dollar tip for both of them, threw his backpack over his shoulder and sauntered out of the building. Chris confused Luming. He could just go to work or visit his friend, Brother. He loves this kind of stuff.

He trotted ten short blocks until he got to the Midway Meditation Center. He stepped through the blue threshold, in time to start the 8:00 meditation. He knelt down, touched his forehead and heart, then sat in the corner to join in the chanting. He started to calm down, the eggs settling in his stomach, and he watched his breathing as he chanted the simple phrases for the day. Emptying his mind was never easy, but today, his mind race was at an all-time high.

If this was the last day of my life, what should I do? What will I do? Do I believe in incarnation? Slowly, breathe, Luming. Pay attention to the words you are chanting. Nothing matters now. Compared to other times, Luming was feeling a lot of discomfort in his third chakra. Having grown up surrounded by Buddhist priests, he found this was a very natural part of living and was used to using his breath to achieve peace within. This meditation center held morning mantra chanting of a simple phrase. Today was the Amitabha Mantra which Luming thought was entirely appropriate as it protected you from dangers and obstacles. "Om ami deva hrih," was chanted slowly by the group of meditators. The combination of deep low voices with higher ones sounded like a concert and the vibrations deepened the feeling of peace. Buddhists designed the center for simplicity. The deep brown color of wood floors offset by indigo mats and ivory cushions gave the place a sacred feeling. Individuals spread in a circle around Brother, who was leading the chanting. The fresh lavender smells, filling the center, were probably from the leaves that Brother liked to burn. While Luming never smelled lavender before coming to America, once he found it, the fragrance obsessed him. It could almost replace meditation as he instantly felt calm and collected. He placed bottles of lavender freshener on his desk at work, in his car and in his bedroom. As the meditation ended, Luming got up, feeling much better, and walked over to his friend.

"Nǐ hǎo, Brother," Luming said while bowing. Brother's Buddhist birth name was actually Brother. Brother rescued Luming from a deep loneliness he felt when he first came to this country. The Midwest was friendly enough but connecting with people was tough. Well-established circles of friends were hard to penetrate. That was also true in Mount

Cangyan, China, his home. His people took a long time to accept strangers outside of his village, especially when tourists started to visit just to cross the famous stone arch bridge, spanning the narrow gorge. This gave him a unique perspective on America. Luming met Brother just when he arrived and he would always be grateful for his friendship and unlimited support.

"Ho," said Brother. "I had a dream about a catastrophic event two nights ago and have wanted to connect with you ever since. It was strange and very real."

Brother often had a spiritual riddle for Luming to ponder. He teased Luming about the inner meaning and how it connected with images he dreamed about. Adding up the coincidences of Chris' game, the Amitabha Mantra and now Brother's dream, Luming was feeling there was some kind of hidden message being communicated by the universe. This felt different. It upset him that Brother would take so long to tell him this news until he remembered he was in New Orleans for five days.

DAN - 8

Dan opened his Blackberry to discover 152 emails, all flagged to him by Martha. In her email, she wrote that she thought the phone messages were in Mandarin, some emails were just blank and some written in Chinese characters. He didn't want to chase this down today. What about Shin? He's in Hong Kong and it was 10:30 PM. Never too late to call him. Shin worked around the clock. He answered on the second ring.

"Hi, Dan," said Shin in his calm voice. "I am so happy you called. We were having difficulty here all day. Just a minute." Based on the background noise, Dan suspected Shin was still in the laboratory. Shin was a researcher at the Shin Institute, named after his father who discovered and patented over 1,000 plastic closures, all filed worldwide, but in China and the US. Practically no location in the world could make, use or sell a plastic closure without infringing on a Shin patent. The Shin Institute's sister company was a law firm that licensed and enforced their patent portfolios all over the world. The principle partners in the law firm, Shin, Shin, Lee and Wong comprised Shin's older brother, Shin's sister, Lee, Shin's brother-in-law and Wong, the oldest Chinese patent attorney living in China. He was eighty-four.

So Shin, Shin, Lee and Wong spent all of their time monitoring products containing plastic bags with plastic closures and any plastic sonographic sealing applications globally. Their success rate in prosecuting patents, defending them and suing infringers made them the number three patent law firm in the world. Shin, not a lawyer, headed the Shin Institute that symbiotically enjoyed the revenue gained from these efforts. These lucrative legal efforts paid for the R&D which created new enforceable patents that the legal team would again turn into financial stability. Their research efforts were vast and Dan had no idea about their current area of focus, but knowing Shin, it was not plastic closures.

Shin and Dan went to school together at Iowa State University and never lost touch. Shin was happy at the University. He had never experienced freedom from his controlling and domineering parents. Dan introduced him to the midwestern culture that he took for granted, which Shin enjoyed outwardly. Dan was thinking of the time they were in his car, smoking pot and driving 80 mph, surrounded by cornfields in an old Iowa back road. Shin was shrieking and laughing while feeling the air pass through him from the open window. That memory brought a smile to Dan.

Dan could hear Shin shouting something and then he came back to speak to Dan. "Dan, I am so sorry. As I previously mentioned, things are a bit off here. We picked up a strange warning signal, bouncing off a satellite and checking this out, along with another 1,000 individuals who read the same outputs we did. They are emailing each other, lowing things down. We cannot identify the source of the warning. It was intentional, but the meaning is vague. What do you make of this? Are you seeing anything?"

Dan thought a moment and remembered Jane's comment about Rosebud Motors and detailed her observations with Shin. "Also, Martha has been monitoring my emails. Actually, that's why I called you. All I know right now is I received 152 emails, origin China, and according to Martha, all in Mandarin. I'm taking a day off and driving around in my car with my granddaughter. Wondering if you have time to help me with this. It's probably not that urgent."

"Not a problem, Dan. We are seeing something similar; it sounds exactly like what we experienced. We'll look. That is interesting. Rosebud? That company is Korean. They make custom parts for satellites and also have a strong presence in Taiwan. I will mention this to my researchers." Shin sighed and said, "So, Dan, it has been a while since we last talked, at least a year. What's new with you?"

"Nothing really," said Dan. "I'm away from the office and it feels like a guilty pleasure. I am half in one world and half in another. It's days like this that I think a lot about retirement. My exoskeleton is wearing thin."

"Hard to believe, Dan. I can see you doing something else. You need a change, bad. You're an entrepreneurial man. You have many ideas. You're a natural born problem-solver. If you left that place today, you would not have to live another boring minute in corporate America. You can pick your people. I know you, Dan. You never pretended to like anyone. I think you like to piss people off, so they don't like you. Think about using all of this knowledge you've accumulated and doing something of value with it. Just think, no more politics."

That was Shin's talent, Dan thought. Cutting to the truth of things.

Shin continued, "Your experience and practical knowledge makes you an awesome partner for a start-up. Come live here. I will set you up with seed money, people, and a beautiful house overlooking Kowloon Bay."

"Right, yep, you know I would. I just have this gorgeous granddaughter who is rewarding me with a second chance at caretaking. I really can't leave her and her mother when they need me the most."

"Okay," moaned Shin. "I will come to you then. Give me your date, and we will begin setting up things per your recommendations. I will get on my plane, just say the word."

"Whoa, what is the rush?" said Dan. "I'm curious. What's the technology area?"

"Agriculture. Yes, yes. We could bring you after the acquisition with Jane goes through. She's been doing such a great job testing our technology, leading a due diligence team and coming with the terms that made everyone almost happy. She's quite an asset for your company. It's rare to have someone so business savvy and technically astute."

"I'm not sure of the details but I know Jane is working hard to make it happen." This was the problem with taking a day off. The phone has a way of disrupting a perfectly good day. "Sounds like an offer worth considering, Shin." Dan looked at his Blackberry and then looked at Lizzy and asked, "I'm having Martha send you the emails we received today. Let me know what you think."

"I'll look. Let's talk once everything is settled. I'm sure you will be surprised."

Dan could hear someone speaking Chinese in the background. "Just a minute." There was phone silence and Dan made himself a coffee. He wanted to spend the rest of the day playing with Lizzy.

Shin got back on the phone and said, "Sorry, Dan." Shin sounded like he had been running and was out of breath.

"What's up?" said Dan.

"Well, we just traced the source of our emails to this strange group in China. They are equivalent to your skinheads. They're a kind of Chinese-race supremacy group called Yamagata. This means small steps are the best steps. At one time, they protested outside of one of our most confidential research labs in the city of Lijiang, in the Yunan Province. They must have highly sophisticated ways of gathering intelligence because we closely guarded the facility and protected it with cameras and multiple security guards. The nature of what we were doing was secret. We were conducting advanced plant cloning activities there, which was not that unique except that the Chinese government weren't controlling the results and would shut us down if they knew what we were up to. They assembled outside the building with banners, shouting, 'SAY NO GMO.' We were not sure why this sect cared about plant biogenetics. It was devastating. We called the authorities. A big mistake. The authorities came in swiftly, fired off rockets of tear gas and literally smothered the protestors as they were scooped up, using a human hauling machine that wrapped up these guys like hay bales. The ending crushed us. Those men will never be seen again."

"What happened to your company efforts?" said Dan.

"We hidour real activities and paid a minor fee for having performed non-licensed research plant detection research. Fortunately, there was no formal reprimand. We then moved our facility to a set of caves near Mount Yulong, just outside of Lijiang."

"What happened to the activist group?"

"They probably went underground, especially if they lost people. No one has heard of them since."

As if on cue, Elizabeth let out a wail-like laugh and smiled to get some attention from Grandpa. Dan looked at his watch and said, "Yeah, Shin, this sounds fascinating. Is there anything I can do?"

"Just send me the emails. I'll call you back when I have more info."

"I have an outside researcher that might help us quickly. I'll ask Martha to send them to you and to Lois, my research consultant," said Dan.

"Gotta go, Dan. Let's talk you later." Shin hung up quickly. Dan rarely found him to speak incorrect English. He must have been pretty upset.

Dan looked at Elizabeth just as her adorable face changed, replaced by her hungry face. Tensed and red, she was communicating with everything she had and was ready to turn on the tears. Once Dan understood the message, he swirled into action. Elizabeth settled down, her mission accomplished. Ten months old and she was already taking care of her needs.

Getting out of the car, opening the back doors of the SUV, Dan pulled out the diaper bag, grabbed the milk and propped it up on a bottle-holding device so Elizabeth did not even need to hold the bottle. "Great," he said, "this contraption holds her bottle for her? I need to talk to Brenda. She needs to hold her own bottle!" As she started sipping and calming down, he sank into the back seat and realized he could relax a little. Were bottle holders such a bad thing?

She laughed and said, "Gan, Gan, Gan," which was her baby talk for grandfather. Dan dreamed about her future as a pitcher and he needed to think about when to start her training. Finally, remembering he needed to send those emails to Shin, he picked up his phone from the dash and speed-dialed Martha.

She answered and said, "Aren't you on vacation? You need to stop bugging me."

"Yes, wise words from someone who never takes a vacation," Dan bantered back. "How are your plans for that trip to Disneyland? When are you going?"

Martha laughed. "You know I love the way you kid. You know as well as I do, I am leaving this afternoon for Orlando, picking up the grandkids at the airport, taking them from their parents for a few days. You remember, right?"

"I seem to recall something like that."

"Cathy Ann will back me up and I have informed her of all of your needs. I'm sure she will connect with you often with many approaches on how to improve things. She's annoying, but she will provide the very best support, especially in a crisis. We have talked about this, Dan, often, and besides her unique way of involving herself, you will love her to death."

"Highly doubtful," said Dan. "I just spoke to Shin and can you send him the same emails that you sent to me?"

"Should not be a problem," said Martha. Martha was a stereotypical-looking midwestern woman, small bone structure, blond hair and sharp blue eyes. She had an effortless work ethic that Dan had grown to expect.

"I have already reported this anomaly to IT, but they didn't respond. No surprise about that."

"Okay," said Dan. "I need to get in touch with Lois. Can you reach her for me and set up a call? She'll be perfect for this project. I'll want to send these emails to her. Martha, let's catch up before you leave today." He looked back at Elizabeth and found that she had cupped her hands around a bright orange nerf ball. She was beaming a wide smile, acknowledging her amazing accomplishment.

LOIS -9

Museumgoers crowded onto the bus. The Art Institute bus ride was popular with the eastside crowd. But Lois got a window seat right away. Museumgoers were middle aged women. They came with friends and chatted the whole time. They dressed seasonally. Because of the light snow, they sported warm scarves and jackets color-coordinated with their gloves, shoes, and purses. They all looked kind and curious, as if they were visiting a different world, like tourists traveling in a foreign country. This bus ride was part of their experience entering into this strange world of people who ride busses. She wondered about their lives, their children and husbands. Did they have enough money to buy anything they wanted? Did they ever yell and shout at their kids when they walked in the door? What would it be like to have a mom that dressed up to get on a bus? What would normal life be like?

Susan, Lois' mother, was pregnant with Lois when she turned eighteen. Susan had no job and no plans to attend college since her parents already gave up encouraging her to get good grades. She was a little boy crazy and Fred and Mary lived in denial that she had a problem until it was too late to change anything. They were Republicans. Fred believed anyone left of God, apple pie, and Ronald Reagan was a pinko communist. He measured his family, friends and colleagues against the principles he held. Working hard and giving thanks to Jesus Christ for sacrificing his life were his yardstick. Mary grew up on a farm. She was a Christian woman and agreed with Fred on everything. Fred held the same beliefs that her parents did and she could think of no reason to question them. Once they could no longer deny that Susan had a problem, they doled out tough love like it was part of a sacrosanct edict. Their solution to the pregnancy was to send Susan away to have the baby and give it to a Christian family. Susan refused to do that. She had the baby on her own. Instead of leaving her parents in shame, she rented a house one block away and crafted a way for her to drop off Lois while she worked at the university.

Susan was parentis-non-grata while Lois was being raised by Fred and Mary until shortly after Lois' second birthday. Susan married a nice man and had Clark four months later. Susan's new husband, Larry, bought a Christmas tree farm for them to live on. Moving to a farm was supposed to be an improvement from the tension Fred and Mary imposed on Susan since she announced her pregnancy.

The truth of Lois' life was painful, her stomach always retched when she was reminded of the cold silence of her upbringing. Lois tried to replace her pain by developing a quiet envy of others who grew up with normal parents. Eventually, the vacancy in her life turned her into a motivated machine. She would make it on her own. She knew what to do. She would help Clark make a difference in the world, without the entitlement of mother love. They would create a future, together.

Lois was a great student. She excelled with ease, always with a book to read, whether it was biology or math or fiction. It made no difference. Her teachers loved her as she was maintenance free. Her ability to concentrate was a notable advantage compared to most of her peer group. Lois' only motivation to excel in school was to move away and go to college. She spent lots of time with a guidance counselor. The counselor was the one who pointed out her skills in both language and math. She scored the top 3% in her PSATs, qualifying her to apply for a National Merit Scholarship, and in the end, she received a full four-year scholarship. When her mother heard the news, Lois detected a smile of self-aggrandizement. Susan was pleased with herself, not because of the hard work that Lois put into her studies, but thinking she had something to do with Lois' success. Actually, Susan did have a lot to do with Lois' success. She propelled her to make a better life for her and her brother.

With the help of her high school counselor, Lois made her final university selection based on her financially challenging situation. She had no money for school. She applied and received enough scholarship money to cover her first year. Her grandparents set up a trust fund for her that could not be accessed until she was twenty-one. Those early college years gave her the independence she craved, but she was isolated and lonely. She shared a house with a roommate who was a senior going into med school. Her roommate came from a farm where they raised golden retrievers. Lois got her choice from the last two of the litter and she raised Suri, her constant companion. Suri was now her surrogate family and cared for her like she cared for Clark.

Now, Lois looked out the bus window. In her last year of undergrad, Clark wrote her that Susan met a widower with two sons. He owned a ranch in northern Montana and wanted Susan be a mother to his sons. How ironic, thought Lois. Letters from Susan came less frequently and cards with a return address were no longer included. Finally, Clark wrote to Lois that he wanted to stay with her.

Lois looked around and found she was almost to her bus stop. It's so amazing how much ruminating a human can do and not be conscious.

MICHAEL - 10

Michael exited Jane's office quickly. He moved smoothly, exhibiting a well-curated behavior he adopted years ago to look busy and important while walking down the hall hoping no one would stop him. He arrived back in his office with voicemails, emails, and texts that he needed to review quickly. His reading priority was VPs and CEO first and, of course, his boss on an as-needed basis. The rest of the emails would resurface tomorrow if left alone. Most people who worked closely with him understood that they needed to contact him to get his attention and they realized pretty quickly that he rarely read anything someone sent him. Another quirk of his was he rarely put anything in writing. Part of a lawyer's credibility required them to be right all of the time. Therefore, not having a lot of written material limited his exposure. He could always find someone else to blame. Did his clients know they were being framed this way? Apparently not, as they continued to seek his counsel.

"I need a personal assistant," he mused, knowing full well the days of having one were over. He was lucky that he found Kelly to schedule his meetings, book his travel, and manage his expenses.

This last meeting with Jane was unsettling. He always took her seriously as she rarely followed his rules. He knew she meant every word and would call him out publicly on anything he was keeping close to the vest.

Michael's true effectiveness was delivered inside the sanctity of a Vice President's office. Using the sincerest tone he could muster, creating a cloud of intimacy and caring, he could massage his message to meet his own agenda, shrouded by the need to protect the company.

He knew that he blocked many deals proposed by managers that did not meet his criteria. He could kill a deal without most people even knowing what happened. People that refused to agree with him were always his first target. Careers could be destroyed, with a few words to the right people. Occasionally, he resorted to carefully written confidential emails, copying only the top executive level of the company, highlighting the issues and the risk to the VP's career if the deal did not get signed. It was a last resort, but an effective one. On rare occasions, the VP would resist, which required him to do real legal work and bring in more heavy artillery to support a position, sometimes including the head of legal and the ear of the CEO.

Ironically, his actions were never connected to lost sales, jobs, or profit margins. No one could pin anything on him. He was just a good conservative lawyer, saving the company brand from risk. He was brilliant that way.

Jane was making a small name for herself and was protected by some invisible shield. She was smart, worked long hours and always came prepared with the support of all VPs, something Michael was trying to change. He knew she was presenting today, and it looked like Dan, her mentor, was on vacation. He thought there might be an opening to dismantle her proposal. If he could plant some well-placed, subversive information to someone before the meeting, he could sabotage her.

He had a few hours. He knew she was proposing the final acquisition of Paradise Lost, the company that invented genetically modified crops with unique properties involving reverse photosynthesis. There was nothing he could do to change it.

Michael stepped out of his office, straight to the elevator and then took the steps down nine floors. He liked to stay trim and knew the importance of taking extra steps during the day. So he scooted down the stairs to the ground floor. He walked clear across campus to the Watson Building. He reached the building just in time to see Dr. McKenzie, a PhD in pharmacokinetics and a smart, politically savvy person, charge out of the building on the way to what looked like a limousine and driver waiting for him.

Michael came up, "What's up, Mac?"

McKenzie, not one for small talk, said, "We're proposing to create state-of-the-art medical labs in the Watson building. If we can cancel our plant projects, the people associated with those projects, and the plots we own to support plant research, IT will save us three quarters of a million dollars. Amortize the loss over 10 years and the tax benefit would be equal to five million dollars in sales. This is a sweet deal for our bottom line. I am running over to finance to finalize the numbers and I will absolutely need your help in influencing others of this idea."

"No problem," said Michael. "I say good riddance. Those projects are such a liability; I am surprised we never had anti-GMO protesters in our parking lots."

"It surprised me too," said McKenzie. "This all started as a bootleg project four years ago led by Jane Witterhouse and kept expanding. I estimated it is now around 1,800 square feet."

"Now that is interesting," said Michael.

"Yes," said McKenzie. "Jane provided me a brief update months ago. I've heard nothing since. I started checking the project out and found lamps, hydroponic feeding tubes, a separate nitrogen supply being pumped in from the tunnels. It is all managed by a few COOP students that rotate in each quarter. She must have received a hefty budget from someone."

"Yes, I understand your frustration," said Michael. "I have found her to be irresponsible and not one I can trust with those big deals. In fact, aren't you at her meeting today? She is making a proposal about this Lazarus project, an expensive acquisition candidate. It would be great to have you at that meeting since it sounds like you cannot afford to supply the resources that she needs to further the research. It would be a shame to have this deal go through and not be able to report cost savings, right?" Michael said as nonchalantly as he could. This was just what he needed to derail Jane's meeting today. What a perfect coincidence to run into Mac.

"How true," chimed in McKenzie. "Just send me the information about today's meeting and I will try to make it. It sounds like you need a little help with her and I'd be happy to support you, Michael. I have a nephew that is finishing law school and might apply here for a job. Could you look at that for me?"

"Yea, sure, will do what I can," offered Michael. Oh great! I hate those quids for employment help, thought Michael. I wonder how Kelly is doing setting up those meetings?

JANE - 11

Jane took off her Pradas and put on her custom combination shoes. They felt great and shaped comfortably around her thinner ankle bone. Shoes were a passion that she turned into survival gear. This latest design should have a nice bounce to it. The rubber platform was stylishly narrow, and the floor of the shoe was red, creating the impression of a Louboutin, hiding the peel-able layer above. The platform portion of the heel could be removed by a ninety degree rotation. Opening the lower half of the shoe revealed a tread that looked heavy, reinforced on the inside, with a blown foam insulation material containing microscopic glass beads, making the shoe lighter than an average running shoe. This specialty polymer provided traction in sand or boulders and heat resistance. The added spring from the new polymer could allow her to leap over burning objects if required. Today's question was could she wear this shoe every day as she would a normal pump?

Jane's survival visions often involved walking up a mountain of rubble. Recently, she had a dream of climbing out of a hole, filled with chunks of concrete that kept falling onto her skin. Every time a rock hit her, it left behind more blood until she was swallowing blood and concrete dust. She felt intense heat all around her. She woke up from that dream, coughing and gagging. Once the fear lifted from her body, she realized the dream helped her imagine what it was like to climb up rubble. She wasn't thinking about heat affecting the shoes until then, so she changed her materials to be both insulating and heat resistant.

This was the test run. As she walked down the inside hallway, she visualized a nuclear event, and knew to avoid windows. Windows would blow out and glass would be swirling as 165 mile per hour winds whipped through the perimeter of this office space. Knowing the safest path to the exit stairway, she also studied where each retaining wall was located. She placed each foot down carefully to test the shoes by walking slowly, planting each foot in front as she lifted the back one. Balancing could be a challenge. She could lower the heel half an inch which would require a major redesign and quickly decided to stick with this for now. Luckily, no one was at work this early to observe her strange behavior.

As she walked, she thought about which way the walls would fall and what desk she would dive under, if walls started to crumble. She imagined crawling in the dark and feeling for each cubical wall. She already memorized the number of steps to the copy machine and the critical right turn to the exit. She kept hard copies of all emergency exit information for each floor for each building she frequented in a vacuum pouch. They were all zipped into pocket number 9 of the backpack, along with an LED flashlight attached to a battery pack. Sometimes she questioned the need she was addressing but did it anyway. It was a puzzle. The art of survival was preparing for the unknown in exquisite detail.

Upon any catastrophic event Jane visualized, she always started by grabbing the Tool Box and her backpack. Each could be lit, using the pendant necklace she wore around her neck which connected to a tracking 'ring' that signaled its location with a high-pitched sound. If she was buried under rubble and alive enough to press her necklace, they could easily find her. As she pressed the pendant twice, two low amperage ropes would light up, running off the batteries, sewn into the fabric. She could charge the lights with portable solar panels, rolled up along the vertical braces in the backpack inches from the built-in connector. The Tool Box had an LED light connected to the solar panel, showing her the forward pathway. She recently added six small wheels onto the bottom of the Tool Box to make it easier to push. Jane had a fire-resistant body suit with gloves, a pair of goggles and a respirator she practiced putting on in less than twenty-five seconds. She never wore nylons and could easily wrap the body suit around any of her short skirts. Her skirts all had silk linings that worked double duty as a cloth for cleaning optical devices. Jane realized a long time ago that there was no end to her obsession and always enjoyed adding new twists to her planning, as inconsequential as they appeared. She wore contacts but had several pairs of glasses as backup. Without glasses, she could not see ten feet ahead of her. She had a pair of glasses modified with a magnifying glass inserted into the right lens. She also had night vision lenses adapted to another pair of glasses that weren't ready. They needed to be smaller. Prioritizing space in the Tool Box was always the struggle.

Six years ago, she started putting together a personal survival kit. Initially, it was a distraction. It was a distraction from work politics and uncomfortable interactions with co-workers. She needed a creative outlet. All of this daily frustration forced her to either quit or find something to distract her from this corporate environment. Solving survival problems allowed her to be unrestricted, unencumbered, and to use the full potential of her creative mind without having to get committee approval to change something.

Her first project involved developing shoes that would help during a catastrophic event. She combed the Internet for elastomeric polymers containing a softer durometer and higher cohesive strength characteristics while still being elastic. She found a small laboratory in town that formulated and cast elastomers. She came up with specifications that represented the properties she needed. With painstaking attention to detail, the scientists worked closely with her and came very close to what she had in mind. Designing the shoe was another challenge. Thanks to her neighbor who put her in touch with a retired employee of Nike, she worked out a way to mold the customized rubber into a standard shoe design. The efforts that went into creating these shoes were now realized. They provided the greatest advantage for any survival situation she could visualize, and she felt good about it.

Shoes were important for immediate survival. After surviving the immediate threat, focusing on sources of food, shelter and clean air required a lot more research. The list was endless. Food was the most fun and perhaps the easiest issue to address. Short term, she refreshed her food supply for immediate use in the backpack on a monthly basis. Fruit from the cafeteria was rotated into the desiccator which fitted perfectly in her file drawer behind the desk. Fruit had a place tucked in the outside pockets of the insulated backpack.

As she paid more attention to the food problem, she observed that a large amount of cafeteria food was thrown out. The legal department ruled that food be removed, reducing liability from sickness connected to contaminated food. This legal ruling prevented the food manager from giving anything to needy shelters around town. As Jane became acquainted with the food manager, Carol, who worked for a large contract catering corporation, she learned a little more about what was happening behind the scenes. Carol brought food to groups in need, a complex process, hidden, to even the food service workers. Jane realized this when she ran into Carol one evening in the tunnels running between the buildings. Carol was pushing a large stainless cart and moving it away from the cafeteria. It did not take long for Jane to size up the situation and to tag along with Carol and help her move the cart. Their friendship grew and Jane helped Carol move food regularly and occasionally drove the truck. She became acutely aware of where all the food was stored, and precisely where the canned food was stored, which was in the subbasement under her building. Recently, Carol mentioned the sub-basement and the special reinforcing I-beams built into the walls and she wondered if they could withstand significant impacts from the weight of thirteen floors above. That gave Jane an idea that there were probably a series of tunnels running under the corporate complex that would provide protection against high impact bombing. There was a sub-basement in the Watson Building where her next meeting was. She could drive there, park in the ramp and enter the sub-basement from there and check for I-beam placements there. There was just enough time to do that.

She placed her beloved Pradas under her desk with a sigh. They were uncomfortable but she loved them anyway. The PowerPoint was polished and she received an email confirmation that Dr. Blue was coming back from her farm and could see her today between four and five o'clock. Jane carefully closed the door behind her and checked her security camera she installed the previous week. Excited about how elegantly that worked, she smiled as she walked down the hall toward the elevator. As she entered the elevator, her phone rang.

"Hi, Jane. It's Dr. Blue." The line went dead as she stepped into the elevator and the doors closed. Jane wondered at the irony of Dr. Blue calling her at this point in time. She would have to call her back.

"You're Jane Witterhouse, right?"

She looked up to this tall man. He seemed out of place, but attractive, wearing a long-sleeved chambray shirt and nice fitting jeans. Everyone else in the elevator, dressed like Jane in their navy blue suits and white shirts, ignored everything around them except their Blackberry phones, even though the internet connections was not available. Jane noticed his naturally coiffed hair. It was refreshing to see what an inexpensive haircut looked like. He kept smiling at her and she reluctantly responded with a shy smile. Thanks to good genes, Jane's smile was a sweet one which made others smile. She knew him but from where?

"Yes, and you are?"

"Jason Kelly, but people call me Jake."

"We've met before, but I can't place you. You went to the University?"

"Yep, we were lab partners once, a long time ago. You probably don't have fond memories of me." Instantly, everyone in the elevator looked up.

Now she remembered this guy from a Chemistry lab she almost failed. He was smart, but not interested in getting good grades. He pursued this time-consuming outlier in their research project that resulted in the two of them turning in an unfinished lab report. The only C she ever got. I wonder what's he's doing here? "Yes, that was a while ago."

Suddenly, the elevator started to shake as it went down two floors. That's strange, she thought. She shifted her gaze to the elevator walls and listened to the cables moving the elevator down the shaft. She thought about what escape route they would use. Elevators were not a bad place to be. Emergency instructions always directed people to the stairs. But if one was in an elevator during a crisis situation, one could get on top of the elevator 'box' and proceed down the elevator shaft more quickly, using the ladder, than going down the outside stairs. She met an elevator repair guy once, who recited every movie that had an elevator escape scene. He told Jane which movies were technically accurate and which movies were completely stupid. He referred to an elevator as a box on a string and there was no reason for anyone to be trapped in an elevator, however romantic those scenes appeared. The elevator reached the ground floor and the doors opened. She thought of a question to ask Jake. She turned to him.

"Catch you later," Jake shouted as he jumped out of the elevator and out the double doors of the building.

"Damn," she said and grabbed her phone. Dr. Blue left a voicemail to call her back.

Dr. Eva Blue had a small kind face with permanently set wrinkles that held forty years of deep listening. Sessions often began with questions connecting her body to her thoughts like, "How are you feeling right now?" or "Where in your body are you feeling tension?" Dr. Blue always started by bringing Jane into present awareness. After reading many college textbooks on therapy, Jane understood that her basic approach to therapy was Jungian mixed with mindfulness practices. Jane struggled with this at first. It was very hard for her to be present since her mind was always on ruminate. Jane spent her free time visualizing catastrophic events, the opposite of being present. Jane later realized that the key to survival was not just good preparation but understanding the situation as it unfolded. Being present was the ultimate survival skill. That was when Jane started a daily meditation practice.

Several sessions after Dr. Blue first observed Jane's Tool Box, she asked questions about how she prepared for her day. Questions like in what order did she brush her teeth? Did she wash her hair before she brushed her teeth? Did she pick out her clothes the night before? Jane trusted Dr. Blue and went along with her. Dr. Blue then shifted to asking about times when she was interested in worldwide events.

Jane, in her comfort zone, did not hesitate and started to tell her story of when she was sixteen years old. She watched every news program she could about the Oklahoma City bombing, April 19, 1995. She remembered national news programs going over the same footage and talking about how the people exited the building, the losses, the injuries, and the missing people. In Jane's senior year, she wrote a paper about the bombing. She specialized on profiling each person in that bombing. She studied what they did on that day before, during, and after the bombing. She spent hours researching information and finding all the pictures she could of the building and the people. She called the OC Tribune and heavily relied on her conversations with a reporter, Maximillian Trotsky, for facts outside of what they reported. After writing the paper, she could not quite let it go. She asked her parents if they would let her go to Oklahoma and they agreed to let her drive there on her own after graduation. She tried to contact Maximillian, but he just passed away from a rare heart disease. She could spend time with his wife, Alva. It turned out that Alva was a photographer, and they spent the weekend poring over photos and stories from that tragic period.

"Are you still in contact with Alva?" ask Dr. Blue.

"Yes, we email and talk on the phone maybe monthly," said Jane. "We developed a special bond."

After this question, Jane realized Dr. Blue had moved and was making tea. Dr. Blue reached down to pick up Jane's hand and gave it a squeeze.

She smiled and said, "Jane, your time is up. We will see you next week."

Jane felt Dr. Blue's soft grey eyes on her back as she approached the door. She turned around to see Dr. Blue waving back at her.

Dr. Blue did not waste any time in the next session. She asked Jane to make a list of her biggest dreams and biggest disappointments. Jane loved making lists, but found this challenging. How long did she spend looking at her blank screen, coming up with one dream? Her one disappointment was easy; not being able to save her mother from dying of breast cancer.

As Jane described her dissatisfaction with the lists to Dr. Blue, she said, "I know you are not going to tell me what you are thinking!"

Dr. Blue said, "I'm not sure if telling you what I am thinking is going to help. I'm glad that you were honest. What was this experience like for you?"

Jane looked at Dr. Blue and blurted, "Are you going to tell me your conclusions from these lists?"

Dr. Blue shook her head. Jane continued to work on her list each session, Dr. Blue listening with curiosity. Eventually, Jane could make these lists more easily as they changed. As she reflected on these two simple questions, she could find older disappointments before her mother's death with the list of her dreams continuing to bubble. She was now realizing how much the corporate life took away from her real dream of starting a new business. Maybe creating a business in agriculture technology. She wondered what Dan would think. He was close to retiring and might want to set up a consulting arrangement. She knew this was a real dream as each time she thought about it, it expanded in a new direction.

Jane called Dr. Blue. "Jane, something has come up and I'm sorry, but I have to cancel. I'll call you back a little later to reschedule. I have to stay at the farm one more day and take my mother to the doctor."

"I hope she's okay. I guess I'll see you tomorrow then," said Jane.

They said goodbye and Jane continued to walk toward her car.

LUMING - 12

Luming still could not figure out if Brother's dream had anything to do with Chris' plan. He explained to Brother what happened, skipping no detail, and mentioned how strange it was, even for Chris, to be acting this way. It was Chris' phrase, "The last day of civilization as we know it," that made Brother tag along and see what would happen next. Luming was thrilled at Brother joining them. However, he was still planning on getting back to work by 11:00 AM. When they got to Luming's home, Chris was waiting for them in an old red Ford pickup truck. He yelled, "Get in. There's no time, let's hurry."

"Look, Chris, just letting you know I have to be back here by 10:30. This is Brother. He's meditation master at—"

"Yes, I know him. You've spoken about him often. Hi, Brother. Can you please convince Luming to get into the truck quickly? Please. We've got to drive to the university to meet someone and I can't miss it. I'll explain on the way."

Brother had the last word. "Luming, I think the fates are telling you something here. I'm not sure what, but if you release the tight grip, you have around your job, you might leave yourself open to something new. If you have to leave, we'll make it happen. I say, let's take Chris' offer."

Brother gave just the encouragement that Luming needed. It bothered him how much work affected his life and how he slaved over PowerPoint presentations, but it was the number of people that depended on him that kept him conforming to the corporate rigor. There was an endless flow of demands that were never satisfied, only to be superseded by a new set of demands. Everyone was together on each project. No one knew how to stop working.

As Chris revved the engine, Brother jumped into the front seat. As they pushed their bodies across the bench seat, trying to avoid the enormous stick shift coming out of the floor, Chris started to release the clutch with his foot. He ground the gears, finding the right gear as they started to jerk back and forth away from the curb. Chris wound up the gears quickly to move into third gear just as he made a tight left turn, trying to downshift and brake at the same time. They rolled against Chris, with Luming holding back, pulling on the safety strap.

Luming started to fire out questions. "No seat belts here. Chris, where did you get a gas-guzzling antique like this? Where are we going?"

Chris was again changing gears to speed up and make it through the first stoplight and turned toward the entrance ramp to the freeway. "I stored this truck for a moment just like this. It's a long story that I hope to share with you later, but for now, let's say that I'm part of a bigger group effort. This truck is an enigma. While it looks rough, it had a complete overhaul a few years ago. The standard transmission keeps things simple. It's mechanical and does not require any board circuitry to run. It has a steel body and very few aluminum parts. It's strong and can carry heavy equipment if needed." As they merged onto the freeway, Chris carefully changed gears to align with the power the transmission was transferring as the truck slowly gained enough momentum to merge into traffic. The three of them were quiet, as if praying that they could gain enough speed to meet the fast moving traffic. The truck grinding its gears, magnified Luming's anxiety and speaking was out of the question.

Once they were safely tucked in the right lane for slower cars, the noise lowered slightly. Chris leaned over and looked at Luming, wide-eyed, and shouted, "What the hell, Luming. This is your great adventure, much larger than I was intending today. Let's reframe. You are going on a long journey and you may never return home. You brought your backpack, right? This will be a journey which, if you are lucky, will save you from catastrophe. Here, take this." Chris threw a tightly rolled marijuana joint across Brother into Luming's lap. Luming picked it up and carefully examined it and tossed back to Chris and said, "Really, Chris, you are too much." Chris smiled, pulled out his lighter, and started to inhale the joint.

"Open the window!" shouted Luming.

"Nah, you've got nothing to worry about, Luming. Within the next two hours, things will change big time. Brother, care to puff?" as he handed the joint to Brother.

Brother took the joint, expertly pulled in the smoke and handed it to Luming. Luming took a long puff and coughed lightly. "Hopefully, my asthma won't react. It's been a long time since I've done this."

Brother looked around calmly, sandwiched in between Luming and Chris, and said, "Journey."

"What? Speak louder!" said Chris.

Brother seemed to have a problem speaking loudly. He put his whole body into it and said, "I said journey. I like that word. What journey are we taking? Can you hear me now?"

"Yes, it's a little better. Okay, now the fact is our journey has already started. You are now an official member, Bro."

Brother was still pushing himself to speak loudly. "Well, if it is a journey, I'm in. I had a strange dream about a catastrophic disaster and masses of people died before escape was possible. I have not slept since. I saw Lazarus, raising people from the dead. It was frightening," said Brother. "As I remember the dream, I still feel the fear that woke me up."

"This is too much, Brother. Give me that," said Luming as he leaned over to take the joint from him. Luming took another long drag off the joint, held it and exhaled. "Wow, Brother. That's a powerful dream. Have you dreamed about the future before and has it ever happened? It makes my OC meeting seem small in comparison." They were now getting used to conversation at a heightened volume.

"OC?" asked Brother.

"Oh yeah, it's corporate lingo for Operating Committee. Chris, you did not answer the question, where are we going?"

"Okay. No problem. The plans have transformed. I received a call from a very close friend from Chufu, a small village outside of Beijing, about twenty-five minutes ago, exactly 9:03 AM CST. He has been networking for the last twenty-two hours, twelve o'clock noon, yesterday. There is a cataclysmic concern of a worldwide nuclear holocaust."

As they continued down the freeway, the truck weaved into the shoulder enough to make Brother and Luming brace themselves. When

Luming heard those two words, nuclear holocaust, it did not immediately register as he was busy adjusting to the truck's ability to correct and stay in one lane. Chris was not smiling, but he had a surprisingly calm look on his face.

"Chris, nuclear holocaust? That is hard to imagine. How reliable is your source?" Luming shouted and wished they could talk naturally. Luming felt an abundance of nervous twitches coming from his neck. "Really, Chris, can we just pull over and talk about this?"

"We're almost there and then we'll talk. Sorry that I've been so evasive, but I did not understand that it could impact us until I confirmed my friend's insight two more ways. It was conclusive and then I got a call to meet Dorothy of Finland, a member of our The Co-op, someone who has arrived with some very special seeds. There isn't much time. I guess my little game ended up being authentic."

"Your game sucks, Chris. Are we still playing it?" said Luming.

"No, that's what I trying to say to you. I've been developing an end of the world app and was trying to get you to play so I could collect information and adapt it to a real-life situation. The idea was what would it take for normal people with boring jobs to believe an end of the world prediction or major catastrophic event and act as if it was their last day on earth? What would it take to disrupt their normal bubble of existence? You were perfect for this trial, Luming. You had a boring job, but I thought you were open enough to try it out. Now this has just become a lucky coincidence for you. I have every reason to believe that this is true and we're racing for our lives right now."

As Chris was talking, the three of them turned their heads to stare at a limousine with blacked-out windows passing them on the left. Luming studied the limousine closely. He adapted to all kinds of changes this morning and allowed himself to be part of this crazy flight of Chris'. He was exhausted. Thankfully, Brother was with him to help steady the situation. He was always the calm in the storm and he seemed to not have reacted strongly to Chris' newest information.

It was at that point that Chris reached over Brother and shoved a bank receipt into Luming's hand. "See, I was serious," shouted Chris. "Here is your bank receipt and cash card."

Luming was a little shocked, but sat silently. Chris started to speed up to come alongside of the limo. Luming was feeling strangely focused as he stared into the limo. No more adventures today! Go back to work.

When a limo is sufficiently backlit, one can see right into it, but at sixty miles per hour, they did not see anything except their reflection in the window. Chris dropped back to a following position. He then pulled out another joint, lit it and filled the front seat with pot smoke which they all inhaled. Luming coughed and opened the window again. As Chris smoked the joint, the front cab was getting cloudy with smoke as the fresh air was replaced with pot air.

Luming leaned forward and said to Chris, "Really, are you serious?" Luming had no problem with smoking but smoking and traveling the freeway in a broken-down truck was a bit of a problem with him. He said nothing further to Chris. He quietly looked forward and said a prayer for their safety and hoped it would be good enough.

Luming knew Chris was a daily pot smoker. Once in a while, Luming could smell it on his breath or his clothing, but Chris never involved Luming in smoking pot. Diagnosed at an early age for asthma, Luming relied on nebulizers in China, and now metered dose inhalers, regularly. While he could drink hurricanes until oblivion in New Orleans, fresh air was the only thing his lungs allowed him to inhale, keeping cigarettes and pot smoke as something to avoid. He could feel his lungs start to gasp for air and he tried to suppress the urge to cough, which tightened up his alveoli and left him gasping for more air. He pulled out his inhaler, which brought immediate relief.

Chris took his fifth hit off the joint, opened the window to blow out the smoke and handed it to Luming. Luming tossed the joint out the window. "Even if it is the last day on Earth, I still have to breathe."

So the trio focused on this limo in front of them. As they headed west, they crossed the river and the limo took the exit at about eighty miles per hour.

Chris said, "Wow, man. That limo almost looked like a black sausage rolling across a table. Awesome! It's taking our exit to the university. That's strange." They followed, making the same turn. Even at a lower speed, everyone was white-knuckled and quiet.

The limo slowed as it reached the university campus, but still moved aggressively through the streets. It finally pulled up to a tall white building and a tall, slim woman, wearing green corduroy pants and a heavy sweater of earth colors and textures, slipped out without looking back at the driver. She had a striking presence, wearing a long scarf of purple, pink, black and spring green wrapped around her neck, covering her throat, and a shock of white spiky hair came straight out of her head. They all stared up at her, her height being the thing, that most commanded their attention. Luming thought she was obviously not from around here and was probably some kind of rock star.

"Wow," Chris said, breaking the silence. "I think that's Dorothy. Get out, quick! Take the elevator to the sixteenth floor. I'll meet you there. Let me park the truck. Tell her know I'm here!"

Brother got out of the truck and bowed to the ground. "I'm grateful," he said. "As a Buddhist, we observe our death and face it as our main teaching. I don't recall when I have had the chance to visualize my death so clearly. Speed and pot are a unique combination that I will consider as a future practice."

Luming laughed, not knowing if Brother was being serious or funny. They started moving toward the Medical Arts Building. Luming seemed to have trouble moving quickly.

"Damn," he said. "The sidewalk is sliding under my feet."

Brother laughed and said, "Luming, you're stoned."

The mystery woman entered the building. She walked quickly without hesitation to the elevator and punched the up button with her leather glove. The elevator arrived and she got on, pushing the people getting out. As this was happening, they ran toward the elevator and Brother jumped on first and held the doors for Luming. Without time to plan their next step out loud, Luming was pressed right next to this woman. Brother pressed the button for the sixteenth floor.

Sweat started to drip down Luming's cheek and spattered onto his jacket where it soaked quickly into the blue fabric. He smelled thyme and sage mixed with the heat coming off the woman's body which started to calm down his anxiety, but the sweating continued in an embarrassing way. Luming then spent the next two floors worrying that he smelled like reefer. The elevator was a slow mover and stopped at each floor. People got off, slowly relieving the pressure of physical contact.

Luming started to think about his last day on Earth. Each day is your last day. Brother said that to me one time. I am living my own dream, not someone else's. Am I in a dream? A journey dream? I'm spending my time racing, running and acting in the moment. Wish I knew what was as going on.

Upon reaching the sixteenth floor, the woman stepped out quickly and they piled out right behind her. If they had not previously raised suspicion, they would now.

Luming, suddenly filled with courage, asked, "Excuse me, miss. Are you Dorothy?"

She stopped and stared back at him. "Excuse me?" she said with a shrilly voice. "I'm sorry. I am a visitor here. I have an appointment to see Dr. Anthony and cannot be of help to you." The accent was crisp and strong and familiar, but Luming could not nail it. Was it Finnish, Swedish or Norwegian? They all sounded alike to him.

While Luming froze at these words, Brother swooped in to help. His cool, patient facial expression and fluid body movements always established a calm feeling with most people. It also helped that he knew basic greetings in many languages. He tried saying hello in German, Finnish and Swedish.

Her face cracked a smile and she laughed at his efforts. "Hei, do you mean? I am from Helsinki, the capital of Finland," she said in perfect English. "I just arrived on a DC-10 from Schipol today. I have to find Dr. Anthony as soon as possible. Are you following me?" Luming and Brother looked at each other. "I am in a hurry," she said impatiently as she turned.

"We can help," said Luming in his most knowledgeable voice and attitude that the Chinese are so adept at. "We came with Chris. He's parking the truck."

She looked at him carefully, "We don't have time. Chris needs to be ready with the truck once I'm done here. Can you reach him for me, please!"

Luming's phone rang. Chris was just entering the lobby of the building.

"That works. I've got to meet with Dr. Anthony now. What's your name?" she said, pointing to Brother. "Wait here for Chris. You come with me," pointing to Luming.

She pushed open the double door to the laboratories. Luming walked next to her, looking for signs on each door for the name Dr. Anthony. He saw it first. She stopped and looked relieved. The window in the door had huge black bold letters that read, Dr. Wolfgang Anthony, Professor Emeritus of Biological Transference.

"Wow, now that is a title," Luming said out loud.

She turned toward them and said, "I'm now okay. Thank you very much. Wait for me." She opened the door without knocking and closed it behind her.

Luming was left, trying to see inside the office, but the window was frosted.

Luming called Chris. "I'm still in the lobby," Chris said, "Just getting into an elevator. No place to park. We have thirty minutes."

"The woman in the limousine is Dorothy. She's meeting with Wolfgang Anthony, Professor Emeritus of Biological Transference," said Luming.

"Bingo, this came together very nicely!"

Luming stared at the closed door. This dream could not be weirder or he must have gotten stoned from the pot. Every word spoken and these white walls, everything, was giving him a strange feeling.

MICHAEL -13

As Michael walked into the lobby of the Watson building, he lingered for a while, looking at his Blackberry and texting his clothing consultant about a Gucci belt. It was important to look busy in a public place to elevate his importance. He had an hour to kill before his next meeting. Eleven o'clock was an active time of day as people left for long lunches or appointments so they could be back by 1:00 PM. Occasionally, Michael was also guilty of a two-hour lunch, but it was to stay connected to outside lawyers that supported him and a way to write off lunch.

As Michael started to move into the glass atrium, he saw his and Marcella's good friends, Malcolm and Deirdre Browning. Wow, such luck! he thought. They walked up to Michael as he finished texting.

"Hello there, Michael. How are you? We saw you talking to McKenzie. That looked like an interesting conversation," said Deirdre.

Michael liked the Brownings. Marcella and Michael first met them at a wine-tasting club and they seemed to be a little helpless in this sea of Midwesterners. They never seemed to fit in, missing the high cultural standards they were used to. The Brownings loved wine tasting and studied it vigorously. Michael thought anyone that spent that much time studying each wine, globally, by region or by varietal, must be good people. He knew they were currently exploring the South African Pinotage vintages as being earthy, almost a muddy wine. Their favorite amusement was comparing the best of Cabernet Sauvignon varietals of Napa versus the 2009 Bordeaux. Marcella and Michael also had a lot in common with the Brownings as they all owned homes on ten acre lots. Malcolm and Deidre went so far as to refer to their estate as being in a double-gated community. Michael thought that was a pretentious statement, but he knew the concept of being understated was not a concept that easterners could easily grasp.

The Brownings tended to gravitate toward people that shared their interest in wine and restaurants. Neither Browning cooked, so eating out was a necessity. As Michael and Marcella took to some of the benefits of empty nesting, they frequently joined them.

The Brownings did not have children. They often spent long hours on the weekend working on numerous projects. They always operated as a team for the same company and commanded high salaries. They chose the companies they wanted to work FOR and smart companies were always grateful for their contributions. Malcolm was originally a professor emeritus at Yale University and was always heavily recruited to work for a corporate laboratory. Deirdre, an agriculture scientist, was one of the original scientists who discovered the method for the transformation of genes into chromosomal DNA for accelerated trait development in a variety of plants, including corn and soybeans. Having been at this corporation for three years, they found their stride and pursued their many interests while commanding two six-figure salaries. Since they had no children spending their money, they had a large safety net that allowed them to change companies on a whim.

Big corporations needed academicians that were flexible enough to appreciate profit-driven initiatives. The Brownings were also able to support the legal department with information on any liability cases they were working on. While they pursued their preferred research, they were on hand to testify in court in support of ongoing legal cases. Michael was always there to show them the ropes and ensure that their testimony would be provided when needed and to coach them if necessary. They always seemed grateful to Michael for his help. They were allowed to conduct research practice around next generational genomics and flexible solar film technology which was their joint passion. The prestige they commanded, the control over others and the numerous technicians that conducted research on their behalf were all part of this unique situation.

Michael suspected that this was not a chance meeting, especially when Deirdre mentioned seeing him talking to Dr. McKenzie. Dr. McKenzie was their boss and well known for strange and weird activities. He rarely shared what he was up to and spent a lot of time traveling internationally with the CEO in one of the corporate jets or taking helicopter rides across the city for lunch. He had the remarkable ability to relate to customers, board members and other CEOs. He was a perfect complement to a high-tech company. He could explain most projects from a technical side and with his photographic memory, could impress just about anyone, including investors, with solid scientific facts. The Brownings never envied McKenzie's job and the more he traveled, the better off they were.

"I hate to be coy, Michael. McKenzie just got back from a trip from China with a renewed interest in saving $1 billion dollars from the R&D budget. We just found out from our sources that he plans to stop the bioengineering project we are working on. He could be cutting a lot of our projects. I'm wondering if he is aware of the number of legal depositions we are involved in? We just thought that you might not be aware of this," said Deirdre. Malcolm was nodding.

So this chance meeting was not spontaneous, thought Michael. Deirdre might have had her secretary find out where his meetings were today.

Michael said, "I heard that your work was going to be featured at the annual shareholder's meeting. That must be exciting for the two of you."

"It depends," said Deirdre, who was never shy and always direct. "We provided the selection committee with Malcolm's research on extending the life of flexible solar panel materials and my research on plant genomics growing plants materials that could be used for solar applications. I recently became aware that the genomics project might get removed due to a space concern in our building. I have also seen signs that McKenzie might be getting rid of all plant projects to sponsor his Equinox project."

"What's that project about?" asked Michael.

Deirdre answered, "It's well concealed from the technical community. I've no idea what it is about. McKenzie hired a Dr. Mueller, from Germany, a renowned hydrocarbon chemist. That may have something to do with this."

Michael was clearly not ready for this conversation, especially after making a significant promise to support McKenzie. Not knowing much more than what McKenzie told him, he better keep it CTTV (Close To The Vest). It was best to soothe any concerns until he could find out the extent of McKenzie's plan.

Michael let some time pass so when he responded, the Brownings would understand the impact of what he was saying. Almost in a whisper, Michael said, "I understand that Dr. McKenzie is under the gun to provide some budget cutting for the next two quarters. Healthcare profits are short and everyone has to do their part. I'm sure McKenzie is overwrought with concern over this issue and I am sure that the last thing he would cut would be your work. In fact, Jane Witterhouse is giving a proposal to our management today to support your project," stated Michael.

"Oh yeah, we know about this meeting and in fact, I am planning to attend. She has been wonderful to work with and so smart. She managed to describe the technology we need to acquire in two slides, so simplistically. I feel lucky to be working with her. She's well connected and has a good track record for helping both parties arrive at a successful conclusion," said Deirdre.

All of this was starting to make Michael burn up. Trying not to give away his position, he said in a somewhat patronizing way, "She is our best negotiator, but part of her job is to discern what's best for the company and not showcase her talents. I just spoke to her and I thought she said the deal is kind of shaky right now."

That was just the response for Deirdre to become agitated. "Why didn't she call me? How can she keep this from us?" she asked.

"No, please don't worry," said Michael. "I also hope to attend this meeting to make sure everyone's interests are protected. You know your funding is supported at the top level, so please understand that whatever happens, you'll have your work." Michael then looked around with his busy face expression and said he was sorry, but he had to leave for a meeting and left the Brownings in a confused state.

LOIS - 13

The bus rolled right into the curb, as busses do. Lois got off and walked up to the Soba Shop for an early lunch of steamed shrimp over noodles in miso broth. This bus stop was Lois' reminder to eat something. By the time she would leave the language lab, everything would be closed and she would just eat the next day. While she hated having a full stomach that drained some of her energy, she always found her chances of surviving a whole day of work in the labs were better with food in her stomach.

She checked her email while eating and looked around at a few students just starting their day at 11:00 AM. Maybe they had a late night with their friends. They all wore black jeans and tops, slightly torn in different ways, but very expensive. They gave the impression of being socially awkward in a cool way, but without this well-curated look, they might look as ordinary as she did.

Lois never experienced privilege in college. She thought her merit scholarship would introduce her to an upper class of people, but she never had time to meet people socially. Was it the lack of expensive clothes, her introversion or just being focused on each task? Was she facing a lifetime of loneliness? It was graduate school when she finally faced herself honestly. She concluded that she was just not that visible to students her age as she held back from opportunities to socialize. She lacked the ability to connect and she lacked the desire to try.

After some lingering and people-watching, she decided it was time to go to the language lab. The sun was shining bright, light snow covered the green grass on campus and she sensed the day was going to be a fresh start for her.

Privileged students had tuition and books paid for at least four years, a car and an apartment if they wanted one. Parents actually bought their kids houses to live in during their college years. Lois felt both envy and disgust when she thought about that. Parents that supported their children produced young adults who believed themselves deserving of privileges and special treatment. As a TA, students often came up to her because they needed extra time to complete their labs. Her reputation developed quickly. She never walked away from being extra tough on these students and never looked back.

Walking to the language lab exposed her to the oldest part of campus. This path always deepened her awareness of the ancient wisdom that originally inspired the building of large universities. Each old building, built in the mid-nineteenth century, dispensed wisdom across the entrances. Wisdom that someone wanted to forward to the future generation in hopes that it would transcend ordinary existence and motivate students to grasp the importance of deep learning. As she walked into the language building, she looked up at the words, "The roots of education are bitter, but the fruit is sweet," Aristotle 384-322 B.C.

She passed by the community bulletin board with requests for tutoring and translation help. She thought about how well her business was going and how easy it fell together. Her Mandarin and Cantonese studies that started in junior high allowed her to test out of first year college Chinese. The summer before graduating in high school, she set up a website supporting Chinese/English and English/Chinese translation services by the hour. This helped her to master both Mandarin and Cantonese. She then was allowed to test out of two more advanced courses, minimizing the credits she had to pay to graduate. Once she understood the market opportunity, her business really took off. She directed her site toward local corporations she met at a trade show that focused on developing business-to-business markets in China. Now there was more work than she could handle. She found that just a few contacts in each company kept her as busy as she wanted to be, making over $40,000 a year. At $100 an hour, she was able to squeeze in four hundred hours of translation with a portion of the work doubling as credit hours. If her success continued, she could fund one hundred percent of her graduate school education.

The lab was never crowded this time of day. Lois found the single cubby she loved open, tucked around the corner between the lab and the windows. It was quieter than the rows of cubbies that would start filling up around noon. No one seemed to realize this spot was available. The language lab had to be as old as the university, over 150 years old. This old brick and mortar university never disappointed Lois in its grand attempts to ignore the necessities of the electronic age. Three computers sat on the floor, all trying to charge from a single receptacle. The plaster lathe walls, with cracks and open seams, felt like they would all crumble and vaporize at any moment. These old walls would have to be replaced one day, she thought.

Lois just started studying Farsi, spoken in Iran, Afghanistan, and Tajikistan, and it was one of those languages that promised higher paying jobs. There was some comfort in studying language, especially one that emerged from ancient Persia. Lois had a strange feeling about speaking and writing languages that touched her soul. She noted her fluency and general language capabilities were unusually good when she felt the deeper meaning from the spoken language. Her teacher was encouraging her to do more, but she was never around to provide much guidance. Lois was considered highly independent, and professors tended to spend their time with the more needy students.

Arabic was more challenging as a culture than as a language. The writing was a little less complicated than Mandarin. The written characters were simpler, and there were fewer of them. She did think that she needed to live the language rather than study it, but she clearly was afraid of the culture because the masculine dominance showed up everywhere in the language. Gender equality was completely missing in this ancient culture and this was the worst time to be a woman in most Arab nations. She chose Farsi because of its connection to ancient times and was developing a thesis of whether or not the language itself also discriminated against women. This was her proposed thesis, but it was subject to her major professor's approval. She either was not interested or just did not have the time to meet Lois yet. Just one of the many frustrations about graduate school.

Her need to take care of herself and not depend on others was non-negotiable. At some point, she might think a little bit longer about what made her happy, but for now, she was doing well. What would she rather be doing? Was living comfortably important to her future? Where would she like to live? Where would she like to visit? What was she yearning for? She needed to find time to think about this. She was too busy holding things together to spend it thinking about some vague future.

As she put on her headphones, she played back a few complex social conversations in Farsi between a man and a woman. She glanced down and noticed a missed phone call from Martha, an assistant of one of her major clients, Dan. She called her back.

"Hey, Lois. It's good to hear from you."

"I was in the lab, studying," said Lois.

"Sorry to interrupt your work, but I am calling about a rush job. Are you busy? Can you break off what you are doing and help us out? Dan is looking for translations and it's urgent. We received a lot of unusual emails in the last twelve hours from China in Mandarin. We need a way to detect if there is a coded message embedded in these emails."

Lois kind of laughed at Martha's specificity, but she knew Martha well enough to understand that she was an excellent support person, but not known for succinct conversations. Martha mentioned to Lois that she would like to send a zip drive of the emails. If Lois could look at them immediately, Martha would offer triple her current rate.

"You don't have to do that, Martha. I'm just sitting down to study Farsi and barely got started. Let's just say I'm always up for a challenge and don't have classes until three o'clock this afternoon."

"Farsi, isn't that the language spoken in Iran? Isn't Farsi the same as Persian? It's a pluricentric language and its grammar is similar to that of many contemporary European languages. That sounds like you, Lois. You are a unique woman and have no fear around learning," said Martha.

"Wow, Martha. You are well informed, but I've never thought of myself as fearless. I want to think about that. Well, anyway, yes, I would love to do this job and maybe catch up with Dan while I'm at it. Would love to chat with him about an article I'm writing for *The Speed*. It's called "The New Glass Ceiling." I'm sure he would get a kick out of it."

"Dan is on vacation today, babysitting his granddaughter. I'll send the emails right away," said Martha. "By the way, I'm on vacation in about two hours. Let me get ahold of Dan. I'll put you on hold."

Lois looked up across the language lab, seeing a few students with earphones talking into the speakers. Their facial expressions always looked stressed, as they tried to hear and respond to what was being said in that foreign language. Short of speaking to someone who knew the language, language lab was one of the few ways to prep for the oral test.

Martha came back to Lois and said while Dan sounded preoccupied, he agreed it would be good to talk it through once the translation was complete. She should call him when she was done. Dan was a cool guy. He was tall, in good shape, nice hair and could converse with women as friends, not objects for sexual consideration. Lois checked herself and was not sure what all that implied. Could she have a little crush on Dan? She did like older men. Well, that would not be the first. Lois checked herself again and said out loud, "Damn hormones!"

Lois was excited about the project. School always seemed to be less exciting than these projects. She would be much happier if she could just freelance projects, knowing she had enough work to support her. What good is a PhD except a method for going broke very early in your career? How many times did she think about this a day! She had no pressure from parents to stay in school and no peer pressure from friends. At least skipping school, if that was what she was doing, helped her gravitate toward those projects that were making a difference to someone.

Lois opened her computer and started reading the first email that Martha sent. The language was Mandarin, but the information seemed to be set in some kind of slang, a newer language. She opened up ten more emails and found certain words were being used out of context as if they were a coded message. She had friends that could be of help. They were Chinese and very adept at creating algorithms quickly. They might find this project to be interesting enough to drop everything and look at it. However, they did have their quirks. One was she could not contact them by phone. She just had to show up, knowing where they were located and trust they would be there. They were also choosy about what projects they worked on. She should call her friend Luming who could help persuade them. She needed to find the Five Guys to help her.

LUMING - 14

The phone rang. "Stay there. We're coming toward you."

Luming could hear Chris and Brother as they came through the double doors and talked all the way to this Dr. Anthony's office. "You can start explaining things to us anytime, Chris," said Luming with a higher voice and he felt his face turning red from frustration.

"Hang on," and Chris went up to Anthony's door and listened in. "I'm not supposed to interfere, but we need to move along. There isn't much time. Let's go over to these chairs and hopefully I can clarify for you what I can."

The three of them sat down in a circle of pristine white chairs, modern and, Luming thought, uncomfortable.

"Luming, we've known each other for over a year, have done stuff together and I've always enjoyed it. What you probably don't know about me is what I do for a living, outside of developing apps. I've studied genetically modified plants for a long time. There's a lot to know about plant genetics and a lot of information that is frankly too complex for anyone but a limited number of scientists to understand. Most people panic when they think of GMOs, agriculture's version of Frankenstein. I graduated ten years ago from the University of Finland with a PhD in human genetics when precise cloning techniques were developed. In February of '97, a Scottish laboratory announced to a shocked world that they successfully cloned a sheep and they called her Dolly, named after the singer, because of her large mammary glands. While Dolly was not the first animal to be cloned, she was the first to be cloned from an adult cell. She started a global ethical debate. It took 277 cloning attempts to produce Dolly and after much analysis, it was concluded that the nuclear transfer technique may never be efficient for use in humans. However, the backlash was significant and people were shocked. Religious groups and scientific futurists created alarm around human beings without souls and Mendelian opportunities for creating a superhuman race. Many researchers recognized the future in this field would involve heavy regulatory restrictions and reporting. A handful of individuals withdrew from academia and industry and exited the cloning field as quietly as possible, myself included. I joined in a practice of genetic experimentation using privately funded labs that eventually were connected in an underground global network. With financial autonomy intact through various benefactors, we did not need to publish or patent what we were doing. As the level of research was increased, we were able to share and advance faster than any one corporate or academic laboratory."

The sudden change in Chris' language and demeanor from his casual, laid-back attitude surprised Luming, but Brother seemed to be listening closely. Chris continued.

"The first focus was to develop principles for our research which we called Planet Positive Principles, The Three Ps. We left mammalian genetics behind and spent our energies advancing plant genetics, using many of the tools that were developed for mammalian cloning. Plants were an innocent and electrifying area of science. Everyone wants to feed the world. Expanding plant habitation to arid regions where nothing grows except for cactus and mesquite was exciting, but our main focus was to build a plant that was nutritionally perfect. A plant containing the amino acids required for human growth and, in addition, an important vitamin not present in plant life, Vitamin B_{12}. An important vitamin to brain growth and one that can only be found in supplements. The complete sequence of amino acids and the nutritional composition of dark leafy vegetables that contain large quantities of vitamins including K, A and C were combined," stated Chris with a passion that Luming never saw before.

"I thought GMOs were bad for you," said Luming.

"You think that because natural food corporations have spent massive amounts of money lobbying Washington to make the public fearful of GMOs and plant research. Their financial efforts outpaced pharmaceutical and gun lobbies ten-fold." Chris enunciated this last part with his carefully placed words. He shook his head and said, "Our group currently has laboratories in Korea, several locations in China, one laboratory each in France, Mexico, Chile and the US."

"This is very interesting, Chris, but I am confused about why we're here. How is this tied to Dr. Wolfgang Anthony?" asked Brother.

Chris got up, checked the closed door, listened a little and came back. "I was hoping this was going to be quick."

"Why don't you knock on the door?"

"No way," said Chris. "Dr. Anthony can't see me. We've had conflicts before. I think he's a complete jerk, but we need him right now." Chris sat back and watched the door. "After spending time in research, I found a way for my passion to translate to a good business model. I started a seed-saver group. Climate-controlled storage facilities were becoming important to groups that were trying to preserve seeds for future use. We accepted any seed, any type of seed, including GMO, as long as the client was able to pay for long-term storage, we accepted everything. If they wanted to protect the identity of the seed, we let them. It started out as a small effort and was compatible with the work we were doing on creating the perfect plant. It was a revenue generator to support the research, in fact.

"We had a client that worked with us a lot," Chris said. "This guy inherited a warehouse after his parents' sudden death and after discovering he had two million dollars from his father's coin collection, he set up one of the earliest, large scale hydroponic grow-ops in the country. It came to be the most sophisticated, clandestine hydroponic pot growing facility in North America," said Chris. "Following that ..." and then Dr. Anthony's door opened.

The woman's face looked flushed, like red paint on concrete. She was not smiling and her demeanor was completely changed. The tall man in a white lab coat who must be Dr. Anthony looked at her, and quickly closed the door behind her.

She looked directly at Chris and said, "Wait." Seconds later, a very large man with big muscles was wheeling two large burlap bags down the hallway using a bright red dolly. As he walked away, a brief moment went by where Dorothy seemed frozen in time as she looked at Chris.

Chris sprinted toward her and gave her a hug that lasted. "Let's get out of here," he said, taking control of the dolly and headed for the elevator. Brother and Luming trailed behind the two of them.

Chris pressed the elevator down button repeatedly. "This is Dorothy, by the way," said Chris, looking back at Luming and Brother. She looked up, smiled, and then looked down at the floor deep in thought. Her long thin body swayed, as deep wrinkles appeared down her forehead, making her appear much older than she first appeared. The elevator doors opened. It was overflowing with post-lunchtime crowds. Chris jumped in, looked back at Dorothy and said, "I'll get the truck and meet you at the entrance." The elevator doors closed, leaving Brother, Luming and Dorothy behind.

They waited at the elevator with the large bags overwhelming the dolly. Luming never used one before and practiced tipping it backwards and rolling it forward. The elevator opened again, empty this time, and Luming pushed the dolly in first with Brother steadying it from the side. Dorothy was slim, but she towered over the whole elevator with her height, accentuated by her white spiky hair. Luming thought she was interesting-looking, but he did not feel any warmth toward her. She was on a mission and was obviously processing something in her head.

Once they reached the lobby level, the doors opened and she turned and quietly said, "Follow me." They pushed the dolly behind her, through tall, thin glass doors, until they got to the curb in front of the building. Her black limousine was still parked in front of the building and Dorothy knocked on the window, bent down to speak to her driver who immediately drove off. Chris was nowhere to be seen.

Luming stepped up and said, "I'm Luming and this is Brother."

"Brother? Is he your younger brother or older?" she said is in a soft sing-songy voice. She was somehow aloof to them, still processing, and Luming was feeling frustrated about how little he knew. How long would Chris be gone? It felt like she was patronizing him in some way.

"No, his name is Brother," enunciating the word, Brother. "Where are we going?"

Chris' truck came roaring up with the muffler sound resonating against the glass building. He stopped right in front of them. Luming realized how this truck stuck out and people around the building entrance were staring. It was old, characteristically heavy for its age, with window frames encased in chrome-plated steel. Luming and Brother loaded the seed bags onto the flat bed of the truck. Each door opened, making the uncomfortable sound of metal against metal. Brother and Luming jumped in the small back seat, giving Dorothy the front seat. Chris started to pull away from the curb, shifting the gears more knowledgeably than before.

"Excuse me, I've got to make a call," she said. She got out her phone and proceeded to speak in her native language. She hand-cranked open the window and lit up a cigarette, still talking. She finally stopped.

"We have confusion," she said. "How far is the Seed Bank?"

"We're twenty minutes away, depending on traffic," said Chris.

Speaking directly to Chris, she said, "I started at 6:00 AM yesterday when we first heard the reports. Dr. Anthony ripped us off completely, by the way. He gave us only two bags and he owed us five. I warned everyone that he was not to be trusted, an asshole." She said asshole with such a unique accent, articulating each syllable as if there were three, making it a surprisingly acceptable word.

"Can someone please tell me what's going on?" said Luming.

Chris turned back to Luming. "We call it the Seed Bank now, but the two-million-dollar facility that contained seeds and marijuana plants was also built to withstand a nuclear event. It's a facility that would be self-sufficient in most crisis situations. The seeds in the back of this truck will feed many people for a long time."

"So is that where we're going? The Seed Bank? A fallout shelter with marijuana plants?" said Luming,

"Luming, not exactly, but you are getting close. I understand how this all sounds. I think you will be thankful once everything unfolds, but for now, you will just have to go with it," said Chris. "Let's sort this out when we get to the SB. I just left a message with Scar that we were on our way."

"I've been in the air for the last ten hours and I have not checked back yet," said Dorothy. She started to tap her Blackberry and never raised her head.

Chris took the corner a little fast and everyone braced themselves against the right side of the truck, forcing Dorothy to look up. She continued to smoke. Luming touched his inhaler, thinking that he might need this again. It was a little thing, but when he loaded his backpack, he never thought about having an extra inhaler. Not having something so small could end his life. For a moment, he wondered if this was all true. He heard of apocalyptic games being played in real time. Maybe Chris was putting on a game for him to not go to work. There were no evidentiary signs of any problem. Traffic was normal and people were walking on campus, looking like they were going someplace.

Chris sped up on the open stretch toward the entrance to the freeway. The truck was noisy and Luming quit trying to understand. Traffic was light and they exited after ten minutes. They wound their way into a warehouse district area that was known for multiple storage and distribution centers. They turned a corner and drove into a large parking lot. Chris drove up to a small red brick building, where three semi-trucks were parked side by side. He pulled up between the last semi and the building, blocking the view of the rest of the parking lot. They got out of Chris' door since Dorothy continued to look at her Blackberry. She waved them on. Luming and Brother followed Chris around the corner of the building and Chris opened a door completely camouflaged by a Linden tree planted close by. He held open the door and they walked down two flights of stairs, with a landing and a door separating each one. As each steel door slammed, loud oppressive sounds echoed off the concrete foundation. The staircases were dark and lit only by gas phosphorescent lamps. At the bottom of the second flight was a large door that looked like a bank safe with a large dial that Chris efficiently opened. The sound of pressurized air bounced against the walls as Chris pulled open the door.

A woman walked up to the door, dressed in a supple black leather jacket with stretch leggings tucked into tall thigh-high boots. She placed each hand on a door jamb and braced her legs across the doorway. She looked tough, like a slender biker without the studs. Her boots were held up with leather straps crossing around her thighs and ending in an intricate knot just below the crease of her leg. Luming was fixated with this knot. Brother was staring at her too. The open steel door blew cool air into their faces, very pungent with the scent of fresh, green budding marijuana plants.

Chris moved forward and said, "We've been shorted. I'm serious. We met Dorothy at the Medical Arts Building, just as you said. Dr. Anthony ripped off three bags of seeds!" Luming realized that he never saw Chris angry.

Not changing her position, she looked at Chris and said quietly, "Slow down, Chris. It's okay. I'm just glad you got here safely. I knew you could do it. Aren't you going to introduce me?" Relaxing her stance a little, but still standing in the doorway, she turned to Luming first. "My name is Scar and who are you two? Do you have identification? I apologize for being brisk, but I have a protocol that requires me to verify your identification. The location of this facility has never been breached. We have a comprehensive vetting process for non-members. This domain is protected by a very small community that insists on absolute privacy. We believe any breach can reveal our location and no one enters without community approval. Due to our special circumstances, it is my responsibility to ensure this is done." She still appeared calm and collected, but Luming thought her body was tensing as she spoke.

"My name is Luming." Luming looked up at the steel door, clutched his laptop," And I don't think I'm staying. I've got a presentation to give and I have to get back."

"And my name is Brother. I don't carry an ID."

Scar stepped forward toward Chris, made eye contact for a long time and they mutually nodded in a way that exchanged important information without speaking. Were they that close, Luming wondered.

"Okay, we're going to skip protocol and Chris has verified that you are a safe risk. I cannot stress how unusual this is, but Chris' word carries a lot of weight around here. We are going to be under siege soon and as a founder, Chris has the right to bring the two of you inside. Where's Dorothy?"

"I'm headed back to help Dorothy with the seed bags." said Chris. "Scar, did you get my voicemail? Is it real?"

"We're still verifying facts. Something must be going on for Dr. Anthony to be releasing his seeds in this manner. What did he say? Why is he holding back?"

"Dorothy spoke to him. I stayed away for obvious reasons."

"Good thinking, Chris. Take the seeds to Stack 4. I'll be there to let you in."

"You guys will be fine now," Chris said as he turned to leave. "Just listen to Scar. I'll be back very soon." Chris ran up the stairs two by two.

Scar paused after that and looked back and forth between Luming and Brother, "Welcome to the Seed Bank. If you would like to step in, we can shut the door and figure out what is going on and what to do about it."

"As I said, I don't like this at all. What's going on? It's like we're walking into a bank vault. Where is Chris going exactly?"

Scar looked into Luming's eyes. They were dark with white lights coming from the center. He felt both warm and cold from her stare. "I thought Chris already told you two what was going on. There isn't much time but if we delay, we will perish. Luming, you may have to take a risk here and assume that you will not be missed at your meeting. In fact, the people sitting in the conference room will probably not survive. I admire your commitment, but you need to decide right now if you are going in or not."

Luming turned toward Brother and asked, "Was your dream a coincidence or not?"

Brother walked through the entrance saying, "My favorite Einstein quotation is, Coincidence is just God's way of remaining anonymous."

"Well there you have it," said Scar. "I'm closing this door."

As Luming walked through the threshold, he again noticed her leather straps as his eyes moved up her lithe, supple body and was reminded of a willow he once drew in calligraphy class, in China. The willow, painted in a dark ink and contrasted against a white background, tended to move with the breeze, but bounced back, tall and sturdy. He then realized how intensely he was thinking about her but could not stop. The attraction to this woman was strong, he thought.

The bank door closed solidly behind them, followed by a hiss of air being infused into the small threshold they were standing on. Well, that's it, thought Luming. Scar went over to a shelf containing wristbands and picked up two.

"Here, put these on your wrists. These wristbands allow you to walk around," she said as she placed a beaded bracelet containing a large stone amulet on Brother's wrist.

"You've selected my favorite stone, turquoise," said Brother.

"This piece of turquoise is pretty old. It has been passed on through seven generations and can be used for healing. I thought you might like it."

Brother grinned and Luming could not remember the last time he saw him smile like that.

"Your stone is rose quartz," said Scar as she placed it around Luming's wrist.

"Is that significant?" asked Luming. The selection of these stones was an interesting detail. It did not seem like an ordinary security wristband.

"It might be. I need to get you oriented quickly as I need to meet Chris in ten minutes. Follow me."

They moved into an enormous well-lit room, the size of a basketball court, with ten-foot ceilings and sodium lights hanging from the ceiling. Green marijuana plants occupied most of the space except for the aisles that separated each set of PVC tubing that held each plant in place. Each plant was uniformly spaced, forming a canopy of flowering buds draping down, being held by green string. No one was in the room as they moved through quickly.

"I'm taking you to Troy. We have nine entrances to this facility, Stacks 1 through 9, we call them. We just entered through the south entrance; you came through from the least preferred entrance for anyone to pass through. I'm sorry about being rude."

"Why is that?" said Luming.

"That door you just entered directly exposes the Grow Room to anyone coming in through that door. As you could tell, the first thing you encounter is the strong smell of the hemp plants. We've struggled with this entrance because this location is closest to what you would normally call the Receiving Department and allows us to transfer large quantities of product quickly when we need to ship out of state." Scar stopped and looked at the two of them.

"You saw the semis parked in the parking lot. Their parking locations were carefully designed to protect the location of the entrance. You would never have found the door without Chris' help. We are constantly improving security and now feel very safe from exposure. We grow hemp because it is the most profitable cash crop, but we could grow almost any kind of plant here. Regardless of what we are growing, we do insist on secrecy."

"It seems strange that such a place exists," said Luming.

"I'm also amazed that you have been able to maintain secrecy. I've lived close by for over thirty years, in fact, I've walked across this parking lot on my way to the University many times. This is very interesting," said Brother.

"Yes, our members are a clever and stealthy group and, of course, with all of this marijuana growing, no one wanted to go to jail. We need to move quickly." Scar continued to speed walk through the room. "All of these plants are fed hydroponically, using a closed loop nutrient balance system that adjusts according to the growth cycle of the plants. You are looking at one hundred percent clones which behave uniformly and do not need to be managed individually. You can see they are all of the same height, width and similar bud proportions. This room would look very different if we were planting a variety of seeds for propagation where each plant requires different scheduled feedings. Chris probably remembers how far we've come from plants growing in soil, hybridizing using diverse genetics resulting in a variety of Sativa-Indica ratios. It was very labor intensive back then."

"How long have you been in operation?" asked Luming.

"Wow, not so fast, Luming." Scar looked a little out of sorts. She looked at him, "I'm sorry, I'm not used to giving tours. It has been a long time since we have had anyone from the outside here. The original founder goes back to the early '90s. Our discretion has been absolute. It is only because of this unique circumstance that you are here at all. Now that you know, I guess I will have to kill you," Scar said as she winked at Luming.

Luming blushed at her attention and quickly recovered. "You said you had nine stacks or entrances. Why are you calling them stacks?"

"Yes, good listening," and she smiled at Luming. "I guess once you're here, there is no reason to hold back information. This facility is connected by tunnels using reinforced concrete, thirty feet below the surface. All of the stacks, except for this one, are designed differently. These entrances to our tunnel system are hidden in various locations above each tunnel. Often, they are hidden in a garage, a home or a commercial establishment and completely camouflaged. The locations are only known by Seed Bank members. Each one is carefully designed to look like something immoveable. They are locked from inside. No one enters without permission from inside unless you hold one of these bracelets. Come, we need to move quickly. Let me get you to Troy as I'm needed," and they walked out of the grow room into a tunnel that was made of smooth reinforced concrete. It looked like any other tunnel between buildings.

"The founders were an extremely paranoid bunch of pot farmers that got together to run an underground marijuana business. The grow room was the first site, created for growing more than one hundred plants. As business grew, they needed creative ways to dispense large quantities of marijuana bundles as unnoticeably as possible. One of the founders was Mexican and knew all about the famous tunnels of Tijuana and proposed that they connect a tunnel system under the streets. Each tunnel would connect in different directions and fool anyone who wanted to track where they came from. This system would serve them well and ensure complete secrecy." They walked further down the tunnel, and Luming was fascinated.

"What are these panels on the walls for?" said Luming.

"You have a curious nature, Luming. These panels are RFID locators, placed in each tunnel every fifty feet. They read the RFID tag on your bracelet as you pass by and map where you have been. You can also determine where you are by waving your bracelet over the map and it will light up that part of the map of the tunnels." Scar held up the tag on her wrist and a map of eight tunnels lit up. It showed their path from the south entrance and that they would soon come up to the center of a spoked wheel. "All of these tunnels are similar and you would be surprised how you can get lost, but mostly, this is helpful to us to know where everyone is located in case we need to contact them in an emergency."

"You said there were nine tunnels and nine entrances. I see only eight," said Luming.

"Right you are. It is hard to explain, but maybe I can show you the ninth later," she said. Luming smiled and caught himself, trying to stop smiling.

"The original purpose of the facility was to grow marijuana plants for product, we got into seed storage later. Everything we do requires water, electricity, light, fertilization or facility maintenance. We are a self-contained, closed-loop facility and have been for about the last fifteen years. Generators have back-up generators providing electricity for the grow rooms, the tunnels, and the area where we are headed, called the Hub."

"Chris started to tell us the history of this place and the combination of seed storage and growing pot," said Brother. "I'm afraid his story did not do justice to the extent of what we are seeing. How long have you been here, Scar?"

"I've been here fifteen years, next spring. I was hired to manage the place."

The smooth concrete walls were no longer an industrial gray, but painted in a soft rainbow of colors, like a light spectrum, barely noticeable. It started in a soft purple and ended, repeating the cycle every fifty feet. Scar stopped and entered a room. They followed and found a tall, slim boy, maybe a teenager, at the computer terminals, scanning small packages into a RFID reader. "This is Troy, our IT genius. He is scanning seed bags into our database," said Scar. "This is the other side of the business. We have the capacity to safely store seeds for our clients under controlled conditions of humidity, temperature, and sterility. Again, we use RFID tags to download extensive information down to DNA records and hybrid history for each bag of seeds. The Seed Bank made a ton of money in the last decade in seed storage. It was the sales of seed, not the marijuana itself, where we received significant profits that allowed us to set up such a sophisticated site. Seed research led to remarkable innovations in improving seed using induced mutation and GM approaches."

"You're saying not just marijuana seeds, but any kind?" asked Luming.

"Right. Seed information is not so difficult, but it was Troy that set up a system to identify each seed, its special traits and the ability to recall it if needed. Most groups that are involved in GMO research find this as a big benefit. Once you mix up your seeds or store them inappropriately, all of the hard work to make them is forfeited."

"So help us understand what is going on," said Luming. "Are we under nuclear attack? We are now safely underground. What information leads you to believe we are under attack?"

"I'm late getting back to Chris and finding Dorothy. Troy, can you help out here?" And she took off.

"This is what an underground city feels like, I guess. I wonder how long you could live here if you had to," said Brother.

"Yeah, it does. It is driving me a little nuts to think that our Chris acted so casual and he really has been involved in such sophisticated secretive activities. What's happening? Are we stuck here?"

Troy turned away from his terminal. "Hi, I'm Troy and you are Brother and Luming? Right?"

"So can you tell us?"

"Sorry, I wasn't listening. What's the question?"

"Are we under nuclear attack?" As Luming formed the question, he looked at Troy's strange facial expression. He was feeling kind of foolish, so he rephrased the question. "What can you say about what is happening?"

"No, I can't tell you anything right now. I'm very sorry about that." He paused. "There's a library in the next room." Troy led them into the adjacent room. The center was filled with floor to ceiling servers, monitors, and individual workstations. The floor bounced on an air-cooled platform and a sound deadener that piped in soft jazz music and a large changing holograph that showed photographs of nature surrounding shelves of books on each wall. Each book had a sleeve that was lit by green LED lights. The center workstation had a monitor and keyboard with a search menu. The search menu already had the word 'Survival' typed on the screen.

"Here. The best thing I can do is let you read about what we currently know. I've got to get back to setting up the scanning program for new seeds."

Brother saw a book light up on the wall of books and pulled it off the shelf. *Survival, Post Catastrophic Living*. He sat and started to page through the book and a phone began to ring. Luming discovered it was his; He was surprised about having service at all.

It was Lois. Luming worked with Lois on conversational Mandarin in the past and they developed a lasting friendship since then. Her language skills were effortless. She graduated with a double major in language and mathematics with a minor in music. She was a post grad now and he rarely saw her. Her true beauty was inside, surpassing the classic definition, with an aura of intelligent curiosity. And she was not afraid of showing her emotions. She was attractive and could be a model if she wanted to. He always wished they had an attraction, a chemistry.

"Luming, Luming," she said in a voice higher than normal and a little edgy. She repeated his name again.

"Lois," said Luming. "Where are you?"

"Hi," said Lois. With a bad connection, they tried to communicate the basics and Lois hung up and tried again. With a slightly better connection, she told him she was headed to the basement of the Physics building at the U and was working on a problem for a client that was high priority. "I'm working on a series of emails in Chinese that were sent to me. Do you have a few minutes to help me?" said Lois.

"I'm in an interesting situation, Lois." He added, "We are in an underground maze that looks like it is a city underground. They grow marihuana. Oh yeah," he hesitated. "I'm probably not supposed to say that. Anyway, there is a really cool woman here that I met. She is in charge of the Seed Bank and is showing us around. However, there seems to be something strange going on. A possible nuclear bomb is going to land here. At least the people here are focusing on that."

"That's interesting," she said. "I thought the 'Seed Bank' was an urban legend. I heard there were a lot of tunnels."

Luming now realized that he was in a lot of trouble by disclosing this information and not really sure why he said that. "I am pretty sure I was not supposed to say that. Can we change the subject? What do you need?"

"We'll talk about that later, Luming. This woman sounds interesting. I might have heard a little bit about her as well. Anyway, let's keep this short. I am working on solving a problem for a client. We're deciphering strange behavior from China and over a hundred separate email messages that suggest we are in danger. We have no idea what this means," said Lois. "I am walking over to the Physics building to meet with the Five Guys. Thought they might be useful in translating these messages. Maybe run a few algorithms. Can you help me if they turn me down?"

"I haven't seen them since the last robotic race party. No problem. Call me back once you talk to them. With everything going on here, this information might help us piece more things together and I would appreciate not feeling like a burden here."

"I'll call you back," and they hung up.

Luming looked at Brother who showed him how the library system worked. On the main frame, he searched the word 'Nuclear,' pressed enter, and got one hundred and fifty-three references and it appeared that he could link to any of them electronically, on the screen. Three book-lights lit up along the wall.

"Yes, I love this part of our system," said Troy as he entered the room. "Long before hard drive storage, the founders wanted an easy system to collect books in the library and find subject matter easily." Troy walked over and pulled each book off the shelf. An LED light turned red each time a book was removed. When he put the book back on the shelf, the light would go green. Pretty impressive, thought Luming.

"Are you backing up to cloud storage?" asked Luming.

"We were already backing everything with memory sticks or portable hard drives. Our system evolved to a somewhat laborious system where we walk twenty feet from the Hub, and back it up with the computers in this room once an hour. It took us less time to do that than pouring a cup of coffee. We decided to avoid the cloud altogether, using this established system. We now use six terabyte drives and have a hundred drives stored for future use. We have successfully avoided the threat of being hacked into the cloud with a relatively simple system."

"One hundred, six-terabyte drives used for backup, is a lot of data," said Luming. "I need to contact Scar. I just received some information about a catastrophic event that is connected to emails from China. I think she needs to hear about this."

"Let me check," said Troy. "Ahhh, it looks like she turned off her tracer, the one that is on your bracelet. That is highly unusual for Scar, we always know where she is. I can trace her steps." He popped up a screen and the three of them huddled over it. "See, she left here to go to the Commons via the grow room which is strange. That is a circuitous route at best. The Commons is a spot that can block any electronic activity. This is only done when we are in lockdown." He looked up, making a strange face. "The Commons Room is kind of like our own Panic Room. Sorry I can't reach her right now." Troy moved to another monitor. "Holy shit!" The screen showed a simple ocean buoy and lots of data with red numbers along the right side of the live picture. Troy gulped and said, "I get lonely for surfing and sometimes look at the wave forecaster in Malaysia. These redlines mean tsunami. I feel so sorry and I know these guys who surf there. I wonder where the earthquake happened?"

Luming was slowly feeling his body tense. The information on the tsunami was real. It was the first data point in fact that something was happening. He was a little distracted by touring the amazing shelter, but he wondered what was going on. How safe were they? He suddenly felt the need to call his mother and hear her voice. What would he say to her without panicking her for no reason? Where was Chris? Chris brought them here for some reason and he needed to know the real reason.

MICHAEL - 15

During the two-hour operating committee meeting, Michael could not sustain a thought. Max, the CEO, fired questions to anyone sitting around the table. As Michael looked around the room, he saw Max's assistant taking meeting minutes. He was good at ducking responsibility, but today, he was not paying attention. All of this was beneath him.

They were talking about a series of emails that people have been receiving and then Max brought up Jane's China project, Lazarus. Great, this meeting is worth my time.

"...with Lazarus, we see a great deal of promise with this acquisition. Due diligence testing supports the decision to move forward. The numbers speak for themselves and the timeline is conservative. Both the strategic alignment and our standard ROI/NPV models make this project important for the new expanding markets we identified in the Five Year Strat Plan. I cannot emphasize enough that this is a new area for us, but the risk can be mitigated by tight controls over the Lazarus organization once the integration teams are in place. We will send our best integration manager and start a five-year permanent position over there to manage the activities closely. Preventing leaks of information or seeds back into the Chinese will be a high priority. Our last meeting this afternoon will seal the deal. We should be good to go," said someone across the table that Michael did not know.

"All contingent on our legal review," said Michael. All eyes looked at him. He stiffened his back, ready for what would come next.

"We completed the legal review weeks ago, Michael," said Max. "You must be behind in your work. Freeman, your boss, provided weekly updates to this committee."

"I know that," Michael said. "Freeman's input was last week and, he is not aware of the latest development in China."

"Now what?" an irritated Max said.

"Don't panic. I know the negotiator, Jane Witterhouse. She has not been communicating to legal all critical points, and we received new information from China just this morning that puts a big wrench in this deal. I am scrambling on how to fix it and not sure I can do that before the meeting this afternoon. Once I reach Jane, whom I couldn't reach by phone today, I'll find what I can do to fix the problem. It's unfortunate that her lack of experience, her poor communication style and weak negotiating skills would put us in this position."

"Sounds like legal gobbledegoop," said Max. "I know Jane very well and have the highest regard for her. Have Freeman call me, today!"

Michael was peeved at this lack of respect. He knew Max pretty well, and this was odd behavior, even for him. Deciding not to stand down, he said, "You're right, Max. Legal advice is never welcomed, but if it keeps you out of trouble, you'll be glad we stopped this deal, instead of having you spending days in jail." Michael was a little shocked at his own response. He rarely used a jail example in public forums like this and rarely struck back in such a visible way to the CEO. What was he thinking?

"I think you will go to jail before I do, Michael," said Max. "Maybe you should leave and go do your critically important work elsewhere."

Michael was mortified. No one ever treated him this way. He stood up and showed a calm and cool response. "Thank you, Max. Don't mind if I do. I wish you the best and I will report back to Freeman your desire to take this direction. I look forward to seeing this conversation documented in meeting minutes. It will be my pleasure in helping you out the door, Maxwell." Michael, only carrying a legal pad with a few minimal notes, smiled to everyone around the room, spreading his threat farther, and left. The room rustled liked dry leaves on an autumn day. The room was silent.

Michael heard as he was leaving, "I think we need to take a ten-minute break."

Michael strolled down the hall, not rushing nor showing any kind of stress, but he was in a big panic. What was he thinking? How was he going to explain to his boss that the CEO kicked him out of a meeting? He and his legal colleagues always showed the utmost respect and public support for Max. They considered him one of their best CEOs in the company's history. Michael needed a moment to relax and collect himself. As he calmed down, he realized that this would pass. He had plenty of damaging information against Max that he could use if he wanted.

Michael was interesting in the reference to heavy email traffic coming from China. Everyone reading emails during the operating committee mentioned this anomaly in passing. If he had only attended his first meeting of the day with the Chinese. He did not trust his Chinese colleagues and here again was another example of that. Were they cooking something up behind his back? Weren't they supposed to copy him on all correspondence into the US for protection of intellectual property? Why was everyone else getting emails from China and his inbox was empty? As Michael's head raced, he picked up speed, turned the corner and ran into Jane.

LOIS - 16

It was good to talk to Luming. She was sure he would help if she needed it. She was excited about the project, but getting a little worried that it might be more important, beyond just Dan. She often read more into signs than the normal person. Her intuition was saying this project was important, but her logical mind was asking why. She walked down the long promenade on campus, walked past two old limestone buildings before reaching the physics building. She stepped lightly up the steps that so many physics students seemed to plod up. Again, another quotation rose high above her head and this one was her favorite: "It is the mark of an educated mind to entertain a thought without accepting it." She was excited to be working on a project with the infamous Five Guys.

She entered the building framed with a brand-new glass atrium inserted into the old building for the millennium celebration. Her eyes naturally looked upward. Suspended from the ceiling was a large brass patina sculpture of a perfectly shaped egg made into a water feature, bubbling water from inside the egg into a large pool of water below. The walls of the atrium were two stories high, made of thin cross sections of granite, probably mined from the great lake regions. The building was a stunning architectural success, but the glass made Lois nervous.

As she took the only spiral staircase on campus down to the lower level. The floor was polished terrazzo, with wainscoted wood trim along the ceiling, heavy quarter-sawn oak doors with frosted glass windows that looked like the glass settled to the bottom of the window frame. Everything smelled old, but with distinction. A hundred and fifty years of smart, knowledge-savvy students passed through these doors for a brief exposure to the complex rules of the universe which they left behind to pursue careers in engineering or medicine.

The Five Guys had a secret laboratory in the building. The Five Guys legend had reached mythological proportions. At the end of the hall there was a bank of computers and three students fixated on the screens in front of them. She shuffled her feet as she walked across the room and they finally looked up like fish gazing at food coming down from the surface of the tank and promptly went back to their screens, showing little interest in her.

"Hello," she said. An uncomfortable silence followed as they again stared up at her. Finally, a very tall, slender boy on the right stood up and smiled.

"Sorry, we are working on an urgent problem that came up last evening. Are you looking for someone?"

"My name is Lois and I have a project for the Five Guys. I need their help translating one hundred emails coming from China for a synergistic analysis, if that makes sense," she said.

"You probably want to talk to Cong," he said. Immediately the person on the left stood up and said very gently, "Hi, Lois. So sorry, I was not ignoring you, but we're very busy with a strange anomaly and are working to solve the problem. I'm afraid I can't exchange many pleasantries. What can we do for you?"

"You remembered me?"

"Yes, you were introduced to us by Luming."

"I just spoke to him. What a coincidence. Well, since you are busy, let's cut to the chase. My client, the V.P. of Asian Affairs, Dan, represents a large corporation, and they have been receiving strange email messages from China over the last eight hours. I copied them on this memory stick. Each of the one hundred emails are in Chinese, Mandarin. I tried to translate a few of them, but they made little sense. Dan wants to have them translated ASAP. My expertise in language is good, but I quickly realized I can't tackle this. It may be a dialect I'm not familiar with and would require analysis way beyond my knowledge. I'm guessing a project like this might interest you. He's willing to pay double or even more."

"Interesting. This is important. It sounds like the problem we are already working on. Follow me." Cong turned toward the wall, pulled a cord hanging from the ceiling and a section of the wall rose. Lois followed Cong as the door closed behind her. There was a staircase to their right.

"Jeez Louise," she said and pushed herself to follow Cong as he sped down the stairs. She stood looking at a mirror image of the room they left. "Wow, now that is tricky," she said. They staged another set of computers along the wall. On her right were four Asian men sitting and staring at the screens.

She looked at the large open space behind them. She also noticed what looked like a Wi-Fi satellite hookup to the left of the door. Without speaking, they all stood up and approached Lois, looking at her carefully without a social filter. They bowed very low, and she returned the gesture, knowing the importance of the depth of the bow. As if they were expecting her, they moved to a large round table in the middle of the room and pulled out a chair for her to sit in. They sat in a semi-circle, facing Lois.

Having only met Cong once, Lois looked at each one of them and could see no difference in their appearance. She remembered Luming telling her the story about how they got here.

The story was about a woman from Luming's village, who gave birth to five identical boy babies. This was such an unusual occurrence and having more than one child was a serious crime. Shortly after they were born, the authorities took them from this woman. They turned them over to scientists who studied them as if they were a human research project. The mother was devastated and tried to visit them as much as she could. Luming's mother said she was an amazing, fearless woman and not afraid of the consequences of her actions. She worked stealthily and got her boys back. She disappeared right after their escape. No one knew how she captured the boys, but some thought she worked as a nursing assistant and timed a rescue when no one was around. Her plan after capture involved finding five trusted families to take each boy. Taking them as babies was easier, and the authorities who were looking for the boys never considered such a simple plan. The boys were well behaved and smart and everyone fell in love with them. The unusual part of their story was as the boys got older, they found ways to be together as much as possible. One woman taught them how to dress and look different, so when they were seen together, they did not look identical. Luming said, "My mother thought they had a special power when they were together as a group. People observed that the villages in which the boys were living had huge crop yields over other farmers. As this rumor became true, the people from these small villages swore allegiance to protect them as much as humanly possible from the authorities."

Luming told Lois, "What was interesting was they could not hide their intelligence, as individuals or collectively. They quickly outgrew their schooling. The villages brought in teachers of architecture, music, literature and poetry to challenge the boys. The consequences of supporting the boys' knowledge resulted in a cluster of five small villages devoted to agriculture and art and as time went on, these towns became wealthier in assets. The boys were eleven when the Party became suspicious of the success in the area. They assumed the villages were committing crimes to bring such prosperity to a remote place. They sent spies to the region and found nothing. The boys were concerned about their own safety and the safety of the villages." Luming mentioned to Lois that he had little information about their escape. The story involved a French university professor, teaching in Beijing. During an international conference, he somehow helped get them out of the country. "My mother was always sad when she told this story."

And here they are, she thought.

"Welcome, Miss Lois. It pleases us that you came and we have a feeling that we need to pay attention to the coincidence of you being here with important information that will impact our current project," said Cong who was sitting in the middle of the five. "Let me first introduce my brothers.

"To my far right is Lou." Lou brought his hands together and bowed slightly. "Lou is our favorite brother and is first born. When things are stressful, Lou will lead us in a centering practice. Please notice today, his necklace has a tiny lotus flower. While we are identical quintuplets, we are expert at showing off individual identities when we need to. We look the same now, but Lou may change into a sweater vest and look like a suburban dad. Lou is the only one of us that works out and you might detect a slightly toned body through his shirt." Lois smiled, now noticing the muscular difference.

"Qiang is to my immediate right and his name means strength. Qiang's preference is to wear hiking boots and plaid shirts. He was born strong. To my left is Hung. His courage has led us through many challenging situations. He loves to blend in, wearing camouflage. And the last born to my far left is Bai. He is the baby, but has repeatedly impressed us with a strong intuition and a quick presence of action. He is who you want to have during a catastrophe."

"Which is why we need to get moving, Cong," said Bai. "As far as your emails go, I think we're entering a catastrophic series of events. My first sense of this was over a week ago, but last evening, my gut ached and I cannot keep food down."

"Let's get going," she said and sat, ready to listen. Once they realized she stopped talking, they started to organize the job rather cleverly. Qiang gently took her memory stick, copied all one hundred emails onto five hard drives in less than a minute, wirelessly. He talked to the others, and they decided that each would focus on twenty emails and run seventeen familiar algorithms. This was all discussed in Mandarin, but Lois could understand a portion of their dialogue. She suspected they used multiple shortcuts in speaking to each other. They immediately started translating and there was a quick feed onto each of their personal computers and onto five projections onto a wide screen where periodically, an email would appear on the screen and be quickly replaced by the next and the next. No sound was being made except for the whine of the computer fans and occasional sucking sounds of lips being pressed or a sigh here and there. Lois walked back and forth, watching each computer screen, but could not decipher much. The emails seemed personal. As the minutes ticked by, Lois started to relax and appreciated being able to just sit for a while. Bai got up and asked her if she was doing okay. As if they already discussed this amongst themselves, they asked for more information about where these emails came from.

"I have limited information. We can call Dan if that would be helpful."

Cong shook his head. "Not yet," and they continued to stare at the screens while typing.

One hour passed and Cong looked up, staring at Lois. "We reviewed the information and it is important that we discuss the results with you and Dan now. It contains an important warning, an impossible one, actually."

Qiang stood up, followed by the other four and said, "Our best guess at the meaning is multiple nuclear bombs are being launched at the United States, including the Midwest."

Lois thought this sounded strange. She wished she knew them better. They were obviously nerdier than herself and they might overreact to situations. This was an inconceivable concept to grasp, she thought. What would Luming think? She did not grow up with the fear of nuclear war like her mother's generation. It wasn't realistic to worry about that. What would happen to Clark and Suri? She needed to warn them. Suddenly helping Dan out with his project meant nothing. All Five Guys looked serious, staring down at her.

Lois, feeling emotion rise into her throat, she blurted out, "So who is sending these messages? Who is responsible?"

"The messages are all different and being sent from different individuals, but the IP addresses were the same. One individual may be sending messages from several locations hoping one message could get through. This is common practice from China where messages can be intercepted. Some citizens have a program that will take one email and send it several times from a variety of different locations. Here, it was sent from a hundred locations as each sender was different. It is a strange idea and message. We have been monitoring the internet, and no one is commenting on this specifically, but there is an increase in internet blogging It could also be a complete spoof, but Lois, please get back to Dan right away. He might have information that could help."

She looked around the room at the grey concrete walls and hundreds of blinking lights from the equipment and said, "Okay, but it sounds like this is beyond getting back to Dan. Shouldn't we be warning someone? I have to contact my brother."

"Listen," turned to Lois. "The work you gave us today is strange, and I cannot validate our conclusions one hundred percent. We're surprised at the outcome and feel helpless about what to do about it. There are two Chinese characters that are rarely used in writing and reserved only for urgent situations. For example, these characters would be used if an earthquake was happening or a tsunami was detected. While these characters existed since the beginning of the Chinese language, we typically combine these characters with a date, a time and a GPS coordinate. We are finding that using two characters in the same message gives them a heightened meaning, translating to a supreme event with significant consequential damages. They are used exactly twelve times in each email, which resulted in 1,200 uses of these two rare characters."

"Stop right there," said Lois, feeling chills down her back. "This sounds intellectually interesting. If we are being notified of an upcoming catastrophic event, how can you make the leap to multiple nuclear bombs. Does it affect us?"

"We have come across a few more items of critical importance that will help you with that question, Lois." All five resettled in their chairs and collectively started to speak to each other in Mandarin at such a fast clip that Lois did not understand what they were saying.

"Look," she interrupted. "Let's get Dan on the phone and you can provide him with your information and then I may understand better what you are talking about."

"I'll get him on the phone," said Lou, with an increase in pitch to his voice.

She felt anxious and wanted to hear Dan's calm voice. He could surely sort through all the information and hopefully come to a different conclusion. As she started to think about it, she realized Clark was probably still sleeping. She should call Clark and warn him. She reached for her phone and called with no answer, leaving an urgent message for him to call her. Alternatively, she could have left the message, "Clark, protect yourself from atomic bombs, please take shelter," which would probably have made him laugh.

She heard Dan's voice coming from a speaker hanging from the ceiling and walked over to the speakerphone and said, "Dan. You've got to hear about this. What are you doing right now? You need to listen to this. We don't have much time." She was trying to sound calm, but she could tell her voice sounded sharper and faster than usual.

Dan's voice came barreling through the speakerphone, vibrating across the cement-walled room like a cannon and said, "Lois, good to hear from you so soon. I thought we just sent you those emails. You work quickly!"

At that moment, a shrill baby cry came over the speakerphone, followed by a silence and then another shrill scream. Standing and speaking into the ceiling speaker phone, she said, "Dan, I'm at the University and we just finished the translations of your corporate emails and the results are alarming. The translators are here, ready to share their conclusion. This is urgent. We need to waste no time." The screeching went up another octave.

"What do you mean by urgent? My granddaughter Elizabeth just started to react to something. What's wrong, Lizzy? I gotta call you back," said Dan.

A deafening scream came through the speakerphone and caused everyone in the room to shudder.

"Try finding her pacifier," said Lois.

"Now why did I think I could do this?" Dan said, speaking in a tone of resignation, obviously not realizing how he sounded over the phone. "Just a minute, I'll see what I can do. You said pacifier, right," he shouted. "Give me a moment." After a minute of rustling, he said, "Now that I think of it, Brenda does not believe in pacifiers."

Bai stood up and pressed a button on the table and spoke softly into the table speaker. "Dan, this is Bai. I am part of the team looking into your project with Lois. I believe I can help you with Elizabeth. I'm pretty good with babies. If you follow these directions, it will make a difference. Take your thumb and index finger and place them on the lower lobe of her right ear and press your fingers together lightly for five seconds. Repeat this until she stops crying."

The screaming prevailed until thirty seconds passed and then the screaming stopped, followed by a kind of half-laugh. A calmer voice came over the intercom, saying, "Problem solved. That was amazing. Thank you, Bai. What was that? Is it like an acupressure point?"

Each of the Chinese colleagues had a smile and a private exchange between them. They had a strange way of communicating. Maybe there were amused at the sheer irony pacifying a baby during a crisis. That kind of detachment was irritating, thought Lois.

DAN - 17

Dan started to arrange himself back into his seat, relieved that Elizabeth's crisis was over. He needed to concentrate on talking into the speaker phone of the car as the cell phone must have slid under the seat, but was synced to the speakerphone. All he needed to do was to maintain his connection and to shout into the speaker on the visor of the passenger seat. As he looked at Elizabeth smiling and waving her hands, it bothered him that the group insisted on talking right now. Shin also seemed agitated around emails from a group in China. What was their name? As he prepared himself for the teleconference, there was a knocking on the window. Betty's voice was sing-songy. "Is everything all right? I could hear screaming in my classroom and was worried."

Dan, still distracted, rolled down the window. "Hey, I am a little over my head today, Betty. There's a work crisis. That was Lizzy screaming. Thankfully, her crisis has passed."

"I thought you were taking the day off," she said in a sterner voice.

"Yep, it's my day off but I have to take this call. My phone is under the seat."

Betty opened the back door and started to speak in soothing tones. Elizabeth reached out to her and Betty unsnapped her from the car seat and reached in to hold her. She bounced and Betty cooed and everything seemed to be fine.

A light bulb went on and Dan asked, "Betty, what happened to your Aikido class?"

"Well, I left them to meditate while I was checking out this screeching that sounded like an owl in hot pursuit of a mouse!"

"Dan, please listen. We have important information. It is life-threatening." As Lois continued to remind him of this, Dan started feeling for his phone under the seat. Without having access to his cell phone, he could not put the phone on mute. Things keep getting more and more complicated today, thought Dan. Betty put Elizabeth back into her car seat and asked Dan for a bottle of juice. He handed her the juice from the bag and Betty gave it to Elizabeth. Betty propped herself in the backseat with the window open and hummed a pleasant tune.

"Are you still there?" Dan said into the speaker.

After a short silence, Lois sounded like she was closer to the speakerphone and said, "Yes, Dan. We're here. We're in the University, Physics building. There are six of us plus our friend Lois."

"Got it." Dan decided that he needed to focus and just hear what they had to say. Thinking about Betty listening in, he thought, oh well, how bad could it be? Having a babysitter at this point in time was an unexpected blessing. "Betty is now in the backseat, helping with Lizzy. Let's get started."

"Great. Betty will want to hear this. Our news is alarming. We need to transmit it to you quickly, and you need to take action," said Lois. She then summarized the conclusions of the Five Guys, a little about their code breaking algorithms, and the results so far.

"Maybe this is a good time to step in now," said Cong. "Dan, our information is grim. Our information so far shows that we will be under attack by nuclear bombs very soon, maybe within the hour. As Lois summarized, we analyzed the emails you provided, we combined them with GPS coordinates that were synced with other sources we have in China and it all points to a shocking conclusion. There is a group called YáChǐ, our word for teeth. They have kept themselves underground, silent, for a long time, but in the last forty-eight hours, we have been monitoring messages about them. In fact, we were working on this before Lois came to us with your information, Dan. This last piece of information concludes that this city is one of the targets. We are just pinpointing the time, but I would say immediately moving to an underground location is the best advice we can give you."

"What? I must reach my brother, Clark," Lois burst shouted.

Dan heard that and thought about Brenda. Where in Washington was she going today?

JANE-18

Jane was going to be in the healthcare building most of the day. The name of that building, The Watson Building, held some irony for her. Watson and Crick were awarded a Nobel Peace prize resulting from x-ray evidence developed by Rosalind Franklin, whose name was not mentioned in the award. She died of cancer four years prior. It was revealed later that she made a significant contribution to the discovery by taking the first picture of the double helix. Would anyone ever name a building The Franklin Building after Rosy? What Jane particularly loved about her story was her signature argumentative, bold style and the fact that people had a hard time dealing with her. It was that brand of feminism that Jane admired but was not able to execute. Her job demands required figuring out how to get along with almost everyone. She could not afford to piss people off.

When Jane first started working here, she could not believe how many meetings people needed to get anything done. Planning and coordinating what they were going to do, then talking about what they did and then planning the next steps were often overwhelming. Granted, projects were complex and required cross-functional disciplines, but no one seemed to come up with a better way. She tried to skip them, but she quickly learned she needed to be there to coax along her projects. In order to offset this part of her job, she planned discovery outings whenever she was in another building. She started to study each building for structural failure from catastrophic events. Some buildings were almost one hundred years old and badly needed upgrades as the tunnels originally built under the buildings were already shifting and showing signs of stress.

She drove into the parking ramp and found her favorite parking place open. No one ever parked here as it was the farthest spot away from the entrance to the building, 252 steps away. It was located in the corner of the garage that was reinforced by three converging walls, next to the exit ramp. Always processing how a parking ramp might collapse and crushing all of the cars parked in the lower ramp, this corner was perfect. She also discovered a secret exit through the animal laboratory to get to her car from the underground tunnel toward the back of the building.

As she got out of her car, carrying her backpack and strapping her Tool Box across her shoulders, she plugged in her car charger. Each parking space had an electrical socket designed for engine block warmers that were used in the '70s before fuel injection was invented. When temperatures dropped below zero, the outlets saved cars from freezing up. Jane used these outlets to charge batteries, mid-day, while attending meetings. Jane was reminded of how old this parking garage must be and how unstable, knowing that pre-1975 versions of reinforced concrete had stability problems after thirty years. As Jane walked toward the building entrance, she noted each electrical outlet, the spacing, the height as they were suspended from the ceiling so in case she needed to grope for them in the dark, she could easily gauge their location.

By now, all of this was so automatic that Jane rarely thought about what she was doing. She memorized large quantities of information. She learned from her study of survival that one small piece of knowledge is as critical to survival as having the gear.

Going into the research building directly from the heated garage into a security-protected elevator was extremely convenient for most employees. Most left their winter coats in their cars. Jane's beef with this entrance was the only way into the building was by way of an elevator. A few years ago, frustrated by this fact, Jane discovered the animal lab entrance. Rather than going up to the building offices and labs, the stairway in this entrance went down. Jane discovered it while chatting with a HVAC guy who was using this access point to perform PM checks. She followed him down three flights of stairs to the lowest level of the building. Thanks to a blogger, StealthForWealth, she figured out a way to copy his ID card so she could access the lowest level whenever she wanted.

It was obviously not a critical part of corporate security, but for her purposes, it was an important find.

Jane scanned her employee pass with the lower level access code and walked down the first set of stairs. She always checked for cameras, but never found one.

Calvin, an ex-military security guard, surprised that she knew about it, told her that the second floor down, a sub-basement, was probably one of the safest places to survive a nuclear bomb in the Midwest. The previous CEO built the Watson building above it. Calvin said there were unconfirmed rumors that he used designs that were adapted from Fort Knox blueprints. Maybe it was an inside joke or maybe he had an intention to preserve technology from nuclear disaster, either way, Jane was very curious about that rumor.

The area fed her fantasies. She studied it as if it her life depended on it. She often wondered if anyone ever heard anything about this sub-level to the building. Most of her co-workers were consciously or unconsciously focused on the politics of the day or how to present their information to management or the latest unfairness that someone experienced. Jane was again under the radar.

As she descended further toward the lowest level, she had fifteen minutes before her meeting and wanted to spend it wisely. Fitting in ten minutes to explore maximized the gap before her meeting perfectly. As Dr. Blue advanced therapy sessions around her survival obsession, she realized how much pleasure survival planning gave her, almost a feeling of serenity. Therapy provided the space for both of them to actively search for why that was true for Jane. Since there were no traumatic events in Jane's life, Dr. Blue was just starting to unveil what part of her personality was driving her actions. Once Dr. Blue asked the question, did she have a strong sense of self-preservation when she designed things like her Tool Box or her backpack? Jane thought she just liked solving puzzles, but realized that there might be something deeper in what Dr. Blue was asking. Obsession was a therapeutic term that covered simple fascinations to fixation and mania. Dr. Blue was probably trying to figure out where on the scale or spectrum, in psychologist-speak, she fit.

As Jane used her security pass to open the door that reached the sub-basement, lights immediately turned on to light the stairway and the tunnel below. Once at the bottom of the stairs, she felt like she was wandering into a different planet. The quiet was a cold one, at least ten degrees colder than the garage above. She felt a damp sensation of what some people experience as claustrophobia, a feeling of being closed in, suffocating, without an escape.

She took out her map for the building which did not reference this level at all. That was a new observation. She took a left and found sections or bays on both sides of her, containing large pallets of what looked like experimental inventory. She stopped to examine a few that were shrink-wrapped tightly and it was not clear what was contained on each pallet. There were large amounts of random-looking boxes that might have been in storage for years, based on the dust caked on top. A few concrete bays down held more unusual stuff, also shrink-wrapped, but without boxes, exposing pieces of chemical-related glassware, like a laboratory on a pallet. What a treasure, she thought: Large 100-milliliter glass cylinders, five liter beakers and a whole host of mixing blades, heating mantles, and old-fashioned scales were carefully stacked. There were also multiple boxes smelling of nasty chemicals of unknown origin stored in dusty amber bottles. Everything that moved around the company was now coded for inventory. Typically, pallets had RFID tags, including dates and a name specifying who was storing the inventory and a notification date reminder. Every six months, a prompt would be sent to that scientist to reclaim the contents or it would be destroyed. Scientists were the worst pack rats and found ways to continue to keep these pallets in case they needed it sometime in the future. Maybe a few scientists found this place to store precious equipment and materials outside the system.

As Jane sat and stared at this pallet, she saw a few tags saying Dr. Maxwell Carnegie on the boxes. Interesting, she thought. He was the third CEO and inventor of resorbable suture material. How old was this pallet? This was a classic example of inventing ahead of your time. These innovative patent applications were filed at the time doctors were still suturing patients from intestines of sheep or cat gut. All of Carnegie's patents expired by the time medical device companies started to realize the benefit of synthetic sutures that dissolved in the tissue, not requiring the painful process of pulling out stitches. Competitors studied the 'Carnegie' patents and were able to commercialize these innovative sutures, making a lot of profit while providing patients with less pain, infection and a smoother skin result post-surgically.

Jane was reminded that Maxwell Carnegie, although retired, was a supporter of the Lazarus project. He sent her a personal note from Oregon. Why he was keeping track of projects was beyond her, but his influence still carried a lot of weight. Nothing ever is that easy, thought Jane. The twists and turns from a corporation this big always held surprises, both positive and negative.

She studied the pallet and wondered what benefit it would have to her as a survivalist. What could be done with the chemicals, condensers, miles of tubing and a plethora of glassware? Not being a chemist, she needed more information and wondered who could help her with this. This was a pretty cool find and spurred her imagination. Her watch beeped to alert her to the meeting with the lab folks. She took a few pictures with her pocket camera and ran back to the stairs. Running up three stairs at a time, she popped back into the elevator and jogged to her meeting room on the sixth floor.

She opened the meeting door and plopped down amongst the scientists waiting for her to arrive. She loved working with this group. They were always on time and prepared.

"Jane, have you heard?" asked Dr. Joy, the most experienced and oldest of the ag scientists. "We were just talking about rumors around strange emails flooding our inboxes in Mandarin."

"Not just Mandarin," said Dr. Calbreer, the blackest African Jane ever met. "We're seeing Korean messages as well. I've been on the phone all morning with Japan and they are experiencing the same thing."

"Now that you mention it, I briefly heard about this from Dan. I wish I spent more time asking questions, but he was on vacation. What have you concluded?"

"It's probably nothing. Okay, folks, we need to get back to finalizing due diligence and sign off on final approval before Jane presents in two hours," said Dr. Joy. "Jane, the Lazarus team has been surveying all of the data provided to us in the virtual notebook rooms. There was a lot of data to go through, but it was all well organized and their results were very advanced from what we are doing. Their study of cross-protection and the communications that are needed for the Integrative T-DNA vectors to produce higher levels of potency leading to a transgenic plant exhibiting higher levels of our target amino acids was confirmed in three different ways."

Dr. Calbreer jumped in with his deep melodic voice. "We're going to try and rein Dr. Joy in just enough to impress the committee, but not overwhelm. This combined with the plant breeding that my lab is capable of doing will provide the perfect marriage of plant science, genetics and genetic modifications that could save the world's nutritional and caloric requirements for healthy growth and brain development in emerging countries."

"There's no need to worry," said Jane. "Present the information the way you see fit. If there are any red flags, please disclose it as accurately as you need to and we'll figure out how to translate the science to the review committee if necessary. I guess I'm hearing there are no red flags." Jane paused and looked around the room. She knew the answer and had been following everyone in the many reports that were generated while the team was taking the virtual tour through the Lazarus platform. The Paradise Lost Company had a unique technology and one which would advance and transform their research by five years. Imagine one perfect seed holding the future that would cultivate high protein plants that could replace beef in the diet and remove a cycle of corn-fed cattle feeding people. This opportunity sold itself. While the population was not ready for this, when it needed it, the technology would be ready. In the meantime, there was growing market interest in meat alternatives.

The meeting continued with multiple presentations by junior scientists with their graphs, pictures, and tables. The diversity of presenters was as vast as Jane had ever experienced in her career. Not just Asian, Indian and South American scientists but equal representation from women and men, conducting research on all aspects of the project. This acquisition was important to a lot of researchers and it was an honor to be selected to do this research. She was fascinated, of course, but could not always catch the innuendos that were being discussed. Dr. Calbreer, Cal, was best at distilling, for which she was forever grateful. She thought about the seeds in her Tool Box and was pleased that she also had a backup plan just in case the project was not approved. These seeds were the future and a survivalist's dream come true.

After the meeting was over, Jane thanked everyone and said Dr. Joy and Cal were joining the meeting this afternoon and everyone would be notified immediately of the outcome. She did not expect any hiccups, but one never knew. The team was going to be ready to go if the deal was approved. It would impact their lives, combining personal passion with good business, a rare combination these days.

As Jane walked out of the conference room, she literally ran into Michael walking down the hallway, throwing her Tool Box across the hallway. Michael seemed quite out of it. There were signs of high blood pressure as his red neck came oozing out from his white collar and he seemed to be talking to himself. Jane thought he looked angrier than usual.

LOIS - 19

Lois tried Clark again. No answer. He got in late. *I wonder if he left his cell phone some place? He could be careless when he was drinking. But then why isn't he answering her landline?*

Dan continued with his questions. "Where are the warnings? Where's the news media? Why have your searches found nothing? The US has a thousand warning systems for attack. Why is no one saying anything?" Dan sounded so commanding and Lois felt a little safer, knowing that there might be a possibility that they were wrong.

"Dan, let's skip to the bottom line," said Cong. "I understand your concern about concrete data. We had the same concerns, but we're good at what we do. Our combined experience in code breaking has made us pre-eminent in this discipline. No one else comes close. We can focus quickly and accurately on the tasks at hand. The information we shared has ninety-two percent accuracy, and the interpretation is at worst ninety percent and the best at ninety-nine percent, depending on how carefully we phrased the questions. We asked a broad question, asking what was common to these emails from China. If we're to address narrow questions like you're suggesting, then we would have to rerun everything through our algorithms again, taking up another hour. Obviously, not an option."

Lois thought Cong was being convoluted with Dan. "I thought we were skipping to the bottom line, Cong. What's going on?"

Cong took a breath, "We think Dan and his family should leave immediately and arrive here in no more than forty-five minutes. You need to stay here, Lois. We are collecting provisions to accommodate a larger group."

A claustrophobic reaction shifted in Lois and she just wanted to run outside and avoid being buried underground. Her mind was racing. How long would it take to convince Dan that he was in imminent danger? "Dan, where are you located?"

"I'm still in front of the Aikido studio."

"Okay, Dan, leave now!" said Lois. "You'll find getting here is straightforward, taking the first university exit from the freeway. You know where the Physics Building is. Dan, confirm you are leaving now."

"Lois, I heard you. Betty is getting out of the car."

"This sounds weird to me,' said Betty as she shouted into the speakerphone. "I'll catch up with you later after I talk to my class."

"Wait, just wait a minute and let's talk rationally," said Cong.

"I think we need to go over the data with them so they will understand the urgency," said Bai.

"We've got no time," said Cong. "Dan, if our reading is accurate, you only have forty-five minutes to get here. Turn on the radio. We are hearing reports of traffic building on the freeway."

Qiang added, "Hi, Dan. This is Qiang. I'm sure hearing this information for the first time is a shock to you and you are probably having a hard time believing what we are proposing will happen. We are in a sub-basement with some survival provisions. Think of your granddaughter."

Lois interrupted Qiang, "Betty, how are you doing?"

"She left," said Dan. "Lois, what's your take on this?"

"Since I got here, they have impressed me with their access to worldwide information. They have a screen with wave bobbers all over the Pacific Ocean, intended to capture tsunamis happening before they hit the west coast. Listen, Dan, there isn't much time and I know the information we provided is provocative. What can we say to convince you to move quickly?"

"I'm looking at Lizzy and I'll do this for her. There is no downside if you're wrong. I hope you are and I think we can make it in forty-five minutes. Maybe I should go get Betty."

"Yes!" they all said unanimously.

The line went dead. The room was silent for ten minutes as the Five Guys continued to monitor communication networks. Lois tried calling Clark and left another message. This was typical of Clark. Her frustration with him was his unpredictability.

The phone rang, "Dan here." He sounded out of breath. "I took your advice and Betty is with me. She let the students know they were in danger. We tried to take some of them with us, but they insisted on using their own cars. They probably went to lunch. It's a tough message to believe in. The day looks sunny with a light dusting of snow. Nothing wrong here."

"Betty here. I agree, when you only partially believe, how can you convince someone else of imminent danger of the magnitude that no one ever thinks is possible?"

"We moved toward the university but freeway traffic is horrible. We're checking radio stations."

"Maybe if Dan had Sirius radio, we could get a news channel. I admit I'm skeptical. Regardless of what is real, I think I can help Dan with Lizzy today. This is all hard to comprehend. If we take this take this seriously, I think we should stop, get formula and diapers and a thousand other staples."

Lois started to feel anxious about this last statement. "Betty, let me take care of that. There is a campus grocery near here and I've seen their selection of diapers and it's pretty good. You just focus on getting here and leave the rest to us." The Five Guys all nodded.

Bai spoke up and said, "Lois, I have inventory and actually, we have underground access to most stores in the immediate vicinity and the supplies Betty mentioned should not be a problem."

"This is strange. The traffic is building up for this time of day," said Dan. "I'm going to avoid the freeway and take back roads. This will be a better way. If this is true, I still can't fully comprehend the full impact of your information. Best case is we had an interesting but unnecessary adventure and the worst case is we can kiss our asses good-bye. Wait, I have a call coming in. Thank God, it's Brenda. Talk later."

"Just in case we get cut off, Dan, we're in the sub-basement of the Physics building. Come here immediately," said Cong. The line was already dead.

The Five Guys shifted their positions collectively around the room, and Lois understood that this meant something, like a swing in focus. Their collective body movement was interesting. It surprised her how much she understood as they discovered new information simultaneously. They emailed back and forth, without emotion but the keyboard speed, picked up.

Lois thought a little about her own situation. Her mother, her brother. "Oh my God," Lois said out loud. "I'm calling Clark again." Lois speed-dialed her home number and let the phone ring in the house and then tried Clark on his mobile again. No answer. Clark enjoyed walking Suri. If he forgot his cell phone some place last night and was taking one of his long walks, this would spell disaster, she thought. The chain reaction in Lois' mind started to implode. Her expression must have changed as the Five Guys stopped what they were doing to get up and move toward her. Their facial expressions all showed concern in different ways and they surrounded her with small gestures like touching her shoulder or hand. Their focused presence was a little overwhelming. Lou poured her tea and told her to drink it while it was warm and she calmed down a bit. A little embarrassed, she nodded in appreciation and slumped into her chair. She had a feeling that a heavy weight rested over her body as if she was sitting in a high gravity room. She wanted to do something useful. The tea helped a little, and she started to sit straighter and looked into Bai's eyes. His eyes were full of compassion and he seemed to understand her fear of losing Clark and Suri.

"Communications will get jammed soon," said Qiang. "I'm seeing a slow buildup of internet activity and our phone calls keep getting dropped. I'll try to get Clark on the phone."

"Thanks, Qiang."

"I hope this is a hoax, Lois. It's a possibility that's what we're dealing with," said Bai. "It occurred to us that we have left an impression on you that nothing disturbs us. We are all thinking of people we love. We have not had a chance to digest what's going on, except for verifying the accuracy of the information. Unfortunately, we need to focus on the action part of our plan if we will survive."

"What can I do? Give me something to do!" said Lois.

Having eased the situation a little, the Five Guys broke up and connected with each other through eye contact and head nods.

"Okay," said Hung. "We have a plan and you can help. Follow me."

"In the meantime, we will locate your brother," chimed in Qiang. "What's your address?" These words meant a lot to Lois. Could the Five Guys do anything about Clark?

MICHAEL - 20

Jane, yes, Jane, a reminder of everything bad that happened to him today. He was a little stunned from the physical encounter and quite surprised at his loss of words. What would Marcella say about this? She often shared a different point of view without forcing Michael to agree with her perspective. That was what kept their marriage so vibrant.

Jane bent down to retrieve her funny-looking purse and adjust her backpack. Typical Jane! She was moving fast with this intense look on her face. As Michael was pushing himself up from his fall, at least ten scientists started to stream out of the conference room. They all offered Jane help while completely ignoring him. Some scientists were still talking about transcription and something about hybrid alleles. He could not track what they were saying, but it sounded impressive. Then Michael heard the key word, Lazarus. They must be leaving the Lazarus meeting.

Jane was now standing composed and she looked straight at him as he straightened up to standing. She wasn't going to apologize for running into him. It was so typical of her. Well, he wasn't going to either.

"What are you doing in the lab building, Michael? Are you following me?" She didn't sound angry at all.

Michael, ignoring her question, said, "What are you up to, Jane? I thought you would be working on your presentation for management."

"We all agreed, no changes to the presentation. We are completing due diligence conclusions and preparing for questions for the Lazarus project presentation in this afternoon's meeting. The team leaders are ready to answer questions and can update the committee with our latest findings.

They are fully prepped on the agreement terms and we are in excellent shape. I am proud of their work and what they have accomplished. I'm not worried."

She was too young to be expressing herself this way. Who did she think she was? "Did you ever ensure the firewall was a hundred percent?" asked Michael. "Everyone is quite upset that you went ahead without approval from our Intellectual Property Security Oversight Committee. Not having a satisfactory answer from you, I had to take this to my boss."

"Michael, the firewall did not have a breach. You wasted all of that worry on a non-issue. We're in great shape. You seem to be popping up everywhere today. I just received an email from someone at your last meeting who told me you had an interesting experience with the CEO. This kind of news seems to travel fast. It seems so unproductive to keep disrupting good projects for personal reasons. I guess I have just come to expect this from you. It's just too bad we have to waste our time with politics for personal gain when we should do good work that benefits the company. Well, Michael, I am sure you have plenty of phone calls to make before the two o'clock meeting. Short of any catastrophic event, we'll see you at the final meeting."

She walked away quickly and rounded the corner of the building. As Michael's eyes followed her passing the bank of windows, he saw birds flying back and forth in strange formation. Michael calmed down a bit as he watched them weave back and forth. He was in a kind of trance when this guy in a lab coat was the last one to walk out of the conference room. He said hi in passing. Michael asked, "How did the meeting go? Does Jane have everything under control? Are you seeing anything strange? I would sure like to know that."

He said. "Yeah, I guess everything is okay. You're from legal, right? You might be interested in this. I overhead Jane talking to someone about the possibility of Seed Capture. The term means obtaining seeds with GMO traits, illicitly. As you know, transferring seeds across state line without a license is a big deal. I was wondering if that is what she meant."

"You are right," said Michael. "And transferring seeds outside of China and into any country violates many Chinese laws with a penalty of death. I sure hope we are not experiencing such shenanigans with our laboratory efforts here, but let me know if you find anything out. Call me if you do."

Michael had to think about strategy. He thought Jane was too ambitious for his taste. If she continued to show confidence in challenging situations, where else could she go but up? He needed to do something about that. Acquiring this Chinese company could present a significant opportunity to the company and some risk. It could be a very positive game changer. Something like this could make her successful and raise her image to a higher level and Michael could just not stomach that. She could lead groups, coordinate successful projects and maybe, grudgingly, make it to VP status where she would ultimately have more power than... he stopped his line of thinking. No way. He knew that would never happen.

In general, women, had too many scruples and tended to focus on the work rather than what it takes to become a VP. Michael was amused at their obvious frustration in getting ahead. Only the super ambitious, well connected squeaked in. Equality was suppressed at almost an unconscious level by men in power. Thank God Marcella held the position of department head and didn't have to deal with anyone challenging her anymore. With her impeccable background, connections, experience and intelligence, she did not have to work hard to be accepted as the top surgeon in her field. She was very different from Jane.

Michael worried about Jane's success. He had to stop her. If he deep-sixed this deal, he could start spreading doubt about her incompetence. She would not end up on a list for advancement. He could make her so miserable that she would weaken, she might spiral down, performing poorly, which was almost better.

Michael almost stopped breathing from the pleasure he felt inside. As a lawyer, they trained him to transfer negative feelings into laser-focused strategy. He suddenly felt a little calmer. It was that moment when Michael remembered the comment about seed capture. Could he suggest this during the meeting to put Jane on the defense? Regardless of truth, that was the angle. He better call Karen to see if she set up those meetings for him.

Michael gazed down over the pond and saw more geese adding to the formation he saw before, coming toward the building and then up to his eye level on the sixth floor. He looked out over the fields of corn and was reminded of his home and the view that he loved so much.

The phone rang, and it was Dr. McKenzie. "I was just thinking about you," said Michael.

"Yes, and I was just reading this proposal by Jane Witterhouse and it sounds ridiculously smart. Unfortunately, it will use the lab space I would like to get rid of, saving me half a million dollars from my budget, which I promised I would do. Michael, I might need your help with this."

Michael, being cautious, said, "Mac, can you meet me on the sixth floor? It's the conference room with floor to ceiling windows with a blue mural."

"Yeah, let's talk," said Dr. McKenzie. "I'll walk up and meet you there. I need the exercise anyway."

Michael stared out the window and thought about his next move. Could he and McKenzie provide a solid front against the deal proposal and delay a decision to go forward that would make the Paradise Lost company withdraw their interest? What questions could they prepare that provided enough doubt to kill the deal? It had to be about the seeds.

"You got here fast," Michael said as he watched McKenzie march down the hallway. He had his white lab coat on which made him appear twice as big. He was well over six feet tall and his large forehead and neck probably meant he was a football player in college.

"I don't have any time. Let me review with you several points in the proposal that bother me," said McKenzie. "We are shutting down the lab that supports this deal. These lab geeks are strange and everyone keeps undercutting my authority. Seeds that are being worked on in this deal have high protein properties that could decimate our livestock industry and my family comes from Nebraska where beef is king. I know this may sound farfetched, but the potential of these seeds is very real and in our current environment, they would have impact on the meat industry forever. Also, why do we hire a Chinese lab? I have lots of guys in my laboratories, at least seventy-two PhDs with 176 technicians. Why would I support going outside to acquire technology that we could do right here?"

Michael thought McKenzie could give a compelling argument against the deal to the committee and it would look like Jane was incompetent. Michael would sit and say nothing. Genetically modified seeds were a sensitive subject, especially when questioned from the head of R&D. He also could carefully place a concern about a rumor of employees moving seed outside of China without a license and the deal would be dead beyond doubt. Problem solved.

As Michael nodded and partially listened to McKenzie rant a while longer, he thought he felt the building vibrate. McKenzie did not seem disturbed at all. McKenzie started to talk about the future of the company and the many paths that research and development could go. They were a technology company and why buy technology they could develop themselves? Michael thought he was a pompous asshole. He was employed to be an expert, but did he have to be such a jerk about it? His pomposity helped keep employees in their place. To be the global head of research, it was critically important that his contributions be well known. As Michael listened, he would go on forever. He waited for a segue and asked, "Are you comfortable saying certain things about Jane at the meeting?"

"Oh yeah. Let's crush her and we don't even have to be subtle about it. It might be fun," said McKenzie.

"Right, crush her."

The building vibrated and the conference room windows were pinched, like a bubble ready to burst. Michael's phone rang.

"Michael, where are you?" It was Marcella. Her voice sounded anxious.

"I'm at work. What's going on?"

"Are you seeing what's happening?" she asked.

"No, I'm in a conference room."

"Go to a window and tell me what you see!" she shouted. "I am trapped in a tunnel leading into the university hospital. Part of the tunnel collapsed while I was going from the medical science building to the hospital. Everything is vibrating. What is happening, Michael? Can you see?" she screamed.

Michael looked down the hallway. McKenzie's phone started to ring. McKenzie grabbed it from his briefcase. It was a goddamn satellite phone. Wondering why McKenzie had such a phone, Michael looked where the geese had been flying around in their pattern, seeing a darkened sky. The phone went dead. He called Marcella back but there was no signal.

That shook him up as it was so sudden. Then he saw three mushroom cloud formations on the horizon and the city skyline lying below. Mushroom clouds, he thought. Michael's breathing stopped in his throat. He could not bring in air as his body was almost stiff with fear. It was like watching a movie from the '40s about Hiroshima and Nagasaki. There were three mushroom shapes high in the sky with a cerulean blue color between the cloud and the cityscape. Suddenly, people came running out of the labs and the smell of sweat immediately filled the small hallway. White lab coats were everywhere. They were shouting while running to the windows. As they looked out onto the horizon, they were all pointing to the mushroom clouds where they seemed to rise. A sea of white lab coats and anxious discussions surrounded Michael about the Chinese bombing nine US locations, each with multiple bombs. Where did they get this information? He wished he could reach Marcella and let her know. Michael was trying to catch the information, rapid firing out of everyone's mouth. No one person seemed to have the complete story.

Someone shouted, "Get to the basement!"

"There's the plane," said another voice. The group started to move toward the exit sign at the end of the hall as more people piled out of the labs. No alarms went off. Just as the confusion was swirling to a higher pitch, Michael saw a low-flying plane go across the horizon and release a projectile close to the field he was looking at minutes ago, only a mile away. A flash went bright before the building shook, followed by a loud, deep deafening clash. Everyone that was standing in front of the large bank of windows started to scream. Some bent down to hide their faces, some put their hands over their eyes and started running. After the initial bright light, Michael realized that he needed to get away from the window and moved next to the cement wall around the corner from the banks of windows. Then a force pressed against the center of the window, spreading glass shards into the room. The stale sanitized air was replaced with a wind that smashed bodies against walls. A blast that powerful will embed glass into any skin, exposed or not. The swirling mass of people moved around and spun down the hallway. As the bodies swirled, they moved toward the exit sign with blood pooling onto the floor. The floor, a highly polished terrazzo, quickly became slippery. People fell onto the hard surface and some passed out.

Michael was watching from around the corner and ironically right next to a first aid kit and fire extinguisher. He made a run for the exit sign to the west along the concrete wall. He tried calling Marcella, but the connection was still dead. As he moved past the conference room, Dr. McKenzie stuck his head out the door and shouted to Michael to come back. Michael hesitated and went back. He was being pulled away from the conference room but fighting his way back. People were crawling through viscoelastic bloody mucus. As they tried to get traction toward the exits, the floor became more slippery. People started crawling toward the exit. Some were screaming, but still moving.

Michael braced along the wall, carefully moving back to the conference room. McKenzie was connected, maybe he could help him get in touch with Marcella. As he fought against the flow of bodies, he almost stopped breathing. The sight of blood closed his trachea and he had the feeling that his stomach was being sucked out of his mouth. He grabbed the door's broken window. Sharp, shredded glass pierced the soft palms of his hands, causing them to flood with blood. When he finally pulled himself into the empty conference room, he saw McKenzie in the corner, holding a large satellite phone, shouting to someone. He quickly ended the call with what sounded like GPS coordinates. Michael wished he had grabbed the first aid kit.

Michael fell into a chair and started ripping off his coat to get at his shirt. It was too tight. Then he passed out.

Michael woke up, feeling cold, realizing his shirt had disappeared. How long was he out? McKenzie wrapped each of his hands with a shirt.

"I wasn't sure what to do, so I took off your shirt to bandage up your hands," said McKenzie.

The halls were silent as Michael looked around and felt the building tremble in waves as the movement dissipated harmonically down to the rebar in the walls. "What is going on, Mac?"

"I have a helicopter coming. If we get to the roof, we'll get picked up. We need to leave before we're quarantined," said McKenzie.

That disturbed Michael. What can I do? I need to protect Marcella. As he looked down at his pants, stained with blood, he remembered the sight from the windows and finally realized that a nuclear bomb caused this. His face felt warm, but he could touch nothing with his wrapped hands. If Marcella was in a tunnel, she was protected from radiation, actually a very safe place.

"Michael, we have to move," McKenzie said as he helped him on his feet. Michael was in shock. The wind in the hallway was blowing, pushing blood around the floor.

"Where are we going? I need to get to Marcella. Can we pick her up?" Michael asked.

"I've got contacts in the government. You lucky you're with me today, my friend. Let's focus on moving and we can talk about her later."

"My wife is trapped in a tunnel. You need to help me find her."

"Look, we are under attack from a group in China. They sent multiple atomic bombs in key cities across the country, maybe the world. The Center for Survival is close and, trust me, they will help you find your wife. Medical care, food and water are available. We are being picked up in fifteen minutes. We need to move," shouted McKenzie right at Michael's face.

Michael nodded in reluctant agreement. Having given the same speech, he trusted no one who said, "Trust me."

Michael and McKenzie cautiously moved across the floor down the hall, crossing a few lifeless blood-covered pods, freshly dead. The place was eerily quiet and Michael slipped twice before they got to the end of the hallway, protected by concrete walls on both sides. As Michael looked back, his lasting memory was seeing three mushroom clouds in the distance as he gazed past the bloody scene in front of him.

McKenzie opened the exit door to the staircase and helped Michael up the stairs. They could hear shouting in the staircase below and Michael thought again about going into the sub-basement. They only had half a flight to the roof and they could feel the building rhythmically roll back and forth in a wave.

They moved slowly up the steps. Michael felt his legs cramp, and he had to think about each time he raised his leg onto the next step. Michael never lost control like this. He was agile and strong. As he collected himself again, with a few deep breaths, he started to get more control over his body and finally could stand and take the remaining steps to the top of the stairs. The Emergency Exit door had a bright red bar written across it. McKenzie pushed it open and stepped onto the roof of the building. He stood, scanning back and forth. All Michael could see was a scene of blackness and fires, burning in every direction. The darkness of night caused every view to be foreboding. McKenzie stepped back and closed the door.

"Where is the helicopter?" Michael asked. "What if this building collapses? What if another bomb lands here? What is your connection with this?"

McKenzie pointed up to Michael. "I've called the helicopter. Consider yourself lucky to be with me, Michael. We are in the middle of a goddamn shit storm."

Michael tried his cell phone, but it was still dead. He only had a suit jacket on with nothing but a wallet in his pocket. Since the explosion, McKenzie's demeanor transformed. He almost seemed prepared for this incident. What could prepare you for this? Why did he have a satellite phone on him? What a strange coincidence that he, Michael, was the only one here being saved? Where did everyone go? McKenzie always seemed to have a mad streak in his behavior.

JANE - 21

Jane had no reason to hurry, except to escape Michael's annoying behavior. She had a couple hours to kill before the Lazarus meeting. She might have overreacted, but she always suspected that Michael spent a lot of energy working against women. Of course, that was impossible to confirm. He almost always won his battles, using his connections at the top. Someone called him a swamp snake, and she laughed out loud at how appropriate that sounded. As she headed down the hallway with these uncomfortable thoughts, she had a beverage in the cafeteria to calm down a bit.

Jane sat down. She was prepared for the meeting. She could now practice Dr. Blue's Full Presence meditation to help stop her mind from racing. As she looked around, the blue colors of the cafeteria were calming. The windows spanned two stories high and brought nature from the outside in. She loved to sit in the back of the cafeteria, staring at the windows from far away. Glass was the enemy for any survival scenario she could imagine and she avoided it whenever she could.

The view was a beautiful showcase of a yellow wheat field surrounding a small pond. The architects carefully constructed this pond to show off a calm and peaceful scene. The golden color of the wheat was effervescent like a Van Gogh painting with the yellow reflecting into the cafeteria. As she looked out southward, geese flew by, close to the window, showing a strange pattern of flight. The flock was composed of twelve geese, five on one side and seven on the other. They flew in formation directly toward the glass and then at the last minute, flew up like an airplane taking off. They returned, repeating the pattern. It caused the few people in the cafeteria to stand up close to the glass and gaze silently. She was reminded of a report about animals sensing pending danger and provide warnings of oncoming disasters. The sun was reflecting against the windows, creating a resonance of light that penetrated the whole room. A beautiful white light ran across the room and reflected against the brass trim. Jane relaxed a little, catching the light and feeling mesmerized by the sight.

Jane felt a strong vibration from the table. She knew that this building normally had a certain rhythm to it, but this feeling was magnified by another source, deeper, in a lower frequency. She placed her hand on the metal table leg and the vibration was enhanced as if something different was causing the structure itself to vibrate. She felt a vibration like this once while waiting for a plane in LaGuardia Airport. Planes took off on her right and landed on her left, each one leaving a unique vibration based on the plane. As she waited for her flight, she tried to categorize the resonance she felt from the building up through to the chair she was sitting on. She knew each plane had a different vibration, but quickly realized how limited her knowledge of planes was in differentiating one from another.

More people gathered in front of the larger window, calling out and pointing at the geese. It was an unusual display of animal behavior, similar to what she saw this morning. Jane walked next to the concrete wall surrounding the cafeteria and felt the vibration amplify. She looked out the large windows, the geese were gone and everyone in the cafeteria were now standing and talking. A man in a blue lab coat passed by her table.

"Jane, did you see that? The geese were flying in a kind of formation I've never seen before. I got it on video."

"What have you heard?"

"We've checked news streams. There is strange activity coming from China. I'm leaving to go to my desk to upload my video onto YouTube. Take care, Jane."

Jane could not remember his name, but he knew her. Maybe he worked in one of the medical laboratories, she thought.

Suddenly, something snapped in Jane. It felt like a meteoric synapse collapsing in her brain. Her split-second reaction was in response to something that just happened. Jane had to force herself to listen and observe. She studied the windows and saw a black plane in the sky, moving straight east. The dots slowly started to connect, the vibration, the drone, the geese, and the people fixated at looking out at the geese.

Jane grabbed her phone, backpack and briefcase. Was she overreacting? This could be a drill. She often created hundreds of drills, convincing herself that something was happening. Was this any different? There was no time to decide. What she needed to do was assess her location and the closest stairs to the tunnels. She never worked an exit from this location before. She rarely sat in this cafeteria. She sensed she was pretty far from where she wanted to be. Did she have time to stop and pull out her map or could she do this en route? But what was the route?

The recurring image in Jane's mind was an ominous projectile moving in an almost horizontal manner across the earth, only fifty feet from the ground. I need a safe spot to stop and connect. Jane thought about those scientists looking at this strange phenomenon. What was their fate?

Saving people was part of Jane's preparation. The catastrophe that Jane was planning for was not one that she could explain to others until the disaster happened. In order for people to take action, they need to react to pain or fear. However, she had no information, so she could only warn them about the windows.

She shouted several times, "Move away from the windows." A projectile went by and she continued to shout, "Move away from the windows."

Personal survival was required to save others. Her ethics were intact, and she knew if she survived, her gifts of knowledge would benefit everyone. Her ethics were not of the captain of a sinking ship, but of a knowledgeable first shipman that jumps into the boat to help the passengers. Jane was not distracted. She knew what to do.

Jane turned and made one last look at this strange sight and exited out of the cafeteria, pushing the double door handle with a forceful thrust.

As she ran down the hallway, people were moving fast in both directions. She thought about what she saw and how it triggered a reaction in her gut. The reaction was visceral, radiating from her solar plexus, something that Dr. Blue mentioned once. Intuition is powerful, she said to Jane one day. You don't have to study it, just be present enough to know when it is happening.

"Can you study the validity of intuition?" she asked Dr. Blue.

"You either believe in it or not. Most religions request blind faith, but none of them request a gut check which is technically more accurate than pure belief." As Dr. Blue talked about this subject, maybe her favorite, Jane became more and more confused. Jane was action-oriented and could not appreciate Dr. Blue's sense of exploration of the esoteric and her indulgence in intellectual discourse. But once the seed was planted, Jane found Dr. Blue's simple suggestion of being present useful. Jane found she had an aptitude for this stuff and paid attention to her gut reaction to things whenever she could.

Multiple national defense mechanisms protect us, Jane thought. How is it possible for a small aircraft to be flying so close to us and dropping bombs? What is this? Was it possible for a terrorist group to penetrate US security? She needed to get online or call someone. Should she get to the tunnel and save her life? Should she seek information and then run to safety? Devices in her backpack could do both. The information phase was important to survival, but that did not make a difference if she was crushed under tons of concrete. Could she make it to safety? How much time did she have? What information did she need to protect herself from a potential catastrophic event? She needed to know the nature of it.

As she was running, she felt the wall-to-wall carpet move. The carpet was a bright purple and green in a pattern that made her feel nauseous. The carpet seemed to take on a 3D image as it rolled down the hallway. She made gut check. Get to the tunnel under the garage with her car, ASAP. She stopped and looked for the nearest staircase.

She did not see an exit sign. As she turned the corner, she saw Jake. He wasn't running. Just having bumped into each other earlier, she ran up to him. "Jake!"

"What's going on? Is this a fire drill? People running out of the building. I'm on the EM committee. I should know!"

"Jake, this is real. I just saw flying objects dropping bombs a few miles from here. Let's get to the basement now. Do you know how to locate the sub-tunnel?"

"Sure, no problem. Is this really that serious?" asked Jake.

"You should act as if this building is coming down on top on you," said Jane. Another vibration turned the building into a wave of molten energy. As they both looked up, the foyer pillars swayed back and forth. Jake turned white. Now alarms blared loudly and everyone was running to leave the building, according to the emergency plan. That's not right, she thought. That means everyone is moving to the parking lots. What if these bombs are nuclear? Reinforced tunnels at least ten feet below the surface are the best protection. The emergency plan takes everyone into the west side parking garage.

Jake snapped into action and motioned her to follow. At the end of the hall, he opened a door leading to the basement level. As she looked down the staircase, she wondered. Is this wise? Her gut answered with a resounding yes, but only if she could get to the sub-tunnel. The icy sound of glass shattering resonated from a distance. The walls were still weaving in slow motion. Could she reach the tunnel she just visited an hour ago which would take her to the garage and her car? They needed to move through areas that supported the six-story building as quickly as they could. It was not ideal, but it was their best option. Jane raced down the stairs. Jake was at the top. Strange, she thought. It was interesting that no one followed him. She was reminded again that everyone was leaving the building to the pre-determined safe places in case of fire. Jane wondered how she could do anything about changing their minds. Of course, she didn't know what course was best. She might be entering into a tomb after the bombing was finished. Wasn't it better to be outside in case the whole building collapsed?

Each decision had consequences. The door to the tunnels below wasn't far. She went right and found the door. It required a swipe to open, and she pulled out her employee pass and it opened. Jane felt a cool breeze rush past her face. I need to check the Internet. She pulled off her backpack and started to log in, and she realized Jake was still not with her. Did he leave? She was now torn between gaining access to information, entering the tunnel level, and rescuing Jake. She ran back for Jake. She opened the door and found him lying on his back with his legs sprawled at the top of the stairs. Blood flowed from his head.

"What happened to you?" she said.

"I can't tell," he said as his body went limp. Another sound of impact made the walls compress with horizontal wave strokes, up and down the walls of the stairway. It was stronger than before, and they both rolled down the stairs. The structure above them sounded like it was seizing against immense pressure. Jane got up slowly, having hit her head and bruised her calves. She looked over at Jake and he was unconscious. Jane needed to get to the tunnel with Jake. She could hear screaming through the closed door.

Speed, she said to herself as she processed her next step. She could only be of help if she survived. She also knew that she could not leave Jake behind. She checked his pulse and his breathing sounded rough. What happened, she wondered? They needed to get to the tunnel before this building collapsed. She tried dragging Jake on the smooth concrete floor, but he was too big. Jake was unconscious, and she needed to move him to the entrance door of the sub-basement without provoking more injuries. They were alone. There was no one here to help. Did everyone evacuate already? Should she try to find help?

Jane had rope and bungees in her backpack. Running down to the sub-basement, she used her security pass to enter, holding the door open with the Tool Box. There was a solution, a wild idea, located right next to the door. Neatly arranged was a stack of wooden pallets, a common transportation mechanism for heavy loads or assorted pieces of laboratory equipment. Why not? she thought. She hauled one up the stairs, dragged it back and found Jake still motionless, but breathing. The bleeding had stopped.

She collected herself and looked at the backpack. She designed it for airports so it could roll around if she did not want to carry it. There were two sets of wheelbases comprising two wheels each. They were a newly designed micro-wheels, used for moving loads in all directions. One of Jane's tech friends told her they were going to put them in luggage soon. They were strong enough to withstand the weight of a man and detachable from the three-inch wide Velcro strips she bought online. She looked at her watch. Fifteen minutes passed since she first reached the tunnel. She grabbed the bottom of the backpack and detached both sets of wheels. She pulled out a three-inch strip of male Velcro and applied it to the wooden pallet. Once the wheels were attached, she had to lift at least half of Jake's body on it. She placed the pallet next to his body and tried to move him onto it. It angled up and threatened to roll away. Bracing the pallet with her feet, she pulled Jake's body toward her, and then onto the pallet, his face up.

She took out three bungee cords from her backpack and secured Jake's body to the pallet. She configured the strap from the Tool Kit as a harness and wrapped it around her body, snapping it on the bungee cords.

There he was, bungeed to a wooden pallet with his legs dragging behind him. It did not have to be elegant. She tested by pulling his body across the floor; it was probably quite a sight, but it worked. She placed her backpack on top of Jake's chest. The bungee cords were biting against his armpit, but the body kept moving a few feet at a time across the smooth concrete floor. She always had a strong feeling that all of her thinking about survival would not prepare her for an actual situation. She looked down at her phone and saw she had a message. She needed information. In all of her research around panic, she knew that keeping focus on the task was key. Twenty minutes went by and they had reached the stairway. Her bruised body was feeling the after effects of adrenaline rushes and she was putting all of her energy toward moving Jake. She grabbed an emergency CPR kit, first aid and fire extinguisher from the wall as she passed emergency supplies and placed them around Jake's body.

As she approached the door to the tunnel, she saw her Tool Kit bracing it open. Now what? she asked. Get Jake to the safety of the sub-tunnel and get him healthy enough to keep moving. Pushing his body to the edge of the pallet, she lifted the opposite end. Grabbing the wheel assembly, she pulled apart the Velcro strips that held the wheels. She torqued his body to the other end and pulled off the other wheels. Taking a very thin, polypropylene rope out of her backpack, she tied it in multiple places around the side of the pallet and under Jake's armpits. She protected Jake's head with an inflatable pillow from her backpack. Wow, she thought, one never knows what will be useful. Pulling the end of the rope around the corner of the door helped her offset his weight. Bracing the ropes with her body, she slowly let the pallet slide down the stairs. She could have used the help of another person.

Once down, she immediately unstrapped Jake and rolled his body onto the concrete floor, keeping the pillow strapped around his head. She checked his blood pressure and pulse. He was still unconscious but appeared to weather the movement rather well. He is muscular and fit, she thought. She covered him up with a fire blanket and set out to sort her options.

This part of the sub-basement was unfamiliar to her, but she was told that these tunnels could hold up under nuclear attack. It was possible that the whole building would collapse on them, encasing them in a lonely tomb. With six floors of research space above them, they would have no chance of surviving. They needed to move quickly. Jane looked up the tunnel and pulled out her map of the tunnel system. Her compass showed her going south, toward the parking garage.

As she walked another hundred feet, she came upon another stack of pallets, used for moving just about everything in the company. Was there a pallet truck? That would be so nice. As she dreamed of a pallet truck and what that could do for her survival, she continued to move down the tunnel and started to recognize where she was. Quickly looking at the map on the wall, she could now correlate her position with her own map. They needed to move at least two hundred yards south from her current location toward the parking garage.

She wanted to call Dr. Blue. Was she safe and could she call her to warn her to move to safety? She pulled out her satellite phone, but there was no signal.

The tunnel shook many times, waking her up to the reality of her next decision but she knew what to do. She wondered about access to parts of the building. What did they need to survive? Food and water to start. As she was repacking her Tool Kit, Jake started moving and groaned and shouted, "Motherfucker!"

"Jake, are you okay? You fell at the top of the stairs. I found you passed out. How are you feeling? What happened?"

Jake started to pull himself up and stared for a while. "Jane. We are in subbasement 28E. What is going on now? I don't remember what happened. I guess we made it. How did you get me here?"

"You sound good for having fallen down a flight of stairs. The next few minutes or hours will be critical to our survival. How do you feel?"

Jake started to stand up and sat back down quickly. He started to pull at the pillow that was taped to his neck. "What's this?" She grabbed her knife and cut the tape. "I think I remember being pushed down the stairs. I was at the top of the stairs with the door open. The corridor was packed with people trying to get out of the building. I guess it shut behind me and I lost my balance. How long was I out?"

"Let me tell you what I know," said Jane. She related the events from the moment she was sitting in the cafeteria to pulling him down the staircase. He was quiet. Maybe he was in shock, but she sensed he was hearing everything she said.

LOIS - 22

Lois was waiting for Hung to return. He was so kind to her. He came up to
her and said he could help. She gave him her address, home phone, and
Clark's number. He hugged her tight, bowed deeply and promised he
would find Clark. Then he was gone. She wondered what he had in mind.

Lois was reminded of a time when they were kids and Clark went
missing. They were separated in the Grand Canyon of all places. After
Susan's divorce, she decided they were driving to the Grand Canyon.
Susan's rebound relationship was with a man named Casey who joined
them on this vacation. Lois, knowing that her mother was unstable, braced
herself against what would happen. This pinnacle incident would define
Lois' relationship with her mother forever. Before the trip, she read a lot
about the Grand Canyon and talked to Clark about its timeless, geological
history. At eight, he was already showing signs of ADD, and giving his full
attention to one subject was difficult. They had never been on a family
vacation and she wanted Clark to enjoy this amazing place.

Lois knew she had to stay close to Clark as he would wander. Casey's
minivan was a nice ride and Lois felt secure, knowing that Clark would
share the backseat with her and had no place to go. Around noon, they
stopped at a rest stop in the middle of the Canyon for sandwiches and a
bathroom break. Susan and Casey were getting everyone a sandwich. Lois
wanted to rush into the bathroom ahead of a busload of school kids from
Arkansas, so she egged Clark on to follow her. She watched as he walked
into the men's entrance, and when she got out, she waited for him. When
he didn't come out, she assumed he must have gotten out before her and

she started to look around for him. She knew he could not go far, but she did not trust his special brand of shenanigans. Casey and Susan returned with the lunches. She asked Lois to go back for the napkins she forgot. She would look out for Clark. Susan was in full panic mode when Lois returned.

"Where is Clark?".

"I thought you said you would look for him," said Lois. "I told you, Mom. We went to the bathroom at the same time and I haven't seen him since. Mom, maybe he was kidnapped."

Her mother continued to wonder out loud where Clark went while complaining that Lois dropped the ball.

Things got quiet at the rest stop and Casey mentioned a desire to get going before it got dark. Lois' gut told her that her brother was just gone, but her brain could not figure out how he disappeared. Susan, finally, just realizing that she might have been neglectful in this situation, called out to Clark as she wandered around the parking lot. She asked people to check the bathrooms and finally, someone called the police. By the time the police arrived, she needed to be medicated, which only confounded the situation. Casey disappeared. Susan's story to the police was she was a single mother with two misbehaving children. She kept saying, "He was kidnapped." The police logged a report. They told her ninety percent of the time, kids showed up in twenty-four hours. An APB on Clark would be filed if he did not return after that. They would monitor information in case they found him somewhere else and let her know via mobile phone.

During this time, Lois looked again, everywhere, retracing her steps many times. Once the police left, Casey returned and Susan started sobbing uncontrollably. Lois wished Clark could appear right then so he could see how much Susan cared for him. She knew how tough he could be. He was a fighter.

Lois retraced her steps one last time and went back into the women's bathroom and looked at the mess the kids from the school bus left behind. She started going through gum and candy bar wrapper. Suddenly she had an idea. Clark got on the bus with them. He could easily have blended in. An eight-year-old like Clark would think this was a funny trick.

She raced back to her mom and told her the idea. Susan contacted the police.

Once Clark was found, he learned a lesson. Many people showed concern about him. He hadn't had so much attention since he was five and he chased a ball into the street, resulting in a broken leg.

A tall, slim teacher wearing a vest and bow tie, introduced himself as the science teacher from an Arkansas Elementary School and was one of two chaperones for the kids. He rented a car to bring Clark back and was apologetic. He said he felt responsible for not recognizing that Clark was not from their group. He repeatedly said that Clark was not kidnapped. This never happened before.

By nightfall, everyone was back and Clark was grinning about his successful pranking adventure, but only to Lois. He was relishing in Susan's guilt-ridden love as she hovered over him for the next twenty-four hours. Predictably, she was colder toward Lois, making sure that this was clearly Lois' fault. That was a turning point in Lois' life, who vowed never to have children.

Hung came running into the room. Lois was still deep in thought.

"Bai just phoned me and said he reached your brother, Clark. Follow me, there isn't much time." They left out the double door exit. After running down a brightly lit tunnel, Hung turned a sharp left where there was no light, transforming this tunnel into darkness. The concrete echoed their steps up and down the tunnel as they ran, sounding more like heavy, rapid fire, gun shots. A blue-colored LED lit a set of rungs that Hung used to pull himself up. He moved a latch embedded into the ceiling and popped an opening the size of a manhole. Lois followed, pulled herself onto the floor and they were standing close together, facing each other, in a small, dark broom closet of a campus building.

"Let's keep moving," Hung said as Lois stared and smelled the nervous sweat on their bodies. "We'll open the door and take a right, passing the men's bathroom. Remember these steps as you will be coming back here by yourself."

"What? Where are we? Where are you going?" said Lois.

"I'm getting supplies, diapers and will check on the status of the tunnels as I work my way back."

"Well, that makes it real. Just that statement makes it real for me." She followed Hung more closely and observed everything around her.

Hung pointed and said, "We're going down this hallway and up one level to the ground floor. Let's keep moving!" The directions continued and Lois memorized the room numbers to help her remember. She was so frustrated, not knowing what was going on, but Hung gave her no choice.

They left the building through a set of large glass doors, trimmed in copper, reflecting light, even on this overcast day. Lois realized they just walked out of the oldest building on campus, the Alumnae building, recently renovated with a new glass-encased atrium. Walking straight ahead to the intersection where light-rails and cars formed an open intersection. It was dangerous corner for anyone not paying attention.

Hung stopped and looked at Lois with a very serious gaze, "Lois, please wait here for your brother. When he gets off the light-rail, you will retrace your steps back to the Alumnae Building. Find the closet in the basement. The one we used next to the men's room. Open the manhole entrance and go down. Move as quickly as you can. Keep moving until you get to the Physics building tunnel entrance. Please take this. Clark will call you," and he handed her a phone. "Now I have to leave you."

"Where are you going?" called out Lois.

"Remember, getting supplies," he shouted. "You have twenty minutes to get back to the tunnel, Lois!"

Hung now left her feeling more shaken than before. With no idea how Clark could get on a light-rail with a dog, her confidence was sinking into her body and draining out from her feet. Was Clark even bringing Suri? Did she forget to mention Suri to Bai? She then sunk down lower and realized there was a strong possibility that Clark would not make it. What would she do then; losing the two individuals that she cared about? At that moment, the phone rang.

"Hey, sis, what is going on? I got this urgent message from a guy who said you're his friend. He said you were on a conference call. Way to go, sis. Trying to bring more adventure into your life. I am so proud of you, branching out and meeting new friends," said Clark.

Lois jumped in. "Where are you? Please tell me you are on the light-rail with Suri." By this time, Lois was fully hyperventilating. She was bent over, could not control her breath and feeling lightheaded. People walked past her without stopping. She started a breathing exercise to calm down, activating her parasympathetic nervous system to offset another dreaded panic attack. Unfortunately, this was going on while Clark was answering her questions. "What did you say?" she shouted into the phone. She then heard a dog bark, sounding a lot like Suri, and the restriction of her blood vessels opened after realizing that Suri was with Clark!

"Yeah, as directed by this funny guy on the phone that called himself Hung, seriously, sis? He gave me this number to call you. Hung, don't you think that is a strange name, even for you. As per his directions, I left the house immediately with Suri. I haven't even had breakfast. Now I am at the light-rail stop and it's complicated. They did not let me board the light-rail with a dog. There is another light-rail coming, I can see it about five blocks away. What's going on, anyway?"

Lois hated pauses on phones, but she needed to think before speaking. Clark could just barge on the light-rail, but knowing him, he could get arrested. Were there other options?

"Wait," said Clark. "I got it worked out. According to Hung, it will take me ten minutes to get to you on any light-rail that stops here. If I board in the next five minutes, I should be there in fifteen."

"Clark, listen. This is not a game or an adventure. I'm right here at the campus station and will tell you everything once you get here. Get on the light-rail with Suri. Take this seriously. I repeat, get on the light-rail." Lois enunciated as if she was talking to a ten-year-old.

"Lois, are you okay? I don't know if you hurt, but I'll be there for you. You have done so much for me. Man, there's a lot of traffic right now. Cars are moving slower, some are making U-turns in the middle of the street. Anyway, I gotta go. The light-rail is here."

The line went dead. Lois watched as several light-rails went by, coming from different directions and each one seemed more filled than the other. Lois ignored everything around her and started to visualize the route back to the Physics building. She checked her own phone for messages and there were none. She started to feel strangely small. Imagine something so big wiping out a population. What is the destiny of people walking past her? The university crowd seemed to exhibit little concern as they looked down at their smartphones. She thought about their families and then she realized her mother might be in danger. Was she still in Montana? It had been three months since they last spoke. She decided to try to call her.

Susan answered on the first ring. "Lois, I hope this is you," she said. "Lois, where are you? I am sick about this!"

"Mom, I am safe at the university. Clark and Suri are meeting me in fifteen minutes."

"I have been following the news on the internet. We just got an announcement that up to twelve major cities in the US are going to have multiple atomic bombs land in the next twenty minutes. Lois, baby, where are you?"

"I'm okay, Mom. I'm in good hands and just waiting for Clark to arrive on the light-rail and then take him to safety."

"What can I say, sweetie. I love you two so much. Please tell Clark I love him and I'm sorry about everything. I know he thinks I don't, but I did, I mean, I do. I'm feeling so bad for you two. I wish I could help. We're safe in Montana. Nothing here except hay and cows!"

That was too much for Lois. Love for others was never in the equation for a self-absorbed narcissist like her mother. Every time she said she loved you, it felt like she was reaffirming her love for herself.

"Mom, does it say where the bombs are coming from?" Lois said, changing the subject.

"Some place in Asia. All communications between Korea, Japan, China and Taiwan are cut off due to underground cables being severed by what they think was a tsunami. It feels to me a lot like 9/11 just before the second tower was hit. A small group called Black and White is an obscure terrorist group that wants to make Americans pay for what they did to Hiroshima and Nagasaki. They have been accumulating uranium over half a century in a small village in China."

"Mom, how did you find this out?" pleaded Lois.

"Our neighbors are big time survivalists and they stopped by with that information. Oh, Lois, something is happening, I have to go now."

The phone connection ended. No surprise that Lois' anxiety was highest after speaking to her mother. She looked down the street and observed a quantum increase in gridlocked traffic. People were running into buildings, talking to their phones, getting out of cars. She was concerned about the jammed-up cars stranded over the light-rail tracks. She hit a button on the phone that said 'history' and called the number

Clark used. Picking up on the third ring, Clark said, "Sis, I'm on the light-rail. Suri and I are disguised as a blind man with a seeing eye dog. What's--"

Lois interrupted. "Clark, how far away are you from the university exit?"

"Close," he replied.

"Are you moving?"

"Yes, and no."

"What is your cross street?"

"Clinton."

She looked at her street and it was Lincoln. With the streets alphabetically arranged by president, Clark was nine blocks away. "Can you run faster than the light-rail right now?" she asked.

"Hell, yes."

"Okay, then. Get off. Run like hell to Lincoln. I am standing on the corner next to the streetlight. Run!"

"You got it, sis!"

The phone went dead and Lois looked at her watch. If he could run a ten-minute mile, he could be here. No problem for Suri. The phone rang again, and it was Hung.

"Lois. How was your connection with Clark? I got him moving toward the light rail station and hopefully, you two worked out a meeting place."

"Brilliant plan, Hung. Yep, he's nine blocks away and I suspect he will be here in less than eight minutes."

"Did the light-rail shut down yet?"

"It doesn't look good. He's running. I am ready to jettison to the tunnels. Any more news?"

"The news has not changed. You know what to do, Lois."

"The crowd confusion has built up and now cars have blocked the light-rails, so they aren't moving. I called my mother, and she told me a terrorist group in China caused this."

"Yes, we saw that. Listen, I will call you when you need to move toward the tunnel, just in case Clark does not make it."

"Great, but I won't leave without him. Appreciate the thought, though," said Lois. The phone went dead.

She turned her head up the street and waited. She waited five minutes and called Clark. There was no answer after seven rings. Not knowing what to do, she decided she had to change her mindset. Assume success. She started a meditation practice she learned for situations like this. Five, four, three, two and one. Observe five shapes, four colors, three patterns, two smells and end with an intention for the moment. She identified rectangular shapes beginning with the high-rise health care building in front of her with tons of windows, car windows, and even the sidewalk. Colors were her favorite, and she focused on finding as many green colors as she could and when she finished, she realized her intention for this moment was to be present for whatever would happen. She started watching a tall man in a lab coat hustling in her direction. He walked up to her and asked her if she was Lois. Stunned, Lois repeated her name as a question, as if she was not Lois.

"Lois, my name is Dr. Wolfgang Anthony, Professor Emeritus of Biological Transference. They named the building you are staring after me. They sent me here to meet with you. I was told there was less than ten minutes before the bombing starts. Let's move into the tunnel, now Lois."

His accent was not British, but she thought he manicured his image as an aristocrat. She was quietly processing this information and took the phone out of her pocket and called Hung.

"Who is this guy?" she said, not hiding the fact that she was pissed.

"Did Dr. Anthony find you? Yes, we directed him to you since Bai is busy right now. I believe he is still staging inventory someplace. It's a long story, Lois. I wish I had time."

"No, you have time," said Lois.

"You know the Seed Bank, right?" said Hung. "They requested that we take care of Dr. Anthony. He may have bags of this special seed that they need and he may have critically important information regarding the growing conditions. He is working with the Seed Bank and they think Dr. Anthony's information is key to our collective long-term survival success. In exchange for his help, we need to provide him with safe shelter."

Lois realized how impatient she was, because Clark was not here. What could she do? She would not leave Clark under any circumstance. Where was Clark? Actually, any more information Hung provided her on Dr. Anthony was only going to compound her ethical dilemma, so she said goodbye to Hung as politely as she could and the phone went silent. She took a moment to compose herself and turned to Dr. Anthony and said, "Dr.

Anthony, I am waiting for my brother and my dog who are very close to me. Please sit tight and we will all get to safety in time."

Probably seeing her unequivocal look of determination, he nodded, sighed and said okay. Lois looked at her watch and time stopped for her. Where was Clark? She called again.

"I'm here! Where are you?" Clark shouted into the phone.

Lois was aware of the same voice around her. She looked across the light-rail tracks and there was her brother, dressed in a jean jacket, holding a leash with Suri, shouting 'where are you,' into a phone. He and Suri were directly across from her. She waved and their eyes connected. Lois recognized that the tracks fell below street level where she was standing. Clark could run over to the intersection and cross or jump down here, a more direct route. She considered Dr. Anthony with a little more consideration of him as a physical asset and decided if he helped, they could save time. Clark instantly figured this out, jumped down onto the tracks and carried Suri across over to their side. Dr. Anthony grabbed the dog, put her down and then gave Clark a hand and pulled him out. When things happen that fast, time has to catch up, so they hugged, even Dr. Anthony joining in the celebration.

MICHAEL - 23

"This doesn't look good. The pilot will never navigate this," said McKenzie. They both were standing on the roof of the healthcare building, underneath a protective awning.

"Marcella is at the university in a collapsed tunnel. I need to find her. Can we pick her up?" said Michael. "It's not that far. Ten miles, if that."

"I doubt it. We are cutting it close. I'm sure there will be a quarantine limit where no one will leave the area until bio-contaminate testing is complete. Damn, I left my secure Sat-phone behind," said McKenzie.

"Quarantine, McKenzie? What is going on? What's really going on? What makes you think we're not contaminated getting into this helicopter?" said Michael. He hated the fact that McKenzie was not sharing a lot. As an important individual of this corporation, Mac should be more respectful of him.

"I'm sure I do not know everything. What I suspect helps explain the suddenness of what is happening and why we have no defense against it. There is a group in China that was under our radar for nuclear proliferation until recently, maybe the last two days. Uranium reservoirs were detected in a large cave in a mountain in China by someone hiking near Mount Cangyan of the Taihang Mountain Range in the Hebei Province. I've been to this area of China several times. I had a meeting last week about it and no one was taking it seriously. China would take complete advantage of a ruined United States, if that is what we have here. I have to get back safely to share my knowledge about these mountains. I have security clearance that will allow us to seek sanctuary in a secure, protected underground location. Michael, I can include you in this, but I cannot help you with Marcella."

"It sounds like you are more than the research scientist I know," said Michael.

"Yes, this job was the perfect cover for me. I guess you'll find out more about me soon," said McKenzie.

"That's strange at my level of responsibility in the company. I should have known your background and everything about you. Are you CIA?" McKenzie increasingly irked Michael. McKenzie's sense of privilege and entitlement was getting old. What good is a safe sanctuary if I leave Marcella behind?

"Your boss helped bring me in. I'm not surprised you don't know anything about this. We always limit information on a need to know basis."

Ouch that hurt. His boss, Freeman, didn't mention something that important! But did anything matter when he needed to find Marcella? "Please, Mac, can you use your influence to go to the university to rescue Marcella? You know what she means to me," Michael said.

"Look, I'm sorry, but I have to get to a secure location causing no harm to myself. I'm very important and they need me to advise the government of what could happen next! Take it or leave it, Michael. You are lucky to be at the right place and the right time." McKenzie patted his coat pockets again. "I need to go back for my phone. I also need to check on Plan B since the likelihood of a helicopter getting here is remote. Wait here just in case," he ordered. "Be right back." And McKenzie opened the steel door which slammed shut behind him. Michael went back inside to wait for McKenzie. It was too hot out there anyway. He still might have a chance at convincing him to go to the U.

Michael thought McKenzie was calm about all of this. Was that part of his training? Five minutes passed when Michael heard a faint, fast clipping sound coming closer. Should he go back? It must be the helicopter. Finally, when the sound was strongest, he opened the door to find black waves of soot swirling before him. He waved, and the helicopter landed on what used to be a circle painted bright red and now was a dull burgundy. Michael expected McKenzie to pop up the stairs and take charge.

The pilot waved at him to stay put and then waited until the blades came to full stop before approaching Michael. The pilot said, "Colonel

McKenzie, my name is Flying Hawk." Flying Hawk was a large man, muscled in a tan, nice fitting orange jumpsuit complete with a helmet, and two long, thin black braids sticking out from the bottom. He had beaded bracelets on both wrists and wore a pair of cowboy boots. All signs pointed to Michael that he was Native American. Michael hesitated and looked back, expecting McKenzie to appear, but he must have gone back to his office to look for his phone and did not hear the helicopter. This was his moment, and he did it.

"Good to meet ya, Flying Hawk," said Michael. "Take me to the University Hospital. I'm on a high priority mission. You must wait for me as I have to pick up my wife to take her to safety."

"That's not our mission," said Flying Hawk with little emotion. "There was no mention of picking up family members. What's wrong with your hands?"

"This is a high-priority rescue mission and if you don't help me, I must stay behind anyway," Michael said as he turned to leave. "We had windows explode on us. Mine got scratched up pretty bad."

Flying Hawk looked a little frustrated. "Let me repeat myself. We're on a mission to get back to the underground sanctuary. My orders state to take you back before quarantine closes. Seriously, we need to leave immediately. Also, there is some preliminary information about the risk of biologics. A biologic threat may manifest after the bombs hit."

"Look, we need to rescue my wife. She is at the University Hospitals." He stared at Hawk and let the information sink in.

"Well, I cannot contact anyone. All communications are down. Are you saying to me that your orders will override my mission? Your level as colonel allows me to make this change. If so, please state the new mission and I can change."

Michael looked away and thought, oh boy. Maybe I should come clean. I'm impersonating an officer and what's worse is I could interfere with an important mission. He looked down thoughtfully, this was his opening. Saving Marcella could put him in jail, but he had to do it. He had no choice. He was taking too much time thinking this through, and Flying Hawk was now staring at him.

"Put this on. I've got bandages for you in the helicopter," Hawk said as he handed him a full jumpsuit identical to what Flying Hawk was wearing.

All he had to do was place his legs into the boots, his arms into the gloves and zip it up. The gloves were flexible, he could still manipulate the zipper. This was a very high-quality protective suit. Hawk gave him a helmet.

As he walked toward the helicopter, Michael scanned the horizon from the roof. Shades of mushrooming black clouds covered the sky. Each wave of darkness, alternating black and gray stripes, were filled with large shiny flakes swirling up from below. The outside temperature, immediately raised his body temperature inside the suit. He thought he shouldn't be here. This was dangerous, but he had to find Marcella. She would do that for him.

Hawk spent a few minutes helping Michael bandage his hands. They looked better after being cleaned. Once the helicopter started to lift he said, "Be prepared for blasts of heat. We have to fly high and land strategically. Seat belts on!" As the helicopter lifted, Michael could not believe what he just did. Screw McKenzie, he thought. How dare he pretend to be a scientist at the cost of the company when he was operating as a cover for the government?

The helicopter felt solid, even in this nightmare. As it rose, it moved decisively above the buildings to where Michael could survey the whole corporate campus. There wasn't anything to see. No buildings were standing except the one he was leaving.

"This may take us over half an hour. Do you know which university hospital building you want to go?"

"The University Hospital." Michael was having struggling trouble with the mouthpiece in his helmet.

"My GPS is down, but I have a set of downloaded maps linked to my manual navigation system. I can use my compass and fly straight east. Once we are close, we will fly low and pin-point the building you are looking for. Then we can try finding a place to land. I'm thinking the football field might be safe. We'll find it once we get there."

As they continued to rise, the surrounding sky was completely covered with impenetrable dark smoke. The only escape from the darkness was minor explosions with gasses and flames shooting below them.

"You okay?"

"Yeah. How extensive was the damage? Were we the only city?" Noise was coming from everywhere, the helicopter blades, the engine, the explosions, but Michael could hear Hawk perfectly from the earpiece.

"I thought they briefed you?" Flying Hawk said. "Well, I heard they affected fifteen major cities. The president was not in a safe bunker and with communications down, no one knows who survived to be second-in-command. Without a chain of command, the challenge will be how to deploy a proper defense strategy. You are one of the few people that we've got to help us with knowledge about the part of China that deployed this catastrophe."

Michael nodded, continuing the ruse. He was sorting out his priorities, and he knew that Marcella was the most important thing for him to save. However, weighing her safety against the future of the country was a bigger burden than he was prepared for. Let McKenzie find another way. He will worry about this later. They could pick up McKenzie on the way back after they arrested Michael for crimes against the state. At least Marcella would be safe.

An opening in the blackness appeared. Below, Michael could see a large, oval black mass that once was probably a lake. He could see house outlines surrounding this clearing, all black so dark that it reminded him of a blueprint for a new development. There was no movement below. The sky went black again; he sat back and thought about praying. Dear Jesus, please help me find Marcella and take her back to a safe place.

"McKenzie, weren't you up in the Ukraine with my friend, Phil?" asked Flying Hawk.

"No," said Michael. This was probably a question trying to catch him in his lie. Hawk was not stupid.

"You're not McKenzie, are you?" Flying Hawk muscled the controls to keep the helicopter aligned while fighting the frequent heat swells. "We're off course a little, but I think we have a better approach from the south."

Michael, trying to cover his shock, shouted, "Well, I guess I'm busted. When did you know I wasn't McKenzie?"

"Right away and confirmed it when you asked what was going on. McKenzie knows more about what is going on than most people in charge. I also heard he was a total asshole. I get selected for the most dangerous missions and no one wanted to take this one. McKenzie is in the CIA and has burned many bridges in his lifetime. My best friend asked me why I would sacrifice my life for such a terrible person and we both knew I had no choice. But I've been thinking. I'm not military, but a hired mercenary. I'm choosing what I want to do. My only crime is stealing this helicopter to take you to the University." The helicopter rose under a strong wind, blazing hot. Flying Hawk immediately rose higher to find a cooler spot. "Who are you then?"

"My name is Michael Kraken, I'm Vice President of Legal Affairs and the head attorney for Intellectual Properties." It sounded strange to be saying that, as the identity he held so closely was fading. Everyone he relied on to hold up his position might be dead. The executive building is gone. Is there a corporation left? Like Hawk, has the game changed his purpose? He has to change with it. Michael started speaking, in a softer voice, barely projecting. "I can't believe I lied like that to you. That's not like me. The last time I spoke to Marcella, my wife, was just after something hit her building and she said she was trapped in a tunnel in the hospital. This opportunity presented itself and I grabbed it suddenly, without thinking it through. I saw no other choice." Michael raised his head and looked directly at Hawk. He shouted, "Flying Hawk, sounds like you are Lakota. What a mess we've made of this beautiful land we took from the Native Americans."

"How do you know Lakota?"

"I grew up in South Dakota with my mother who studied Native American history in community college. Your bracelets are familiar to me, especially the placement of the jade at the beginning and end."

"We're coming up to the southern part of the university now. I'm not sure where to land. I'd rather land on a flat surface on the ground, but the ground is now covered with a foot of ash that could jam the engine and cling to the blades. Let's check out the football stadium. I could slowly lower onto the field and blow the ash away by flying low and then land."

"Sounds like you know what you're doing. Let's try it. I suspect I must walk a way to the hospital, but this seems like the safest approach. Thank God for this suit and respirator," said Michael.

"Let me set down the copter and then we can plan," said Flying Hawk. As they approached the precisely oval-shaped black space, Michael realized that Flying Hawk had expertly found the old football stadium. It was a deep glossy impenetrable black color surrounded by very dark-gray bleachers. As they descended, the ash became denser in the air and was flying all around them. Flying Hawk suddenly took the helicopter up again and hovered. "Well, this ash is heavy and could start gluing itself to the blades. Once that happens, more ash will stick and start weighing us down to where we will never lift off again. This here is a bowl of black bean soup!"

Michael laughed. "I wonder. The university has a helicopter pad on the top of one of the medical buildings. It might have a better landing position. Can you find it?"

"Yes, let's try that." The helicopter lifted again and started more slowly toward the south. "According to my map, we are coming close to the pad. Do you see anything?" As they descended lower and lower, they saw no buildings. Then they saw the distinctive Medical Arts Building logo pitched on its side, laying on the ground, confirming the fact that the building no longer existed. The building next to it was the hospital but the tops floors were open like a doll house.

Michael gasped. "Oh no! We must get down. She's in the tunnel. I have to see if she's okay. Just let me down and you take off, Flying Hawk. None of this looks safe."

Flying Hawk seemed deep in thought. "We're going back to the stadium. I have an idea!" The helicopter rose and quickly reached the stadium again. Now there was a small bare spot where the rotor blades loosened the black tar. Flying Hawk skillfully dove, hovered for a few brief moments, and lifted to reveal a larger area. He did this two more times and then landed the helicopter in the space he created. He turned off the engine and the blades slowly stopped. The silence was notable. The intense heat combined with the sooty air was a reminder that walking on this ground could be riskier than flying in a helicopter.

"I need to perform helicopter maintenance before I leave. I want to check everything out and see what I can do to protect the blades," said Flying Hawk.

"I think this location works," said Michael. "I believe the university has some kind of tunnel system that possibly includes the stadium. Once I'm underground, I have some hope of finding Marcella. I cannot thank you enough, Flying Hawk."

"Michael, nothing is guaranteed. The engine would normally cool when it is turned off, but I'm concerned that the heat will damage parts the longer I stay here. Keep in mind that your protective clothing is completely contaminated on the outside. Take it off once you get inside or you'll contaminate any survivors with the radioactive particles that adhere to you. Bring back water or anything else that could be useful for survival if you can. I'll come back tomorrow. Keep your respirator on and take a second suit. You'll need it when you find Marcella." And Flying Hawk winked and smiled.

Michael nodded and looked into Flying Hawk's deeply creased, kind face that was filled with compassion. He agreed with the advice and appreciated Hawk's ability to think about details that Michael was not prepared to grasp. He now had a better chance of saving Marcella. He adjusted the respirator and adjusted his breathing for a minute, now realizing the enormity of what he was about to do. As he stepped off the helicopter onto the black sticky goo that was once artificial turf, he thought about football games he and Marcella attended here. As he started to progress across the field, the ash was about six inches deep and sometimes deeper. It was like black snow, with light airborne pieces of lace. Michael needed a huge amount of energy to just walk through the ash as his protection gear was heavy and hot. Particle contamination was not a pleasant thought. I think I am in hell; he thought. He held tightly to the garment bag. Flying Hawk was right, the ash had a stickiness to it and became heavier as he walked. He looked back at the helicopter and saw Flying Hawk scraping the blades clean. When he reached the entrance to the stadium, he thought about all the young college students that died or were dying right now from these bombs. It was too terrifying to think about. He needed to focus on Marcella and where she was. He needed to walk a significant distance to get to the hospital. What he needed was a map of campus.

As Michael entered the stadium through the concrete tunnel that opened to the hallway, the temperature dropped inside his suit. He immediately saw people lying down, covered with burns, being treated by just one medical person in a lab coat. No one was interested in his presence. Across the hallway was a huge locker room, one used for football players. He backed up into the concrete tunnel and took off his respirator. He stripped off his suit and carefully rolled it, so the inside was not exposed to the contaminated outside. He took off his gloves and placed them next to the suit. He grabbed the clean suit and crossed the hallway. He looked around at the row of lockers, a perfect place to store the suits. Michael opened a locker and found several large equipment bags in school colors. He picked up two bags and carefully placed the clean suit and respirator in one. He went back and placed the contaminated suit in another bag. After he put the suits in two lockers, he left the locker room. He felt satisfied he was safe and could take on finding Marcella. The people bombarded pushed against him as he walked slowly down the hallway. The people lying on the floor, along the walls, were not moving. The outer corridor of the stadium was a closed loop. He must find the tunnels.

A group of students rushed past him, looking out the tunnel leading to the football field. They studied the tracks he left and one boy asked if anyone saw the helicopter land and did they see anyone walk in. The man treating burns shook his head without comment.

Michael felt lucky that he missed engaging with this group and headed toward the exit sign. He realized there was a tiny map in a plastic folder underneath. He grabbed the whole piece of plastic and studied the map. There was no sign of a tunnel, but he noticed a solitary set of stairs that did not connect to the upper portion of the stadium. It was opposite from his location and he set out without noticing what was before him. More people lay lethargically as if they were drugged, but not dead. As he approached the spot on the map, there was an exit sign above the door. The tension in his body relaxed just a little. He raced down the stairs and found an unmarked door before him which he opened and then smelled and felt cool untainted air. It was moist and slightly stale, but a wonderful departure from the heat. According to the map. the stairs down to the tunnel were long, over one story. As he hit the bottom, he heard an echo, the sound of complete emptiness. Thinking about the direction of the hospital from the stadium and assuming he did not get turned around, he started running down the tunnel. Now he could move quickly and find Marcella. He continued on, looking for maps on the wall, but this tunnel seemed more like a maintenance tunnel than one for ordinary traffic. He reached another tunnel going perpendicular. Not knowing what direction he was heading, he could not decide which way to go. He went left and continued to move fast. It felt like the wrong way but he kept going, thinking he would see something that would help him. He came to two double doors that had a cross bar that said Emergency Exit. He plowed through the exit and found a gurney with supplies laying on top of it. Strange, he thought, and continued forward.

LUMING - 24

The facility used twelve walkie talkies, a style of communication fashionable in the '60s. These people were used to being here, comfortable with what it takes to manage a catastrophic event. Intentional movement filled the site. Luming did not understand their shorthand way of speaking, but he did his best to relay anything to others when needed. Critical information, updates from the Hub or anyone calling was given his highest priority. It felt great; he was contributing.

The only goal he knew of was to be ready to seal the nine stacks. Three gongs would sound before the stacks would close. Nothing would hinder closing the stacks. That would be it. Access codes would be reset and no one could enter after that.

Scar initiated the declaration of significant disaster about forty-five minutes after they arrived. She sent a code to all Seed Bank Members that lit up their RFID tags. Only Members within a radius of seven miles from the bunker would reach the Seed Bank. Troy told him that Members included growers, maintenance, geneticists, plant technicians, biologists, physicians and even an accountant. Every resource they had was deployed toward getting people into the tunnel and closing the tunnel to the outside before the bombs hit. The RFID tags provided GPS coordinates for the closest stack to each Member. Each stack entrance was hidden creatively; under furniture, inside an armoire and even inside of a dumpster. Once the sensor on the tag came within fifty yards of the stack, a beeping sounded and opened the stack for the Member to enter quickly. No one could enter without a tag.

It was Luming's communication with Lois and the Five Guys that convinced the Seed Bank to start The Code. Lois and the Five Guys were tracking information that confirmed nuclear bombing would take place with only thirty minutes remaining. Lois told Luming that her good friend Dan and his granddaughter and a woman, Betty, would not make it to the university. Dan's situation was dire when he left the highway and tried making it to the university, using back roads. Once Lois shared the absolute, undeniable gravity of the situation, Scar approved their passage to the Seed Bank if they could make it. Luming was to make direct contact with Dan. Luming remembered how worried Lois was about her dog and her brother, Clark. He would not know if Clark and Suri made it until they the university contacted them.

Luming went into action first by understanding the locations of the nine stacks from a map of the city. This was all detailed in a spiral-bound booklet Scar gave him, both with GPS and Latitude/Longitude coordinates, a residual from the past. Old technology was now useful. He needed to help Dan locate the nearest stack. With the number Lois gave him, he called him.

"Dan, can you hear me? This is Luming."

"Yes, barely. What is this about? I'm off the freeway and making my way to the university. It's going slow."

"Dan, the current situation is as follows. You will not make it to the U before T zero. I have been in contact with the Five Guys about the data you circulated that triggered this emergency and we are forever grateful. We have fourteen minutes to get you to a place of safety." Luming made sure that Dan understood.

"Good, no, not good, but I am relieved that you know the enormity of what is going on," said Dan. "I'm currently on Myrtle going north and crossing 21st Street."

Luming had his map with a search engine ready. "Based on your location, you now have ten minutes to get out of your car and walk half a mile to our secure location. We may lose contact on our phones, so listen carefully and I will provide you with directions." As they worked out the exact directions, Luming realized he needed to get to the stack and open it manually so that it would allow a non-member to enter. In fact, according to Lois, Dan was with Betty and his granddaughter and he needed to figure out how to override the system for all three.

"Where is Scar?" he kept asking to anyone that would pass him.

"I can help," said Brother. Luming rattled off the situation. Taking that time away from finding Scar raised Luming's anxiety to an even higher level. Brother's quiet demeanor calmed him down a little. He needed to get to Stack 3 and figure out how to open it and let these guys in.

Brother said, "I'll get Scar and meet you there," and ran off.

The tunnels, thankfully, were well marked with you-are-here stickers, on maps every fifty feet against the full diagram of the facility with the stack location identified. Luming walked past Stack 2 just before two women and a man came crashing down a slide. They were well versed with the routine and looked at Luming strangely, probably recognizing that he was out of place.

"My name is Luming. It's a long story, but Scar has approved two people and one baby to have access to Stack 3."

"No time for formalities, Luming. My name is Bill. We're headed to Scar right now. We'll let her know that you need her. You realize that they cannot enter without one of these," as they flashed their RFID tags.

Having spent enough time here, Luming understood the military aspects of how things operated. The sole mission of this operation was to preserve seeds and plants. Everyone he met was dedicated to this purpose. The stacks were an elaborate system put in place so everyone could routinely enter the facility without calling attention to themselves. He needed to figure out how to override the system. Where was Scar?

Luming called Dan. "Where are you?"

"We got here faster than expected. I am in an auto body shop called Raymond Auto. No one is here."

"Sit tight. Once you hear a beeping sound, follow it." There were digital clocks at each stack, showing a countdown of six minutes.

Brother was working on Stack 4, just down the hall. Luming could hear the sounds of the stack opening and a person coming. "Take these supplies," the female voice said. As each bag dropped to the ground, the tunnel echoed. "Grab that cart," said a familiar male voice, sounding like Chris. Things were loaded quickly and wheeled away, leaving an echo of silence behind. Luming was curious, was that Chris?

Brother came back to Luming, out of breath.

"They're here," said Luming. "They're ready to enter. This is a fucking catastrophe. I don't know what is going to happen after the countdown, but I don't think I could bear to let them die. I will go out and die with them!"

"We have time. Scar is coming." Brother stared at the clock that gave them three minutes.

"Luming, I'm headed your way." That was Scar calling him on the walkie talkie.

"Over here on three, quick! I need you right away."

Scar showed up, her hair partially unbraided across her face. She looked more beautiful than before. "Okay, quickly. I located Dan and Betty above in the auto repair shop and they're waiting for guidance on how to enter!" said Luming.

"They're here. That's great," Scar said with an intensity he had not heard her express. Her face showed she had parallel thought streams going on. "Good job, Luming. I'll take care of the rest. Try calling Lois and let her know they made it."

Luming watched Scar as she pulled her handheld out, entered a code, and the stack opened. Dan shouted, "We're here. I can see the red light." First a large cloth bag with handles came down, landing on the concrete floor, followed by a stroller that crashed perfectly onto the bag with no harm to the stroller. Scar rushed to move the stroller away from the stack entrance. Then a woman's leg showed wearing soft shoes, then black pants, followed by an orange tunic, draped with purple scarves and beads. Her face was framed with shocking red hair. She squirreled down the rungs of the stack and bounced down from the last rung. Luming thought this was probably Betty. She impressed him. "Watch yourself, Dan," she yelled up. Dan followed, carrying another bag on his shoulder, a baby in one arm and hanging onto each rung as he carefully moved down until he stepped onto the floor. The clock said thirty seconds when they closed the stack door.

The clock countdown was ten seconds when Luming called Lois and after one ring a crushing sound reverberated off the concrete walls, up and down each tunnel. The stacks were sealed. An underground coffin sealed them off from a toxic, lethal environment. Luming's phone was dead. They all just sat under the stack and stared. Elizabeth started to wail. She screeched harder and stronger each time she opened her mouth. Betty brought Elizabeth close to her, pinched her ear, and she slowly started to quiet down. But she was still whimpering while they all huddled in silence.

The place shuddered, and the temperature kept rising. No one moved. They would die! Their bodies would be found in tombs of concrete. It was a strange feeling as time went on and they could hear repeated sounds of destruction farther and farther away. No one spoke for a while.

Luming realized that there were people being pulverized as he stood safely, for now, underground. If you're gonna die, an instant death would be a blessing, he thought. He pulled out his mother's jade locket, and he gripped it tightly against his chest.

Scar spoke first. She wisely looked over to Brother and asked him for a blessing. "Though he should live a hundred years, not seeing the True Spirit; yet better is the single day's life of one who sees the True Spirit within us." Luming would never forget Brother's words and never forget the lost feeling of complete annihilation.

Scar spoke, "We notified twenty-one people, eleven made it. In addition, there were two people on staff, when Luming, Chris and Brother arrived." As Luming looked around, he saw Chris huddled with Dorothy. It seemed like Chris was a key figure in this operation and Luming wondered about his relationship with Dorothy. It made him a little nervous to realize how much he didn't know about Chris.

Then everyone went to work. Scar directed the Members toward tasks relating to water, electricity or plant maintenance. That left Luming, Betty, Brother, and Dan. Betty agreed to check all water valves for leakage and radiation in each tunnel. She handed Elizabeth over to Dan and took off. Dan said he had lots of practical knowledge and he could walk around, helping with any problem solving. Scar liked that and took the walkie talkie from Chris and handed it to Dan and said, "Keep in touch." Luming knew he would sit and monitor communications and took Elizabeth from Dan. By this time, Elizabeth was exhausted and sleeping, undisturbed by anyone that was carrying her.

Luming had no siblings, so he surprised himself when he took Elizabeth from Dan. Then she suddenly woke up and belted out a loud, strong scream, reaching her hands out to Dan, screaming, "Da Da," as he was leaving the room. She was going red quickly and her face was covered with nose mucus, mixed with tears. Dan came back to soothe her and reached for a juice bottle from the bag, but she still kept screaming. After changing diapers, giving her more food and milk, she still would not settle down. Dan tried pinching her ear again, and that didn't work. Finally, Luming thought of something. He reached into his pockets for his Jade locket. He slowly swung it back and forth while Dan was holding her and she went limp and crashed again into a deep sleep.

Scar was standing in the doorway, watching this, and smiled. "That was amazing, Luming. May I touch it?" She held it in her hand, possibly feeling the warmth it always provided when he held it. There was energy in this stone. She looked up, smiled at him again and placed the stone back in his hand. "Do you guys need anything else? Otherwise, I will bolt. Brother, I need your help," and they quickly left together, deep in conversation. Luming felt the warm stone and thought about Scar. Was it possible that she was feeling a deeper connection too? What an awkward time to discover that he had feelings for someone.

Luming put Lizzy in the stroller. As he started back to the Hub, pushing the stroller, he found Chris and Dorothy standing next to the burlap seed bag Luming recognized as the one they retrieved from Dr. Anthony.

"At 2 minutes, 15 seconds, she had not entered the building. I went up the stack and sat there and waited," said Chris.

"He grabbed my waist and this bag and we slid through the hole, on top of the seed bag with that creepy sound of the stack closing behind us. This bag contains our future," said Dorothy. Chris and Dorothy finished loading the bag onto a cart.

"Later, dude," shouted Chris back to Luming. He remembered that Dorothy disappeared when they got there. Where did she go? What was her relationship with Chris? They knew each other.

Luming thought either Chris had an extraordinary capacity to be calm under pressure or he was just well versed in what was happening. It was only five hours ago that he was having breakfast with Chris and Luming was worrying about his PowerPoint presentation. He realized he still had fifty thousand dollars in cash from Chris in the bank. Cash, not exactly helpful in a survival situation, but seeds might be.

Luming's mind raced. They were thirty feet underground, but Luming felt heavy in his body as if the gravity was greater here. What was going on in China? Would he find out about his mother? What was going on in this world? On the way to the Hub, Luming visited the plants. As he entered the grow room, he saw Bill checking water lines.

"Oh, how amazing is this little person," said Bill, coming right up to Lizzy's lazy sleeping posture. "You know, Luming, we have lots of baby supplies." As soon as Bill said that, his face turned down affected by a memory. He was fighting tears. Had Bill lost a child or a partner? Maybe the question was too obvious as everyone here lost someone.

"She's finally sleeping." Luming took a moment to look around and smelled the heavily scented air. "What an amazing set-up."

Bill collected himself and sat down. "This room was part of the original network of tunnels. They planned the whole site much like the tunnels that cross the Mexican borders. The original founders, before we created the Member group, were a paranoid bunch of pot farmers who got together to run an underground weed biz. As demand grew, they needed to create ways to dispense large quantities of marijuana bundles as unnoticeably as possible. One founder was Mexican and knew all about the famous tunnels of Tijuana and proposed that they create a grow room that was connected to a tunnel system under the streets. The stacks were created to manage distribution, supplies in and product out. Multiple entrances were key to the operation. Eventually, strict guidelines were worked out on how to protect everything connected to the facility. This system served us well and ensured complete secrecy."

Luming took it all in and looked around the grow room with renewed interest and realized every inch of the whole area was lit by LEDs, providing high wattage light at a very low electrical demand. Ironically, Luming's Power Point presentation today was about developing new alternative light sources for the growing indoor kitchen herb market. People wanted to grow herbs all year round at home. This new light source could change the way people used herbs in their kitchens. Here, his ideas were already being used and scaled up, only for a different herb.

"I know that the two generators started up immediately upon impact. Air flow must blow air throughout each tunnel, cooling everything down," said Luming. "You've got to have a lot of power to run high pressure sodium lights or metal hydride, but these LEDs are not even on the market yet."

"I'm impressed, Luming," said Bill.

"I was just working on a project involving these lights. This technology is crazy," said Luming.

"Sounds like you'll be helpful, Luming. Let's catch up later. I've got to keep looking for leaks," said Bill as he went back to checking the water lines. "Talk to Scar about the baby things." That was it. It was ironic that a place designed for such a specific purpose would provide advantages for sustainable living. He was already thinking that switching from marijuana production to food would be a necessity.

Luming continued his way to the Hub, pushing Lizzy in her stroller. He didn't look, but no fuss so far. Luming wondered about Bill's tender reaction to baby things. What was that? Maybe there was a Member close to Bill that didn't make it and had baby supplies stored here. He had not thought the Members. There was much to learn and understand more deeply, but everyone was busy and distracted. He kept thinking about his mother and living in their remote village. Was she safe? She survived many hardships in her life. What will happen to her? She worked on basic survival her whole life. Her life was simple. How can I get a message to her?

As Luming entered the hub, Troy still hadn't moved from his perch on a stool facing a computer screen. Luming asked him why the growers were double-checking each water line for leaks. Troy said there was a developing concern about radiated water leaking into the bunker. An impromptu meeting ensued that Dan started so Betty and Bill could report on their findings. Troy said they ended up checking on anything that came in contact with water. An old Geiger counter showed up from some place and Dan started to check each room for any breach in the lines. I guess staying active sure beats thinking about what was happening above surface and how lucky he was, Luming thought.

Luming knew the signs, so when Lizzy started crying, he checked her diaper and yes; she was full. This was the final stage of awareness that they were down below a nuclear bomb, safe and without an endless supply of diapers. Her bag held a good-sized stack of disposable diapers, fused together in a neat bundle.

"Troy, can you help me?" he asked. "Is there a good place to change these things? I think we may have to fumigate after I'm done." A little humor could only help. Troy was not flustered and walked ten feet outside of the hub to a door that opened into a large bathroom complete with a concrete cubbyhole that looked like it was set up for changing diapers, complete with a box of wipes. A baby was definitely changed here recently. He changed, fed, and sang to Lizzy. She responded by laughing and holding her feet in the air. She was a beautiful baby, and she reminded him how vulnerable to radiation someone so small could be. He put her back into the stroller and she started to play with the plastic music box where she pushed each colored button for a different song. "There," he said to no one. "I've made my contribution."

Luming went back to the Hub. With Troy's help, he collected all maintenance checks around the facility. He set up a spreadsheet, compiled the data, noting any issues. Other than an elevated temperature and higher humidity in most areas, nothing showed up. They were safe, but for how long? Everyone was busy with specific jobs which offset the sadness of being stuck in this bunker without knowing what happened. Two big questions: Did they have a future? What was it like on the surface?

Lizzy fussed, and he gave her the last bottle of juice from her bag. He needed to find Scar about her food. They would run out soon.

"Troy, I have not picked up any satellite communication. Maybe you can help with this. Can you take over? I will look for baby supplies." Troy nodded, absorbed in something deep.

As he walked down the fifth tunnel, pushing Lizzy's stroller, Luming questioned if he was really adding value as a communicator. He felt restless. Troy sitting and staring at a screen was stressing him. All of this was very challenging. While his physical body was safe from contamination and heat, his mind kept spinning negative thoughts. He entered a room he had not seen before. Chris and Dorothy were weighing seeds into small burlap bags, labeling them and scanning information with a large wireless gun.

"Each RFID tag contains extensive information down to DNA records and hybrid history for each bag of seed we scan," said Chris as he looked up at Luming. He added, "Luming, are you okay? We'll need your help once we get a satellite link that works."

"No, I'm pretty sure I'm not okay," said Luming.

Chris and Dorothy looked at each other in silent communication. Dorothy started to play with Lizzy and picked her up. Lizzy was happy with that.

"I think you need to explain everything to me, Chris. How did we end up here? I'm grateful, I think. What did you know when you knocked on my door this morning?"

"A lot of this is a coincidence. I really thought we would play a game around my newest app. Until I left you, I was hoping to convince you to spend the day beta testing and figuring out variability ratios for random actions. Frankly, I was completely stunned at the news I received. They directed me to take off immediately to meet Dorothy at the university and help her collect these seeds." He pointed to the large bag of seeds they were working on. "I could not stop to explain things to you. I couldn't say exactly what was happening because I didn't know much myself. The Seed Bank was on the highest alert possible. It's called Purple Haze. When that alert is set, everyone is given a job and that's it. No questions. I either had to leave you behind or take you with me and I made that choice pretty quickly. Bringing Brother worked out for everyone. He will contribute in a special way. You probably know that about him already. Lucky, eh? Now, why are you feeling bad? Survivor's remorse?"

Once he heard that term, Luming thought about how it resonated with him. Chris's glib way of stating it was strange; like the feeling he had when he ate Mexican food. He was experiencing indigestion. Was he naming this rotten feeling in the pit of his stomach? Was he feeling bad because he survived where others were obliterated?

"Luming, do you know what it means to be here? The Seed Bank, I mean," asked Dorothy. She was bouncing Lizzy in the air as Lizzy was reaching for her blue and gold beaded earrings, shockingly beautiful against her short white hair. "The Seed Bank is famous around the world, for having made good investments. People wanted to study this facility and how this community worked." Knowing English was not her first language, he realized her interest in exaggerating each word slowly. "Most money was made from the sales of seed, not the marijuana plant buds," she continued in her Nordic-sounding accent. "Seed research led to big innovations, using induced mutation and GM approaches. They sent seeds to growers to select what worked in their climate and specific climatic conditions. This brought high dollars. The original founders and later, the Members lived understated Midwestern lives. Not unlike my home in Finland. They were not interested in changing their lifestyle to match their income but reinvested their earnings in an infrastructure to continue to research seed modification and provide a stable place to preserve seeds of all kinds from around the world. Supporting the mission of growing good bud was never dropped. This facility became a world class seed bank with the mission to preserve the future of seeds, the secret of life itself. Ironic, isn't it? The founders never knew what future they were saving for. Now it's clear." She looked exhausted, having to tell this story. What a fascinating piece to the puzzle, thought Luming. Seeds from all over the world stored here and an infrastructure to grow plants, wow!

The small lit up drawers interested Luming. He walked around looking at the Red and Green LEDs. Dorothy smiled at Luming with a thoughtful look on her face. "There's a library, Luming. With a huge collection of books and each book has an electronic, searchable backup. Check that out."

Feeling a little dismissed, Luming said, "I already know about that. I'm looking for baby stuff for Lizzy. Is there some place to check?"

"Oh yeah, they're pulling that together in her room. Check with Scar."

Her room? Lizzy has a room? Everything was feeling surreal. So many levels of sophistication. Dorothy put Lizzy back in her stroller and Luming said goodbye. She was asleep again. Chris ran after him and said, "It's too much to take in, I know. Check out the library. I know you will love it. It has comfy chairs to sit in. There is a meal planned for later. I'll see you then." He patted him on the shoulder and said, "Later, dude."

While Luming was hungry, he was a little shaken that a meal was being served. Sitting down to eat while people were dying slowly from radiation burns was a little strange. Luming had not eaten since their breakfast. What happened to Stanley, I wonder? The expression, 'life as you knew it', was poignant. Stanley may never serve breakfast to his neighbors again. Maybe the library will help me sort out my place here.

Luming went back to the Hub, wondering where they were preparing Lizzy's room? There was a piece of paper with a handwritten note that said, "Multiple bombs were dropped above us only miles apart, wiping away all exposed humanity in the city. Expect days of aftershocks and long-term radiation damage on the surface for several years." Luming wondered who wrote this. Was that by a female hand? Was it Scar? Being alone did not have a calming effect on him. He went next door to the library. He sunk into a deep chair with large arms that surrounded him completely, Lizzy sleeping by his side. He paged through a book that was laying out on the table before him, thinking about the message. He stretched a little and felt the tension radiate from his neck to his sacrum. He knew that wheels were turning slowly in his head and his neck muscles clenched against his vertebrae.

Here is a place that was safe and secure, while millions of people were pulverized from heat or radiation? What did survival look out there? If you lived, the exposure to radiation had to kill long term. What did that mean to him?

Luming looked around. Each wall contained books, floor to ceiling. Two monitors with keyboards inhabited opposite corners of the room. The search menu must be on one of these terminals. Luming sat down at one terminal. He typed 'effects of nuclear radiation' and got three references and looked up to find three blue LED lights corresponding with books directly above them. Wow, he thought. How did they do that? He typed in another search word, 'survival,' and now seven blue lights were lit. He got up and pulled one book off the shelf and the LED turned red. After returning the book on the shelf, the light would go out. Impressive, thought Luming. Instead of a sophisticated system that monitored theft, this system assisted in finding the book and helped in returning it to its correct space. This was also a kind of search engine not connected to the Internet, but to an actual library with books.

The cover of the book he pulled, *A Man's Guide to Survival*, was black, white, and red. The book was more manly than militaristic. It was geared to survival of non-nuclear events, but reminded him of how many aspects of survival involved drying fish and building shelters. He found a fascinating chapter about eating polar bear and why you needed to avoid eating the liver. He thought about all the times he was passing time with his friends. He could have been learning practical survival skills. Other books were oriented toward being adrift in the ocean or building a raft to cross a river. He needed to find something more relevant. He started to think about their situation. This bunker was designed as a hydroponic marijuana grow-op and a temperature-controlled seed bank. Why did it feel like the perfect survival shelter? How long, years or months, would he stay here? They would eventually run out of supplies, water, maybe even electricity, once the fuel ran out. How safe is the water and would they have an uncontaminated, source? Would rescue teams come down and transport them to safety? Were there regions of safety now and who would control them? The focus on the plants was the current priority, and plants could provide them with lots of sustenance. He repeated the search to look for drought and water conservation. Another random thought came to him about medical care. How many bathrooms were available? Will the plumbing handle this capacity? How much water did the bathrooms use? Did anyone have a degree in medicine? How long did the radiation last? Was anyone thinking long term yet? What value could he bring to a survival situation?

Luming took his books and sat down, paging through them. The radiation question was the critical issue to focus on. He read where an initial blast contained the most radiation. If protected by a bunker of ten feet or more, no radiation would penetrate. Not knowing where the center of the bomb landed nor the height of the bomb, the level of radiation could be high. That there were multiple bombs meant they were miles away from any free zone. At least they had a way to measure radiation. Residual radiation, contamination in the tunnels from outside visitors, was going to be a big concern.

Luming went up to Troy. "Any luck?"

"No," said Troy as he continued to look at his computer screen. Luming was really not the guy for this job, but maybe Troy wasn't either. Just because he was quiet did not mean he was smart.

There were no surprises here. You could hear voices or walking well before they got to your area. A single set of footsteps brought Dan into the Hub.

"Hey, Luming," Dan said as he spoke at a quiet volume. Looking at his stack of books, he said, "So you discovered the library. I've been back here twice. The search engine is amazing. I found blueprints of this place and downloaded it onto my tablet, using an USB port, and walked around, finding each water source. I guess because of the demands on the seed bank archive, they have a room dedicated to servers. The secrecy this place demanded required them to become independent of cloud storage. As long as we have fuel, we have electricity. Fuel and non-radiated water are the keys to survival. It looks like we are sustainable for food for a long time. Lizzy sure looks content."

Changing the subject, Luming asked, "How was Lois when you spoke to her today?"

"I think she was okay. We conferenced with her just before we headed to the SB. Praise Jesus for this place. I was having a pretty nice vacation day with Lizzy. I asked Lois to check out strange emails that were coming from China. She called me back with information the Five Guys processed in an hour. We were on the freeway just when the information hit. Eleven cities were being targeted with multiple atomic bombs, five miles apart, that could wipe out everything, including people and any communications. The prediction I heard was the heat and the radiation from multiple bombs could put North America back one hundred years. The news came out and we had a twenty-minute warning while we were already seeking an alternative route off the freeway. We were headed to the university to join Lois and the Five Guys when we realized the gridlock of traffic prevented any movement at all. You know the rest."

"You left me that note, right?" said Luming.

Dan shrugged and continued, "The network of people associated with this place is wild. The dedication to maintaining it is almost inhuman. The Five Guys have been in touch with the Seed Bank since they first came to the US. Scar trusted very few people, except for the Five Guys. She told me they exchanged a lot of information during the ongoing construction of this facility. Once I trusted the information that the Five Guys obtained, I was convinced to take action. Lois was very helpful to set a sense of urgency. She and Cong called Scar and received permission to bring us to the closest stack to our location. How are you doing, Luming? You don't look so good. How's Lizzy doing? We have a room set up."

"I'm okay and thanks for filling me in. I'm still in shock, I guess. I also feel inadequate to handle anything specific. Scar wants me to work on communications, but the satellites have been dead since T zero. I have tried to tie directly with a satellite for a simple connection that is just jammed or maybe scrambled somehow. This is not my area of expertise." Luming's hands were shaking by now. He tried to calm down, but his racing mind was a real problem. Dan sat down in another chair and fell asleep.

Luming sat and reflected on the last hours of adrenalined-frenzy. This was the first time he was alone, except for watching Lizzy sleep. He looked at his watch and it was three hours from when they first entered the Seed

Bank. Each moment was filled with quick decisions and twenty-one people all doing something important.

It was strange to be here. Sometimes he was filled with fear, followed by a numbness left behind from the extended adrenaline surges. Synapses kept snapping in his brain. The chaos preceding the bombs required quick, accurate action which did not stop. Now they were all contributing toward the fine-tuned operation called survival, both short term and long.

JANE - 25

Jane and Jake did not move. Something just happened above them. The tunnel rose a few inches and then set down. It felt like a wet noodle being tugged in opposing directions. Would this squirmy worm stay intact at least until they cleared the area? What's the plan? Jane wondered.

"I think we may not be okay here," said Jane. "We should keep moving toward the parking garage where my car hopefully sits unharmed. I parked it next to a load-bearing beam so it wouldn't get crushed."

"Jane, you knew about this?"

"No, but I plan for catastrophic events, even though this is my first one. As I was saying, optimistically, my car might be safe. It's equipped with additional batteries, water, food, medications and a lot of small things you might not think of as items for survival. This sub-basement is thirty feet below the surface. Someone told me it could survive an atomic bomb. I guess we'll soon find out if there is any life above us. How are you feeling, Jake? Your fall down the stairs was scary," said Jane.

"Is that what happened? I have no recollection. I was walking down the hallway for a coffee to fill my thermos when I ran into you," Jake said as he pulled out his pocket thermos from his tool belt. "Let's assume we are safe for now. The tunnel would have collapsed from the initial bombing." Jake started to pour hot steaming coffee from his thermos and handed it to Jane.

"Jake, I would rather keep going. It's not a good idea to stop. You can catch up with me later." She studied compromise in her job and knew that survival situations were not conducive to it. Survival decisions were black and white, needing to be quick and decisive.

"Nah, let's stay together for now. What's in your various bags?" said Jake. "I always saw you in the halls, carrying them. They seemed odd, organized in a certain manner."

Jane sensed that something about Jake was not right. "Look, Jake. We can talk about this later. I strongly suggest that we keep moving," With her teeth clenched and her hands opening and closing, Jane knew she was showing signs of deep stress. Jake was aggravating her.

"I know how you're feeling, Jane. I'm stressed too. We can set off in an infinite number of directions right now. Let's get a plan in place. Then future decisions will be quicker."

He has a point, thought Jane. She recalled one of her deeper moments with Dr. Blue was a discussion when she realized action was her antidote to stress. When Dr. Blue pointed that out, she asked if that was something Jane wanted to control? She said control starts with being aware of the behavior. She brought the cup up to her nose and noticed the aroma of the coffee steaming from the cup. Dark roast coffee smelled like heaven. She took a sip, and it did not disappoint. She expected the thermos would taint the coffee. She felt the warmth of this cup against hands. Her shoulders dropped down as she relaxed, sitting cross legged and breathing. She was suddenly more aware of her surroundings, Jake and feeling the rhythm of the building above them. Jake was looking at her with less concern and her mind was uncomfortably blank, just settling into the moment. Being aware can start with a cup of coffee.

"Jane, I used to spend a lot of time in these tunnels a decade ago. I had a project that required me to update all the wiring and plumbing. This forgotten tunnel is ancient, built in the early fifties. I was a new employee, assigned to assess the old tunnels. I often thought about the project. These tunnels are speedways for getting around."

"Interesting. This place caught my fantasy too," said Jane.

"For good reason," said Jake. "This whole tunnel system is over thirty feet below the surface. It spreads across the whole campus and has its own independent generator. I imagine we are running on generator support right now. The lights have already switched to LED and the cooling system has kicked in to offset the heat from above. Jane, do you have any idea what is happening? It's the end of the world as we know it!"

"And I feel fine," Jane laughed at the homage to REM, a song often running through her head. "I was upstairs in the cafeteria when I saw a small plane moving across the glass windows in the cafeteria. I did not stop to watch and ask questions. I just took off. That is when I saw you. My colleague, Dan, left a message and said atomic bomb clusters targeted eleven cities in the US. He did not say who sent them, which is why I think we should keep moving."

"Jane, you are as safe as you can be here. Trust me," Jake said as another crushing sound landed above them and elastically moved the tunnel, again, longitudinally. Jane was mindful enough to catch the irony, the timing of this statement and smiled at Jake.

Jane was prepared for long-term survival but only if she could reach home. What's the probability of that? She grabbed her radiation sensor from the side pocket of the backpack. She just completed a redesign of her Sitka-Pac, tearing it apart and putting it back together. She sewed non-woven Velcro fasteners in two directions, three inches apart. This would allow her to tightly pack any device while charging and reposition it easily. Most items were accessible, without taking the whole thing apart.

Once home, she'd be able to sustain an independent existence for years. She had supplies, but more importantly, she had a way to grow plants from the seeds that were tucked away in her Tool Box. If she could maintain 66 to 87% sustainability, she had a chance to live at home for decades off the grid. Some things you could not plan for, but she was a genius at adapting to changing circumstances. Dr. Blue showed her the excitement she felt about adapting to change. She always commented on Jane's preparedness, but also her ability to think on her feet.

As she sipped her coffee and read the radioactive sensor, she realized how much she needed to reflect and plan. Jake was right, they needed to talk about what was needed for short and long-term survival. Between the two of them, they covered a lot of useful knowledge. Jake also seemed mindful of being present and aware of what they were doing. He might be helpful in finding a way home.

"Jake, thank you for the coffee. It helped me sort things out better and cleared my mind. I can't believe that we are safe. The sensor shows that we are below normal levels of radiation. No breach in the tunnel so far.

Assuming we are safe, communications are the number one issue for us right now. How can we find out what happened?"

"I agree with that. Going to your car seems like a good idea. As we move around, we may encounter others. Additional information might come from other survivors," said Jake.

"I am happy to hear you talk about moving. The thirteen-story building above us concerns me, so moving away from this point makes sense," said Jane as the sound of the building creaking under stress continued. This time, the ceiling moved, and some concrete started to fall onto the floor.

"Let's get to the parking ramp and locate your car. That'll give us a chance to see if we can connect, using a satellite phone, which I assume you must have in your backpack."

She nodded, and they moved just as a large piece of plaster fell on the floor where they were standing. She thought Jake was a really nice guy, but didn't he just say what she had been saying all along and now he said it as if it was a new idea; always an annoying male trait. His knowledge of these tunnels made him indispensable, and they needed to work together.

Jane had an idea about what was happening above them. Total fatalities were a function of population density and distance from the original impact. A corporation this size contained the same number of people as a New York City block. This building contained 300 scientists that were either dead or packed into the tunnel above. I wonder how many scientists went to the parking lot? Those individuals standing near the large window would now be in various stages of decay. That thought triggered a deep sigh across her body and she found Jake staring at her. She stopped moving, thinking only about the people that died. All the consequences left her frozen in place, blocking her from moving. She took a breath and quietly said, "Jake. Do you realize what we are facing? Most people have not studied nuclear war. Frankly, most Americans thought they were immune from it ever taking place on American soil. Nuclear failsafe security protocols started in the '50s. Jane collected those brochures as keepsakes. The lack of valuable information about nuclear warfare surprised her. Specific information about exposure to radiation incited fear. Was that why no one wrote about it? Or was our government confident that it would never happen?"

"Where did these bombs come from?' asked Jake.

"Attempts at negotiating nuclear de-escalation with China, Pakistan, India, North Korea and Iran were ongoing but had a feeling of uncertainty. China is a vast country and finding nuclear activity in every corner of that country would be tough. What is startling to me is our lack of defense and awareness when this happened. Where was the warning? The emails? I'm shocked!"

"Jane, you wanted to move. Now we are standing and talking."

"We need to stop to anticipate what could happen. There are people in floors above. No one knows these tunnels exist. We can think more clearly and take steps to ensure our future and those of the survivors above. Our long-term prognosis is not good. We are surrounded by lethal radiation, depending on how far we are from the impact, firestorms from every combustible on the surface, followed by what some scientists call nuclear winter from the residual particulates in the air which will block out the sun and force temperatures to subzero. Not to mention that the lack of sun would mean the lack of plants, throwing us into an ice age."

Jake stood still and choked.

"Let's move toward a safer part of the tunnel. Then let's take another break and talk about our next move." She got out a protein bar from her Tool Box and split it with him. "I think we need this. As you chew this bar, remember that food and water will be our priorities for our survival and others. We are on a raft in the middle of the ocean with no rescue mission in sight. I'm estimating that there will be about 150 to 300 people in the tunnels above. We need to think about this situation and how to diminish wrong moves by people who might hurt chances for survival. Think about someone taking out a knife to kill a fish for food and ending up piercing our life raft."

Jane surprised herself, summarizing the situation so succinctly. She realized she needed to talk to sort out her thoughts. Most people in survival mode are not aware of the need to think beyond their own needs. She needed to come up with ways to provide direction and collaborate.

Jake stood up and said, "Jane, you have my support."

"Let's go to the ramp, find my car." as she fist-pumped up toward the ceiling. She remembered the seeds. "Gosh, the seeds. I can always use lights and generators if we run across them." Jane looked at her watch and realized they spent over ten minutes just talking.

Finally, they moved and came to a map. Jake showed Jane where they were and the direction of her car garage. It was the one farthest away from their location. He also pointed out access points to the upper tunnel. "I know that these entrances to the tunnels are electronic access only," he said.

Jane was reminded of a survival issue. How to survive while others are suffering. "Let's keep moving," she said. A weight was sitting on her heart and panic radiated outward. Keeping busy was her familiar friend and would sustain her in these moments of struggle.

She never envisioned being slowed down by another person. They continued to walk together down the straight, concrete passage. Jane kept looking for more cracks in the walls and ceiling. No signs of stress so far. A pipe running along the ceiling caught her eye. Each building had a similar set-up. It was gas! If that broke, she wondered, and then erased that thought. Another reason to move. Jake walked slowly and was not keeping up to Jane's pace. She waited for him several times.

Finally, they reached the storage tunnel where she had found an interesting pallet of things just a few hours before. Getting to the parking garage will be easy from here. She started to visualize where her car was located, the two access points to the garage and what she would do when she got there.

Jane saw the pallet. Did she need glassware and tubing? Jake walked over to the second bay and cut the poly wrap and started opening up boxes that revealed dozens of surgical suits. The next box was filled with respirators. He opened another box of what looked like surgical masks. These prototypes came from a project started five years ago. The materials used for the suits were coaxially oriented to provide a high sterile barrier. The product worked perfectly, but it cost hundreds of dollars to make each suit. Could they be used to protect against radiation exposure? If she was going to make it home, they needed radiation protection.

"Jake, this is great. I knew of this project. These respirators will be useful. We should grab them," said Jane.

"How about this?" Jake shouted. He pointed to a dark corner of the storage bay, revealing a pallet truck tucked in the corner.

"Jesus, you're good, Jake." Jane threw down her backpack and said, "Stay here and I'll bring the truck close." While she walked toward the truck, another vibration coursed through the building, sending piles of dust to the floor and fogging up their visibility. Jane found the keys in the ignition. Oh boy, she thought. Now what? Looking at the controls, she found a toggle, and she tried going back and the truck moved, making a large divot in the wall with concrete dust adding to already cloudy air. "That must be forward," she smiled as she reversed the truck. Another control moved the pallet forks up and down. Pretty simple, she thought. Jake was laughing. With a little backing up and turning at different angles, she moved the truck around the obstacles and planted it in front of the pallet of supplies they wanted to move.

"Let's put all of our stuff on the pallet of surgical suits and hopefully, we can move this stuff toward the stairway leading to the garage. Jake, with your bad leg, we can create a spot for you to ride."

"Boy, you are a little tough on a guy's ego," said Jake.

Jane thought, there is that male machismo again, but he was laughing at himself when he said that. Then she realized the solution. "Jake, why don't you drive the truck and I'll run alongside." Jane moved the pallet fork under the pallet and lifted everything a foot in the air. She jumped down and threw her backpack on top of the boxes.

"Here," as she motioned for Jake to hop behind the controls. He limped over and started moving forward and they were off. Now speeding down each passageway, they finally arrived at the door that would take them to the parking garage, one floor above.

Jake stopped and carefully stepped down from the truck. It occurred to her that Jake might still be a little dazed from his fall. He did not know what to expect outside. She'd have to help him with that.

Jane started to unpack the boxes on the pallet. "This material will protect you as long as you do not tear the fabric. It's designed to be disposable, so it's fragile. Once radiated particles enter inside, you are exposing yourself in an occlusive environment which will multiply the effect significantly." The white surgical suit combined with the respirator looked strange. Jane remembered the original project was making surgical protection more comfortable while preventing exposure to viruses and bacteria.

"Got it," said Jake. "I also grabbed a few gloves we can use. I learned with these, if you put on multiple ones, you can take them off as you need to."

"You're a pretty savvy survivor, Jake."

"Oh, yeah? Well, I was a Navy Seal for ten years until I broke my foot in four places. I guess the survival training we received was helpful, but the real training was how to approach the unknown. That fits here, doesn't it?"

"Really, you're a trained Navy Seal? What're you doing here?"

"Long story, Jane. Let's just say I followed my heart."

Jane smiled. "Well, we can leave that discussion for later. This is what I'm thinking. We're at the edge of the southern part of the building complex that may have a better chance of remaining intact for a lot longer. Since the ramp is not completely enclosed, I'm assuming we will encounter radiation. Let's suit up and leave the pallet behind, until we know what we need."

"Roger, Jane," he said. Sarcasm was not his style. He was legitimately following her orders.

As they finally got everything together, Jane realized she needed to protect her Tool Box and backpack from contamination. She also realized that there would be extreme heat. She didn't want to use a surgical suit for this purpose, but realized she had no alternative. She also flipped open her sensor to monitor levels in real time. She checked the readings as she strapped it across her body. Still normal. She draped another surgical gown securely over the backpack and the Tool Box. It was clumsy, but it would work. She looked up at Jake, "Any ideas?"

He hobbled over. "Nah, I think you've got it right."

They used Jake's security pass this time to open the door. She took more readings and again the radiation level was normal, but the temperature was already ten degrees higher. Will they overheat? She motioned to Jake to drink some water. She looked down at the Tool Box wrapped inside of the protective material and saw a light flashing. Odd, she thought. What is that? She carefully unwrapped the Tool Box and saw it was her phone. Her phone showed it had one message.

It was from Dr. Blue. "Jane, I am at the farm. I need your help and..." then the message went silent. The time was 12:01. Jesus. Where is the farm? How can I help her when I can't leave here? Jane felt like she was going crazy, but she knew that she needed first to connect to the closest satellite, her only means of communication. Her satellite phone would help. The temperature was climbing higher, the tunnel shook again.

LOIS - 26

The entrance was close. "This way," she shouted. Lois was leading, followed by Clark and Suri. Suri was on high alert, pulling Clark like she was afraid of losing Lois.

People were bunched up next to the main intersection. The Metro, now stuck, with cars on the tracks backed up for blocks, was surrounded by people getting off and looking at their smart phones for information. Suddenly, a small, black plane, flying low, flew overhead coming from the north. The once self-absorbed crowd started to shout, "Look at that!" and pointed and screamed, some running to the Medical Arts building. Clusters of groups formed and were madly talking and pointing.

Clark caught up to Lois and said, "I feel like I'm Will Smith on the set of Independence Day."

Lois stopped running. "We have a plan, Clark. Just follow me. We're going to the Alumnae building, now!"

"Clark's in. Lead the way."

Lois was never sure about Clark. He liked to compare life events to movies and often acted like he was in a movie. He needed the context of a movie to know how to behave. Real life did not provide the answers he needed. When he dropped into a third person point of view, Lois knew this behavior pattern very well.

As Lois started to push against the people headed for the medical building, she wondered if Hung was correct. Did they have only fifteen minutes to return to the tunnels? If he was wrong by ten minutes, they wouldn't make it. How could he be so precise?

Upon reaching the Alumnae building, there was a group positioned directly in front of the double doors. She moved to the right but found those doors locked. She had to push into the crowd. Several groups were shouting about what they were reading on their Blackberries. It seemed to Lois that this pod of people were talking about bombs, maybe a nuclear event, and someone shouted they needed to move to safety in the medical building.

She had to stop. She tapped a short, razor thin woman, standing alone and reading a device positioned very close to her face. "What's happening?" said Lois.

Not looking up, she said, "I think multiple nuclear bombs are going to be deployed very close to this location," she said. "Where are you going?"

"We're going back to a tunnel. Do you want to come with?"

She looked hesitant, but Lois touched her shoulder and said, "Come!"

Lois made eye contact with Clark and he nodded. They finally got to the entrance of the alumnae building with its tall glass atrium. Suri was showing signs of stress, having been compressed by human bodies. Dr. Anthony was not around. With this woman's confirmation on the same information they received, Lois knew the last minutes were nearing. Why are people still standing around? She tried to open the large glass doors, and they were locked. She pushed the handle a second time and then Clark came over. He pulled the doors and they opened. He even held them open for her, Suri, and this petite woman and gave the woman a big smile as she passed through last. He is practically effervescent, she thought. She was madly trying to remember the scene in Independence Day.

The building was empty. Lois started running as fast as she could and they followed. They flew down the stairs to the basement level and turned to the right where halfway down the hall was the janitor's closet. Lois opened the door. It was then that Lois remembered they climbed up using these built-in rungs sunk into the concrete. What about Suri? We can't carry her down this thing.

"Clark quickly, check the elevator. Is there a floor below?"

Clark did as she asked and reported back, "We are on the lowest level, level one. There is nothing below this level."

Strange, thought Lois. Was this tunnel hidden and only accessible from this hidden closet entrance? Overtaxing her rattled brain with this stressful situation did not lend itself to a lot of solutions and she felt the urge to just throw everyone down the shaft. She was breathing hard and then bent down to hug Suri, feeling the soft, creamy fur cover her face. Suri leaned into her. Suri then moved her whole body like she was preparing to shake off water.

Lois then noticed the thin woman and Clark taking down a few things off the wall of the janitor's closet. She thought that was odd until she realized they were creating a pulley system out of ropes and threading them through the eye ring of Suri's leather halter.

Clark shouted to Lois, "Go down to the bottom of the shaft, and we'll lower Suri down to you." She felt skeptical and knew her face showed it. The thin woman touched Lois on the shoulder. This gentle gesture woke Lois up to move quickly and she started down the concrete tube into the tunnel. As she landed on the ground safely, she looked up.

Clark shouted, "Okay," and she heard Suri's whimper as she was being lowered down. Lois started to climb up each rung until she was close to Suri. Once she connected with her, she could steady the ride down. Once down, she untied the ropes to her halter and thought, Nice Job! It was then that the sound of a door closing above echoed down the cement tunnel. She did not have to wait long to see the petite woman and Clark appear and land solidly on the concrete floor. Clark did not seem tired but looked almost exhilarated.

Lois said, "Thanks. We need to move fast now!"

The darkened tunnel looked familiar to Lois. The finality of the door closing reminded her of Hung and Dr. Anthony. Was Hung safe? What happened to this Dr. Anthony? Taking care of him would be repulsive. He must have changed his mind. Her phone rang. It was Hung.

"You in?" he said.

"Yes, we just got to the tunnel. Are you okay?"

"Yep, and I have Dr. Anthony, if you were looking for him. I found him with a group of medical professionals. I needed someone to help me lift a few boxes and he did. We just entered a tunnel under the medical building. Are you seeing anyone else in the tunnels?"

"No. No one was even in the building. Everyone was outside getting a better reception," said Lois.

"It is strange. They are all standing outside," said Hung. "No one wants to be underground because of 9/11. Radiation will kill them instantly. Imagine, we are minutes away from a bomb hitting."

"I hope you're wrong," said Lois.

"Me too! Get to back to the Five Guys ASAP! I'll see you soon after I store more supplies. If you see anything in the tunnels like..." The phone line was quiet.

Suddenly, a force came up from her feet and through her body. The sound of the impact followed. As the tunnel twisted in an elongated wave, Suri barked. She jolted into action and they followed, running away from the closet toward the end of the tunnel. Concrete started to crack slowly and then a few chunks came down, creating a dust cloud. A large chunk of concrete landed right in front of them, creating a white haze that filled their lungs.

"I can't see," choked Lois. "Let's go back!" Now Suri, covered with concrete dust, stopped running, walking with a heavy burden on her back. Clark grabbed her leash to pull her back. As they ran back, chunks continued to fall and suddenly, the ceiling broke open, just missing Suri and Clark. They continued to run and finally stopped at the closet where they started. All four poured in and closed the door. Clark put his arm on the thin woman's shoulder, so tenderly.

"Are we safe here? Please God, not this," cried the petite women.

"God?" said Clark. "I wish I had your faith. Just in case, let him know we don't want to be buried alive, please. Hey, what's your name?"

"My name is Karey," she said. They sat silently as they listened to concrete coming down and puffs of dust coming up from the bottom of the door.

"Sis, what's next?" Clark said in a shaky voice.

They waited until the sound of concrete falling and the waves of dust stopped blowing up into their faces. "We needed this tunnel to get back to the Five Guys. If the tunnel is caved in, we are really screwed as that means the sub-basement above will have a gaping hole down to this floor. I don't want to be walking on top of this rubble."

Lois could hear a creaking sound above their heads. The hatch started to lift, "Hello," was a sound from the floor above. "Hello, I can hear you."

"Hung, Hung? Is that really you, Hung?"

"Yep," he shouted. "Are you safe?"

"So far, we're safe," Lois shouted back.

"I'm coming down."

As Hung lowered himself smoothly, he squeezed his body between them slowly from the last three rungs. This movement sent more dust flowing up into their nostrils and lungs. Everyone started to cough. Once they all adjusted to the closeness, Lois finally asked, "How did you find us?"

"Once the bombs hit, the tunnel collapsed. I had to check on you. I just walked across the edge of the collapsed floor. It's passable. This tunnel was built long before the building and it wasn't reinforced like the Physics building was ten years ago. We know this because we tried to make them do it when they built the Alumnae building. I will guide you back up to level one and backtrack the way I came." Hung looked down at Suri, "Hmmm, someone came up with a genius plan to get Suri down here." He patted her back.

They hooked Suri's harness to the ropes. Hung and Clark went to the top to lift her up. The cobbled-together pulley system worked perfectly. Lois was calmer, saying encouraging words to Suri as they lifted her back up. What a trouper, thought Lois as she followed up the ladder.

Once everyone was on top, they walked toward the edge of the collapsed floor and saw the problem. The pile of rubble looked ominous, illuminated by a white cloud drifting onto their faces. Lois wondered how much asbestos was in the air. Two feet of flooring was left along the wall. Is this where Hung walked? Lois felt scared just looking down.

"The alternate route is climbing on top of this big pile of rubble below," said Hung pointing to the floor below. "I think this will work."

"I'll go first," said Karey. With less than four feet of an intact floor, she quickly walked the fifty feet, braced against the wall, and made it look easy. Clark followed her, flying so quickly that Lois thought his feet did not touch the surface.

"Just letting you know, I'm afraid of heights. How can I cross with Suri?"

"First things first, Lois," said Hung. "Let's get you across and we'll worry about Suri later."

"Impossible," she said.

"Don't look down. Just look at Clark and slide one foot in front of the next."

She had no choice. This was difficult for her. Heights manifested a reaction in her whole body. With her back leaning against the wall, she inched each step sideways while practicing a special breathing pattern she learned in yoga. She looked at Clark and his encouraging smile. Breathing in, she slid a foot, and breathing out, she kept her balance. Sliding a foot at a time, she finally got close enough for Clark to grab her. He pulled her to safety. Suri started to whine, pulled on the leash from Hung and, in four strides, came across and started to lick Lois' face. Hung crossed easily and they were safe.

"Now, you need to keep moving," said Hung. "Take this hallway toward the Physics building as fast as you can. There'll be a stairway to the tunnel level where we all will meet later. Find the entrance to our place with the double doors. You might remember them when you first arrived. Remember, this is not the way you came, Lois, but I'm sure you will find it. Take this security card, you may need it. I'm helping Dr. Anthony and will be picking up things that might be helpful to our survival." Instructions given, Hung ran across the gaping hole and disappeared around the corner.

They walked slowly down the hallway and found the double doors and stairway to the lower tunnel level that Hung had described. People were crammed against both sides of the tunnel with space down the middle. Some people had bloody bandages, some were screaming in pain, and some were pushing past the slower people. About half were medical professionals in white lab coats, some helping and some needing help. This was the hospital basement, thought Lois. A sign said Medical Arts left and Physics right. Moving against this crowd will be challenging. Orderlies were moving supplies from the inventory areas in offices along the tunnel. There was equipment, carts, bed sheets, and bandages everywhere. All signs of normal, clean efficient hospital activity were unmistakably absent, replaced with an overload of sick people in need of help.

Another explosion went off above their heads. The sound jolted the building and anyone standing balanced themselves against the moving floor. Once it ended, waves of people continued to move as if the bombing overhead was just another distraction. Strange, thought Lois. Why was no one panicking? Lois saw an older woman lying on the floor. Was she dead? Lois shuddered at the thought of just walking past her when no one stopped to help. She inched toward an abandoned gurney with a white sheet tucked into a mattress parked next to the wall. She looked at Clark and he must have read her mind. They grabbed the gurney and started pushing it against the stream of people. Karey followed with Suri and they all stopped where this woman lay. Karey bent down and pulled a stethoscope out of her jacket, taking vitals. Something that Lois had missed. Was she a medical professional?

"This woman will need to be triaged," said Karey. "It appears she may have had a stroke. Normally, I would not suggest that we move anyone, but I think leaving her on the floor is worse. She weighs well over 200 pounds. Do you think the three of us can lift her?"

"Yep, there is a technique though," said Clark as he lowered the gurney to the floor and showed how two people can lift from opposite sides. A guy stopped to help them. He looked almost out of place except for the bloodstains on his fancy suit, tie, and Italian shoes. Obviously, some kind of lawyer or business person. The four of them lifted the woman with Karey protecting her head. The guy said there was a line for medical help. He offered to take her in that direction. She was staring in space the whole time and never responded to anything they said. Lois felt they needed to find the Five Guys as promised but did not want to leave her. Karey pointed out that they could not help her and this would be the best approach. Lois was still not sure.

"I'll take her," said the man. "I'll get her in line for treatment." Finally, Lois agreed and watched as the man disappeared, pushing the gurney toward the Medical Building. Clark distracted her, and she caught his movement passing through a door marked Pharmacy. Lois followed with Suri and Karey behind her. They looked into the dispensing window and saw the pharmacists had completely abandoned the area. The pharmacy shelves were locked up, but Clark already slid through the dispensing window and was wandering up and down the aisles loading various bottles of pills into a steel basket that was already overflowing with boxes.

"What are you doing, Clark?"

"Hung did ask us to pick up supplies," said Clark.

He's right, thought Lois.

"I can help with this," and Karey slid her small body through the window and started to name generic drugs and categories. Antibiotics, Cipro, steroids, Hydrocortisone, anti-hypertensives, ace inhibitor, calcium channel block, beta blocker, opioid narcotics, antidepressants, Prozac, Valium. Lois knew they could not stop long but found an abandoned cart with bandages and loaded up the cart with drugs as fast as Karey and Clark passed them on. Clark placed three large bottles of Paxil, Prozac and Zoloft on the cart and smiled at her. Drugs for depression would come in handy. Then it really hit home for Lois. What were they doing? How long would it be before they would have normal modern lives? What were their long-term prospects for survival? What right do they have to stockpile drugs for themselves?

Wanting order, she took charge of organizing the cart, covering the contents from on-lookers with blue surgical drapes she found in a corner. Now, they could finally make progress, moving toward the Physics building. She had Clark and Karey walking ahead of the cart with Suri, as she pushed the cart. They moved slowly through people moving in the opposite direction. No one noticed the cart, but continued to move, bumping against Clark and Karey instead of the cart. Finally, there was another sign pointing down a dark hallway that said Physics. At the far end of the hall, Lois thought she recognized the double doors. Finally, able to run, they quickly reached the end of the corridor. Lois fumbled for the security card that Hung gave to her and the doors did not open.

Another blast hit hard and small crumbled pieces of concrete dropped from the ceiling. It was then that Lois noticed the difference between the corridor they were in and the one that they left. It was obvious the Medical Building was newer and was holding up under the stress from above. There was no time to think. Pushing harder was the only option.

Now what? She remembered that there was a similar door they could use upstairs. Maybe her card would work there. "Wait here," she shouted. Running upstairs two by two, she recognized the glass atrium that gave the Physics' building its elegant appearance. She found a strange scene of students, clustered together, in lab coats with the word 'Physics' labeling their pocket protectors. They were all talking in an agitated way about the effect of nuclear bombs. Lois thought it was ironic that students of physics would be the only people here that really understood nuclear disasters. There were about a dozen of them, all talking at once, seeming on high alert. She also noted one woman with raging red, curly hair who stood out in the center of the group, seeming to lead an intense discussion. Lois wanted to stop and talk but realized that she needed to keep moving. She tried the double doors and her card let her in. She was almost there. She quickly ran down the stairs and pushed the doors open to let the others in.

One last challenge, thought Lois. Suddenly, the Physics building shook and crumbled with an intensity like one hundred thunder blasts. They stopped to brace themselves and then moved on. This was the worst. As she looked back, she saw the walls resonate rhythmically, in a wave pattern.

"Quick. Fly!" she screamed. They were being propelled by the collapsing of the walls above them. As they rounded the turn, she saw the staircase and where all Five Guys were standing at the bottom, ready to receive them and break their fall. Leaving the cart behind, they flew down the stairs. Cong and Bai shuttled them to the far end of the original room that Lois left just an hour ago. There, they waited for something to happen.

Lois was shivering or shaking; she was not sure which. The full burden of the last hour came crashing down on her shoulders and shook her body, releasing a massive delayed reaction. Clark was composed, eyeing the room, observing the residents. He looked at the Five Guys with wonder and then returned to Karey who was exhausted and breathing heavy and finally at Suri who was licking Karey's face. Lois went over to Suri for affection. Suri turned and jumped on her. She sat down and they collapsed into a ball of body fur with Suri sitting on her lap like she did when she was a puppy. Lois started to cry into Suri's fur.

"We cannot communicate with anyone without a satellite upload. Let's fill each other in. There are conflicting stories and we're not sure what's true. Hi, I am Cong," he said as he nodded to Karey and Clark.

It was then Dr. Anthony came forward, showing a more compassionate face than before. He helped Lois to her feet, gave her a hug and looked directly at her and quietly said, "Thank you, Lois."

Lois could not react to Dr. Anthony. Was he sincere or did he just have a shallow personality? Nothing matters, thought Lois. Her mind released the most desperate thoughts of complete destitution on the surface. I wonder if Dan made it, was her first thought. How seriously did he take the information and was he able to react quickly enough? Was Betty with him? I guess Luming is all right since as long as the Seed Bank holds. They would have lots of resources to help Dan out with Lizzy, if they made it.

Multiple impacts were continuing and shaking the building, but this room, the pod, felt insulated. Cong motioned for everyone to move toward a circle of seats. Someone put on some music, Fleur de Lis, lending a calming effect. They sat for a while quietly and Qiang prepared some tea and served it to each person. It had a fragrant odor of spring flowers and had a surprising relaxing effect. Lois stopped thinking for a while and closed her eyes. She was not sure if she was sleeping when Dr. Anthony and Clark came back with the cart of pharmaceuticals. She smiled, not thinking too much about when they left or how they got that stuff down the stairs, but she remembered the cluster of physic students and sighed silently. Where were they?

"Where are the students?" she asked. "Can we save them? Has the tunnel collapsed?"

"Yes, it will probably collapse from fatigue, but I don't think we could determine how deep the collapse is," said Dr. Anthony. "We must protect ourselves when we go out. We also have to prepare for significant radioactive fallout from anyone coming in from outside."

"If we take too much time, they may die. Why do we have medical supplies if no one here is sick?" said Lois. "I'm going out!"

Cong jumped down from his high chair and said to Lois, "I understand your passion, but we are a group now and we are all locked in here together. You are feeling survival guilt, we all feel that. We need to pause and discuss this. What is the best way forward for our group?"

She looked around and, still feeling uncomfortable with waiting, she said, "You have ten minutes to plan this and then I'm going out."

The Five Guys quickly came together in a tight circle, talking quietly. Cong's head popped up and asked, "Where are the people located?"

"They are one floor above us, down the hall going south and toward the west in the atrium," said Lois.

"Yes, the atrium. We might have a plan for rescue. Give us a minute. I apologize; we can brainstorm faster between ourselves."

They moved toward a monitor and Qiang grabbed what looked like a gamer's remote. He moved it as the black-and-white image changed. It seemed like some kind of robot searching the tunnel, equipped with a camera. She recalled the many robot races conducted each year and how the Five Guys won this each year until they had to drop out of the competition. Now they were using them for a real application. I wonder how that feels to them, she thought.

Everyone started to fixate on the screen above and finally started to see the extent of the damage. Dust filled the air space and quickly covered the lens of the camera. As the robot moved through the debris, they could see the outline of a collapsed tunnel.

"Where are we?" asked Clark. Clark was observing everything. Lois recalled that he had a fabulous sense of direction and could almost always remember a location where something happened. It suddenly struck Lois to think about everyone in the group and how critically important it would be to understand their individual gifts.

They were all silently watching the black-and-white screen and then it went black. "I was afraid of that," said Qiang. "We have several robots stationed around the buildings, but this was the only one close to the atrium. Let's review the tape and see if we can find the closest robot." He backed up the video and applied a blue filter to the film which blocked out some dust. There's an opening at the end of the long tunnel. Large shards of glass lying around meant that the glass atrium collapsed where the students were convening. Qiang saw something that no one else could even detect. "There's one. I recall we left it here to monitor sound expansion in the atrium. I think I can get it engaged."

The robot was on a tilted surface and started to walk forward slowly toward the opening where the light had a greenish tone. What they saw were bodies covered in debris, probably radioactive, some moving slightly, completely covered in white dust. Many bodies were lifeless, and some were just moving back and forth, probably from pain. The glass must have severed arteries because black liquid spots appeared around mounds under what looked like a couple of feet of white dust. A patch of curly red hair partially covered in dust came into view. Lois was sick suddenly and vomited into a wastebasket.

DAN - 27

Dan stopped a moment in an empty tunnel. He had just completed checking a gas line, leaned against the wall, feeling a tightness around his chest. Luming was walking toward him with Lizzy in her stroller.

"I've got to find Lizzy's diapers and food as I just ran out of almost everything," said Luming.

Dan straightened up. "How's she doing? You've got things under control? How has she been for you? You know, someone is working on a room for us to settle in with her. I still haven't been there. While this place seems simple, it has many hidden spots. It shocked me to hear that they had baby formula and diapers, not just the disposable kind. Then I realized that Members were also parents which led me to wonder about the Members that didn't make it."

Luming looked at Dan. "I've thought that too." Dan picked up Lizzy. "Betty told me that Lizzy reacted badly for her, screaming for no reason, but now she's smiling and waving her hands a lot."

Betty also mentioned that to him, but the hand-waving was new, Dan thought. Someone must have taught her that. Dan felt an immediate loss of having to share Lizzy with so many people, but he trusted Luming or Betty to do the right thing in his absence. She looked happy, putting her arms around Dan's neck, but as Dan knew only too well, a baby's contentment could change in an instant. Lizzy had shown him that several times. Dan swayed back and forth while she looked up at him. Luming was looking at them. He must really love children to be taking care of Lizzy for so long.

"You know what I need, Dan?"

"What do you need, Luming?"

Luming took a breath before he spoke. "I need more information about what happened. What is radiation poisoning like? Do we need to worry about it? I want to know what radiation is. What are we measuring when we use a Geiger counter? How does radiation come from a nuclear weapon? Where does the heat come from? How much protection do we have from what just happened? I know the basics just like everyone else. Spitting the atom, releasing energy that causes damage beyond what is imagined possible. What happens next?"

"I understand," said Dan as he lightly touched his shoulder.

Luming sounded stressed as he spoke. Stress was in everyone now, but no one talked about it. This was hardly a situation ever experienced before by anyone. It had been six hours since the stacks closed. Their work was still focused on basic preservation of the facility and measuring for radiation leaks. Every decision needed to be based on a general knowledge of what happened. Dan thought Luming's idea was a good one. In order to bring everyone to the same level of knowledge, maybe he could pull together some basic information.

He'd have to ask Scar who to ask. "I think I get it," said Dan. "Let me see what I can do. I'll be back. Do you want to take Lizzy around again?" Luming nodded and Dan handed Lizzy back. She waved goodbye as she hugged Luming around his neck.

That was a good decision as Luming looked a little less burdened with Lizzy in his arms. As Dan was walking away, Scar came around the corner with a shopping basket of baby supplies. Luming smiled at her as she instantly started asking him about how Lizzy was doing and giving directions on where to find the living space they were creating. There was energy between them. Scar seemed to have shed a bit of her tough persona. Dan thought there was a spark between them, but Scar was so consumed with every detail, he could be wrong. When have I ever been right about romance, he mused? Yes, consumed was a good word. She made time for the constant list of immediate needs, problem-solving, hand-holding, and she even delivered an occasional hug. Scar was everywhere and everything. She held things together. Dan thought it was amazing that everyone understood that Scar was in charge and honored that. What she was not doing was taking care of herself. It's still early, he thought. There'll be time. Maybe they'll be able to come together as a group at this dinner. Gosh, I would love a beer right now. What are the chances of that?

Everyone was thinking about survival first and then loved ones. How long do they have? What happens next? It impressed Dan how organized everything was and how individuals supported each other. Was this a learned behavior of the Seed Bank's organization?

As Dan walked away, Scar caught up to him from behind. While she was only five foot eight-ish, her stride had no problem keeping up with Dan's long legs. Her toned, slim body showed a readiness to tackle the next thing.

He stopped to talk. "We were just talking and Luming asked me to explain what's happening on top. What do we know about radiation?"

"Dan, we can speculate, but knowing will be hard. Based on the information we collected so far, nothing has changed down here. Seven to eleven major cities were hit, but we lack any communication from the outside that confirms or denies this. I've been thinking a lot about bringing together this group into a true community. Something based on individual needs collectively. I know, naïve, right? But how do we plan long-term survival while addressing day-to-day needs? Who's in charge? How do we cohabitate? We need to work these things out. Yes, I am holding us together, but I think we could improve by sharing the leadership load. We need co-leadership and find passion around how we lead. It's great that you want to step up, Dan. That would give us a chance to get together, ask questions and dialogue on what we know and what we speculate about knowing, based on science. Maybe we can even talk about our feelings," she said as she laughed at her own comment. "The Seed Bank has a few rituals we developed that might be helpful in developing a meaningful lifestyle and even create time for reflection. What is our purpose? What is different? Can we adapt to the destitute environment above us?" As they entered the Hub, she went right up to Troy, sat down, and they engaged in an amazingly fast dialogue. Dan had never heard Troy say three words before.

Dan sat down and looked around. She surprises me every time I'm with her. She's kind of like Jane. As Dan thought about Jane, he was reminded of Brenda and even his ex. Thinking about them brought him to a place of darkness. Everyone down here must be grieving about their losses and the guilt they feel over having survived. They're all healthy but what's the long-range perspective? Would survivor's guilt have an eroding impact and damage long range health? So many outcomes, he thought.

Dan got up and walked into the Library. Betty was reading out loud from a book. "The initial signs and symptoms of radiation sickness are usually nausea and vomiting. The amount of time between exposure and when these symptoms develop is a clue to how much radiation a person has absorbed. After the first round of signs and symptoms, a person with radiation sickness may have a brief period with no effect, followed by the onset of new, more serious symptoms."

"Jesus, Betty, I was just coming to look up this information. This kind of information is going to help everyone come to understand what is happening above us."

"I agree, Dan. By the way, I'm an RN, graduated from the university nursing school in 1973. I'm here to help anyone needed some medical attention." Dan thought she was some kind of plant scientist and a teacher of martial arts, but a nurse as well? How lucky they were to have someone with that background. Betty told him she was trying to focus on being present. Catching herself when she started to think about people dying slowly on the surface. If she was thinking this, everyone else was also going through very dark thoughts. Getting information about what to expect was helping her balance negative thoughts. She and Brother might be good at starting practices to counter such stressful thoughts. There, he landed on a forward-thinking idea. Something he could act on.

At some point, he could bring the group together and find an expert to share the information Luming requested. Maybe start creating common ground between the SB people and the newcomers. They were all survivors. He wondered if the SB members were accepting the non-Members.

He started to think about how to present nuclear technology in a way that increased awareness without causing more fear. As he started to formulate questions, Brother poked his head into the Library.

"Everyone okay?"

"You can help us, Brother," Dan answered immediately.

"What is your question?"

"When we get together this evening, we want to bring the group together. Connect the Members and the 'new members' and lower survivor anxiety. Can you do that?"

Brother's eyes brightened. "I think we need to bring nature into our community. Thank God we have plants and seeds. Green things should help us imagine the patterns of our lives and how we can find our centers to do that. I'm surprised at the many talents around this place. I think the harsh admittance policy left quite a few people upset. Something no one could prepare for. I also don't think the word 'survival' is the one we should be using. Survival is what it takes to stay alive. If we raise our awareness beyond survival, I think we might find some healing ways and discover our path toward humanity. Whatever it is, we have to include all living things like plants and animals?"

Scar walked into the room. "Scar, you spoke about existing rituals. Can you share them with us? It might help us prepare the evening activities," asked Dan.

"Isn't there a sacred place? I thought I saw it on the map," asked Brother.

"Yes," said Scar, looking intently at Brother. "I'll show you. Dan, can you look at the rituals, specifically the Ocha rituals? There's a small hardbound book under the podium that identifies all of our rituals developed over that last decade. Just read them. Let me know what you think."

Scar's and Brother's eyes continued to lock on to each other while she was talking. Scar's body appeared relaxed. She took Brother's arm as they walked out. Dan was happy to see that change in her.

Dan thought about leadership. Her slight shift surprised him. Scar exhibited a fluid style and was receptive to other colleague's ideas. This was Scar's facility. She was in charge, calling the shots. He just witnessed a change in her. Vulnerability is not a sign of weakness and Scar just proved that. Flexibility, in body and in mind, was Scar's strength. Dominant power did not seem like a part of her personal equation. She was almost a reluctant leader. How interesting, Dan thought. Somehow, this new living situation needed shaping, like a clay pot on a potter's wheel. They needed to start with a crude concept and then continue to refine it until it was a beautiful blue and white pitcher ready to carry water. Was that possible?

Dan pulled a rough looking book from under the podium. This must be the Ocha ritual book. It was covered in a dark Indigo blue with white triangular white shapes evenly spread along the length of the book. This looks interesting.

He sunk into a bright turquoise sofa chair and thought about the craziness that led them here. Each moment counted, and they had such a slim possibility of surviving, but they did. What were the chances? Just above them, their flesh would be blistering and boiling. Poor Lizzy would not survive two minutes. Brenda leaving Lizzy with him to apply for a job, saved her life. Otherwise, they would not be living in an underground marijuana grow-op while millions were dead. Where was Brenda now? How did her early flight to Washington end? He had to stop thinking about that. He was sure that Lois made it if she stayed with the Five Guys below in the Physics building. Jane was probably trapped in a conference room somewhere in the Health Care Building. When was her acquisition meeting? Was she safe? He then remembered the message he left Jane. He was overcome with grief, losing her. Losing the uniqueness that she held in the world. I hope she is safe and listened to my voicemail.

Now, back to the task. He wrote two pages about how the impact of radiation is a function of how far away they are from the center of the bombing, the degradation that happens to bodies that survive the first impact, and how quickly secondary effects can waste away the body in days. You can pulverize completely or walk away and have long-term issues like cancer. But what types of cancers?

Dan was concerned about what to share. He thought about approaching the whole subject from a historical point of view of how weaponry steadily increased starting with forged iron until scientists created the ultimate weapon. Why would they care about that? Technology always paced faster than the society could handle them. Weapons, always a means and never a solution to solving differences. Are we the end of the line? Would they want a philosophical approach or just clear answers? What helps the long process of grieving?

"Hey, Dan," said Troy as he walked into the library.

Dan looked up. "Hi, Troy."

"Scar said you might need my help."

"That's interesting. I am trying to summarize information about nuclear technology. Like what has happened, what kind of effect it has on surviving and get those questions behind us before we tackle our next steps."

"That sounds intriguing, Dan. I think I already know how I can help. Did you know I'm a cartoonist? Probably not. For example," and Troy started to sketch a picture of a stick of dynamite and showed it breaking. He drew an image of gas and objects blowing out and buildings collapsing in line drawings.

"That's fantastic. Cartoons have a way of symbolizing ideas succinctly and add some lightness to the subject," said Dan. "I think I know what Scar had in mind when she made that suggestion to you." He handed Troy the two pages he wrote. "Can you do something with this?"

Troy's eyes widened. "Hmmm. Probably. Let me see what I can do. It would be faster digitally, but I would like to try a low-tech approach like sketching." Troy read the words out loud. "If we appreciate the context of how mankind has evolved and where we are maybe, we can change the pattern of destructive living. Healing eventually follows destruction in this constant changing universe. We need to pivot from our past outlook and change to our new one." Troy stopped reading and said, "Sounds hokey, or I mean philosophical, but I will see what I can do with this." He shook his head, deeply immersed in thought, and said yes to himself a few times. Troy was back in his own world. Dan envied the ability to turn everything off.

"Thanks, Troy. We can provide a few technical facts, using your sketches, and then we just ask the group for their questions. Let me know what you need."

Troy already sat down with his sketchpad and was oblivious to Dan. Dan started to think about the benefit of knowing history. He walked over to the wall of books and found a whole section in the library dedicated to SB History.

The SB History section was fascinating. The facility was an old creamery room that originally processed milk in the 1900s. Then was converted to make moonshine during prohibition. They forgot this underground facility, as the city grew. No one realized it existed below as buildings surrounded the area.

There was still a circle that once held the distillation equipment, carved into the concrete floor into a deep two-foot ring in the floor. The equipment, removed long ago, left a natural circle for seating. The natural gas line that was hooked onto the still was re-engineered into a flame burner. This heated the water for tea ceremonies. The space is called Sacred Center.

What an improbable place, thought Dan. I feel like everything here has potential. What will happen? Do we stay? What is the long-term capacity? Will we let other people in here? Well, those are healthy thoughts. Openly thinking about the future by asking questions and not sitting in fear of the unknown of what could happen to them.

MICHAEL - 28

Home, thought Michael. His mind wandered back to the moment this morning, before he tied his tie, as he looked out onto the prairie view he loved. That was today? He sighed as he realized he stopped wandering the tunnels and was staring into space. Where're the kids? Kay would be in school at her college in Wyoming. How long did they fight about that? She could have gone to his alma mater, Duke, with an amazing jump start to a successful career in finance. Instead, she wanted to go to a small liberal arts college in the middle of nowhere. Max used to wander through southwestern towns in Nevada and jumped trains to Mexico, until he recently took this IT job at the university. His location was someplace across the river, in a huge windowless building. The unsettling thought that Max was also trapped forced Michael to stop walking. The present is a cloudy mess, there is no infrastructure. There is no one to help him find his family.

Was Hawk right? The US was obliterated by nuclear attack? Was there government? Hawk was certain that ten major cities, and hundreds of others, were bombed enough to have no survivors. Where did that leave him, persona non-grata? What can a lawyer do without a constitution?

As he stood, letting his mind float away from this reality, an idea stopped all other thoughts. I need to take a new approach in finding Marcella. Instead of wandering the tunnels, like a hundred other people, looking for her and asking if anyone knew her, he needed to do things differently. In truth, no one even showed the slightest interest in helping him. He was starting to think his carefully curated tie and suit were hindering his cause.

Did he have any skills that he could use to help others? Michael strained his dehydrated head for a while, thinking about that question. He would need to find water soon. People had water bottles and were filling them from a tap in one of the bathrooms. There was a line for water. But Michael sensed that it would not be advisable for him to cut into line because he was dehydrated. He must look pretty bad, however, as a young woman came up to him and allowed him to drink from her water bottle. She did not look very good either. Her head was covered with a scarf and her complexion was ruddy, showing how much stress her body was in.

He was staring at her when she said, "You don't have to stare. I was here for my weekly chemo treatment and I guess I won't be having that to look forward to. Come to think of it, I could go outside and get radiation. Ha! What's up with you? You look different."

Michael turned to look at his suit, torn with splotches of blood pressed into the fabric. He was sure he looked scary too. As the water started to work on releasing his brain from the stress of dehydration, he sat for a moment to re-evaluate.

"Where are we? I am looking for the Medical Arts building. My wife is a doctor here and I have to find her."

This woman's face suddenly appeared in front of his, with only a six-inch separation. "You and everyone else is looking for someone. What makes you so special?"

"Right, yeah, you're right," he said to the empty space in front of him. She already turned and left. He felt confused. As strange as her curt reaction was, it was the first time someone made any gesture of kindness toward him. He felt so inadequate, so ill-prepared for this scene. People were injured, helpless and needing attention, and here he was, selfishly looking for Marcella so he could feel better. That thought struck him hard. He worked hard, raised a family and that was it. His outside interest was drinking wine with the right people, people of status, and taking vacations in the right place so he could talk about wine over dinner. Does that matter anymore? What does matter? For once in your life, Michael, do you think you could think of someone besides yourself, sitting in your own little world? Then an idea came to him. And something he could do for others.

After that, everything fell into place. He searched the tunnels for a cart with two carboys and found both, abandoned in a small clinical laboratory full of test tubes and surgical gloves. The cart looked like it was headed for some experiment, but the large plastic container with the two handles said D.I., probably meaning deionized water. What he needed were two pieces of tubing to get the water out with a clamp to adjust water flow. All of this reminded him of high school biology and days of confusion of not knowing what he was doing in a laboratory. Lab work was messy and smelly. At that time, Miss Margaret, one of the librarians, showed him a copy of the Federal Register for the first time. He could not believe it, but it was published daily. He then turned to reading the history of the constitution, realizing how great it was to understand the rules of this country, how important they were to controlling society and the important role of a lawyer. Fast forward, he was now working out a way to pass water around for others to hydrate.

He found a closet with a basin, a source of water and filled up the two carboys with water. He even found a large stash of Dixie cups in the cupboard. He then started down the hall, handing out water to whomever came toward him. It took him two hours to complete one tunnel. The whole time, he looked for Marcella, asked hospital personnel about her and felt very informed about what happened as people told him their stories. It was the elderly that were having the toughest time. Sometimes overweight, they were destined to sitting or worse, lying on the floor. He noticed a tiny woman trying to treat one very large woman. Some people with a yellow lab brought a gurney to her and lowered it. As each person took hold of her, they were able to put her on a soft mattress. That dog seemed so connected to the group, paying close attention to what they were doing. Michael offered to take the woman for medical help. Marcella would be proud of him, once he was able to tell her what he did. As he approached the entrance to the hospital, he found patients lined up to get in. He was told that no one could enter the hospital. Sick people were triaged by two nurses and set along the wall, outside of the double doors. He asked the first nurse, who looked completely exhausted, if she knew Marcella. She was not interested in engaging with him until he offered her water. She accepted two cups, one for a patient and one for herself. She did not know Marcella, but was a radiology nurse, working in a diagnostic lab. She could not provide Michael with any useful information, but she told him there was a massive hit to the south side of the building. Many people lost their lives and there were rescue efforts ongoing to find survivors. She did take the woman on the gurney, thanked him, and then shooed him off. There was nothing unique about him. Hundreds of people were waiting to be treated or looking for survivors. At this point, it made no difference to Michael. What choice but to keep pushing his water cart?

He went back to fill the carboy again. As he started the filling process, he looked into the janitor's closet a little further and found an opening in the floor that looked like a manhole cover. This was the older building, he thought. He just saw a sign that said Anatomy Building. Maybe this would lead him to another tunnel below that would connect to the hospital. He looked at the cover and tried turning it in a counterclockwise direction. Pulling a mop handle from the wall, he used what muscle he had and moved the cover. Once it got started, it moved smoothly and the cover opened up hydraulically. He looked down and it was dark and smelled like moist, moldy air. He could see rungs along the wall leading down. Dropping the mop into the hole, it sounded like it landed on a concrete floor.

LUMING - 29

As Luming walked toward the end of Tunnel 6, he thought about how strange it was to be alive in this environment. The temperature seemed tightly controlled so they never felt damp or cold. The plants breathed life into the stark environment and at times, the air was thick with the aromatic smell of marijuana.

"Hey, Luming, can I borrow Lizzy?" said Betty, as she walked toward him. "While we were finishing her room with baby supplies, a few questions came up. You don't mind, do you?"

"Of course not. I was thinking of doing some exploring on my own anyway."

"Great. You'll find us at the end of Tunnel 9, if you're looking for her place."

From the time he started to make a living at this corporate job, he spent most of his free time in pursuit of a type of risk that resulted in a feeling of pleasure for him. It was not really rebellion, but developing experience in handling freedom, something that was removed from his strict upbringing and his mother's domineering ways. She would be horrified if she knew how he spent his time and how he wasted large amounts of money. The money he sent home was more than enough for her to be comfortable. She hated the idea of wasting money on something as trivial as dry cleaning or buying pizza. She understood the value of his education and the opportunities he had from studying but she harshly criticized the way he frittered away the money on non-essentials.

He loved freedom, meaning he was in charge of what he did from moment to moment. His lack of experience with risk meant that his intuition was not tested. He needed to build a set of experiences that would teach him how to listen to intuition. The reason he was here was from having made a very strange and risky choice involving Chris.

Chris always seemed to have less ambition than anyone he knew. But in this environment, he was in constant movement. Thinking about Chris made him want to talk to him, so he got on his walkie talkie and called him. There was no answer. He then called Scar and she answered on the first ring.

"Luming, here, over."

"Hey, I was looking for you. Where are you?" she said.

"I am taking the last readings at the end of Tunnel 6. Nothing but baseline so far," he said.

"That's great. No news from the outside. We even got out a shortwave radio and tried that. Something will work eventually," said Scar. She sounded almost chatty. "I'm coming to you. I'll meet you where Tunnel 6 winds down into the reservoir. It's not far from where you are."

"Where is that?" asked Luming, wondering how she knew where he was.

"Just go back to the end of the tunnel and open the door. You will find a surprise on the other side."

Luming, intrigued, walked back and found the door that Scar spoke about. He opened it up, pulled up on a latched handle from the floor. He peered down into complete darkness but could hear a waterfall. He left the latch open and climbed down about thirty rungs. As he descended, lights turned on to show a smooth concrete surface below. He jumped off the bottom rung and turned to face a large mass of water surrounded by a limestone outcropping. It was as if he was standing in an underground cave. It was a waterfall. Staring around in wonder, he heard a thump when Scar jumped down about twenty feet away. With everything going on around him, he still noticed her hair braid was no longer pinned up and her thick jet-black hair was swinging well past her waist.

"This clean, natural reservoir of water was an ideal location for the Seed Bank. Marijuana plants grown hydroponically require a great deal of clean, neutral pH, non-tainted water. An old, underground distillery utilized this space during prohibition and put out moonshine to supply the masses during the depression. They also made a fabulous beer, I'm told. Based on maps from the early 1800s, the area above was a dairy farm and someone discovered this old cistern during the dust bowl drought. This reservoir saved lives in watering and feeding the cows as well as the farmers in the area. An underground spring feeds this cistern, otherwise, it would eventually be full of contaminated water from the runoff above ground. It now is our lifeline against radiated water. We plumbed water from here for our plants and general everyday use very early in the operation. This natural formation has about fifty feet of limestone between us and the surface which provides a natural filter for anything passing through the rock. See the images on the wall. They are cave drawings from 5,000 years ago." Luming studied the rock and noticed a smooth area. He focused as the lines revealed themselves, then they combined into patterns. They looked like fish, swimming in a spiral up toward the ceiling. Images danced as the water reflected against the rounded walls. He never felt paintings so alive, so pleasing.

"We were initially concerned about the impact from above, but it stood up to it beautifully. In the past, one of our architect students mapped it out. She determined it is designed like a roman cistern, only natural. While she never ran the impact measurements, archeologists have studied this structure in Mycenae, Greece. They believe this cone structure will survive extreme conditions, including strong earthquakes," said Scar.

"Who were the artists?" said Luming.

"I'm not sure, but I think it comes from the original indigenous people before the farmers were here. Probably the Sisseton, Wahpekute, or the Mdewakanton tribes. My guess is it was the Mdewakanton, due to the many drawings they left in limestone caves all around this area. They tell the story of time in the history of the land. They capture my curiosity, but I never have the time to study this. Shall we sit for a while?" She pointed to a spot on the floor that had several flat colored pillows laid out in a circle with the charcoal remains from a fire in the middle.

They sat and listened to the sound of water in silence. Luming thought that this place was beyond imagination, but he was distracted by Scar. She was a very sophisticated woman. He was used to women who took sexual charge of the situation with him. He hated that but had to tolerate it because he was shy. His mother warned him of bossy women who are 'Road Chiefs.'

"What do you mean, Road Chiefs?" Luming asked his mother.

"Road Chiefs, like me! They push the husband around until he has no soul. The man goes to the corner to pick up groceries. Imagine that. That is not a man's work! Be warned, you are going to meet a Road Chief and you will end up losing your heart and your manhood. You'll be a nobody, period!" she said, emphasizing 'nobody' with her spoon aimed at his head.

Later, he understood what she was saying. Girls that were attracted to him were strong, aggressive and eventually started to tell him what he should do. It started with simple things, like where they should go. He would be polite, respectfully asking the woman where she wanted to go. One woman, Kathryn, answered the question with such detail, he was exhausted just listening to her. He liked smart, attractive women who followed their own individual ways. It was so much easier when things were equal and he did not have to take charge of everything, but his mother's words resonated with him, leaving him to question when he was pushed around. He'd end the relationship if he thought that was happening. Of course, the fact that his mother was bossing him around about his girlfriends was not entirely lost on him. His father was quiet, but wiser about things. His favorite memory was when his father brought Luming to their temple to quietly sit and talk about his travels as a youth.

Luming found Scar to be smart, in charge of everything, but not bossy. She was straightforward. Direct without being demeaning. She earned a lot of respect in his mind. Do I want to kiss her? he thought.

Oddly, Scar broke the silence and said, "What a strange set of circumstances we are in, Luming."

His heart pounded when she said his name so gently.

"Our families may be destroyed. I know I have many friends that were probably decimated in the bombing. Surviving is almost worse than dying. What's worse is they might still be living and need our help and we can't go out to save them," she said.

Luming nodded. He thought about how special he felt and all the coincidences that brought them together. He remembered a sophisticated phrase he researched as he studied advanced English in high school. It was sacrosanct synchronicity, a sacred coincidence. He was, yes, he believed he was, living it right now.

"We still do not know what happened. We can only speculate on the extent of the damage, who is responsible and why. I have been in doing mode to forget," she said. "Just to forget my shame as a survivor. We are all lucky and now we are survivors with the day-to-day burden of surviving. I act fearlessly, but I don't feel heroic. I realized my purpose quickly and did everything I could to save a few people. Someone had to make that choice and it was on my shoulders to make. People need things to do, to forget about the immediate moment. I was afraid paralysis would set in. Short term, I had to invent a few extra things to do to make sure everyone was busy. Sorry about asking you to search for satellite communications. Troy has been doing that from the beginning." She looked down.

"What?" he fired off. "Is that why no one seemed to care what I was doing?"

"I'm guessing this makes you mad. Good, I was wondering if you could get angry. This is one of my big faults. I'm often immersing myself in anticipation and vision. That means sacrificing others for some of these objectives. I know it was wrong not to tell you."

Luming's head or maybe his ego was flailing about. She was a road chief, right? But not the manipulating version his mother talked about. Her intentions were to consider not just his feelings, but everyone's feelings and finding something for everyone to do, taking them away from dwelling on the truth of what happened. That was pretty insightful, he thought. He started to cool down.

She paused for a while. Then she said, "I have an American Indian background. I am one fifth Oglala Indian, Lakota to be exact. I am a descendent of Crazy Horse, the dark-eyed fighter of the indigenous Oglala tribe."

Luming was aware how she was able to change the dynamic between them with her soft voice. "That is fascinating, Scar. I know so little about indigenous people. Are your parents living now?"

"My mother is and she is probably safe, wherever she is. The last time we were in touch, she was in Utah, exchanging history with a native group there and leading white people on vision quests. She predicted disaster for a long time, as her mother did. She is fifty now. She had me at eighteen. I think she wanted to become free of responsibility to pursue her personal vision as early as possible and got the baby thing done right away. She was lucky. She feels Crazy Horse in her bones and the magic of his soul. She became an elder at a very young age and is part of an important motherline. I stumbled on the beginnings of the Seed Bank when I was twenty-five, long after my mother left me for her own pursuits. This Seed Bank is my life and these people are my family. I am glad you are here. Will you forgive me?" Scar said as she reached over and squeezed Luming's hand.

That's strange, Luming thought. No mention of her father. I'll ask about that later. They got up at the same time and stood face to face. Luming leaned in for a kiss and she responded in the gentlest way. After the kiss, Scar was blushing and she looked at him with her deep black eyes as they penetrated his heart. Scar broke the silence. "What a time to feel something like this!"

"Maybe this is perfect timing," said Luming. He pulled her body into his and she wept.

Now he was experiencing another shift with Scar, an exchange of thoughts and feelings. It was a dance of understanding of timing and changing the mood around the context of the situation. He smiled and said, "Normally, I would ask you for a date. I'm kind of an old-fashioned guy."

"I think I like you, Luming," She dabbed her tears and turned to leave. They climbed the rungs out of the cistern. Luming thought about questions he could have asked about her. What is a motherline? That, hopefully, will be the long and interesting process of getting to know each other. He reached into his pocket and felt the warmth of his mother's jade locket in his hands. Interesting, he thought.

JANE - 30

They decided to wait until the tunnel stopped shaking. Their hopes were dashed by sounds of boulders hitting the door, one after another, with dust puffing right through the doorjamb. After some settling, Jane could not resist opening the door, but it was barricaded by masses of concrete on the other side. The elevator door next to the stairway that Jane always used was bent outward. This was bad, she thought.

"Damn, maybe the whole ramp has collapsed." As she talked, she again felt that uncomfortable feeling of loss. All of her preparation for this moment only gave her a very bad feeling in her gut. And her heart felt like it was pumping against a barbell laid across her chest.

"If we backtrack about two hundred feet and head north, there is another door we could try," said Jake.

"Really? I'm unfamiliar with that one."

"It does not directly feed into the ramp, but you can leave the building and walk about fifty feet to the eastern side of the ramp right where your car is parked. We'll need to go up a level to access it. Of course, that fifty feet will expose us to massive radiation."

"Well, we've got plenty of protective gear." It felt better to focus on the next task, but she felt shakier than before. She now realized what they would find outside could be a dead end. Her car might be demolished. They might be trapped inside this steel corporate building full of offices and conference rooms for a long time. How she longed to get home. "Let's take only essentials with us until we know more."

Jane pulled out another compressible stuff sack and they packed seven suits and respirators. Jake slung the pack over his shoulder and she picked up her Tool Box and backpack and they started to look for a door to the upper level. As Jane walked down the tunnel, she could still hear and feel the sounds of the building creaking. As they entered the northern tunnel, she felt the temperature increase. She kept thinking about the photograph of the World Trade Center collapsing. The heat in the upper floors melted the steel which weakened the structure and multiplied the weight so the whole structure fell in on itself. Wow, she wondered, could this happen here? Not unless there was a plane stuck in the top floors. This was different.

Jake stopped and pointed at a door she must have missed. Jake tried his badge to open the door, but the security pad flashed two red lights. "This door needs higher security than I've got," said Jake. Jane jumped into action and swiped her badge with the same result.

"Strange," said Jane. "Wait a minute!" Jane put down her Tool Box and snapped open the top pockets. She lifted out a tray and beneath it was a set of plastic cards. "These were sold by a security hacking company and are supposed to remove security clearance restrictions. I used them in a hotel one time and they worked for each door I tried on one floor. Hmmm, that was a good time!" She slid the card and three green lights flashed. Jane beamed, opened the door and Jake high-fived her.

They cautiously went up the steps to another door that was also locked. Once again, she used her security-hack card. They looked at each other as they both pushed open the door. This was the lower level basement. It was brightly lit, warmer than below, showing very little damage. They heard voices in both directions, but could not see anyone. Lucky, thought Jane. Realizing interacting with people might create a whole new set of problems, she knew she wanted to stay focused on finding a way to her car. She was not sure how Jake was going to react.

They closed the door behind them, moving south, according to Jane's compass. "The ramp should be south and east of us," said Jane. As they came up to the end of the basement level, it expanded into a larger space that contained offices and chairs and there were many scientists in white lab coats everywhere, talking in small groups. Some were shouting at each other, some were crying and terror was a smell oozing out of people's skin.

This was uncharacteristic of the calm scientists that Jane knew. At the opposite corner of the room, Jane noticed an area for medical treatment. Jane immediately noticed Deidre Browning. Deidre always showed support for Jane's projects. She always asked great questions and helped her through political issues she ran up against, especially the ones Jane knew nothing about. Jane thought she looked withdrawn and detached from the chaos around them, but she was still triaging injuries as people lined up. As Jane approached, she could tell the injuries were minor, and Deidre was behaving like she was in a fog. That's strange, thought Jane. She looked stunned and was not interacting with the people she was helping. She was just treating them.

"Deirdre?" said Jane. She looked up and showed a faint sign of recognition. "Are you okay?" said Jane.

"We're isolated from the other group that were exposed to radiation. Had to. Otherwise, this whole place would be contaminated with deadly radiation. People running over each other to get to the lower level, walking on broken glass. Where are you coming from? I don't recall seeing you here before."

"Oh, we just came from another tunnel below here," said Jane.

"Interesting. You have to show it to me later. You'll need to be scanned over there for radiation if you are going to stay," she said, pointing to a woman sitting down in a torn dress and a Geiger counter in her hand.

Jane and Jake walked over to this woman who looked familiar. "Don't I know you?" asked Jane.

"Well, I know you. You are Jane Witterhouse. We met in my lab one time. I'm in charge of the animal lab in the basement. Your name was all over some tests we did for you many years ago."

Jane blushed a little, reminded of a dark time she wished to forget, when she was asking to have animal testing done on biomaterials. They implanted them in pigs that ended up being sacrificed at the end of the study, without her permission. "Oh, so you are Marnie Ferguson?" she said.

"In the flesh." She smiled. "Since I'm the only black woman scientist in the building, I would have thought everyone knew my name. Not many people pass through the dungeon to check out what we do."

"Not true," said Jane. "I was down there every day when I ran my experiment. I just never met you."

"Sure, Jane, I believe you. There's this idiot Dr. McKenzie, a self-important executive running around, trying to find a helicopter or something. Who does he think he is, CIA? Another Vice President of marketing came by to be checked for radiation and he was a hopeless mess. All these men with their big salaries and enormous egos coming apart and not being able to get it together to organize something as simple as a water line." She turned on the Geiger counter and scanned Jane's front, back and arms, around the face and the bottom of Jane's feet.

"You're in the normal zone," said Marnie. "Please take precautions to stay that way. Don't go outside!"

Jake stepped forward. "Hi, I'm Jake."

"Yeah, I know you too. Now you're the precious commodity," she said, speaking slowly and emphasizing you're. "With knowledge of building maintenance, you could be a very important person around here. I'd listen to you rather than any VP like McKenzie. In fact, everything has changed. We are no longer employees of a corporation. No one is in charge and no one cares about anyone else but themselves."

Jane was struck by Marnie's clarity. She obviously thought through many of the issues facing them. Who's in charge, what skills are valuable, what are the rules and how does she fit in?

As Marnie scanned Jake's tall, taut body, obviously experiencing great pleasure in doing so, Jane asked, "Where did you get a Geiger counter?" She didn't want to let on she had the same one in her backpack.

"My lab. Our studies include the use of radioactive isotopes and our safety protocols require us to take daily readings."

"So you've been back to the animal lab already? Any damage?" said Jane.

"Yep, I was there and no damage. It's all locked up too. I made sure of that. I'm not going to deal with any of these dweebs getting an idea that they can just walk in and start eating my animals whenever they want. Once the true survival situation becomes clear, they are going to have to deal with me." She stood up, suddenly looming taller than Jake. Protecting lab animals did not sound like a bad idea, but her attitude felt like retribution against the treatment she received and Jane knew what that felt like. Here was a woman who could take care of herself and be a valuable future asset to others.

Jake and Jane said goodbye and wandered down the tunnel to an area where a dozen scientists were sitting in a tight circle. She noticed their lab coats and the PhD insignia displayed on each collar. She recognized some of them. Some were famous, receiving awards for various contributions to big million-dollar product launches and some were quiet, introverted and their talents were rarely showcased, but they were always there, helping to solve technical problems. One woman, who Jane recognized from her dark burgundy hair contrasting against the white lab coat, was talking about some kind of call to action. Jane could not hear what she said, but as soon as she stopped speaking, someone else started talking. Everything seems different, thought Jane. Jane sensed passion coming from the group. As they approached, she could now hear they were talking about the effects of radiation. The red-haired speaker seemed to be an expert on the Hiroshima radiation sickness. She actually read translations from Japanese scientists that gathered medical information for three decades post-catastrophe. She spoke about her father, a physician who volunteered to spend time in Japan after the war and became aware of data collected secretly right under the American's noses. After she spoke, there was silence. It was like they had all the time in the world to explore and cover many perspectives. Looks like an interesting group to work with on problems, thought Jane. Someone mentioned McKenzie's name and she moved closer. Apparently, some people were suspicious of McKenzie. Someone heard him fight with someone about a helicopter that was supposed to pick him up. Late-breaking speculation was McKenzie had early warnings of a nuclear attack and had a plan in place to leave that failed. Someone took his ride? It was hijacked? He also prevented anyone from coming back into the tunnels because of radiation contamination. Some scientists expressed concern over how the people exposed to high levels of radiation were being isolated, locked out, and that led to ideas of what was going to happen next.

After listening to this, Jane and Jake walked away. "I'm getting uncomfortable," said Jane. "I think we know enough about what is going on. Let's return to the ramp and find my car."

Jake smiled. "Yep, let's go. What a zoo! Locked up in a place where you work is the ultimate hell. These guys seem okay, but it only takes a few a-holes to change things dramatically." Jane knew he wanted to say the other word that went with pompous, but was being careful around her. How unique to show old fashion manners during a crisis.

"There was something about McKenzie's failed escape plan I found interesting. A helicopter landed here to pick him up when the bombing started. What happened to the helicopter? Is it coming back for McKenzie? If only we had a helicopter, we could make it to my home," said Jane. "I prepared a home sanctuary for various catastrophic events. We would be safe and have a chance to better prepare for an uncertain future."

"Getting to know you, Jane, has been interesting," said Jake.

"My therapist has a name for my personality type, which I forgot. Bottom line, I'm mildly crazy, so you better watch out." A smile came over her face as she tried to simulate a crazy person facial expression.

"Can't we call the helicopter using your satellite phone? What we need is the phone number of the helicopter. Can we find McKenzie and somehow get it out of him? Copy it from his phone?"

"Now that is a plan of a true crazy person. I like it! Of course, but that will only work if the satellite is working and connections have not been destroyed," said Jane. "Once we reach the ramp, we can try it there. How do we find McKenzie?"

They talked about Deirdre's strange behavior. Jane thought she could do a deeper exploration with her and find out McKenzie's whereabouts. McKenzie and the Brownings were the highest ranked management here. They must be coordinating their activities. Jake wanted to walk the whole sub-basement until he found him. This was a longshot but after some discussion, they separated, Jake to find McKenzie by asking around and Jane to work with Deirdre.

"Everything will be okay," Deirdre said to herself as she worked on a patient, treating a superficial wound on her right leg. She looked tired from crying and her left eyelid was drooping. Jane thought it might be from an injury to her eye.

Jane approached and said, "Do you need a rest? Should I find someone to relieve you? I can get Dr. McKenzie for you. Maybe he can help out."

She looked up, but not at Jane, and started speaking as if Jane wasn't standing in front of her. "I've been trying to locate him. I just tried to call him again. See," as she held up the satellite phone high in the air. "It won't work here. This thing is worthless. He left it with me and promised to be back soon."

"If you've got his phone, how can you call him? Maybe I can help." Jane gently grabbed the phone and acted knowledgeable about how it functioned, pulled up the most recent phone numbers, wrote them on her arm and then gave it back, saying, "No signal. The satellites are down now. You'll have to wait. In any case, it sounds like Dr. McKenzie will be back for his phone and that should provide you with some relief."

"He promised. I want to go home. I wish he would hurry up," she said as she lowered herself onto the floor.

Jane could tell she was not herself. Her eyes were moving back and forth too quickly while she was trying to focus on what she was looking at. Jane wished she could do something to help. She sat down next to Deirdre and held her hand for a while and pushed hair out of her face. That was about all she could do. She needed to find Jake. This was the philosophical edge, self-survival versus group survival. Jane got up to leave, wishing she knew what to do to help Deidre. Where is Doctor Browning? He should be here at her side.

As Jane thought more about the moral dilemma, she walked down the tunnel in the direction that Jake took. So far, no one was paying attention to her, but a smaller group of people in business suits formed to talk about running cause and effect programs to predict the best outcome. Jane stopped and asked if anyone saw Dr. McKenzie and everyone shook their heads, while still talking amongst themselves. The intense dialogue moved to the subject of nuclear winter and Jane wished she could stay, but she needed to find Jake so they could get to the parking garage and try out the phone numbers she copied down. There was no way to reach him.

She decided to quit walking and just wait. She slid down the wall and dropped to the floor. The backpack provided a nice support and she fell asleep instantly. A dream developed as she was crawling up rubble and small pieces of concrete started to fall on her. As she struggled, she sunk even deeper and when she stopped, the pile started to fall over her body. She heard someone calling her name. Jake was touching her shoulder to wake her up.

"Oh my. What a dream!" Pausing a moment to realize that the dream was almost reality, she searched for an ordinary question. "Any luck, Jake?"

"No. It's as if he disappeared. When I asked about him, I got a lot of very agitated responses. He's chaining down all doors to the outside and from other levels, preventing people from coming in and contaminating the place. People that need medical attention the most are being locked out. What a beast!"

Jane, still foggy from her dream, suddenly felt very sad and then she remembered. She lifted each sleeve of her shirt that revealed two numbers and smiled. She pulled her satellite phone out and entered the numbers. No service. "Let's get to the ramp." Jake helped her up and they proceeded to walk east according to her map. The challenge was to find the southeastern door that would take them to the ramp.

Finally, they found the ramp with a professional punched out sign showing Parking Ramp Exit across the door. Something was strange. The door was warm and there was a chain wrapped around the door handle, preventing it from opening all but six inches. "It looks like McKenzie was here, Jake." It was easy to take down with her bolt cutters as the intent was to keep someone from entering, but it gave Jane a heavy feeling in her gut.

"Jane, what an act of a kind of domination, authority and control. What would possess anyone to do this? I don't like this guy," Jake said in a neutral tone, lowering his voice, sounding casual. "Let's put on our suits and get out of here."

Jane started to tremble. Nothing was falling in place as she thought it would. Uncertainty was the norm, but she knew enough to keep moving, focus only on the next task. She pulled on her protective suit and found it was heavy, but manageable. It gave her a secure feeling that she could hold up against heat and radiation. Jake was initially having trouble getting it over his larger build and she helped him. Once the suit got past his upper muscular torso, the rest slid into place. Respirators went over their heads and, lastly, insulated gloves. Jane wrapped her backpack and Tool Box with some plastic bags and Jake did the same for the stuff bag. Without ceremony, she pushed open the door. This was the first time seeing what it was like outside. Jane's first impression was thick heat, everywhere. She worried about burning up, but realized the level of protection from the suit should be fine. All they could see was the parking ramp, a hundred feet directly across from the door. They had to cross over and find the opening to the ramp. Concrete debris was everywhere, reminding Jane of her dream. A dense gray fog was swelling up and down over the waves of heat, at times blocking their view. Jane thought about the word dense to describe everything, dense heat, dense air and dense oppressive feelings. She started to walk forward with Jake right behind her. The door slamming shut reminded her if McKenzie came back, he would lock them out of the building. After walking thirty feet, she finally noticed the opening to the ramp. The ramp was intact!

They crossed over piles of debris made up of sharp pieces of glass and concrete. Each step was a challenge of multiple proportions. The heat, the unsure footing and hearing loud explosions became an absolute truth, the overwhelming reality of a catastrophic event. What were they doing out here? This could be their death sentence, even with these suits. How long would they be protected? They came within twenty feet of the opening and Jake shouted, "Yes!" as he recognized the location of the opening. Jane thought about his accident and appreciated how well he was coping through each transition. The fact that he did not see the opening until now made her realize his senses weren't normal. Was he going to tell her? As they entered the ramp, they found the space was clean from any debris. I don't know what's next, but this is a wonderful feeling, thought Jane as she stepped in, aware that they crossed a small divide from the deadliest radiation and heat known to man.

Without discussion and under the safety of the ramp, Jane and Jake walked to the opposite side. This was their first chance to see what buildings were standing. "Look at the shadows of crushed buildings. They are the ghostly remains of a lost corporation," said Jane quietly.

"Jane, are you okay?"

"Yes, I think I am. I have imagined this scene so many times, but now that it is here, I am filled with sadness. Futurists are always thinking about catastrophic events and this would be a reasonable scenario. They would call this a low-probability, high-impact event." Jake looked at her strangely. Jane surprised herself. She learned to not say much to people about her passion for futurism and the complex calculations she used to assess risk. Determining risk and uncertainty about the future was not exactly great conversation. Jane studied these principles so she could start thinking about the risk associated with each possible action. The action of leaving a safe environment, exposing themselves to high levels of radiation and heat was a questionable decision. Their risk just increased a quantum leap higher.

As they turned toward her car, they remained sheltered, with no signs of any structural damage above them. The far end of the ramp had collapsed reminding Jane of the uncertainty of what could happen next. Jane pulled out her keys and remotely started her car. The sound of the engine resonated across the ramp, like something was coming alive.

"Hop in. I'm going to see how far we can drive," she said.

"Jane, that's crazy," said Jake, but he got in anyway.

She drove toward the exit and they started to see the desolation before them. Driving a car across deep crevasses with overbearing heat was hopeless. She backed up, away from the exit. Jane instantly lost all her energy. That was a stupid action, she thought. She sat with tears as random thoughts passed across her brain. She wanted to drive home. That was the plan. It was not going to happen. How could she leave her car behind? The Hummer might have been useful in this situation, but her car had more useful batteries and survival gear. What was her gut telling her to do? Dr. Blue's lovely voice was inside of Jane's head and was repeating, What is in your gut? What is in your heart? How many sessions did Dr. Blue start with a quiet meditation of observing the feeling of her gut and her heart? The grief still lived inside of her, but having Dr. Blue in her head steadied her and she looked up to see Jake staring at her. This was a personality trait she liked about Jake. He studied her with no pretext about knowing what she was thinking. Unless he knew what to do, he stayed pretty quiet. She could deal with that. His dashing good looks helped that as well. She checked herself. That was not a sexist thought, but one recognizing him as a whole person. She would have to study that line of thinking later.

Jane pulled out the phone and dialed the first number for the helicopter but it did not connect. She tried the second number, which rang, but no answer.

"Here, you try," she said. She lay back against her familiar leather seat and tried Dr. Blue's body scan meditation. Her mind was on fire, red hot, needing a cool-down, and her gut was surprisingly quiet, but warm. She felt her stomach sink into her vertebrae, leaving a space between her pants and her skin. It was her heart that was absent like never before. All she could feel was a strange, cold, absent feeling. While this was a practice she worked on with Dr. Blue, she never felt an emptiness this deep before.

Jane was not sure how long she drifted when Jake's face appeared through her open window and said, "What do you think about that plan, Jane?" It was clear by Jane's 'huh' response that Jake was going to have to repeat everything.

"I reached McKenzie's pilot, Flying Hawk. He was headed back here to pick him up. I filled him in and he said he had a lot of information that could be helpful to us. He needs batteries, a lot of them, and kerosene jet fuel. He did mention that as far as he knew, he still worked for the CIA, but he didn't care anymore, knowing what he knows now. Apparently, he was coming back from the University Hospitals which was a complete diversion from his original last mission. He helped this lawyer locate his wife who was trapped somewhere in the tunnels under the hospital. He's heading back here, probably arriving in fifteen, twenty minutes."

"Interesting," said Jane, now recovered from her pause. "It would be amazing if he can bring us home. We can get him batteries from here and I've got lots of fuel stored at home. Will he take us there?"

"I think so. He didn't ask where we were going. I told him about McKenzie's antics, not sure if he understood the subtlety, but he said he would land in about half an hour right next to this parking garage, in front of the atrium, over there. We need to prepare," said Jake, using slow determined speech. Jane was amused. He's probably thinking I'm in some kind of shock. Was she? It made no difference. They needed to take action and prepare.

"Let's start unloading the batteries from my car." Understanding the magnitude of what they needed to do in such a short time, Jane was happy. A chance, a good chance at reaching her home, her sanctuary.

She took out a large canvas sack from her trunk that had wheels attached to a plywood base with multiple pockets and Velcro attachment points on the outside. She had three large, heavy lead acid batteries located in the trunk which she lifted, using a pulley system attached to the trunk that she was quite proud of. She saw these pulleys at a mechanical engineering demonstration at the U and modified them for easier battery deployment. She was able to lift three twelve-volt batteries out one at a time and stack them onto the concrete floor. Jake lifted them into the sack.

She selected three more batteries that were high electrical drain, used in cordless appliances and very handy for drills and power tools for short periods of time. The final battery was her pride and joy, and one which she only recently procured from a junk yard. Evidently, a Tesla was totaled and the owner, who was a good friend of hers, called her and told her he had one undamaged Modual. One lithium battery Modual was worth 230 amp hours and 403 volts, a precious commodity since it was completely rechargeable. She hoped this Hawk person would appreciate it. This left the sack very heavy so she added a few lightweight survival things of interest. Flashlights of every shape and size were Velcroed to the outside of the bag, and a water purification system that consisted of a five-gallon, insulated water bladder. She was missing the stand holding the bladder, but knew they could improvise if needed. She smiled when she took out over one hundred packages of compressed freeze-dried food. She had sixty daily allotments of nutrition, translating to thirty days of food for Jake and herself or twenty if she included Flying Hawk. She pulled out another kit from the glove compartment of over one hundred pharmaceutical drugs, rolled up in a plastic tube and tied with a Velcro tape closure. If she could just get home, she could use the seeds in her Tool Box and start growing plants that could feed both humans and animals. Her smile faded. Did she ever stop to think why she was preparing for a disastrous event? Wasn't it just a game for her to focus on?

Suddenly, the adjacent building creaked loudly, as if in pain. It was an unmistakable sound setting an expectation of something worse. Is the Research building going to collapse? Putting aside her racing mind, she came back to her task and looked at her watch. Hawk was already late.

They rolled the large black sack toward the interface between the atrium and the ramp. She thought she could have retrieved over a hundred lead acid batteries from the cars in the ramp. She also knew they could not haul all of them into a helicopter. Jake finished wrapping the sack and all of the bags with a big roll of plastic they picked up in the tunnel. He had a plan for protecting the contents of the sack which could be removed once they reached her home. She had not thought about this aspect, which surprised her. Jake was an important asset. Her planning process only involved herself with marginal attempts at understanding her own limitations. They finally sat quietly and watched the atrium to the building where the helicopter was supposed to land. Jane went back to the car, for the last time. She was sad. She dug in her pocket and left the keys on the seat, just in case someone could use it in the future.

Hawk was late. The frequency of explosions outside increased. Could this be the fatal one? The outside sounds reminded her of war movies she watched. Well, we are at war, I guess, she thought. Movies did not reflect the reality of sitting in an oven in a sticky, smelly hot suit, swimming in sweat. The grief she was feeling was becoming more comfortable, almost a sanctuary for her to be in. It kind of grounded her and helped her decide what actions to take. Is there a purpose waiting for her in the future?

"I hear it!" Jake shouted. He pointed toward the sky. Jane could almost read his body language. She liked that about him. There was a trust between them now. "Are you still up for this? We can go back."

"I have a bad feeling about staying. I think we should go."

"Yes, I also have that same feeling. Let's do it!"

The helicopter was able to land in a spot at the building entrance which was next to the ramp. The windows of the atrium were gone. No living species was around. They walked outside, Jane with her backpack loosely strapped to her back and carrying her side of the battery bag. They moved slowly toward the helicopter as it was winding down. Flying Hawk jumped out and looked at the large bag they were carrying.

"Hi. My name is Flying Hawk, Hawk for short. You've got quite the load here. I'm impressed." He was dressed in a heavy green camouflage rubber suit made with large zippers, and a massive head respirator. He's prepared, thought Jane.

Jane enumerated what was in the bag and added she had an underground storage of jet fuel, if they could manage to get to her home, twenty miles southeast of here. He plainly said, "I need that jet fuel." Jane realized that this guy was a straight shooter. In one simple comment, she had confirmation of the plan to leave for her home. Jane thought the helicopter already looked damaged. The exterior had splotches of black gum melted into the surface that made the aircraft look almost reptilian.

Jane handed Hawk her water bottle and discussed with him a plan to transfer fuel from her underground tank. He looked at her in instant appreciation and said, "You must have quite a place, Jane. Okay. Let's get moving. I am getting an uncomfortable feeling," and grabbed Jane's handle of the bag and, with Jake's help, lifted the whole thing into the back storage area of the helicopter. Jane looked up. She thought she saw stars against a black sky, but it was quickly replaced by a dead gray cloud moving quickly across the ground. The wind was starting to blow again. What time was it? Her watch was deeply embedded inside her suit.

Flying Hawk and Jake struggled lifting the last heavy bag into the back. She estimated the weight and conveyed that to Hawk. "Will we be safe?" asked Jane.

Hawk smiled for the first time. "Jane, there is nothing safe about anything we're doing."

Jane nodded and pulled herself up to sit in the front seat with Jake following behind. "Here are the GPS coordinates of my house. I suspect we're still going to see the basic roads, but they might also be in black. There are a series of Indian burial grounds we can also use as a reference as we get closer."

"I've got maps downloaded on my computer and I'll fix the destination there. Otherwise, GPS will be of no use," said Hawk. "Here, put these on," handing both of them helmets with radios. He started the propellers and the engine was choking significantly and stopped. "I was afraid of this. Turning off the engine allowed it to cool, but probably caused waxy build-up, clogging the fuel line."

"Try it again and this time, pray a lot," said Jane with as much optimism as she could muster. She was living in the moment now. The propeller turned again with the engine sputtering but came up to a semi-satisfactory sound of engine stability. Hawk lifted the helicopter ten feet high to check out the balance as the engine settled into a rough rhythm. To keep her mind off the sputtering engine, Jane looked out across the horizon as they rose.

"We will see best flying high above the clouds, but the chance of surviving a crash from that height is very low. What approach should we take?" Hawk looked at Jake's and Jane's frozen faces. Jane processed the two options and decided to make the call and said reluctantly, "Low and slow."

"I like the way you think," said Hawk and they rose slowly toward the top of the building. The satellite phone signaled a call. "Pick that up," shouted Hawk. Jane pressed the button to talk and an agitated voice came on. "This is McKenzie. I'm right here. I can hear you. You pick me up, now! I'll have you court-marshalled, Hawk!" Thinking about all of the chains he put in place, that bastard, she thought and hung up the phone. Hawk gave her a thumbs up and as they cleared the building, they flew right over him, frantically waving, all alone. That feels good, thought Jane.

As they rose in height to scale any of the remaining buildings, the degree of the devastation was thorough. Nothing was living below them, nothing moved except for the intermittent swirls of debris as buildings collapsed, slowly, almost undetectably. The ground was the deepest black color, no light escaping, and vision was no more than 50 to 100 feet. Hawk suddenly pulled up, just clearing a tall building that was still standing. Jane screamed and Hawk laughed nervously.

To calm down, Jane thought about the survivors in the building below. They were going to be safe and had a good chance at survival if the right people were in charge. Maybe it was safer to stay behind. As they flew a mile without any change in the scenery, they kept going, feeling the intense heat rising up as the wind blew across the thick glass shield. She noticed all of the cars below were parked, sitting with no signs of occupants. I wonder, she thought, if they had any chance at all. Were they barricaded from entering the building? Her stomach turned when she thought about Dr. Blue. Was the farm safe? How could she reach her now? She sat, fully saddened by her circumstances, for her friends, Dan, Martha, Dr. Blue, and for humanity. Survival was a cruel master. It was what you have left after you survive.

We are a fragile bird, she said to herself. The engine struggled to keep a consistent rhythm, but continued to kick out horsepower. The sky was changing into a deeper black in some places. The black flocked carpet of sticky ash below held no light. The only color was a rose red against black, reflecting the fires burning whatever was left. The longer material burned, the more toxic it was. She could not tell how far they traveled as the surface of the land was indistinguishable. She could detect roads only from the abandoned cars. Finally reaching the freeway, most bridges were compromised with portions left standing. She now knew where she was.

Was that movement below? Something was moving on four legs. Was it a dog or a wolf? Wolves are known for being survivalists. As those figures ran out of her view, they now passed acres of what were suburban houses.

All vanished, replaced by repetitive black dots with no sign of movement anywhere. Again, cars were black fixtures, pulled up to face houses that did not exist. Another similar group ran in the same direction. These were dogs running in a pack, she finally realized. Were they moving toward something safer or away from some kind of danger? What could be learned from them, she wondered. "I think we should start to see the Indian burial mounds. At least I think I know where we are." The engine now sounded like an epiglottic sputter from sleep apnea. Were they losing altitude?

"Prepare," Flying Hawk said with the finality of not willing to engage in any more dialogue. "We're probably going to crash land. I feel it in my bones, I can't explain it. Here we are," as he pointed to their location on the map. We've gone ten miles straight east. Jane quickly calculated the distance to her house. If they crashed here, they would have to walk ten miles to her house. Any farther west, they would be in the suburban hellishness of black tar.

"We can walk," she said. "Go as far as you can. We can walk."

They started to brace themselves in a different way.

"Get out when we touch ground," shouted Hawk.

The helicopter didn't fall from the sky, but swirled back and forth as they lost power. The digital display went out first as the engine continued to run slower and finally stopped with a gasp.

LUMING - 31

Karyn, the cook, was collecting extra chairs for the table and stopped to let Luming know that dinner was now at midnight. Her eyes were a cerulean blue, but it was her smile that brightened up Luming's attitude when she spoke to him as if he belonged here. Strange, he thought, there was a plan for something so ordinary as eating a meal. He then realized that they needed to eat, but maybe more importantly, they needed to be with the whole community. Maybe someone wisely thought that they needed to share, possibly to express sorrow. Then Luming's stomach growled like a tiger and that said it all.

"I have been cooking with Chris and Mina. It takes my mind off what is going on," Karyn said. "Constantine, my husband, left this morning to give a talk on Peruvian Nazca lines. He had our son, Cahoke, with him. They were going to meet my parents who live in San Diego before the conference. I put them on a plane and I'm beyond worried, overwrought is a better word for it. I know I'm helpless to do anything."

Luming placed a soothing hand on her back. "I can relate to that. We don't know the extent of the damage and are of course thinking of worse case scenarios. What kind of retaliation was made? I have a mother in China. We have not spoken for a week. I have a friend, Lois, at the university and she might be okay. My body is heavy and sluggish. It's like another organ was added to my body, crushing me from my heart to my gut."

Karyn looked up at Luming with a strange smirk on her face. "Luming, that kind of sounds poetic. If I know Scar, I'm sure she'll be looking for a poet in residence. She was very close to Adam until he died, suddenly. You know, come to think of it, his poems are still located in the library somewhere. She never talks about him. You know, we planned for catastrophe many times, but never thought it would happen, at least not this way. How many times did we conduct drills with different scenarios? I was getting kind of sick of it. Over here," as she pointed to wall of the dining room, "Constantine and I painted this fresco. He designed it and painted it with the vegetable dyes I grew in the greenhouse. That was such an innovative time for us, just before we conceived our precious Cahoke, who's still the best example of our collaborative accomplishments."

Luming handed her a handkerchief he carried in his pocket. He comforted her with his hand on her arm as tears fell from her eyes. Comforting words and actions were going to be important in these situations, thought Luming. She finally stopped with a deep sigh of exhaustion.

"There's a lot to do, Luming," she said. "Work will not fill the gap in my heart. I had no idea that I've already started to grieve as if my family was dead. Up until now, I was holding on to hope, but in reality, I'm probably wrong. We were just in our backyard last evening, playing catch with all of the neighbor kids. I did remember to pause and appreciate that unbelievable moment of happiness we all enjoyed. It sounds ironic now."

"Do you feel better, recalling that moment?" asked Luming.

"Not really. I still feel hopeful, but I might be suffering from confusion from what happened and what I'm assuming happened. There's no need to be certain about death, what's the hurry? Why am I here alone? I always thought of something happening, but never without my family. This is so new. I better keep myself occupied, Luming."

"Let me help," he said. He moved the folding chairs around the table and Karyn kept opening cupboards and handing him centerpieces, placemats, candles, plates and silverware, which he laid on the table, not knowing what she wanted to do with all of these things. He turned and said, "Where is everyone? Who have I not met?"

"Well, I am not sure who you have met," she said, grinning at the stupidity of his comment. Sometimes he just said stupid things just to offset the heaviness of the moment. "You've met Mina in the kitchen, right?"

"Yep. I've also met Troy."

"That's great. He's Sharme's son. He's quiet, but indispensable. He started doing software development as a hobby and then went to freelance for a living. He just helped me out about an hour ago. He hooked up a battery system for me on the spot so I could move my boxes around using this electronic dolly. You know, there is a lot going on in the sub-tunnel. I should bring you down there. This can wait," she said as she waved her hand over the large oak table.

"Don't go out of your way for me."

"Don't worry, I won't. I think you might be useful anyway."

Karyn started walking down toward Tunnel 3 and Luming followed. Karyn twisted and lifted the handle of a large round manhole cover that Luming missed completely, having walked over it several times. As Karyn stepped down, a light turned on. "This should be easy for you, Luming. There are eighteen rungs," and she disappeared down the hole.

It seemed like a lot more than eighteen rungs, but Luming managed to get down with his dignity intact. As he jumped onto the concrete floor, an echo resonated. He sensed the room was like an empty concrete container, a completely different environment than the cistern. With the exception of pillars every ten feet, Luming looked out at a room so large that he could not see the end of it. In the middle of the room was a long table where both men and women sat with keyboards in front of them. A sea of hard-bound books were piled in the middle of the table. As Luming followed Karyn toward the table, the people did not acknowledge the echoing footsteps announced their visit. A large man, older, was talking.

"Frank, it is because of the lighting that I am thinking we need to reorient the beds to accommodate the new seeds, which is why I keep asking for the growing conditions before we germinate one seed." He stood up from the table, slowly, with wobbly knees. He started to walk around the table, stretching out his calves and lifting his knees waist-high.

"Can't everyone see what has happened? We are subsistence living now. We can't afford to grow pot anymore. Every possible space needs to be converted," a gray-haired woman said, her body motionless in her chair as Frank continued to circle.

"Trudy, we need to do what we do best. A barter community will spring up and our product will be needed to fill a variety of medical and recreational use, more than ever. We do our best when we are future-focused and building those scenarios that got us to this place. Granted, we need to seek balance and grow plants to survive, but not sacrifice one for the other. Let's do both."

"Bill, we are almost full circle for the millionth time. Let's start figuring out what we can do. Let's put two plans in place and then decide. Who wants to do both?"

"McLane, what are we, in third grade?" said Trudy. "If we keep talking, I think we'll begin to see what emerges and then come out without having to tediously analyze each data point. Our minds and our bodies have already done that. I suspect we are not going to change if we stop and do all of this analysis. We just keep at it until we see something new and create our future from there. I think we need to reach deeply within ourselves to find our answers."

"This is survival, Trudy. Until now, we were behaving on a very superficial level," said Frank. "We need to work differently."

Trudy sighed. "Frank, that's what I've been saying. Lincoln, you have been very quiet, what do you think?"

"We have visitors. Welcome to our dungeon. You must be Luming." said Lincoln.

"Scar thought it would be a good idea to bring Luming here," said Karyn.

Luming was surprised at this introduction but looked around and sensed that the reference to Scar shifted everyone in their seat. He wondered why Karyn used Scar's name at this time. It happened so naturally. He had no idea she was behind this visit. It was not fear, but it seemed like her name elevated them out of their own personalities and into a fresher space.

"Luming, I'm Frank, in charge of Production. Around the table is…"

"I think we can introduce ourselves, Frank. I'm Trudy. I guess you can call me a plant breeder. I cross and hybridize plants and have been doing that for thirty years. I grew up in a farm in Iowa and worked for the Steineford Seed Company which my uncle founded in the early '60s. I… I'm sorry, I am going on quite a bit. This is all so new to us. We are not really acting like ourselves. We were focused on immediate survival and started to grieve a lot, each in our different ways. Scar came around and gave us a project which shifted our perspective and now I believe we are looking forward, somewhat."

"I can relate to that," said Luming.

"Thank you, Trudy. Bill, do you have a few words?" said Lincoln.

"I'm Bill. I work closely with Trudy, taking her hybrids and matching them to the right genetics, which Francine is responsible for." Bill pointed at the corner of the large table to a short, younger woman, with white and purple hair.

"Hey, Luming. I have been trying to figure out how I know you. I am thinking we met at a SURF club meeting, with Bai, one of the Five Guys. Does that ring a bell?" said Trudy.

"Brother organized community meditation classes with Bai. I might have attended one of those classes. I know Brother was into Pokeman but I don't know much about SURF."

"Maybe that was it. Oh yeah, while I'm the resident plant breeder, I also love Beethoven, but can play Chopin competently. Actually, I can play most of the masters. I love classical music, would rather play it than listen to it. I like to experience the music as it was written and feel more intimate with the composer while I'm playing. I've been wondering what I'm playing tonight, if asked, that is. I could select a more recognizable piece, but Mendelssohn keeps going through my head. We are underground and I suspect we are going to be here for a very long time."

There, she said it first, thought Luming. The elephant in the room.

"My name is George William McClane. GW for short. We've been sorting out our future, using limited, almost non-existent information of what is going on at the surface, locally and globally. It was the only way we could do what Scar asked us to do when she said, "Plan for the worst future. Assume we live, but only with a life expectancy of five more years." That assumption seemed strange at first, but it has provided a very useful timeline. Maybe after five years, we can leave or maybe after five years, we are dead. It has an interesting finality about it. We decided it oddly gave us some relief and support around what to do next... for the next five years. It's still a little mystifying."

"Five years does sound fatalistic," said Luming.

"Based on Trudy's calculations of where we think the bombs landed, she estimated the half-life of each radioactive isotope in each region and determined we would have to live down here for five years to survive in a healthy way. We have to set up an endogenous society that will not depend on the surface for survival over this time period. We're already off the grid which may prove to be a big advantage to our choices in the future."

Bill stood up and again started to walk around the table. "Look, Luming, you are extremely lucky to have come across our little enclave and, sure, things happen for a reason. We are democratic in every detail of this operation and we believe this will continue regardless of what we end up doing. Our gang, including yourselves, represents all points in a continuous circle. We will fit you in as an equal voice once we get ourselves sorted out." Bill reversed his direction. "I have bad knees. I used to run marathons and need to move around a lot. I suggest we all eventually find a physical routine, right, Trudy?"

"Don't go there!" she said.

"All right, children," said Frank. "Lincoln, what do you think?"

"I think we had a nice break. Luming, please feel free to come back any time, but we should resume working the question. We'll have a meal at midnight that should relax us while we hold new places for a new group of people. Trudy, please play your Mendelssohn tonight. You're never wrong about your selections. Your repertoire is a Hallmark card of musical options."

"Thanks, everyone, for this introduction. I would love to contribute at a deeper level, but right now, I think I will continue to roam. This room was a surprise to me. I've been in all of the tunnels and the library, the grow room, the kitchen and the cistern..."

"Wow, the cistern, that is interesting," said a woman walking in from the shadows.

"Oh, yes. Luming, this is Sharme," said Frank.

"Sorry, I have not been observing for long," she said. "I found it interesting to watch everyone's body language toward Luming. The words were kind, but I'm not sure about the bodies. I'm wondering what that means, but more about that later. Yes, the cistern, Luming, is very special. It's our most vulnerable place and I am surprised that you were already taken there. By whom?" she said, extending the last word like an alto French horn.

Trudy interrupted, "Don't worry about Sharme." This exchange was frightening to Luming on a number of levels different from anything he experienced so far. He was not used to talking about anything personal and it seemed like Sharme already knew the answer. The deep flush he started to feel rose from his chest to his neck and head.

"Scar took me to the cistern," said Luming. There was an unusual silence in the room. Everyone was looking at Sharme for her response. "I found it very peaceful and was intrigued both by the engineering and the symbolism of the images on the wall," he added finally. Was there anything else to say?

"Luming, never mind. It's none of my business. I was just curious. We are often troubled by others who do not share in our commitment, especially anyone with an ego that supersedes the good of the group. As far as I can tell, you are nothing like that, especially if Scar shared one of our most scared places with you already. I understand you have a corporate background, I'm sure you're going to be very helpful." Sharme then turned and left.

Taking this as a good time to leave, Luming backed up, taking in the scene of a table of people with amazing intellects, obviously comfortable with each other, solving their future, he said goodbye and then turned and walked away. Karyn followed him across the vast space toward the rungs. Luming felt slightly hopeful that he could find a way to contribute. Every contribution was necessary. What syndrome is the opposite of survivor guilt? Survivor independence? Guilt, in modern times, is almost a physiological term. Luming once heard his English professor quote C.S. Lewis, "I side impenitently with the human race against the modern reformer." He was living for the human race now. Was this home? Not really, but he was moving in a slow state of emergence and mystery that held the meaning of what was next. His previous life was in the middle of society. Now he was living in a fringe community which potentially could protect him far better than any modern life he thought he led.

"You are deep in thought," said Karyn. "There are plans to build living quarters out of this space." She twirled around, looking up at the lower ceiling and then at Luming. "Are you worried about us?"

"Hmmm, I've had no less than ten thousand thoughts since T zero. I'm not sure what to think. I think we are going to have lots of challenges in living out our future. What do you compare it to? The life we had before? I know I wish I had a toothbrush with me and a dog. I think a dog would help me feel a little bit more human," said Luming.

"Good to know. I need to get back." Karyn left him at the bottom of the rungs. Luming wasn't sure what was coming out of his mouth. He needed to find a quiet space.

DAN - 32

Dan walked toward the library, still unsure of what Scar wanted him to do. She asked him to review the Ocha Rituals. He knew that ocha was the Japanese word for tea and he even took part in several tea ceremonies while doing business in Japan. It was a very precise practice and often very nerve racking for him. He had to pretend to like it, while never feeling comfortable. Throughout the ceremony, there were a lot of awkward pauses. Protocol dictated that it was important to compliment the tea cake. He remembered a very awkward silence after his comment on how spongy and white the cake was. Well, hopefully, they are more casual about it here.

As he headed down Tunnel 9, he heard female voices speak with overtones of frustration. A corporate technique he found useful was to spy on conversations. It was amazing what you could hear just hanging out in the hallway, pretending to be studying papers or shuffling a briefcase. Spying allowed him to know what was in people's hearts as they spoke to friends and colleagues they trusted. It was a clean, non-disruptive way to understand things without a social filter. Midwesterners made it prohibitive to confront situations head on. For him, spying illuminated problems and helped him understand how to work in various situations. He was convinced that this was a helpful technique when used honorably.

Dan waited patiently around the corner to hear the debate. They spoke freely, like people talk when they are not concerned about being overheard.

"How much is enough?" said one female voice.

"What was she thinking?" said a second voice.

"There is nothing we can do now," said the first voice. The conversation was congealing in Dan's head. Maybe Scar's decisions were not being supported? Was her compassionate gesture of adding people with no connections to the Seed Bank in question? What was Chris' role in bringing Luming and Brother here? As Dan continued to listen, it sounded like there were multiple objections about the new people. Typically, an arduous vetting process was used to add members. Who was this Luming guy who walked around, looking busy? Was Scar having a relationship with this guy? "Unheard of," said one voice. "Scar has not been romantically involved since Adam."

Dan thought about what he was hearing and realized how important talks like this were. There was a need for people to share their worst thoughts, get it out and clear their minds of the rubble knocking around in their heads. He wanted to interrupt, but realized how devious his spying looked. Maybe the Ocha Ritual could help ease tension at the Seed Bank.

He did not feel what they said was challenging Scar's leadership. The closed stacks shut out Members that did not make it to the tunnels. That was a harsh but necessary action, and no one disagreed with the decision. They needed to acknowledge that and accept the people that were allowed in.

Dan also recognized the combination of circumstance, grief and hope at the same time. God knows how many times he thought about where Brenda was this morning. Was she alive and struggling to survive some place? Washington DC was probably a big target. Estimating her timeline, she was probably taking a taxi from the airport to a conference center mid-morning. That's a horrible thought. Can one grieve without knowing if someone died? What if your son was on the bus; what if your wife was in the basement or what if your mother rode her motorcycle that day? So many circumstances would determine if they were living or dead. How long would it be before they could find answers? Will information be there to find out? The irony was, everyone was grieving, but Scar focused them on tasks that minimized time to dwell on feelings.

Saving the seeds in the SB and cultivating plants for future civilizations must make these people feel valuable. With that thought, Dan looked for Chris.

Dan addressed Troy as he entered the Hub. It was conveniently set up right next to the library. "Troy, I need to talk to Chris right now. Do you know where he's at?"

"Are you asking where he is right now?" He was nervous about the question. "Okay, take a look at this." The screen summarized the whole complex. He typed in Chris and it showed he was in the kitchen.

"Thanks, Troy. That is amazing and could be very helpful in the future." Troy impressed him with all of things he did so effortlessly. He had respect for him and his quiet ways, although he seemed to respond to questions literally. As Dan set off for the kitchen and got closer, he started to smell an unbelievable aroma coming through the door. Dan was sure he never passed this area before, as he would have remembered seeing a door this unique. It was a solid cherry wood painted with a scene that looked like an Italian landscape with tall cypress trees lining a road up a green hillside. Knowing that something good was behind the door, he opened it into a full commercial kitchen. Warm waves of bread smells hit him in the face as several dozen fresh baguettes were being removed from the oven. Pies were laid out on all the surfaces and a woman stood on a stool, assembling what looked like an enormous pan of lasagna. The way he salivated as he opened his mouth to speak embarrassed Dan. "Hi, everyone." Right in the middle of the kitchen was Chris, stuffing a turkey.

Chris smiled and said, "Hi Dan. Yeah, please meet Karyn. She and Mina are the geniuses behind this dinner. I'm not sure where Mina went. I'm just the sous chef. According to our survey, we have from eighteen to twenty-one people to feed. Half are vegetarians and five vegetarians are gluten free, so we have been changing things like crazy to make everyone happy. At least for this dinner."

"Why so extravagant?" asked Dan. "Shouldn't we be conserving our resources?" Chris looked wilder than normal, but he was extending a strong, positive smile with an energetic bounce to his step. He had to be tired.

"I'm not sure how to answer that question. I'm just following orders. Maybe it's the last supper," said Chris.

"I hope that's not what we're calling it," said Dan. "What can you tell me about the Ocha Ceremony? Scar asked me to check it out."

"Right," Chris said matter-of-factly. "Are we going to incorporate that into the dinner? That would be interesting." Not waiting for an answer, Chris smiled, took off his apron, and waved goodbye to Karyn. "Let me help you with that. Come, follow me."

Chris crossed the kitchen to another door that led into the dining room, a large oval space that had a table set up for twenty people. The table was a long and oval shape, reflecting the shape of the room, with four serving trolleys set out around it. Dan noticed the walls immediately. Greek Minoan images filled the wall in the color of oceans. Dolphins were swimming around the room from all angles. It gave a feeling of being surrounded by water, as if they were sitting at the bottom of the ocean. Mobile track lighting was placed onto areas that made the blue shades glisten and sparkle in and out as the lighting angle changed. The quality of this installation was a complete surprise to Dan.

"Amazing," said Dan.

"Two of the original Seed Bank founders, Constantine and Karyn, completed this mosaic the first year of living in community. Constantine was a trained mosaic artist, having just studied in Rome and Karyn, a pottery artist. He prepared the mosaic shapes, and she created the glazes. The design says a lot about how they fell in love. They also had a hand in designing the Sacred Center."

"The Sacred Center? What's that about?"

Chris sat down at the table and pointed to the chair for Dan to sit down. "Let's start with the Ocha Ritual," he said. "We'll visit the Sacred Center later. The Seed Bank has been involved with marijuana since the beginning. We've had lots of experience dealing with the Bank members working here high. We've been breeding all kinds of marijuana plants with Sativa and Indica mixtures. Our quality-assurance staff tests for the percent of THC and its analogs. They also try out each new strain and make recommendations for medicinal and recreational use."

"How do you monitor people getting high while working?"

"There is little tolerance for making mistakes. If someone cannot handle the stone level they selected, they take themselves off the shift and find a replacement. This subject has been hotly debated over the years and members are comfortable where we landed. While rules for working were carefully debated and constructed, we also wanted to create a ritual that honored this as a spiritual place in our lives and the deepened experience of sharing it in community. We added a ritual around drinking Ocha which involves carefully selecting the correct potency."

I'm thinking nothing gets missed around here, thought Dan.

Chris then reached over to a small teapot sitting on the table and said, "Try Ocha-O. Drink it slowly, and I promise it is pleasant, like a ten-year Bordeaux."

"No, sorry, Chris. I'm too old for this. It's just not me. I'm a beer drinker." He was feeling a little strange. Regardless, Chris was relaxed and did not show any concern.

"In case you change your mind, this is the weakest tea, specifically designed for inexperienced users or anyone who enjoys a breezy lift to their day. Ocha-O is a tea that is a combination of Peppermint-Pine and Serenity^R, the lowest level of THC, containing more Indica than Sativa. Ocha-O is refreshing and relaxing, much like lying next to a calm pool with a waterfall next to the woods. If the waterfall sound did not calm your nerves, the sweet smell of pine would."

"I'm sure it's fine for others, but not me," said Dan.

"That's cool, man. Most of us are familiar with the social stigma to using so we would be the last people on earth, no pun intended, to shame anyone into partaking," said Chris. He looked serious and continued. "We have what we call Ocha-B. This is our medium strength tea, having a higher THC level equal in Indica and Sativa, combined in an earthy mixture of black cherry and rum flavoring close to feeling, tasting and smelling earthy. Ocha-B is balanced for maximum cerebral stimulation that takes the edge off. This is by far the favorite of the group."

"I'm sure it is," said Dan, feeling uncomfortable, thinking of Lizzy being exposed to such a dangerous environment.

Chris continued, "The strongest tea, Ocha-T, is 100% cerebral, all Sativa, and if drunk on its own, provides an energizing lift to the mind. This one is hard to reproduce each time and its potency varies widely. Our current strain is one of the best."

Dan was slow to recognize the meaning behind the ceremony. He mistakenly thought the ceremony was about tea. I wonder if I should warn everyone about this, he thought. The seriousness of how Chris presented this caused Dan to pause and think about how little he understood these people he was cohabitating with.

"It took the SB five years to complete and clarify this ritual. We also have abstainers in our group, which is perfectly acceptable. What people used to call contact high is an actual phenomenon we've documented. You'll find that study in the library. If the tea ceremony is done properly, a spiritual connection is made."

He thought about what Chris was saying. He could not take a chance with his responsibilities with Lizzy and Betty. He came to the party with pre-established ideas about marijuana and he would stick with them. "Chris, there's too much going on. I will pass, but I'll still support the ceremony."

"Dan, appreciate your position and I must get back to the kitchen. I'll leave you with some music and some Ocha. I'm pretty sure it's the teatotaler version. This music sequence is called Ocha-O and was designed by one of our Members, now missing. Enjoy and see you later."

Dan thought about everyone now living in the Seed Bank. Had he met everyone? I wonder if I know all of their names? Mina and Karyn were joining them and eleven other people, including Chris and Dorothy. He must have forgotten names already. With thirteen people from the Seed Bank and four non-members, they could enjoy an amazing meal, get to know each other and form connections. He thought about Brother doing a meditation at the beginning. He'd never meditated in his life. Another shift in his value system. He was sure that Betty had.

Differences were overwhelming to him. He was old and drinking marijuana tea or meditating were best left to younger generations. He read many times that there were advantages to meditation that would benefit most people. He could not even speculate who meditated and who didn't. What if they meditated in a group and then moved to a tea ceremony? That would emphasize differences between the SBers and his group. This could get interesting, very fast.

As he sipped the tea, he looked at the detail of the mosaic surrounding him. Dan started to notice the music. The notes of the piano were played softly, part classical and part jazz. The flute playing was light, and was mixed with a strong, slow drumbeat that offset the flutiness of the music. Flutiness? he thought. Is that a word? He now looked at the oceanic scene and was sure the dolphin's skin was glistening gold from a sun and not a light source. As he mused about the wall, Brother, Betty and Lizzy came in and Betty chirped, "Hi, Dan." Brother came up and hugged him and Dan felt a shift to a higher energy level.

"I'm starved," said Betty. "Here's Lizzy. She just had a nap and I am sure she would love to be held by you, Dan." Dan took Lizzy from Betty and thought they both looked exceptionally beautiful.

Brother leaned over and gave Lizzy a pinch on her cheek, which made her look at him and smile. "Anything I can do to help you?"

"I am not sure," said Dan. "There is a teapot of Ocha here. It does not have any THC, Betty. Have you tried this?"

"I recall trying Ocha-O for the first time several years ago. I remember its lovely fragrance, but did not recall much of an effect," said Betty. "If this is plain tea, I'll try it.

"Let me pour you some," said Dan.

LOIS - 33

Lois was awake, meeting Clark's green eyes of concern. Her head was pounding as she heard voices speaking behind Clark.

"Look, she's awake. She should be okay. I'm sorry, but I had to stop her before she hurt herself and us," said Dr. Anthony.

"We've been through this already. There was no need to hit her on the head," said a softer female voice.

As if he was reading her mind, Clark said, "That was Karey speaking," and frowned. "He whacked you over the head with a book. A rather large textbook."

"Whom are you talking about? What was I doing? I remember nothing."

"Do you remember watching the pictures the robot was taking? You puked good into a bucket, stood up and ran to the doors. It looked like you wanted to open them. The good doctor grabbed a book from a shelf, ran up to you and hit you before you opened the doors. He claims you would have exposed us to radiation, which isn't true. He's a little crazy, if you ask me. There was no need to hit you. What if he gave you a concussion? Just lay back for a while longer."

Suri came up to Lois and started to lick her face. Lois grabbed her fur down to the softest downy hair and pulled Suri into her arms. Suri sank to her knees and lay down beside Lois, pressing against her as close as she could. Lois felt the deep connection she needed. What started as an overwhelming moment changed into a heavy numb one that weighed on her body through the blankets under her, as she felt the hard surface of the floor. She was disoriented. She couldn't move her jaw up and down.

Typically, the strong one, she needed to accept the dullness she felt. The life she knew was gone. Did Dan make it out with Elizabeth and Betty? The lasting image of those physics students branded her soul.

Lois woke again with no one hovering over her. Suri was still tightly bonded to her body. She had a strange feeling, but could not put her finger on it. She wondered how much time passed. The clock said 8:05.

"Lou here, how are you feeling? We worried about you. I know you are recovering. Wanted to let you know we finally received some information from a satellite and have been planning to reach the Seed Bank while you were out. There's a strange message being repeated in several languages. Three words."

"How long have I been out? What three words?"

"About three hours. The message repeats Patience, Compassion and Simplicity in a loop," said Lou.

Lois sat up and was irritated by the buzzing from the florescent lighting. Everyone in the room was engaged. Three of the Five Guys were staring at computer screens. She could see that one was a split screen of several building blueprints being panned back and forth between screens. She saw Dr. Anthony and Clark working on something that looked like a space suit with goggles and Karey was heating water on a Bunsen burner. Seeing Karey, lining up the teacups, pulling teabags from her many purses, gave Lois a peaceful feeling. She slowly moved around with intention that almost seemed ceremonial, Lois lay back to stare at the ceiling and the cracks and fissures embedded in the ceiling. Is this structure going to hold? There were frequent sounds that shook the building, but the force of impact seemed less than before.

Qiang walked over, dressed in his blue plaid flannel shirt and hiking boots. "We hooked up to a satellite for fifteen minutes. Other than that, there is a communication blast every 120 minutes that repeats three words, Simplicity, Patience, Compassion. Bai is sure it is from an old text from Lao Tzu, but we have been too busy to research this. My calculation shows we'll have access to one satellite every sixteen hours, but there may be others. The blasts took out most satellites. There are very few that were not damaged by nuclear blasts. Most satellites at 22,000 feet were affected."

"Too technical for me," said Lois. Her head was pounding.

"Sorry. I'm a communications nerd and can't help myself. We'll try to keep this as simple as possible for you."

Cong got out of his chair, wearing his familiar vest and corduroy pants, looking like a 19th century poet or professor. "How are you feeling now?"

"I'll get you some water," said Qiang, leaving Lois alone. She saw they were all making quick observations of her as they communicated to each other silently.

As Lois looked around, she saw the large screen hanging from the wall that had impacted her so strongly. Now, the only picture the robot's camera was taking were motionless shapes, covered by cloaks of gray flocking.

Karey came over, leaned down and gave her a hug. "Lois, I'm so glad you're better." They stayed in their hug for longer than Lois was comfortable, and Lois pulled back first. "When you are feeling like getting up, I could use some help making tea. We should update you on all the things that have happened since you were out. Your brother has been amazing. He is so helpful and innovative in finding solutions to a multitude of issues." She got up and walked back to the kitchen area. Lois thought, Clark, helpful, innovative? What's happened?

Lois felt some peer pressure to stand and do something as Cong, instead of Qiang, came back with her water. Cong had a flaxen shirt with a knitted vest on, an ascot and pants with loafers. She appreciated their attempt, now more than ever, to communicate their identity in such a humorous way. Everyone seemed to be strangely calm. Was that for her benefit? Here they were, survivors, for now, surrounded by extreme decimation of matter and disconnected from humanity, including the people trapped in tunnels. This immensely talented group still operated with a sense of purpose. As she stood, she looked over at Clark and he smiled at her with his just-a-minute hand wave that typically meant not to bug him right now. When was the last time Clark focused or engaged in anything? She pulled herself up from the floor and walked over to Karey with Suri moving tight to her left calf.

"What can I do?" Lois said.

"I'm making Lavender Dream tea with biscuits and jam. I selected this tea due to its calming effect that does not make you sleepy," said Karey.

"Is that why everyone's so calm?" asked Lois.

"Could be, but I doubt it. You might be confusing that with intense concentration. I've only known the Five Guys through their reputation, but there's something strange about being around them. They somehow get us to focus less on personal issues and more on the greater good." After a small pause, she said, "Except for Dr. Anthony. He is the strangest character. In fact, he's darn creepy," Karey said with a laugh.

They worked together quietly and finally brought two teapots to the center of the circle of chairs they originally sat in hours ago. They added chairs, creating a larger circle. Lois brought the tray filled with an assortment of mismatched bone china teacups and saucers. Some were blue with pink flowers and some were cream-colored with golden rims. The cups reminded her of her grandmother's set of bone china she used for special occasions. Oh no, she thought. What happened to them? She wished nothing bad to happen to her grandparents. She never wished them harm.

Without a word, everyone stopped and assembled into the circle, all nine of them. Karey poured tea into each cup and Lois passed them out and then sat down in the chair next to Clark. Clark put his arm around her and then held her hand for a moment. She could not get over the change in him. Even the lines of his face were set deeper.

Karey passed the biscuits around the circle, starting with Cong and ending with Lois. Karey finally sat down in the remaining empty chair. Bai was wearing his flowing cotton shirt with linen pants, a la sixties hippie, Hung was in full military camouflage, and Lou was like a suburban dad in Dockers and a polo shirt.

Cong leaned forward and looked around at everyone. He turned to Lois. "How are you feeling?"

"You can all stop asking me how I am feeling now. I puked in a bucket, irrationally raced to open the door, was hit by a book and passed out. Let's cut to the chase. What's going on?" said Lois.

Dr. Anthony stood up and walked over to Lois and picked up her hand. "You reacted emotionally to what you were seeing on the screen, I felt I had to stop you. There is no excuse for my bad behavior. I wanted to act fast before it was too late. Please accept my apology," as he bent his head to kiss her hand.

Lois pulled back her hand. "I don't know you, Dr. Anthony. What universe supports hitting someone on the head with a book? In fact, why are you here?" Dr. Anthony went back and slid sheepishly into his chair as if an angry woman was an impossible situation for him to handle.

An uncomfortable silence took place, followed by, "Lois, let's get back to that question later. Let's get you up to speed," said Qiang. "While you were out, we connected with a satellite and found out many things." Lois settled down into her chair with this information. "We now know that all major cities around the world were attacked by nuclear bombs. No one knows the extent of the damage, nor do we know how this was even possible. There are groups, like ourselves, leaving messages using the remaining satellites that survived the blasts intact. Attempts are being made to connect these sites in order to assess the damage, understand the politics, and even look toward trading assets. It is a common conclusion that the cities affected will have unacceptable radioactive levels for a minimum of two years. Anyone within a ten-mile radius outside of most cities are advised not to enter the cities without complete body protection from radiation. Blockade may be already formed to limit access to heavily bombed areas."

"Lois, I'm not sure we know what is going on, but we have been doing a lot of speculating," said Cong. "Dr. Anthony has been an asset to us so far, despite the fact that he behaves like a pompous asshole."

"Hey, Cong, be gentle," joked Dr. Anthony. "I have something precious. I have access to seeds. Seeds that are beyond remarkable. Seeds that may be a key to our survival. You know the Seed Bank, Lois?"

"Yes. We were just in contact with them before the bombs hit. Luming was there and contacted us. Do we know if Dan, Betty and Lizzy made it?"

Cong shook his head. "We don't know, Lois but we will find out soon. Dr. Anthony, can you share with Lois what is going on with the seeds?"

"Ah, yes. Dorothy Jarvinen, the Growth Coordinator and my contact from Finland, came to see me today with information about a catastrophic event that would happen within hours of her visit. Because of my arrangement with Dr. Zhi, the inventor, I was the only US citizen who took his seeds and put them into production, and scaled them up, using an engineering term."

"I thought you were a physician?" said Lois.

"Yes, but I grew up in Iowa, and I have been planting these special seeds each year, increasing the numbers exponentially, that can be distributed and sold once they're approved by the USDA, FDA and EPA. I've produced enough seeds to plant 800 acres of crop, albeit illegally, but we were sure approval would take place. Dorothy was at my door today, asking me for as much as I could give her. I provided what she asked for. She wanted to bring all the seeds she could to the Seed Bank as a lifeline against what would happen. That state-of-the-art facility should be able to propagate them sufficiently to feed survivors after this horrible holocaust."

"What's so special about these seeds?" asked Lois.

"They have been genetically modified to produce complete protein, including Vitamin B_{12}. This is a revolutionary breakthrough. No plants to date have been able to provide complete protein. Because they are modified from soybeans, they are also nitrogen fixing and do not require a lot of fertilizer." Dr. Anthony paused for a minute. As if on signal, he nodded to Qiang. "Dr. Zhi also has a new line of modified plants that I've been working on just one year. Zhi modified the genes of these plants to grow by respiration instead of photosynthesis and gave them to me to scale-up." Dr. Anthony paused again. "I have a bag of them hidden to take to the Seed Bank."

What a drama queen, thought Lois. "So, tell me, Dr. Anthony, what does that mean?'

"What that means is you can pair two kinds of plants underground without sunlight. Instead of photosynthesis, these plants will breathe oxygen just like humans. Grown together, they can sustain forever without sunlight. This was Dr. Zhi's most amazing innovation and something he shared with very few individuals. I'm pretty sure that even the Seed Bank is not aware of them. But seeds are seeds. Once they are in someone's hands, anyone can take them and grow them without Dr. Zhi's permission. The idea was clever, if you ask me." The room went silent. The Five Guys moved in discomfort and looked at each other, naturally communicating in silence.

"You mean to tell me that Dorothy was given the seeds containing the complete protein, but you held back the seeds that could save civilization in times of nuclear winter? This is new information," said Cong. "Why would you do that?"

"Well, Dorothy's story sounded fantastic. Nuclear bombs would hit hundreds of cities. She needed to take the seeds to the Seed Bank. A place that will store them under controlled conditions. She wanted the Seed Bank to grow them underground, in case of this catastrophic event she described. She said they would have a perfect home. I thought her story was preposterous, so I held them back."

"Dr. Anthony." Cong stood up with his chest pushed out and his hands on his waist. "I don't believe that story for a minute. If you did not believe her, then why did you contact us to move this bag of seeds for you into our bunker? You acted as if you believed the bombing would take place. Dr. Anthony, your information is new and we're very surprised. In fact, it disturbs me that you are now just disclosing this information. What we just learned from Dr. Anthony is critically important," Cong said as if Dr. Anthony was not even there. "We need to get these seeds to the Seed Bank."

"Exactly." The twisted smile on Dr. Anthony's was disturbing to Lois. She sensed she was not alone.

"Dr. Anthony, are you blackmailing us to provide transportation to the Seed Bank?"

"I must have missed something," said Karey, now standing and looking directly at Anthony. "How could anyone think only of himself when they hold technology that could save the future of the planet?"

"Look, I need not answer to you, my dear." Dr. Anthony tilted his glasses down his nose and stood up to look down at Karey. "The Seed Bank has an amazing capacity for survival and they've planned around it for decades. I need to be there to provide them with the seeds and pass on important information on how to grow the plants."

"You're an asshole," said Karey. Clark grinned and nodded.

"I'm torn, Dr. Anthony." said Cong. "Let's be clear. With this absurd threat to hold the seeds back unless you get transportation out of here completely changes our plans. I'm sure the Seed Bank would not welcome you under any circumstance if you are operating on a moral compass of a scam artist. The only reason, I mean the only reason, we would provide you transportation would be for the good of the whole, the people who can use these seeds to grow plants for the future. Hmmm." Cong looked like he ran out of energy or was deep in thought. He never lost his cool. Again, a long silence transpired.

Hung sighed. "To change the subject, let's fill Lois in about where we're at with the rescue in finding Michael and Marcella. Lois, Flying Hawk contacted us we during the time of our satellite connection. He was searching channels and connected with us. Apparently, he's been flying a government helicopter since the bombs hit and dropped off this guy Michael who was looking for his wife, Dr. Marcella Brown. He asked us to locate Michael who is somewhere in the University tunnels underneath the hospital and bring him to the Archibald football field where he will be waiting tomorrow."

"Incredible," said Lois. "I can't imagine the bravery it took to fly into this tragic mess. I wonder what that was like? It must be hot, swirling winds, soot with toxic levels of radiation."

"Hawk picked up our signal just when he was leaving the stadium. If we find Dr. Brown and Marcella, Hawk will pick them up. He also promised to bring some provisions that we could use. Mostly food, in return for medical supplies, which we have an abundance of. He said his fuel supply is fine."

"I get it," said Lois. "It sounded like a reasonable tradeoff and helps everyone involved. We reunite Michael and Marcella in exchange for additional supplies. Hawk must be an amazing guy."

"Now it should be no problem for Hawk to drop me off with the seeds at the Seed Bank on their way back," said Anthony.

"Why would we allow Anthony to use up a space on a helicopter to the Seed Bank?"

"Well, listen, Lois," said Anthony. "You have no choice. Not one of you would hold back this technology, critically necessary for survival underground during a nuclear winter. Unless you want to jeopardize human lives, you have no choice but to take me to the Seed Bank."

"This is extortion. There's no other name for it!" She was angry. She stood up and faced him. "I think you need to leave."

There was complete silence. "Let's take a break," said Cong. He walked across the room. Karey, Clark and Lois followed. They left Anthony sitting by himself, out of earshot.

"Lois, we've spent a fair amount of time, in fact, the last few hours, talking about this. We need provisions and cannot pass up on the opportunity to get more food from Hawk. During the last hour before catastrophe hit, we obtained many basic supplies, but it will not help us long term," said Hung. "Our plan was to find Dr. Marcella Brown and Michael and connect with Hawk. We were also interested in getting transport to the Seed Bank without Dr. Anthony, but he got wind of that plan and is holding us hostage with these seeds. Where are the seeds anyway? Do we know if he is telling the truth? We need to figure this out. We need to find out where he has hidden this bag of seeds."

Dr. Anthony was still sitting alone, crossing his legs and did not seem too bothered with any reaction against him. Clark moved back and forth on his feet struggling with something.

"Let's do something about him. We are eight and he is only one," said Clark.

"Nine, including Suri," chimed in Lois. It thrilled her that Clark brought this up, and she did not have to be the antagonist.

"No, I don't think he has the upper hand. If we throw him out of here, he has nothing but a bag of seeds and no place to go. I wish we knew if those seeds were legit. Who can trust him? How can we accept him as a member of our survival group?" They all nodded in agreement with Clark.

"Let's be strategic," said Cong. "We'll work the plan as we discussed and start with three teams. One team stays here, doing communications. That's you, Qiang and Cong," said Hung, directing his attention to Lois. "The second team will go back through the tunnels toward the Medical Arts Building. That will be me, Bai and Dr. Anthony. We'll stay close to Anthony and see what he is really up to."

"I see the wisdom in that," said Lois. "There is no reason to kick him out now. Just so we are all on the same page of not keeping him around nor going to extraordinary lengths to protect him. Where are Clark and Karey going?"

Karey, Lou, and Clark will take a direct path to the hospital. We have protective suits from a chemical supply laboratory and they should be able to enter the hospital since the underground entrances are closed. According to Dr. Anthony, Marcella will probably be treating patients in the hospital. Lois, your team will manage communications between the two groups, using good ol' fashioned walkie talkies."

Lois felt lost as she looked at Cong. "How could you agree with this plan?"

"I suggested it."

"Let me get this straight. You are sending my brother out in intense heat and radioactive fallout to find this woman so her husband can reconnect with her? Is that worth risking a human life?" She stopped and realized what she said. She then lowered her voice slightly. "I know we want to connect with Hawk and work with him, but shouldn't we wait until things have stabilized? Won't there be opportunities in the future that would allow us to do this in a safer manner? No one wanted to go out and rescue those physics students, but now we're willing to execute this plan? Why isn't Dr. Anthony going outside and exposing himself to radiation?"

The room was silent for a while. Lois realized how stupid that comment sounded. The tunnels might not be safe. Radiation could be leaking from the outside. Clark picked up Lois' hand again and whispered, "It will be fine, sis. I've carefully worked on a plan that is safe. Believe me, I would not do something that would cause you any grief. I know I can do this." Always charming when he wanted something! She was worried, he seemed almost elated. Was this bravery or bravado? The others seemed fine with the plan.

Dr. Anthony looked up as they stood, surrounding him. Cong reviewed the plan. "Frankly, I think this will work out very well." His automatic acceptance of the plan made Lois immediately uncomfortable. "I'm going to be a big asset in the tunnels. I'll retrieve the seeds to bring to the Seed Bank. I'm hoping that the building is still standing; otherwise, there are no seeds to save our future."

"That sounds like a bunch of crap, if you ask me," said Lois. "We don't even know that you have seeds, that the seeds will do what you are saying they will do. We are all acting as if it is true." There is nothing more frustrating than this kind of bull, thought Lois. Here we are, stuck in a situation where we have to deal with this jerk. I wished we decided to just kick this guy out. If they were to stay here long term, she could not tolerate his presence. Settling in tight quarters might be tough, but living with such an unscrupulous, self-important, offensive man here would make her take her chances elsewhere.

"Lois," Cong said tenderly, "we understand your concern and share your frustration. There are a lot of risks involved. Having transportation like this helicopter will be an advantage going forward. I wish we had more time to talk about options around collaborating with the Seed Bank. We need to act, now! Dr. Anthony knows the tunnels and, more importantly, knows Marcella. While he gets the seeds, he can also help us find Marcella if, indeed, she is in the tunnels." Cong looked at everyone as he said, "Everything we do has to be calculated against our future. Supplies for us are critically important. To ensure long-term survival, we need resources and we need an escape route, a secondary residence."

No one had anything more to say as the circle separated. She had faith in the Five Guys. They were smart and ethical. Would they knowingly put people in danger? Her head hurt. She was not sure she could think.

Karey, Lou and Clark finished dressing in bright orange rubber suits. Where did they get them, thought Lois? Hung connected the oxygen to the respirators and continued to teach the team about how oxygen worked, the dangers, the interlocking device and safety protocols around radiation. He also spent some time talking about how not to contaminate others when re-entering a non-contaminated space. Clark was absorbing everything and making alternative suggestions that everyone seemed to agree with. Lois looked at her watch. The time was 11:02 AM, almost twenty-four hours since the first explosion.

Dr. Anthony, Lou and Hung were facing three computer screens and combing over original blueprints of the campus. They finally confirmed a path that would take Clark's team directly to the hospital from the main entrance through the atrium. It would expose them to radiation, heat and building wreckage, but it was direct.

Lois was proud of Clark, even though he was putting himself in unknown danger and taking Karey with him. As Lois tapped Clark on the shoulder, she thought carefully of what she would say. "Hey, do you have a minute?"

"Yes, sis," he said. "How are you feeling? Have you been hydrating?"

"Yes, I'm fine. Clark, I'm so proud of you. I know this is a big sister thing, but I want you to know, you do not have to do this. We are caught up in these incredible moments and everything seems urgent. We need to think about other people and what we can add to everyone's chances of survival. However, it does no one any good if you hurt yourself taking extraordinary chances." Lois looked at Clark and knew she was not connecting. This look was a new one. His whole body tensed up with resistance to what she was saying. She changed tactics. "Okay, let's think about Karey. Do you want to put her in danger?" Now his body relaxed as he looked at Karey with his kind eyes and slight smile, a look that she thought was reserved only for her.

"Sis, I know what you are doing and it ain't working. Look at Karey, she is holding her own, as tiny as she is. She is her own person and I would protect her as I would my big sis. But I would never tell her what to do. That is her choice."

Lois, feeling a little dizzy, started to feel the tears again. "Clark, better get back here safe. I demand it!" She sat down as the room swirled around her, but she did not faint. Clark kneeled down next to her, held her hand and rubbed her arm.

"You need to rest, sis," said Clark. Cong and Bai came over to check on her.

"I'm okay," she said. Clark stayed with her for a while and they sat there silently, but soon, she could tell he was anxious to get back to his task. "I'm okay, honey. You get back to the planning. Please be careful." Clark jumped up, unable to snuff his enthusiasm, and walked toward Karey, who seemed to watch him closely as she worked through her tasks.

Lois understood that there was a growing relationship with the two of them, which already seemed far more mature than any of his previous ones. She smiled at the thought this horrific situation could bring people together, maybe even quicker. Clark might have found 'the one', a good person.

She still could not figure how strange everything felt and the focus this group had in completing this incredibly dangerous quest. She was eager to help. She got up and walked over to Cong and Qiang who were listening for satellite messages and testing and retesting the walkie-talkies.

"Where did these come from?"

"Interesting question, Lois," said Qiang. "Actually, I've been a collector of old communication devices for a long time. I found the walkie talkies one day as I passed a garage sale. I also picked up an old ham radio that day, which I am eager to set up. I used to know lots of individuals using ham radios, but with the Internet, not so much. We must set a tower up, which requires getting up on the roof. We could send and receive RF signals if someone else was out there doing the same. I have another technology that would open things up for us too. Stay tuned." Qiang's energy felt so positive.

"Okay, give me something to do," said Lois. Qiang jumped up and gave her his seat, and with limited guidance, she was scanning networks for signals.

The first group was ready. Dr. Anthony, who showed very little connection to what they were working on, suddenly became interested. They tested the walkie talkies and gave one to Bai for all of them to share. Dr. Anthony wanted one to himself in case he became lost to the rest of the team. Cong decided they had an extra one and gave it to him. It wasn't clear when Hawk was coming back, but they had to find Michael and Marcella before he arrived. The satellite connection was not due for another two hours. Being in a university environment and a medical facility created opportunities for survival, but they all felt uncomfortable that the buildings were not stable. A constant reminder came from ceiling cracks spreading concrete dust over everything. As this odd team of three, the tall indifferent Dr. Antony, Bai in his embroidered shirt with linen pants and Hung in camouflage, left through the stairway to the tunnels. Finalizing Clark's team prep was their last task.

After working to ensure the walkie talkies were inside the protective suits, Clark, Karey and Lou opened the double doors that Dr. Anthony chained closed.

Karey came up to Lois. "Do you remember times when you wished things would change? A better life was always in the hands of others, policy makers, people in charge."

Lois nodded, tears now in her eyes.

"Within the ashes of this catastrophe, we can create something better. It is now within our grasp to do this."

Karey's voice was soft and gentle. Lois felt her body relax slightly as she thought about what she said. These words struck Lois and transcended her to an important intention to focus on. They had to think about living forward and what that would look like. It was a big thought with a tiny beginning that came from the heart. This was the only purpose that made sense. Thankfully, we have Karey with us, she thought.

They all said good-bye and Cong stayed close to Lois and Suri. Clark hugged her and reassured her they would be fine. Lou was encouraging everyone to depart soon and so they did.

The camera mounted on Clark's head showed the same white-gray scene unfold that they watched from the robot. She could see Karey's petite body struggling to keep up with Lou, while Clark brought up the rear. She hoped she would not fall. Clark shouted out to Lou to slow the pace. This is good, she thought. They came upon a steel barrier, angled from the ceiling above. Lois wondered how safe it was as she could not tell from the computer screen. Karey showed amazing flexibility in finding a path around it without disturbing the beam and then took the lead, finding an easier route through the debris. They seemed to make better progress with her guidance around large structures that were bent over from heat. Once they were in the atrium, there was no sign of life except for the robot that was stuck in a corner, wedged between two broken steel beams. Karey brushed the white gray flakes of debris off the robot and directed it toward what used to be the atrium. Clark spent an inordinate amount of time looking at Karey and Lois wondered what Lou was doing.

"Clark, show me where Lou is," Lois said into the handpiece.

Clark slowly moved to the right and Lou was making progress across the atrium. He seemed to be looking for an exit to the outside.

"Catch up to him, Clark. Show me what he is seeing. Qiang has the blueprints ready to assist."

The camera moved up and down as Clark nodded. He looked back at Karey and she nodded back to him as she started to walk away from the robot she was studying. The same robot that took the pictures when Lois collapsed. Any hope that they could save a physics student was gone. She noticed how the scene of the atrium gave the same feeling of serenity of a new snowfall. She noticed the brass patina egg sculpture half-buried under concrete rubble from the ceiling it detached from. Those poor kids, standing in that glass atrium, engaged in research and hoping to create a better future, were all dead. She wondered how many families were even alive to worry about their sons and daughters. Then Lois rested on the thought at least she had the most important part of her family with her, now surrounded by incalculable danger. Suri was still sitting next to her at attention, no sign that she would sleep.

"Lois, look at this," shouted Qiang uncharacteristically. "Luming sent us an SMS message from the Seed Bank. Can you believe this? A new satellite passes over the five-mile area we share, and it says, "WE SAFE. U2?"

"Did you respond?" she asked.

"Yes. Hope he gets it. We sent him timing for the closest satellite connection. That's when we should speak directly with the Seed Bank."

She was relieved and anxious. Was Luming speaking about Dan, Betty, and Elizabeth too? Did they make it from their car to the Seed Bank?

"Once we retrieve Michael and Marcella and Hawk picks them up, how are we going to deal with Dr. Anthony?" said Qiang. He did not show frustration very often.

"Hmmm, we still got options. Let's see what happens," said Lois.

"You're right, Lois." That's odd, she thought. Qiang always seems in control.

They turned back to the monitor while Clark's team was walking through the atrium doors and onto the campus plaza. Sticky black substances covered everything. They lifted their feet up and dropped them as if snowshoes hung from their feet. She wished she could whisper in Clark's ear to be careful but decided against it. The space they were traveling through was not recognizable, it looked empty, maybe where grass used to grow. The parking garage was to the left and looked like it collapsed completely, black ash, with an occasional explosion from cars parked underneath. As the trio headed toward the hospital, Lois thought about how many times she crossed such streets with health care professionals and patients swarming in and out of the entrance. Well, if they were outside, they were dead now.

As they walked toward the building's entrance, Lois said calm, soothing things like, you're getting close, look around and listen to what is going on. Now she realized that Clark no longer heard her voice. The walkie talkie was not transmitting, but it might be receiving. Then the camera stopped working. Lois looked at her watch, 1:02 PM.

Suddenly, Suri walked away from her to sit in the corner. Strange, thought Lois. Maybe Suri sensed that Clark was in danger and maybe even blamed Lois for it. She thought, get used to it, Suri. Clark has changed. God knows what he will do next. She would not panic. She had no choice but to pray for his safety.

My God, she thought. Things were changing quickly. She looked at Qiang and Cong in a moment of silence. Her shoulders lowered, she took a few breaths. Qiang seemed to work through the problem quickly.

"Let's find a solution," he said. Cong got up from his chair and the three of them started brainstorming their next move.

"I don't know how many more of these adrenaline rushes I can take in a day," said Lois.

Dr. Anthony called and reported, "We have not found Michael yet. Bai and Hung are canvassing everyone, but the tunnels are crowded, I'm not sure if we'll find him. Without a picture to show of him, this will be much harder. It's interesting that Geiger counters were found and several people are using them in the tunnels to detect radiation. I'm not sure they know what a bad reading is. I ran into a colleague about half an hour ago. He said that parts of adjacent buildings were evacuated hours ago. Since the parking ramp collapsed, this building started to sway, and the tunnel was cracking like crazy. My friend located larger cracks near the hospital entrance and everyone poured into the tunnels. There is no order and people started running back into the building, grabbing things, knowing it might collapse."

"Are you by yourself?"

"We split up," he said. "It made sense to do that."

"You didn't stick to the plan! You are supposed to be with Bai and Hung!" said Lois. Lois had to take a few breaths and Cong make a funny face and puffed his chest, doing a decent imitation of Anthony walking around the room. Lois had to laugh at him.

MICHAEL - 34

A tunnel below, this was intriguing. This might take me to the hospital. Would this tunnel be similar? He quickly dropped into the dark musty basement. There was no sign of any life as he walked toward a light, an old design with a wire cage protecting a large, elongated bulb. This small fixture lit the tunnel for about thirty feet. It looked like light placement was regular enough where he would not be in the dark unless electricity was down. If that happened, he would be in complete darkness. He needed a flashlight, but he would try to get by without one. This was probably a not-well-known tunnel. It was forgotten for decades after a new building was constructed above it. I wonder how old this is, he thought. There were no signs or maps on the walls. The walls were old plaster-like concrete, smooth with many cracks, crossing diagonally. The tunnel seemed to be oriented perpendicular to the floor above, not in the direction of the hospital. Was this a waste of precious time? He was far from the rendezvous point with Hawk. He stopped and listened more deeply and felt the tunnel itself creak, bringing more stress to this old structure. These sounds concerned Michael and were far more disturbing than the sounds of human chaos he experienced above. He thought about 9/11 for the first time and remembered the building disintegrating unexpectedly. I wonder, he thought, maybe I'll breathe my last breath here, alone. As feelings of depression crept into his body, his claustrophobia also increased. Claustrophobia was something he avoided in daily life, but if he let it, it could have a paralyzing affect. Michael started to walk fast, taking less notice of where he was going. Now he was bolting down the hall. Marcella must be in the medical building and I need to get in. This tunnel was easier to travel in, but the damp smell was annoying. Finding another tunnel, he had three choices. He finally chose the one to the right, using some strange logic around how he felt about which direction to take. Finally, he found one heavy fire door. He turned the bolts and saw a sign on the door stating, Anatomy Building. According to the brass plate, the Anatomy building was over eighty years old. It was like any building with offices, storage rooms and an exit sign at the end of the hallway. Strange, he thought, this tunnel was blocked off from any traffic and I wonder if they did that for safety issues. I wonder if I'm close now? He passed by another door with the word Morgue and realized that there were cadavers there used by medical students. Of course, they would put a morgue in the lowest level. Avoiding the use of the elevator, he found stairs and went up a flight to find the hallway from the Anatomy building to the Medical Building completely caved in.

Michael slumped to the floor and was feeling... hmmm, he wasn't sure what he was feeling, but maybe hopeless was closest to describing the thing inside him he couldn't grasp. Had he never experienced failure? Why was it so hard to find Marcella? He was left immobilized. Just sitting on the stairs, looking at the collapsed rubble piled high, covering the entrance increased his patent disappointment. He listened to the building creak and explosions from the surface shake the walls with plaster coming down in spots. This building is in pretty bad shape, he thought. He got up, now feeling exhausted, the last drop of adrenalin having passed out of his bloodstream, and peered up the staircase. Was that natural light? Typically agile, he could only walk up the steps, taking frequent breaks after only a few steps more. He kept climbing and rising past each floor. The stairwell was sturdy, and it felt safer here than hanging out in an antiquated tunnel. He went to the top floor and looked out to learn what to do next.

On the sixth floor, he opened the heavy fire door and looked down both hallways. The one to his left should face the Medical Building. He turned into a large room with test tubes, beakers, and strong-smelling chemicals, looking like a technician's nightmare. The windows were not blown out. I wonder if new windows are sturdier than old ones. Michael went farther down to the largest corner office. He heard a noise and doors being opened and shut. He opened the office door to find a tall man pulling a large burlap bag in his arms from a metal cabinet. He was completely startled. Michael's instant assessment was something's not right.

"Who are you?" asked Michael.

"My name is Dr. Wolfgang Anthony, Professor Emeritus of Biological Transference. This is Jeff Goldberg's office and I am retrieving something he needed." Dr. Anthony looked strange, acted strange, but Michael could not figure out why he had this impression.

"Where is Dr. Goldberg? It looks like he is the head of the Anatomy Department, according to this nameplate."

He stood and squared his body toward Michael. "Listen, I am wondering what you are doing up here?"

"Oh, I'm checking on a way to get to the Medical Building so I can find my wife."

"Oh, really? Well, I can help you with that. The entrance in the basement where the nurses are triaging patients has collapsed and it now looks like the Medical Building might collapse as well."

"How do you know this?" asked Michael.

"Well, I'm leading a team from the Physics building and looking for Michael Kraken. Maybe you've run into him. Wait a minute, you're looking for your wife?" Anthony looked a little pastier in complexion. "Are you Michael Kraken?"

"Yes, I am."

"Well, we must go back and meet with my team. I'm separated from the group that is looking for you and they will be thrilled that I found you. You cannot believe the efforts we were making for Flying Hawk to find you. We have another team... no, wait," and Anthony darted toward the window to look out. "Look, see those three bodies moving through the debris below? They are trying to access entry into the hospital, the first floor of the Medical Building, to find your wife. The nurses managing the triage were not going to even let me into the building. I later found out the entrance had collapsed. We split up, looking for you in the tunnels."

Michael was uncomfortable with this guy. Something was not right here. "So why are looking for me in this office?"

Anthony started to act kind of animated. "You've got the wrong idea. You know, Michael, I have an idea. Let's call the other guys looking for you. They will be successful in getting into the Medical Building. Give me a minute, and I will bring you to the team that is communicating with them. It won't be long until they find Marcella."

His voice speaking her name gave him chills. "How long will this take?"

"Just give me a minute," Anthony said, shouting impatiently. "We are going to extreme measures to accommodate your passage back with the Flying Hawk guy. You should be more patient since so many people are helping you."

Suddenly, the building shuddered a little and then continued to vibrate at a stronger frequency. The frequency accelerated until windows started breaking and a wind blew through the hallway. Michael looked out into the hallway, concerned. "I'm not waiting. I'm leaving."

"Yes, go ahead. I'll catch up. Just head toward the Physics building and ask for the Five Guys."

"What does that mean, Five Guys?"

"Well, they're five Chinese students who are very smart and look alike. You can't miss them."

"Great." This rude man would say nothing useful. The whole situation was weird. Michael could not wait to speculate as the building was now doing more than creaking. He went down the hallway and peered down at the three people Dr. Anthony mentioned. Something changed. They were running away from the Medical Building. It looked like it was swaying and more windows were blowing open from the higher levels. Michael decided he needed to get out. He needed to move fast, but the only exit was the tunnel he came from. He took the stairs, holding onto each handrail as his feet skidded downward. Once in the tunnel, all the building stresses were translating to degradation of the lowest tunnel. He had to slow down while dodging concrete coming on his head. Once the tunnel transitioned to another building, everything changed. The floor was smoother and the lighting better. Once he got to the transition point, he pulled himself back into the janitor's broom closet. He sat for a moment. Nothing was stable, and he needed to think straight. People are looking for me. Praise Jesus, he thought. He had help to find Marcella? Flying Hawk was trying to make contact? To think Hawk was doing this for him. I wonder what kind of impression I left with him? He now was a lot more optimistic about finding Marcella. He saw the water container and thought, I even did a good deed for others. Let someone else hand out water. I need to find the people looking for me.

Michael set off out down the hall and started to look for signs to the Physics Building. I wonder what happened to this Anthony guy? That guy was weird.

JANE - 35

The three of them sat in the helicopter, stunned, looking around. No one spoke. Jane braced for the worst, realized that Hawk had already set them down. How did he do this once the engine sputtered and died? No one was injured, as far as she could tell. But that seemed immaterial. Their real problems began now. They were in a sea of black sludge. It was the heat that was unbearable. Jane was more frightened than she had ever been and all she could think about was how were they going to walk in this burnt-out landscape. Their suits were heat tolerant, but was that enough? Her second thought was how practical was it to bring the supplies with them on foot. Maybe she could fashion a kind of sleigh to pull the supplies. Lastly, Jane stopped and thought about the loss. As she scanned the horizon that held so many fields of corn, barns and horses, there was only black to be seen. No signs of civilized life.

"Jane, do you know where we are and how far we have to go?" said Hawk.

"My home is ten miles from the freeway and that is just behind us. I could walk this blind. What about the helicopter? What's wrong and should we fix it first?"

"Show me on the map where you live. I'll meet you there. I'd like to stay and work on the helicopter and go back for more supplies. I promised to pick up some people at the university and transport seeds to the Seed Bank. I've got to get this helicopter running to do that."

"What? What seeds?" asked Jane.

"Well, it's a complicated matter. There is a professor at the University. He has a big title. Someone like this McKenzie dude you guys were dealing with. Someone so full of himself, so self-centered that he could not dig himself out of a compost pile. Well, anyway, the Seed Bank bought seeds from him just before the first bomb landed."

"Seed Bank, I know them. At least, I believe the urban legend of a grow-op located underneath the streets for miles and miles, growing pot and storing seeds for anyone interested in long term preservation," said Jane.

"Well, I made a promise. I'm supposed to go to the Medical Center and transport Dr. Anthony and his seeds to the Seed Bank. I was already picking up Michael Kraken and his wife Marcella, anyway. We had a poor connection and I'm not sure I understand the urgency, but the request sounded important."

Jane could not believe what she was hearing. "You know, I know this Michael you speak of very well. Correction, I know him too well. How did he get to the university? I also know of Dr. Anthony. He was supposed to produce large quantities of Dr. Zhi's seeds."

"I brought Michael. I thought he was an okay guy. Loving his wife so much that he impersonated Dr. McKenzie, flying into the worst area you can imagine instead of staying behind in safety. I took him to the university hospital to find her. That was a major act of valor, if you ask me."

"That's where we differ," said Jane. "There are very few things he does that do not involve his ambition to dominate everything he is involved in."

"Tell me what you know about the seeds," said Jake.

"I know they originated in China and were genetically modified by Dr. Zhi. His group produced soybeans that contained all required proteins, the same as meat, which includes those vitamins missing in your normal vegetarian diet. For example, they contain vitamin B_{12}, an important vitamin that is normally missing in strict vegetarian diets. I know about this because I have a large quantity of the same seeds. I also have something else that will be very useful to us. There is a strain of seeds that symbiotically grow in the dark. It's a complex growth cycle and you would destroy them if they are not in an environment that allows them to proliferate. This recent development involves two strains of plants. One grow under the normal conditions of photosynthesis and another grows by respiration, the same as most living beings. These seeds represent plants with extraordinary genetically modified attributes that grow in dark conditions. No need for light."

"Sounds interesting, Jane. This scientific breakthrough could not come at a better time. Our situation is getting more complex by the minute," said Jake. "How about this solution? We all try to fix the helicopter together, whatever it takes. Then if we get it going, Hawk drops us off at Jane's and he will come back after he is done with the trips he needs to take. If the helicopter does not lift, we all start walking together in this mess the rest of the way."

"Agreed. We're yours, Hawk. What do you need?" said Jane.

Hawk jumped down and grabbed his toolkit. Jake assisted him and seemed to be able to brainstorm a few ideas. Jane stood by, ready to help. While they diagnosed the problem, she stared at the sky. It was 5:35 PM. The western horizon was visible and reflected a muddy orange light that revealed what might be the sunset. The sky above was a changing dark eddy, a downward swirl mixing blacks and grays. Jane sensed they were going to work well past midnight. But it pleased her they did not split up. They had a chance to get home, no matter how bleak it felt. She felt hope.

DAN - 36

Vibrations were less frequent. The walls still held up, but cracks were appearing. The mural seemed to have changed slightly with a little more texture being added as cracks crawled diagonally across the walls.

Dan was sitting with Lizzy, making faces and letting her crawl around the large Oriental rug that surrounded the massive dining room table. Considering everything they experienced, she displayed amazing resilience. He was not sure about anything. He realized that everyone in the Seed Bank was healthy and untouched by this catastrophic event and would probably be healthy for a while. At some point, someone would go outside, leaving through a portal, and expose themselves to radiation. I wonder if there are other pollutants to be concerned about? Toxic fumes or biological organisms? How could he protect Lizzy from that? Would she ever see her mother again? What was their purpose now? How could a group work together? Did everyone have an equal say in what happened next?

Dan was grateful to be safe and healthy, but how were they going to fit in? Did he have any other options for Lizzy, Betty and himself? More people were coming. Who were they and would they contaminate the group? He needed to protect Lizzy. He wished that everyone would feel protective toward her. Dan needed some time to think. He was wondering about how marijuana affected judgement when Chris walked back into the dining room.

"How's Lizzy doing? She looks fine."

"Remember, she is only 10 months. She's doing fine, but she's not always this calm. She has her moments."

Chris was looking straight at Dan and then relaxed his posture. "Let me share more about what is happening."

Dan was frowning deeply by this point. He was so tired of having limited information. Based on his eavesdropping, this tight group was not used to interfacing with outsiders.

"Keep in mind, Dan, we still don't know that much. There are a lot of questions and we can't trust unvalidated sources of information."

"Your behavior told me you knew something would happen way before the rest of us," said Dan.

"Oh, yeah, well, you won't believe it when I tell you I didn't have any idea what was going on until I got a call from Dorothy to help her out. She was already on her way to the University Hospital to meet with Dr. Anthony."

"I think I can help vouch for Chris," said Dorothy as she walked into the room. She bent down and picked up Lizzy, making a warm cooing sound. Lizzy seemed to accept her without fussing. Most babies were wary of strangers, but Lizzy seemed to love the attention. "It was not a coincidence that I ran into Chris. I needed his help, and he took a chance as he could have just gone to the Seed Bank directly. We've known each other for a long time and I knew he would help me, actually, it was for all of us. I guess you could say, but for me getting Chris involved, Luming and Brother would not have come to the Seed Bank."

She sat down in a chair and bounced Lizzy on her knee. "I'm part of an organization that was created in Finland, shortly after the Nagasaki and Hiroshima bombs ended World War II. Since that time, a small group of pacifists began monitoring nuclear events. It was September 1945, when twelve individuals got together in Turku and created the TNA, The Nuclear Alliance. They decided they would study each nuclear test, each movement of uranium, the purchase of high-strength aluminum tubes and tracking scientists involved in building bombs, globally. They compiled every study that looked at the effect of nuclear exposure, starting with the clandestine clinical data collected by the Japanese after the war. More recently they were heavily involved in studying Chernobyl and Fukushima. Our diverse locations allowed us to study these events and collect information surreptitiously. We have been maintaining fastidious records and have an accurate picture of this world's nuclear history, year to date."

"That's impressive. I find it hard to believe, but go on," said Dan.

"Yah, I appreciate your skepticism, but it's surprising what they can hide in remote places. Most governments are spying, doing the same thing, but we see everything. While the US is monitoring Iran, Pakistan and North Korea judiciously, we know of activities of very, tiny entities. Our purpose is not just watchdog, but also preparation for an inevitable nuclear holocaust and providing survival skills in case this should happen. We established several small groups, carefully placed by location, to prepare for such an event. The Seed Bank people have been the longest standing members. They were perfect candidates because of their preservation of critical seed lines, infrastructure, and technical expertise. I've known Chris since we first met in Helsinki at my first forum."

"Of all of our scenarios, this was one that took us by complete surprise. Once we started to evaluate suspicious emails coming out of China one week ago, we knew possible catastrophic outcomes could happen. Once we realized what would happen, I got on a plane to get the seeds Dr. Anthony produced for us under contract--"

"Who is this Dr. Anthony?" asked Dan.

"He's full of BS and is quite a scoundrel but he knows his stuff. I've spent quite a lot of time with Dr. Zhi, the developer of the seeds. I worked with Troy to translate growing conditions for Anthony, as a contract grower, to produce seeds for our purpose. He has been well paid, an understatement. A unique strain of seeds were provided to him to grow, and I was supposed to get them when I picked up seeds from him. These special seeds are grown from genetically modified procedures. Certain desirable traits are insert into the DNA, producing seeds that grow into plants, like humans, requiring an intake of oxygen instead of carbon dioxide. These special plants work symbiotically with normal plants that grow by respiration, for example, carbon dioxide. I suspect Anthony is trying to leverage his way with this information into the Seed Bank, knowing what a safe shelter this will be in the future. Chris and I just finished logging the seeds into the database and he did a lousy job of relabeling the bag we wanted. Fifty pounds of these special seeds are missing. When we met, he sized up the situation and tripled the price. I had to do an additional electronic money transfer before he would release them. And then, I didn't get all the seeds we ordered, anyway! Beyond frustrating. I want to kill him.

"The person I am interested in is Jane Witterhouse. Betty mentioned her name when she talked about sitting in your car, overhearing your conversation with her. She said Jane is a friend of yours, Dan. Dr. Zhi and Jane are close collaborators and she was putting together a deal where her company was funding further research for Dr. Zhi in exchange for completing the required testing to commercialize the seeds. I believe Dr. Zhi gave her some unique seeds. Is there a way to contact her, Dan?"

"Hmmm, I know where she was when she left me a message. She was going into a meeting to complete that deal you are speaking of. It was called the Lazarus Project. The irony of this name does not escape me, Lazarus is a code name for projects that were raised from the dead. So many projects are named Lazarus because of the number of times projects are terminated, only to be revived because the team won't let it go." Dan paused, feeling his throat tighten, pushing back on the strong emotion rising from his heart. "There is no one better suited for catastrophe than Jane. It all depends on how far she was from nuclear sites. It would be good to find her."

"Let's go talk to Troy and Luming about locating Jane," said Chris to Dorothy.

Dorothy got up and handed Dan a sleeping Lizzy. That's amazing, thought Dan. Everyone is so comfortable taking care of her. So many people are caring for this little person. The more adaptive we are to having a baby around, the better. How would Brenda react to this? "I think I'll stay here. Lizzy seems to be happy and I think I'm dealing with a little indigestion."

Dorothy and Chris walked out, deep in conversation about expanding the planting rooms. Dan moved Lizzy to where he could be with her and sat down on the floor to be next to her, grabbing the ball from her diaper bag.

JANE - 37

The sky was a deep black. The curvature of the earth stood out as a faint line, profiling the ground meeting the black sky without interruption. No light was coming through, so it did not matter that it was eight o'clock in the morning.

They gave up fixing the engine around 4:00 AM and decided to sleep. For Jane, as she lay down, she felt adrenalin escaping each organ of her body, like a plant wilting from cell lysis. Jake and Hawk gave her the whole back seat. They talked to each other about a few technical things, but she was detached and weary. There was just too much uncertainty, uncertainty that she thought she was prepared for. Had she read about this kind of fatigue and what to do about it? How ridiculous reality felt, compared to all the devices and plans she made in preparation. She never once thought about the emotional consequences of a major catastrophe. Maybe Dr. Blue brought it up a few times, but she couldn't grasp what was meant by that. Jane, this never happened in the earth's history, so don't be so hard on yourself. There, she could close her eyes and sleep now.

Suddenly, something moved below the helicopter. They all heard it. The sound was a creature, but when Jake pointed a flashlight beneath the helicopter, there was nothing. They waited in still silence for quite a while. Nothing made a sound.

Jane woke up later and remembered experiencing a moment of fear. "What was that?"

"That noise," said Hawk, who sounded like he was up, but not moving. "No clue."

She looked around. It was 8:10 in the morning. They needed to get moving. "What's changed," said Jane, "is the beginning of nuclear winter. Overnight, the atmosphere has been collecting nuclear ash from all bomb sites and has made the sky an impenetrable sea of tiny black particles. Darkness will make our movement difficult, but not impossible. Hawk has the downloaded maps and I am very familiar with the area; however, it looks like a moonscape right now. I can recognize the basic contour of the landscape, but without the trees and farmhouses, it all looks different. I have driven these roads home for a decade."

Jake and Hawk seemed tired but did not express their fears about this next step. "Before we crashed, I saw footprints of farmhouses and barns that must have burned quickly, reduced to piles of ashes," said Jake. Even in this darkest of mornings, she was still optimistic that her home would still be standing, if they could only walk there safely.

"I built my home inside a hillside and is primarily underground. I made it with reinforced concrete and is super-efficient at heating and cooling. The only thing I'm worried about are trees that may have fallen over the entrance," said Jane. Jake nodded and Hawk seemed a little disengaged. He is either a moody person or a deep thinker, thought Jane, recognizing how little she knew about either guy.

"It would sure be nice if we had some protection against those creatures we saw yesterday and heard below us," said Jake.

"Just a minute," said Hawk, and he felt under the pilot seat and pulled out a 9 mm semi-automatic Glock. "This old thing should do the trick! I've had this since Iraq and never thought I would use it again. It has good range. To stop a creature from attacking up close, you need to put several shots into them all at once. This 9 mm will do that."

"Hawk, you are quite the mystery!" Jane smiled. She didn't know what else to say. She knew being armed was a very special part of survival, which she could not muster much interest in. She had a few rifles at home. "Let's put you in charge of weapons, Hawk. I trust you will figure out what we need if any attack happens to us. Who knows what we are facing?"

"It will not help us if we run into a pack, especially if they tear at our suits," said Jake. "A calculated risk we have to take, I guess," answering his own question.

Jane reached into her Tool Box and pulled out two large aerosol spray cans and handed one to Jake. "Here's something else. Spray this directly into the eyes of the attacker and then stand back. It will immediately immobilize them for about two minutes. I think we are as prepared as we can be."

Jake nodded.

"I've been thinking about animals running away from a forest fire. They will instinctively run in the direction away from the insult. From what I could see yesterday, fire had almost surrounded those creatures, and they were running in one direction, away from the insult. Where were they running?" she said. "I wonder if those were the same creatures that were below us this morning?"

"Okay, enough speculation," said Jake. "Let's stop talking about creatures, okay?"

Jane took Jake's response as information she needed about him. Was he squeamish? He was acting brave, but there were limits. Not the typical male response, but she was okay with that. The whole psychology around survival was something she missed in her research. Locating Dr. Blue will be a priority. Where was the exact location of her farm?

They decided not to pull the sled with supplies but leave them behind and focus on their own safety. "I'm still reluctant to keep the supplies behind," said Jake. "We went to all of this trouble. When are we going to get back here? I know it seems like a wise idea, Jane, to not burden us, but couldn't we devise a system to pull it behind us?"

"I have to return and fix the helicopter," said Hawk. "My promise to Michael and the Five Guys is important to me. They will be waiting. We'll figure out a way to bring this stuff back to Jane's place. Jane, you must have some tools I can use to fix the helicopter?"

"Yep, I'll take care of you, Hawk. Getting back here is not a problem. I have the perfect solution to get back here quickly. Let's first get moving and see if we can walk ten miles in this mess without killing ourselves. Exposure to radiation makes me uneasy. The fresh suits and masks we brought should protect us, assuming we don't tear anything. However, we cannot lift our respirators to drink or eat, so let's hydrate as much as we can."

Before putting on their masks, they passed the water around and drank silently. Each one put on helmets that Jake passed around with built-in respirators. Jane helped Jake lock the helmet, respirator and suit together. Her back hurt from sleeping on it wrong, but it was nothing that a much-needed stretch could smooth out. Hawk jumped down onto the ground and black ash floated up to surround his body. "Let me help you down slowly, Jane," said Hawk. Once they were all down, Jane did a few stretches and signaled the direction. They started to move slowly, Jane in the center, flanked by both men. Hawk tested their radios with a suggestion that they communicate only when necessary. Jane understood and said, "Good idea, Hawk." Jake nodded with a thumbs up, already following protocol.

The ground was flat, and it was strange for Jane to get her bearings, other than the compass on her wrist. She knew where she was, but there were no recognizable signs. No trees, houses, barns or livestock were left to use as a gauge of where they were. She knew that the land was part of a river valley and that her home was located in a protected gorge, but they had to cover miles of rolling landscape until they got there. She thought they could take the road, but she noted it was about two miles west. Four miles added to their total trip, would make it fourteen miles total. They probably could make better time with the direct route. She hoped she was right.

As they walked, the ground was warm and still smoking in some areas which they avoided. The ash was a deep black color, but not sticky like they observed closer to the center of the blasts. I wonder why Jane thought. It could be crops and trees burned cleaner than artificial building materials. The thought of the tar substances they scraped off the helicopter yesterday started to make her sick again. With the respirator pressing against her face, it was no time to be nauseous. She suppressed it and moved her attention toward listening to the blackness surrounding them. They made no conversation, but from time to time, they pointed at things. They almost fell over tree stumps not burned to the ground, completely hidden by ash. While they carefully navigated around dangerous barriers, Jane realized each step burned calories and created sweat that was accumulating in their suits. Jane knew these suits were to be used for experimental purposes, for evaluations, which was why they found so many of them in lab storage. Something was wrong, they were supposed to be breathable.

What other construction defects were here? As they established a rhythm of walking, they moved slowly, but more deliberately. They went back to walking in a line with Jane in the middle, supporting each other by crossing their arms together. They needed to conserve their strength for the long term and not burn out. Jane was dehydrating quickly and was sure that was the case with Hawk and Jake.

They stopped after one hour. Nine miles to go according to Jane's pedometer and it was 9:30. How disappointing. Could they handle nine more hours of walking? They had to do it. Jane knew that this was it for them. She had provisions, her seeds, and a sustainable resource to manage food for a long time. There was fuel, batteries, water and the perfect vehicle for getting through messy areas, if only they could get there. She could not wait to see the surprise on their faces when she showed it to them.

"We've got to take a chance and take water, Jane," shouted Jake through his respirator.

"No, I do not recommend this. Exposure to radiation at these levels would be life-threatening. People have survived without water for at least twenty-four hours. We need to prepare ourselves, walk conservatively, and keep our heads. Unless you see someplace, a cave, a house, maybe that would not expose us, we should keep going." Jane realized the strain of communicating itself was sucking energy from her body.

Hawk patted Jake on the shoulder. "I'm sure we can find a protected location where we can take off our respirators. Then we can take a real break." They looked at each other and Jake's shoulders relaxed a little. Jane thought of the various tests she and Jake already experienced together. Jake had been more resilient before they left the building. Hawk wasn't showing the signs of stress that Jake was. She realized how easy it was to work with Hawk, going along with everything and was completely committed to her suggestions. She wished she spent more time describing her place and the benefits to him. It sounded like he would leave once he got to her place.

After a brief rest, they kept going, now keener on finding a protected place where they could stop and hydrate. Jane suddenly felt something behind her and she turned around. It was a coyote, at least the head, teeth and size looked like one. She screamed, "Coyote!" and continued to scream as she noticed that the animal seemed to be afraid of the sound. Black with ash, it opened its jaw to reveal a mouth full of large black teeth. She kept screaming and Hawk turned around and kicked it away before it could bite her. He took out his gun and stopped. Jane stopped screaming as they both stared at the creature.

"It's not a coyote. It's not a coyote at all," said Hawk. "This is a large dog! Maybe it's a Great Dane. Remember how it cowered at Jane's voice."

"I know the feeling," said Jake. Jane thought that was a horrible attempt at humor. Oh well.

"Are you sure?" said Jane. She slowly approached the dog, and the dog kept walking backward and Jane was sure this was a female. "She's probably a lost survivor from a farm nearby. Let's walk away and see if she follows. It wouldn't hurt to have a dog around. Looks like maybe she could even fight a coyote if we ran across one."

They continued to walk while the dog trotted behind them. It disappeared from time to time but came back. There was something reassuring about being around something so ordinary. They continued to walk slowly through debris, Hawk leading and Jane going last for another hour. Jane clocked two miles, eight hours more to go. They were all moving slower, shoulders were down. Jane was feeling depressed. She now realized that the road would have been a better route, but they now needed to stick with it. If she was on her game, she would have calculated the advantage of the road and speed would mean at two miles per hour on the road, the trip would be only seven hours. But she was brain dead and dehydrated. Plugging forward was all they could do. The sky seemed lighter. It was almost noon, and they were deep in a gorge. Looking up and down the gorge, they could see a few trees and green plants. Encouraging, thought Jane. Once they climbed up from the gorge, the stark black landscape returned.

Each mile clocked created more sweat building up inside and the temperature of their bodies was also rising. They needed to find a shelter immediately. Then she realized she had an answer. Why had she not thought about this sooner? She was definitely off her game. With her hand up, she motioned a stop. Jake looked at her face, his face showed strain. Hawk looked up, alert.

"I've got a tent. In here," as she pointed to her backpack.

"Brilliant," said Hawk, immediately knowing the significance of this idea. He helped her unwind the backpack made out of a lightweight Teflon microfiber fabric. The tent poles rolled out easily, and they had it set up in minutes. It was tall and could just fit a body standing up. They could each go in, remove their respirators in safety, hydrate and cool down a little. She explained how it worked to Jake. Closing the zipper, then removing the respirator but dropping it on the ground. Contamination of the mouthpiece was critically sensitive.

"Jane, you never disappoint," said Jake while he nodded. Jane motioned for him to go in first. He went in and they zipped up the tent for him.

"Take your time, Jake," she shouted. "Hydrate, eat a bar and take big cooling breaths."

They watched the shadow of Jake who took half an hour and finally came out smiling beneath his mask and gave thumbs up to Jane. Jane realized her faith in her ability to solve problems must have increased. She was feeling optimistic. She knew that she was a little crazy, but her obsessions were her world and this was the complete cathartic experience. I wonder what Dr. Blue would think right now. She wanted to talk to Dr. Blue. Maybe there was a way. At that exact moment in time, the dog came up to her and licked her gloved hand. "Blue," she said. "I'm going to call you Blue."

Jane and Hawk took turns and were able to keep it to fifteen minutes apiece. They were off again, refreshed. They left the tent behind, knowing that it was too contaminated to bring along. No one looked back as they were placing all of their energy forward, toward the future.

The pace was faster. They moved without a break for several hours. Everything seemed flat, black and empty. Hawk was pointing to something ahead of them. Jane looked at her pedometer and said, "Four miles to go." It was 2:30. She could start imagining what was close to her home. Besides corn and hay fields, there would probably see the remains of two farmhouses. She strained to see what Hawk was pointing to. As they got closer, she realized what made Hawk look so grim. This was the remains of a farmhouse with the concrete basement intact. She did not look closely, but it looked like human remains were located in the corner of the home. The barn next to the house was burned to the ground with only metal tractors resting on puddles of rubber. Farm implements were laying on their side and showed no signs of life. Blue walked up and started to bark. Who knows why dogs bark? Was this Blue's home? They needed to keep walking and not think about what they were seeing.

With three miles left, each step left them with less energy. Jane knew they were close, but the pace was slow and they were physically running out of steam. Jane signaled a break and told them they were close. The thought of being safe helped her motivate them in the last push. She took the lead. This was it.

Jane's confidence in the plan did not falter. As they walked, she realized that they could not see anything until the last hundred feet as they would climb toward the top of the gorge and look down. The terrain was now very familiar.

And that was when she heard it. A familiar sound. "Yippee!" she cried and threw her hands in the air.

Both looked at her and then around looking for something special.

"Listen," she said as she pointed to her ears. They both shrugged and then Hawk heard it.

"What's that sound?"

"My generator, my generator." She jumped up and down. Now the significance was appreciated and they could all celebrate. This meant something. Her home was not damaged. They would be safe. Safety was important, but they also had a space to build something for the future.

The pace improved. Jane led the way until they climbed to the top of the ridge and looked down to a cement walk at the bottom of the gorge. The path led to a building embedded into the side of the hill, lit up from inside, radiating out from a bank of windows. Her home was intact. The lights were even on! The trees deep in the bottom of the gorge were still alive. Seeing green lifted Jane's heart.

She showed them the way around the gorge, using a familiar dirt path that led them to her driveway. They now faced a four-car garage. The rest of the house was not visible. Jane entered numbers into an electronic display and the farthest door opened. As it was opening, the standard garage door opening had fat vertical, plastic panels, like in a big box store, covering the opening.

"Wow, Jane very impressive," said Hawk.

"I'm not surprised, Jane. This is an amazing way to protect the inside of the building from the outside elements," said Jake.

"Yes, it's a long story of how I acquired this but right now let's focus on taking our suits off here," as she pointed to a space outside the plastic doors. "I'll go first. Think about zipping up your suit completely, so the outside does not contaminate the inside of the suit before you hang it up. We may use these again." She took off her respirator and laid it face down on the ground on the apron of the garage, unzipped the suit and stepped one foot past the plastic panels onto the interior garage surface, followed by her other foot. With a gloved hand, she zipped the suit up completely. She was gone for a few minutes and came back with hangers, a rolling coat rack and a box full of gloves. She hung up her suit, brought a garbage bag up from the feet to the head and tied it at the top. "Limit your exposure the best you can. We're going to shower right away."

Jake was a little wobbly on one foot, but soon followed the same procedure that Jane did. Hawk observed quietly and did the same procedure twice as fast as Jake.

"Show off," said Jake.

Jane disappeared and came back with a gallon jug of water that she drank from using a stainless-steel cup. The act of having water and not being bound by a suit was freeing. Jake and Hawk were looking around at their surroundings. Jake responded first by taking the container from Jane and immediately shared some with Hawk. Jane looked out onto the driveway and Blue was nowhere to be seen. Jane thought that was okay as she had no plan for a dog. She put out a dish of water and closed the garage door.

"Jesus, Jane, what the hell," said Jake. "I can't believe this. This is a total surprise. I had no idea."

"Jane, there is much to do," said Hawk. "I need to get back and work on the helicopter."

"Right, Hawk. I can help you with that. Let's first completely decontaminate ourselves. Based on what I'm smelling, I can tell we all need a shower." She walked them over to an industrial shower with an attached hand spray and drain directly below. "I installed this originally to wash my German Shepherd, Sam, who passed away, almost to the day I moved in. It was then when I realized this would be a perfect way to decontaminate.

We need to take off everything and shower so any residual radiative particles are removed from our bodies, hair, nails, anywhere. One of us will hold the hand spray with these plastic gloves, spray the body from the side, keeping the water contained over the drain. There are soaps, scrubs you can use, and we will rinse completely. That is the best we can do right now. Sorry, there won't be any privacy here."

"Jane, this is amazing," said Jake. "Let me propose the following. Hawk and I can work with each other in cleaning and holding. Why don't you get us towels and then we coin toss who gets to hold your shower spray." Jake was smiling sweetly with an expression of concern for her. Jane appreciated the gesture.

"Jake, that's sweet, but there's no problem." She took off her clothes and Hawk grabbed the shower handle and Jane started to wash her hair while Hawk worked the spray up and down her body. When she was done, she jumped out and said, "I'll get the towels," and she was gone.

She came back quickly, wrapped in a large white towel. Jake was still washing his hair under the showerhead with Hawk holding the hand shower. She set down four large towels. "Come on in when you're done. I'm going to make scrambled eggs and bacon."

As Jane walked away, she finally allowed herself a moment of joy of being home and having the design of her home reaching its full potential. There was much to do, but the simple task of cooking gave her great pleasure.

Finishing a six-egg scramble, she was pleased that she built a chicken coop using reinforced concrete. It resided on the top of the building near the garage, looking down on the gorge, almost directly on top of this room. Now the chickens would sustain them with protein for a long time. She needed to check on them, make sure the rooster was okay and put out some food. Assuming the coop survived the bombing, the chickens would be fine and not radioactive. A series of metal fences protected them from coyotes and predator invasion. She could hear the door open from the garage. Jake and Hawk walked down the travertine steps and through the hallway tiled in white marble. It was probably the smell of bacon that they were following, she thought.

Jane had this feeling of excitement, being in a place of safety. It also pleased her to share it with her new friends. "So, what do you think so far?"

Hawk, who rarely showed any enthusiasm, spoke first. "Jane, I was sure you were the real deal, but this is incredible. Was that a real Oglala headdress in the wall display off the stairs?"

"Yes, I was honored with that at a drumming ceremony ten years ago. I've been going each Labor Day since I was ten. My father was Oglala."

"And you ended up as a big deal corporate executive," said Jake.

"I'm not, or wasn't, to be accurate, a big deal there, that's for sure. I struggled with my job for a long time. Ironically, it feels good to be done with that. This is a sad time. I never wished for people dying. However, survival is my obsession or passion, as my therapist would say. I've spent a decade planning for a catastrophic disaster. I think it was the only thing that kept me sane through all the politics, pressure and insanity that comes with the corporate territory. Well, let's eat and we can talk after that." Jane took two beers out of the cooler, knowing that beer would eventually be in limited supply. Home brew was always a possibility, which made her realize her hops were freeze-dried and never been tested. She needed seeds. From now on, everything has an enhanced meaning. The importance of each item consumed, being the last, was their new life. It was also the time to enjoy being alive. Sharing this incredible story of survival, through a landscape of desolation, with two amazing men was an unexpected but welcomed outcome.

They were sensitive, manly, vulnerable, smart, and each one showed support in ways she never thought possible. They reminded her of Dan. Willing to take on any task, be collaborative and not disarm her contributions, even when there was lots of uncertainty.

Ironically, they ate in silence. Jane started to feel her body relax and was fighting a need to sleep. She got up, made a pot of coffee, as the conversation opened up.

'Jane, this was amazing. My brain thanks you and my body is highly indebted to you and to your gifts. I think that is the best meal I've ever eaten, and it's not just because I was starving," said Jake. He seemed reserved when he was saying this. It sounded like he was truly expressing a deep feeling inside of his words.

"I agree, Jane. I'm in awe," said Hawk.

"Now when you two just come down to reality, we can study our next steps." She smiled as she spoke because she knew they meant it and she was flattered by how they expressed themselves. She shared that awkwardness of expressing deep feelings, and she felt they had a lot in common already. "Reality check. Just making sure, is everyone feeling okay physically? Hawk, you were exposed to radiation a lot longer than we were. I have some vitamin D3 that we will take in a tincture form." She put five drops in everyone's coffee. "That is the best I can do at this time, but D3 should pump up our immune systems and, with the added antioxidants, help us navigate through this time of stress."

"What an amazing place, Jane. We need a tour," said Jake. She wasn't sure about Jake. He seemed sluggish which he was entitled to. She was dragging after the meal herself.

"I need to get back," said Hawk.

"Yes, of course. I'm thinking a priority is to set up communications. Let's find out if we can connect to a satellite."

"I can do that," said Jake.

"Good idea. That would be great. Hopefully, we can set up a system before I take off," Hawk said.

"Let's take a quick tour and I'll show you where the communication room is." She got up, and the men loaded the dishwasher. Jane smiled, never expecting that to happen so easily. Using the dishwasher would not be a good use of energy in the future, but she saw no harm in that now.

To start the tour, she brought them back toward the garage and showed them the hidden doors on the way toward the living quarters. One door led to storage and one was a tunnel to the chicken coop. She told them of some research involved in each detail, but eventually, she gave less information, realizing there would be time for all of that later. Basically, the house was built with the garage on ground level and all the living space on one floor, underground, facing the gorge. The long bank of triple pane windows, floor to ceiling, held up from the blasts. The gorge protected the windows and she detected no signs of damage. They walked back to the end of the living room and Jane opened another fire door into what looked like a large arboretum. It was set up for both natural and artificial light. "I now have the seeds, with time, they will grow into vibrant plants to help complement the food supplies stored right under this room. Let's look at the communication room." She opened another fire door that had stairs going down and up. "All bedrooms are in the basement which doubles as a fallout shelter. I'll show that to you later."

She took the upward staircase that opened into a room packed full of electronic equipment, screens, even a short-wave radio. "I recognize this stuff," said Hawk. "This will become very useful, Jake."

"We are at the top level of the shelter, and you can adjust the satellite direction by adjusting this throttle. I'm assuming you know what you're doing, so we'll leave you to it. Hawk and I will work on transportation back to the helicopter," said Jane, and they left.

Jane led Hawk back through the grow room, the expansive living room, the kitchen and up the stairs to the garage. She had quite a few vehicles from two four-wheelers, three ATVs and an old Vincent Black Shadow. She turned and looked at Hawk.

"There is a Hummer in the exterior shed, but I have a better idea for transportation. This will sound weird... hear me out."

"Jane, I have no issues with your ideas. You are amazing," and he smiled, looking at her a split second longer than she was comfortable with, although he had these soft brown eyes.

"When I was young, my father had a weekend job at the local WWII armor museum. It was a collection of weapons that you would probably see at the Smithsonian. My father served in WWII and the museum was a big passion for him. What he felt was missing in his collection was an M4A1." Hawk looked confused. "Yes, you are right if you think I mean a World War II military tank. He purchased it for less than five thousand dollars, an armored tank that was called The Sherman. It was a key draw to the museum in the '70s and just before he died, he took part in a big event where he started the tank up and showed it off by rolling it up and down the street of Riverton. Shortly after my father's death, the museum closed, and the tank sat there for almost ten years. I went to check it out, Riverton is only two miles from here, and it wasn't hard to buy it. It cost a thousand dollars. They let me store it for another ten years until they demolished the museum. I was already prepared for the event, having worked with WWII vets still living who had either driven or knew enough about the tanks to help me get it started. I had to get all kinds of permits to even drive it two miles, but it was worth it. It started up just like the day my dad drove it up and down Riverton."

"Jane, let me play this back to you. You purchased a Sherman tank and drove it two miles to your home?"

"Yep, that I did. It has its own garage about a hundred feet from here. Do you want to check it out?"

"Yes, I guess I do. What are you thinking? Taking it back to the crashed helicopter to fix it?"

"It's worthy of consideration. Let's go look."

"This is wild, Jane. It's like you saw too many movies and are working on the edge of reality."

"Yes, I realize that, Hawk. That's exactly why I've spent the last three years in therapy."

Jane was amused and realized how openly she was sparring with Hawk. He was an impressive guy. She opened the garage door and reached for their suits.

LOIS - 38

Lois never got headaches. When she finished speaking to Bai and Hung, she realized her headache might indicate concussion. That's probably why I was so angry. Just thinking about Dr. Anthony treating her for concussion was enough for her to stay quiet about her condition. Her mind was ruminating on getting rid of him. She was not exactly proud of her more violent thoughts about that. Maybe another sign of concussion. Unfortunately, he was so tightly connected to these seeds, they had to behave more strategically, and then she could cut his throat. Hopefully, the Seed Bank will know if his seeds grant him a rite of passage. Lois looked at her watch, it was twenty minutes before connecting with the satellite and finding out if Dan, Betty and Lizzy made it safely. There was a lot to talk about and they needed to fit it all in. Her head was pounding.

No word from Clark's group. Hung and Bai called.

Lois let them know about Clark's group. "We never checked Clark's batteries. We should have thought about that," said Hung.

"What are you finding?" asked Cong.

"A few people remembered someone handing out water and asking about Marcella, but nothing recently. We ran into Anthony right after the old tunnel to the anatomy building collapsed." Hung related the story of finding Anthony pushing a fifty-pound bag of seeds with a cart and being covered with concrete dust. He was hardly recognizable from the smudged gray dust on his face. He seemed agitated and Bai soothed him with his soft voice. According to Bai, he was upset and eager to get the seeds to the Seed Bank. Anthony also mentioned running into Michael but lost him once the tunnel started to collapse. He told a frightening story of looking from a window of the sixth floor of the Anatomy Building and seeing three suited figures, probably Clark, Karey and Lou, enter the hospital building. He said they were slogging through several feet of black ash just before they entered the front entrance of the hospital. Lois remembered being near the same entrance, where she waited for Clark to arrive from the railway. Hearing where Clark was, in the hospital, sent momentary relief to her aching head and she was able to take a few deeper breaths.

"Where are they now? They may have a better chance of finding Marcella there. Where is Michael? It figures that Anthony dropped the ball in not bringing him back. I wonder what really is going on?" she asked. The strong feeling of distrust gave her a stomachache.

Bai continued with the story. Anthony took off with the seeds, saying he thought he could locate Michael. He repeated several times, almost unconsciously, that he needed Michael and Marcella to complete the plan for his departure. Bai thought he was acting unstable and might have suffered some kind of shock. So what, she thought. I'm just tired of this drama. Knowing Clark, Karey and Lou were temporarily safe in the hospital, maybe closer to finding Marcella and would come back soon, filled her with hope. Clark would find batteries in the hospital, if that was the problem.

Bai also confirmed that many people told him the hospital was isolated, and no one came out of it since T zero. That also meant if Marcella was there, she was trapped.

Qiang pointed to his watch. "We've got to connect with the satellite. Let's talk again. We'll call you."

When Lois released the transmitter button, she looked at Qiang and then back to Cong and noticed the smiles on their faces. The news about Clark was good. She needed to compose herself again and prepare for the call with the Seed Bank. She got up from her stool, took a few breaths and realized her breathing was shallow. She decided that she could afford a few yoga moves, the first time since she got there, to calm down a bit and be ready for speaking with Luming. She hoped the connection worked. Would the news be good?

"Lois, how are you feeling now?" said Cong.

"I have this headache that won't go away. Other than that, I'm fine. I guess the headache reminds me of you-know-who. What are we going to say about Anthony?"

"Well, we will just have to see. Let's make sure that we find out about growing conditions in darkness. We need to speak Dorothy," said Qiang.

"Yep, we're on the same page with that," and then the satellite phone started to vibrate.

"Cong here. We only have fifteen minutes and quite a few items to cover. Myself, Qiang and Lois are here. We are sequestered in a sub-basement room in the physics building on the university campus. We are surrounded by massive destruction from several nuclear bombs in this location. We just don't know anything. We're not sure about survival rate, but there are hundreds of people stranded in the tunnels."

"Lois? Are you there? It's great to hear that you are okay. There are only three of you?" asked Luming.

"We have a group of nine here. Six are looking for Michael and Marcella," said Cong.

"Yes, I'm okay and I just found out that my crazy brother is okay. Did Dan make it?"

"Yes, he, Lizzy and Betty are all safe here. They made it with only seconds to spare thanks to your heads up. There are quite a few people from the Seed Bank that did not make it, however." Luming paused for a moment. Lois let the silence continue before she spoke.

"We have very little time, Luming," said Lois. "We need to inform you of what is going on." Cong, Lois and Qiang took turns telling their stories of what was going on with Hawk, Michael and Marcella and none of them scrimped on words about Dr. Anthony. Cong presented a summary of Clark's bravery, intelligence and innovation around what he'd done so far. That was a cool thing to say, thought Lois.

"Sounds like Clark showed great bravery contrasting with Dr. Anthony's antics," said Luming. "I've been broadcasting this conversation so everyone at the Seed Bank can hear first-hand what was said. To summarize, you're looking for Michael and Clark's team is hoping to find Marcella in the hospital so Hawk can pick them up. You spoke to Hawk shortly after he dropped off Michael and have not been in contact with him since. You are uncertain that he is even coming back. Dr. Anthony has held back a bag of seeds he is using to gain passage to the Seed Bank, if Hawk shows up. Does that sound right?"

Lois looked at Cong and read his mind. "Yes, that's perfect. I'm not sure if we have thought through the fact that Hawk may not show up. Does anyone know what Anthony is talking about? Are these seeds that important?"

"That would be Dorothy. She's right here," said Luming. Cong and Qiang looked at each other and pointed to Lois. She was okay to speak to the Seed Bank, and she knew Luming.

"Dorothy, good to meet you," said Lois. "You've heard our story so far. Just to restate this situation, Dr. Anthony did not give you all the seeds, he left a fifty-pound bag behind and he is somewhere in the tunnels, pushing a cart with the bag on it. He's been telling us that these seeds will allow you to grow plants in the dark and that you will need to use them with the seeds you have already purchased."

"Yes, I realized that when Chris and I documented and stored the seeds. I agree. He's a complete scumbag. We were desperate, out of time, when I picked up the seed bags. Unfortunately, Dr. Anthony was the only producer in North America with the quantity of seeds we were looking for. That was disappointing information! We had to buy large quantities of this seed quickly and could not take a chance to take such a large amount through customs. Dr. Zhi knew Anthony increased seeds yield each year since he received them and paired them with local plants to accommodate a variety of weather conditions. He uses his family farm in Iowa to do this. I've been there often, to consult with him. He did all of this without a regulatory body overseeing his operation. Their grow-op has the largest square footage of a greenhouse in North America. This allowed his family to multiply yield once a year from the original fifty seeds. We estimate that he should have over one hundred and fifty pounds of seeds that could plant forty-four acres. Dr. Zhi noted his strange idiosyncrasies, but he was the only person Zhi knew that would plant the seeds illegally, knowingly breaking the law."

"So Anthony must have the exact knowledge of proper growing conditions," said Cong.

"He does, but so do we. Dr. Zhi was a smart man. He requested that someone from the Seed Bank be inserted in Dr. Anthony's field crew, so I trained Troy, who took careful notes and made observations about the operation. Is Anthony claiming he held back the seeds that process by respiration instead of photosynthesis?" asked Dorothy. "What did he say about that?"

"He said he needs to provide this special bag of seeds to be grown in combination with the seeds you already have," said Lois.

"Interesting," said Dorothy. "We don't need Anthony. Dr. Zhi provided the same seeds to the Seed Bank and to Jane Witterhouse. I guess Dr. Zhi's intuition was correct in not trusting Anthony." Lois heard laughter on the other side. "Thank God we don't need what he's selling! The Seed Bank's expertise in GMO plants is well known to a few people. No pun intended, but we are definitely an underground operation. If that's it, if that's what Anthony's got, we don't need him and we don't need that asshole hanging out here either. I'll say goodbye now."

"Bye, Dorothy," said Lois. "I'm not sure if I can handle this much good news."

"We have a few minutes," said Luming.

Cong said, "Regardless, would it be helpful to pass on anything to you when Hawk arrives? We have a few things that might interest you." He looked back at Qiang and they exchanged a significant silent communication.

"Qiang here, Luming. I'm our communication expert and I dabble in robotics. I can't believe this myself, but I found two experimental drones developed by one of our physics students. Can you believe that? I'm wondering if you could use one."

"That would be amazing. Scar here." She paused for a long time and said, "Also, if any of you were to come on that helicopter, please know you're welcome anytime." A long hesitation ensued as if the phone was on mute. She got back on. "The invitation remains. I might have spoken a little too soon, but we've got capacity to add more to our group. We'll figure it out. The Five Guys have always been a valuable resource, and we hope to combine our efforts going forward."

"Thank you for your generous offer to stay with you," said Cong.

"I think we have one more minute," said Lois, watching the clock carefully, then looking at Qiang. "Have you been listening to the broadcasts? What do you think about the three words?"

"We heard it too. Brother found that..." said Luming, and the line went dead.

They sat in silence for a moment. What was Luming going to say about the three words? Finally, Cong said, "This changes everything!"

"Yep, Anthony is history!" shouted Lois.

"Do you still have your headache?" asked Qiang.

"Nope."

"Let's talk about Hawk. We need to establish a way to communicate with him," said Qiang.

The walkie-talkie light turned on again. "Lois, Hung here. Bai and I are with Michael. He does not want to meet with you. He wants to keep looking for Marcella. I told him you are in contact or were in contact with Clark who just entered the hospital building. He wants to go there too. Here, talk to Lois."

"Hi, Michael. My name is Lois, and I'm coordinating things here between the groups. My brother, Clark, is part of a group that entered the hospital building from the outside, a very treacherous attempt to find Marcella. He successfully made it with the help of Karey and Lou. The three of them are searching for Marcella in the hospital. If she's there, they will find her. However, we have no way to communicate with them. We've been out of contact for almost an hour. I've no more information than that."

"I have to go to the hospital to find her. I have to see if she's okay." Michael's voice did not sound stable. Lois was a little concerned that he was not just physically spent, but emotionally spent. She knew so little about him and could not tell what would sound normal.

"Michael, you must be exhausted. Have you had any nutrition?"

For a brief second, there was the scratchy silence coming from the large speaker of her phone. "I'm fine, but frustrated. Bai was telling me about this Anthony guy. He gave me a strange feeling when I met him, like I caught him doing something dishonest. He was tearing apart an office when I found him. He never said what he was doing. Once he realized who I was, his whole demeanor changed. Hung and Bai just explained things to me and Anthony's role in this intricate plan. I guess it was your brother I was looking at entering the hospital. Frankly, I only care about Marcella right now and I have to keep looking for her. I cannot sit and wait. That's it."

"Bai or Hung will bring you back here. That way, you can hear Clark describe conditions first-hand when he leaves the hospital building with Marcella. We're in a safe location and you will have access to satellite communications if you need that."

"I still want to get to the hospital and know how to get there from the underground tunnel system. What have you heard from Flying Hawk?"

Lois sensed that he was calming down and his breathing was not as short. "He contacted us shortly after he dropped you off in the university football field. He's providing passage for you and Marcella back to your home. You must have left quite an impression on him. He's willing to risk a lot to come back for you." As Lois hoped she convinced him of coming to her, she heard loud, repeating snapping sounds.

"Lois, Michael just handed me the walkie talkie and took off."

"Great," she said, looking up at Cong and Qiang as they heard the news at the same time. "If he is so determined to do his own thing, give him one of your walkie talkies. Let him know the batteries may run low and to check in frequently. Lois, over."

"We'll run after Michael and get back to you. Okay. Out."

"Out," said Lois with a smile on her face. She felt a small inkling of hope. We found Michael and now know Clark entered the medical building. Suddenly, she needed more information. Why can't she speak to him now? What is wrong with his walkie-talkie? Is that building even safe? I'm feeling so tired, she thought. Suri walked over to her at that moment. Lois sat on the floor with Suri, laid her head down in her golden plush fur, and immediately fell asleep.

LUMING - 39

As Luming and Brother started to push their way to the outside of the crowded room, Scar joined them. Everyone standing in the small communication room, listening to the broadcast with the university, made the room unbearable. Scar was under a little scrutiny for inviting the Five Guys group to share their space. As the comments broke out, she handled it gracefully. She stated being open was important to the survival of the SB, reminding everyone of the significant advantages to having them here. More concerns about the others that were with them hit a sensitive nerve for Luming, still feeling scrutinized himself. How were they fitting in so far? He still felt that the tension was not going away.

"Where did you last see Dan?" asked Scar, looking at Brother. Was she concerned or just trying to change the subject, wondered Luming?

Brother looked at Luming and said, "It was a few hours ago for me. He was with Betty while Lizzy was taking a nap. They were in that room close to the plants."

"I've not seen him since he visited me here when I was working on the transmissions," said Luming.

"Maybe we need to grab Betty. She might know."

"Brother, there's so much going on now with communications. I feel frustrated. Face it. We are outsiders and I felt tension in the room."

"Luming, take a few deep breaths. I know this sounds cliché, but we are our best selves if we can just live in this moment. Take a moment to settle into your chair, your feet on the ground. Close your eyes and relax your shoulders."

Luming knew Brother was right to relax. Maybe tension was coming from him and not the others. He was now part of a group. It seemed like everyone was interconnected and that few actions could be taken independently. He valued independence, so how was he going to survive in this controlled atmosphere? They were lucky to be alive, safe, and in this amazing place that was prepared for a catastrophic event. Living with so many people meant a lot of interactions and no foreseeable downtime.

Scar walked out of the room, followed by Dorothy who was in deep conversation with Betty. They all looked a little worried.

"Chris and I left Dan playing with Lizzy in the dining room," said Dorothy. "He was pretty happy there, except he did mention having a stomachache. That was when we walked back to hear the satellite broadcast. He wasn't interested in joining us, I guess."

"Wow, that's good," said Luming. "I started to worry since he was the only one that was not in the room. He's probably been listening to the broadcast from the speakers."

"Yes, that's good to know," said Scar. "Let's go find him, anyway. It would be nice to take a break and relax a little. Dan can convey such calmness."

Betty added, "Every time I see him playing with Lizzy, I count my blessings to just experience someone with that ability to exude common sense. He thanked me for helping him when I left," and she blushed.

Luming picked up on that. "It must have been a very special moment, Betty," and she blushed brighter.

"I guess so. I enjoyed it for what it was. I'm an impulsive person. The impulse to grasp, to hold it close and experience pleasure, is strong in me. But realistically, it's just friendly banter."

"Well, let's go find him," said Brother with a smile.

It was a much-needed light moment, thought Luming. His memory of the brief time he spent with Scar at the cistern seemed like a long time ago. So much has happened since then. He was constantly learning about how things were done. He already made a few suggestions of what needed to change. Their lives now depended on everyone's engagement, and he hoped they appreciated him for his ideas.

They started to walk down the hall, Scar next to Luming and Brother with Betty. Dorothy returned to the room. Betty kept talking, but Luming was now quietly fixated only on Scar. He looked over at her and she smiled. Her black braids had partially come apart and he could see how thick her hair was. He imagined what it would be like to unbraid her hair. He remembered the initial physical reaction he had to her lean body standing in her black leather pants, tall black boots and the loose gray top. She moves so gracefully, I think I'll call her Willow, he thought.

As they walked, music was coming over the loudspeaker. Soft jazz piano music relaxed Luming and Betty gave a whoop. As they entered the tunnel for the dining room, Luming heard Lizzy.

"Ma ma, mama." They turned the corner to find Lizzy, sitting up, crying with a face as red as a tomato.

"Dan? Dan?" shouted Betty as she started to run. They all followed and found Dan, laying prone on the floor. Brother picked up Lizzy to get her to stop crying. "Dan, what's wrong?"

"I'm okay, I just need my pills. They're in the pocket of my jacket. I was feeling sick to my stomach, almost vomiting. Then these darn chest pains started. I think my jacket is hanging on a hook in the kitchen. Is Lizzy okay? She's missing her mother."

"What are you taking, Dan? Ace inhibitor, calcium channel block, diuretic and beta blocker?" asked Scar.

"You got it, the cardio quad," said Dan, looking up. "How d' you know?"

"Well, these are the four most prescribed pills in the world. They treat hypertension. This makes me sad, but we had a pharmacist as a member of the Seed Bank. He made up most of our tinctures, but he also made sure that our facility would have a variety of drugs we expected needing in case we were cut off from the world, which we are, only in a different way than he imagined. Daniel was climbing Mount St. Helen this week, so hopefully, he is safe. I hope he is. Anyway, we have large supplies of these drugs, especially since they were all generic, they were really cheap to buy. We also have a large amount of nitroglycerin. I will grab the medical kit." And Scar left the room.

"I'm grateful for that," said Dan. Betty came back into the room with Dan's jacket. "Look in the front pocket. I should have four pills in the bottom."

Betty pulled out the pills and a lot of cloth piles came with it. "Dan, this is your lucky day," said Betty. She handed him the pills and a water bottle.

"Do we have anyone with a medical background?" asked Brother.

Scar entered the room with a large blue First Responder Bag and pulled out the blood pressure cuff and stethoscope. "No," said Scar. She checked his blood pressure. "It's 190/110."

Luming knew this was not good news. Dan needed medical help. Ideas were spinning in his head about what to do next. He must have arrived at the same conclusion when he and Scar said, "Marcella!" in unison.

"Who's Marcella again?" asked Dan.

"She is Michael's wife, the one they are looking for that Hawk is picking up to take to their home."

"I must have missed a lot. I might have drifted off when Luming started broadcasting. That is when I started feeling chest pains. I must have passed out or something."

"I'll fill you in later, Dan," said Betty. "Right now, I suggest you stay here for a while and we will find some blankets to keep you warm. I'll take BP measurements every ten minutes."

"There's a quiet place to sit in the Serenity Room," said Brother. "Once Dan feels better, let's move him to that spot. I promise you, Dan, it has a special quality there."

They exchanged more ideas as no one wanted to move Dan but laying on the concrete floor with blankets would not be the long-term solution.

"I'm okay. I feel much better already," said Dan.

"Yes, that's great, Dan. But let's err of the conservative side," said Betty.

"Ma ma, mama." Lizzy was now completely calmed down, but saying mama in a very drowsy way. Betty found her second bottle and gave it to Brother. While being fed in Brother's arms, she was sleeping by the time she was done with her bottle.

"Hey, Lizzy. Are you okay?" Dan said with feeling and a smile just for her. She slept right through.

They waited for half an hour and Dan seemed to be feeling okay. Luming and Betty helped him get off the floor. They slowly walked to the sanctuary and found a futon with pillows in the corner.

"I think it's best if we let Dan rest. Betty, let us know if anything changes," said Scar. Dan was already asleep. Betty and Lizzy stayed behind while Luming, Brother and Scar left.

Brother said he would head back to the library to look up information on heart attacks. They said goodbye and Scar and Luming stayed behind outside the room.

"Is he going to be okay? That was a close call. I never thought about the need for pharmaceutical drugs. Scar, you and your group are incredibly disciplined and prepared for every worst-case scenario. How did you stay committed to catastrophe? What else have you thought about? Why does everything seem so strange? And why did the seeds come from China from this Dr. Zhi?"

"Wait, take a breath," she said. "To tell you the truth, there is a lot of coincidence mixed up with a plan that had nothing to do with us. We are just plain survivalists. There is no end to preparing for a catastrophe, and we had the finances to fund it. It kept us challenged. It's an interesting point of view. It keeps you focused on what is important in life and taking the steps to ensure basic needs are met. Luming, I'm afraid I don't have all the answers. All I have ever done here is keep our group together and focused on what we collectively do. I'm like an executive director. I have my thoughts about what is going on, but I have no answers."

"Let's see what we can do to get Marcella to come here. We've got to figure out a way to communicate with Lois. We need to intercept Marcella and Michael before they get on that helicopter."

"I thought. I will check for a few things in the pharmacy," and she was off.

Luming walked into the Hub, finding everyone had left the room except for Troy. Luming let Troy know what happened to Dan. They needed to let everyone know, and they needed to contact Lois.

"I've researched satellite communication. There is a great deal of interference with the cloud structure and the number of satellites that are left in the sky. I'm thinking our problem is a combination of both hindrances," said Troy.

"We've got to reach Lois now. If we sort out how we connected with them last time, maybe we can figure out how we can get in touch with them sooner. How far away are they from here, five miles? Let's break this down."

"I will look at any conditions different during our communication. We should look at SMS texting and using Wi-Fi. They are close to the hospital and that might also lead to another communication network. Let me keep studying."

"I'll go back to the computers and see what I can find by roaming satellite channels," said Luming.

Luming went back to the library. Brother was deep in thought, surrounded by a stack of ten books in a soft red chair in the corner. Luming started his search for answers in satellite communications.

MICHAEL - 40

Michael felt better just running. Hung and Bai were very caring, but Lois wanted him to come back and wait until her brother Clark returned. He just could not sit idle. It was Hung who reached him and got him to slow down. He handed him a walkie talkie and showed him how to work it. It was obvious he wanted to come along, but Michael refused. He knew what he would do, and it was possibly very dangerous. He agreed to call every thirty minutes, as the batteries might fail.

Knowing they were connected to Hawk, it made finding Marcella that much more urgent. The fact that Hawk confirmed he was coming back for him was a surprise. Hawk dropped him off hours ago. Anything could have happened to him. It did not matter. He just needed to find Marcella. Even if they weren't rescued, they would be together. He would brave the radiation if he had to. She was in the hospital. She was probably busy saving lives right now. Her years working in an ER would have made her very useful. She was in the hospital for a scheduled surgery she talked about last night. Was it a Mohs surgery? That was a tedious one, requiring slicing the skin like a microtone and testing each slice for cancer cells. She also could have been in the pathology lab. Realizing he never visited her at work, it depressed him he had no idea how to find her lab.

As Michael walked away, Hung's sincerity touched him in finding Marcella. He was the same height as Bai but wore a rich green version of camouflage that reminded Michael of his childhood. Hung was direct and informative, but his soft touch on Michael's shoulder gave him a deep sense that he really cared.

Michael stopped to lean against the concrete wall and continued to think things through. People were moving back and forth along the tunnel. These tunnels were wide and could handle many people. There seemed to be clusters of groups forming now. Some groups were medical technicians, some university students and there were also groups in scrubs looking like interns. With the physical connection to the hospital severed, Michael realized that hospital workers could not do much. There was nowhere to go, but a lot of people moved around, checking out every corner. Food, maybe even water, would be in short supply soon unless they could dig their way toward a cafeteria. Michael wondered if cafeterias stored much food anymore. Weren't there sophisticated caterers delivering meals each day and making them in off-site locations? What would happen to these people? Once he got home with Marcella, they could live in the basement wine cellar if his house was destroyed. We buried it deep to keep wine at the perfect temperature. We could grow our own food. He had a deep well, a surplus of fuel he kept in underground storage tanks and an abundance of trees. Maybe they would find seeds to grow. How funny, they could live like pioneers. So much for progress, civilization and practicing law. Marcella's medical background would prove more useful than his twenty-five years as a lawyer.

Michael noticed a map in a plastic laminate pocket, bolted to the concrete wall. He walked across the stream of people moving in both directions to look at it. It was a map of the tunnels, but as he pulled the map out of the sleeve, a second map behind it fell out. Having carefully studied the maps once before, he realized that the hidden map showed a complete diagram of the tunnel he used to get into the Anatomy building and the second tunnel he suspected would take him to the hospital. As he looked closely, the lower tunnel ran to the Gabriele Hearst Heart Center, which was also connected to the hospital. He pulled out the walkie talkie and pressed the green button.

"Qiang here, over."

"Oh, this is Michael. How do I speak with Clark?"

"Let me get Lois, over."

"Michael, where are you? We'll help you find Marcella. We have not spoken to Clark for a long time. I'm not sure why, but we suspect it's the batteries."

"Lois, I'm finding another way into the hospital. I am going back into the tunnel I just left and see what they destroyed. There was one tunnel I did not have time to explore. These tunnels are ancient and underneath the existing tunnels. If one tunnel did not collapse, then I can get myself into that building without exposing myself to radiation."

"Michael, please wait. I'm sure Clark will be back soon with Marcella."

Michael turned off the walkie talkie and felt a little guilty. He knew Lois and her group had the best intentions. He did not believe that Clark would materialize, suddenly. He did not want his efforts compromised, nor did he want to put anyone else in danger. He could do this and he felt energized about it already.

He started to backtrack, running toward the janitor's closet, bumping into people that were walking. He passed a new area where people were injured and a few medical people were moving around, treating injuries. Not a pretty sight and he was relieved that he could leave this place, hopefully, with Marcella and return home, regardless of what they would find. At least it would be his own land, not shared with needy people, grasping for things. He heard someone scream in agony and he heard several men and women asking anyone in a white coat for methadone treatments. This situation could get much worse, he thought. There could be drug issues, food issues, and acute injuries. Maybe the worst thing that could happen to someone was to survive a nuclear blast.

He stopped a man in a white coat and asked if he knew, Dr. Marcella Brown. He shook his head and said he was only a pharmacist helping out, but to please keep his identity quiet in case a riot for drugs transpired. As Michael inquired about Marcella, he finally reached a woman in a tight-fitting business suit who she said she knew Marcella, but not well. She worked in personnel. She agreed, Marcella was probably in the hospital, but none of the hospital staff were seen so far. She confirmed no one knew what happened to the hospital building, just that the entrance from the tunnels collapsed several times and no one could enter.

Michael finally reached the janitor closet from where he first entered the tunnel. A small group had formed directly across from the closet. He needed to be careful. He did not want people going down there while he was looking for Marcella. He needed all of his senses and did not want people around to cloud the situation.

He waited for a while and watched them. They were students, medical students, based on their scrubs. He listened as they talked quietly amongst themselves. They were mad and seemed to blame the government for everything that happened. The information that was held back, how ill-prepared the university was and just how did this happen with all the defensive actions the United States could have taken. Michael soon realized that they were oblivious to his presence. But would that be true if he casually walked by and opened the door to the closet? He had a better idea.

"Hey, how are you doing?" he asked.

The tallest man had a superior air about him. He looked up as his glasses slid down his nose. This didn't bother Michael as he was a master at doing that himself to people asking questions. The man said, "We're like everyone else here. Angry and getting hungry."

"Aren't your services as physicians needed somewhere?"

"Not sure what you mean by that word, services. We're interns."

"I'm sorry, but I saw quite a few people that need medical help back there. There were people asking for methadone, maybe they were going through some kind of drug withdrawal. I know some have wounds that needed tending. What kind of medical professionals are you?"

A rather small woman spoke up. "We just took a break after working non-stop for the last six hours. We have no supplies left, there is no one supervising anything, it is complete chaos. People are making demands on us and we just can't do much for them."

"You're healthcare professionals. You signed the Hippocratic Oath. Doesn't it say something about you're a member of society with special obligations to fellow human beings, those sound of mind and body?"

They now stopped talking to each other and listened to Michael. A large, muscular man moved to the front of the group and said, "Who do you think you are, talking to us like that? As if you know what you are talking about. What gives you the right to judge us for taking time out from a stressful situation?"

"My wife is a doctor in the hospital, Dr. Marcella Brown. She is trapped in the hospital and probably has been working to save lives without taking a break and she's twice your age." Michael stared at them and did not stand down.

The small woman said, "He's right. Let's get back to it," and they moved down the hall slowly, looking like they were lost and not showing the crisp, clean positive attitude that Michael was used to in a physician. He wondered if this was normal for this new generation of doctors. He always assumed anyone in medicine dropped everything to help people in a crisis. What was happening to society? He thought of his son. Max was probably safe in a high security room reserved for programmers across campus. How long would it take for them to connect or even see each other? Michael wavered back and forth, realizing he was stuck in a mind treadmill.

He walked over to the closet and closed himself in the room. He grabbed a large flashlight from the emergency supplies and a first-aid kit. The portal door was still open, and he flashed a light into the tunnel. He could see lots of particles in the air. He brought himself carefully down and closed the portal behind him. When he reached the bottom, he saw a lot more rubble on the floor than before. He thought he could at least find his way to the intersecting tunnels. A compass would be nice as he recalled seeing the hospital from the eighth floor and knew that this building was west of the Anatomy building. The tunnel was now different. Large chucks of concrete covered the floor and each step he took, he had to ensure that the rubble would not move under his feet. He did that once, and his foot slid alongside the concrete, cutting his upper leg right through his pants. That was not smart. He got up and felt some blood flowing down his legs as he stumbled along. He was mildly aware that he was feeling a knot in his stomach. He thought if he got to the intersection, he could take that tunnel to the hospital and definitely find Marcella. If this was the only way in, he needed to take it. He could not wait for Clark to get back. It was possible that the hospital itself was damaged, and Marcella was dead or injured. The only way for him to stop his mind from racing was to keep moving.

He tried to move faster, but it resulted in taking more time and he continued to scrape his leg and cut his hands when he fell. He started to feel a little sick. The blood flowing down his leg caused his feet to slip, and he fell again, this time harder as his head hit a large, jagged piece of concrete. He was dizzy and thought he had better stay quiet for a while.

Maybe this was not such a great idea. I should call Lois, he thought. He reached down and pressed the button on the walkie talkie, but there was no response. He pressed a few times, but he heard nothing. He forgot that he turned it off to save batteries and now had to find the power switch. He decided to just lie here for a while and get his blood pressure back up and then press the power button. He knew that a nauseous feeling was a sign of shock. There was no sense in calling out, no one was in this tunnel. He was a real idiot sometimes, he thought. He should have asked Hung to join him. He'd tell Marcella, once he found her, what a big mistake he made. Once he felt better, he would make sure that he got her back home. Where he could take care of her.

Michael started to feel cold. I should grab the first aid kit. There is probably a bandage I can use to stop this bleeding. He looked down and realized that the blood was running through the concrete rubble and pooling around his legs. It was impossible to react since he could not move much. The blood was flowing from a deep gash on his leg, his pants were soaked. The blood was now coming out of him fast. He never felt a thing except the warmth of his blood down his leg. This must have happened with this last fall before he hit his head. He thought he was having a mild concussion, but he might have also severed an artery. That would not be good. He looked at the blood pool and doing a quick calculation of how much blood was in the body, he realized he would die. He would die soon. What did Marcella tell him? It would take ten minutes or was it half an hour? He was feeling sleepy now and cold. If he could rest awhile, things would be okay. The building shifted a little and pieces of concrete started to fall around him. He could not even raise his arm to cover his face. His only thought was he wanted to redo the last half hour. If he had not messed with the interns and closed the portal. Refusing help was a bad decision. That was so rare for him to make serious mistakes like this. I'll just go to sleep now and get my energy back. The building moved one more time and then there was silence.

JANE - 41

They were in the air, looking forward to seeing her home lights again across fields of blackness. Jane could not believe how smoothly everything worked out. Their combined effort in starting the Sherman Tank was pretty incredible. Hawk ratcheting the levers, rewiring the starter while she read the schematics all contributed to making it happen. Once they got the tank running and filled it with fuel, they raced into the house, collected a few things, informed Jake what was going on and in a quick hour, reached the helicopter. The next challenge was fixing the helicopter which Jane could only watch with fascination. Thankfully, her complete set of power tools and Jake's military expertise got it running. Leaving the tank behind was a key decision. Hawk suggested that after completing the repair. The debate started with taking the tank instead of the helicopter to pick up Michael and Marcella. Why risk this journey in a broken helicopter and just pace it slow with the tank? It became clear that the space was small, the treads were gummed up with the black goop over everything and it could get caught up in some debris field. "I think it will be an excellent roadster for us, but until we work out the maintenance from radioactive goop, I think we should take the helicopter," said Hawk.

"Okay, I see your point, but I hate to leave it here," she commented. "A lot can happen and I'm not sure how to lock it up. I have a key, but someone could seriously contaminate it if they just go inside."

"Yeah, I agree that would be terrible. I was just calculating how much time we have before dark. We are behind in getting back to the Five Guys and if we delay even one hour, we might not get there in time to fly them to the Seed Bank. I'm getting uneasy about that. We have seen no one wandering outside since we arrived."

Jane, also anxious about the dark, was persuaded to leave it. It was a risk they would have to chance. They'll pick it up on the way back. They loaded the supplies they had left behind and secured them in the backdoor hatch.

Hawk started up the helicopter, lifted and headed back to Jane's fueling up for the journey to the university. She was not ready to play it safe yet. Taking a risk with the tank was hard, but she felt it was important to support Hawk's mission. He made all of this possible for them and this was the least she could do. Being on his mission to extract Michael and Marcella was exciting and an opportunity to learn more about survival in current conditions.

Hawk put down the helicopter in a large turnaround spot off the driveway where Jane had one of three underground storage tanks buried. She had sufficient fuel to support five people for five years with solar and three years without. If nuclear winter set in, they would have to think about alternative energy supplies sooner. The work they had in front of them made her eager to get started. They needed to work on long-term survival strategies. She could feel the excitement in her bones.

Hawk filled the helicopter tank and Jane grabbed the remote and opened the garage door. The plastic panels were swinging back and forth, but she could see that Jake was waiting behind them. With Blue jumping up and down around her, she realized they now had a problem with keeping the dog out of the garage. She could easily slip between the panels, which was worrying Jane. How could she control this dog? Jake was aware and threw her a package of beef jerky. She found a place away from the garage and left more food for Blue to eat. She made it a little challenging to reach so Blue would be distracted while she spoke to Jake. She quickly ran back to the garage and Jake closed the door behind her.

"I've been wanting to do that since you left. Blue has been running around outside and looked starving," said Jake.

"That's so thoughtful, Jake. We must figure what to do with her later. She can't be in the house. Well, we've got working air and ground transportation now. The tank got us there smoothly, but the helicopter is running a little rough. It's funny that I had the tank, but never processed exactly why I would need it. Isn't that worth celebrating!" She filled him in on the details while standing between the garage panels and the garage door, not wanting to take her suit off. Jake shared that he was also busy, having successfully connected with the university. Once he heard about the Seed Bank's need for a doctor, he was trying to communicate with Jane the sense of urgency for Hawk to get there ASAP.

Jane paused, hearing the news for the first time. Luck was running out. Dan was suffering chest pains, maybe a heart attack. They needed to bring Marcella from the university to the Seed Bank to treat Dan. That had to be done. "The only problem is finding Marcella," said Jake. "I guess they're not sure where she is, nor have they seen Michael."

Jane trusted once they arrived at the university, something would work out. There were many doctors in a hospital. If Marcella was not there, they'd find someone else to take care of Dan.

Finally, Jane calmed down to think about their trip. To prepare a trip first to the university and then to the Seed Bank, they needed additional survival supplies for the people they were picking up. She had enough to last comfortably for six months in the bunker, and if they planned correctly and planted crops, they were in good shape for a long time. Her well, drilled to a depth of two thousand feet, would remain untainted for a very long time, the limestone bedrock being the perfect filter media. They needed a lot more protective suits.

As she heard the engine start up and the blades whip around, she felt excited to take this adventure. Jake walked halfway into the garage, grabbed a cooler, and slid it past the plastic panels. "There're sandwiches, apples, and two coffee drinks." She laughed at the forward thinking he exhibited. "There's a black folder with information on how to run communications from the helicopter to reach me and the university. Here are seven protective suits hanging in the garage attic."

She was shocked at the planning. Jake was becoming a perfect survivalist! "We need to go then. Anything else? I'm almost afraid to ask."

"Yes, something weird is coming over the communications satellite. A repeated message comes every 120 minutes. It is a repetition of three words, Simplicity, Patience, Compassion. It was broadcast in English only. Any idea what that means?"

"I think that comes from a book by Lao Tzu. He wrote the Tao Te Ching. That's both interesting and surprising. Directing world-wide annihilation and broadcasting an ancient poets mantra. Could anything be stranger? She thanked Jake, turned as the garage door opened, grabbed the folder, cooler and suits and turned to walk toward the helicopter. I hope Blue does not jump on me, she thought. Any smell of food would attract her.

As she looked at the blackened helicopter, her mind flashed on everything she did so far. Finding the lower tunnel, getting a helicopter, crashing a helicopter, getting home, and then driving a Sherman tank to repair the helicopter. As she got closer to the helicopter, she steeled her thoughts against crashing again. One more trip and she would be back in the safety of her home.

They survived, they went through incredible challenges, decisions and depended on each other. She was right in so many areas of survival about what was needed, but the most important one was being able to trade risk for trust in others and feeling the uncompromising support of community. Belonging to a larger group that survived because of their combined intellect, heart and capability was pretty amazing. She could look forward and be satisfied that this new thing was now her life work. She would spend one hundred percent of her effort surviving, anticipating and growing green things for the future. She was feeling like she was part of something, but she was not interested in losing her independence. It will be a delicate balance, she thought.

Looking across the horizon of blackness, she now knew what each shade of black represented, having walked through this very field. The darkest black was actually flaky and wispy charred pieces of grain. She wondered if seeds survived the temperature of an atomic blast? She wondered what the future held beyond the next twenty-four hours for humanity. She could think about her own personal survival, but what about those that weren't prepared for it? What did that feel like? Were there groups working on saving people, bringing them back to safer places? Right now, the future did not seem much different than the present. Would the future be filled with despair or with hope? She felt free, being in a helicopter, even having the fuel to run it, but what was her responsibility to the rest of the survivors? She and Dr. Blue always spoke about her obsessive behavior, but never recognized this could be an actual event, possibly a vision of sorts. She needed to find Dr. Blue. Would Hawk help her do that? Could they find Dr. Blue's farm? They talked about the concept of saving friends and family versus survivors in general and what role she played. Right now, she was of no use to anyone unless she was assured of a future first. Then she could help others take care of their own future.

LOIS - 42

Lois woke again. This time, no one was watching her as she opened her eyes. She felt rested and Suri's weight was still comforting, heavy against her legs. As she sat up to look around, Qiang and Cong were both fixated on the large viewing screens. Lois tried to focus her eyes, wondering about the gray slow-moving blobs.

"Is that Clark?" she said groggily. "Why didn't you wake me up?"

"We thought you seemed tired and needed sleep. How do you feel?" said Cong.

"I'd feel much better if you tell me what's going on."

"I think you were experiencing an extreme drop in adrenaline. Our bodies can produce only so much Lois. You had an adrenaline crash." Cong was not as calm as before. He was probably worried about her.

"Isn't that Clark?"

"Yes, we finally chatted with him briefly. His batteries ran low, and he turned off the walkie talkie until he had something to report. We only spoke a few minutes, but he is with Marcella. He knows that we connected with Michael and Marcella agreed to come back for Michael. They all are safe at this point. Karey fell over while entering the building, tore her suit and strained a tendon in her leg. She has been slowing the return significantly. Clark was carrying her at one point."

"Oh, no. I know how those things can hurt. What else did Clark share?"

"He was pretty excited to be spending time in the hospital. It was all hands-on deck and our group spent some time to help set up more rooms for advanced procedures. Most injuries were fairly recent from the tunnel collapse, but still insignificant, considering what could have happened. They also confirmed that there is no passage between the hospital and the tunnels. A group tried for hours, clearing debris to get back here. They have isolated everyone in the hospital since the first bombs brought down the surrounding buildings. They spent the first eight hours triaging people affected and then started to organize around various medical needs that might arise," said Cong.

"Marcella is not the only doctor there, and she said they could spare her. She sounded like she was anxious about Michael and could not believe that he was here, looking for her," said Cong.

"So, is she in the group we are watching on the screen?" said Lois.

"Yes, she's one of those gray blobs. She's wearing the spare respirator and suit Clark carried," said Qiang.

Lois stared at the monitor. Could it be true? Could Clark be safe? Did he also bring back Marcella? Is it even possible to be sealed off by a catastrophic event and still have everything work out? She looked down at Suri and smiled. The day started so innocently. A soft layer of snow on the ground, walking Suri and thinking about leaving grad school. She was going to start her career as a full-time business entrepreneur. Was her mom okay? What was the future of the world? She walked around to settle herself. She needed to calm down her mind race. She thought about what was next. Getting Michael and Marcella on that helicopter seemed like a priority now. Connecting with the Seed Bank seemed like a smart idea and one that could nurture an alliance. While she walked around, she realized how protected she was by the people around her and honestly wondered if she carried her weight. A new idea started to shape in her mind.

"Where is Michael right now? Have we heard from him?"

"No, we haven't," said Cong. "I've tried to call him on the walkie talkie, but he isn't answering. Wish we had a cell phone that works. Hung and Bai are combing the tunnels systematically for Michael. So far, there is no trace. Bai said Michael talked about a tunnel below, but they could not find it or anyone who knew about it. They're just returning now, without Michael."

Lois thought, what's next? They resolved the virtually impossible problem of finding Marcella and now Michael is missing? What could she do? They needed to find Michael before Clark and Lou returned with Marcella. What would they say to her if Michael was AWOL?

"I've got an idea. I'm going out with Suri and we'll look for Michael. I've sat around here long enough. Everything is under control and we just need to get Michael back here. Anyway, I'm curious about what it's like in the tunnels. We cannot isolate ourselves forever. I'm tired of sitting and doing nothing!"

Cong looked at Lois and then at Qiang. They nodded to each other in that infuriating way. "There's one other thing, Lois. The Seed Bank sent an IM. Actually, Luming sent the message that Dan had a heart attack."

Lois' knees shook a little as she sat down. "Come again?"

"Yes, he is resting, but needs medical help. They requested that we deliver Marcella to the Seed Bank as soon as possible. They also encouraged all of us, except for Dr. Anthony, to go there as well. We've contacted Hawk who should arrive soon, but we really have no idea when."

The thought of Dan having a heart attack without medical assistance, made her crazy. All Lois could think about was Dan. How old was he, sixty-something? She was fighting a lot of surging emotion and settled on the need to do something constructive.

She stood up. "The need to find Michael is urgent. I'm going."

Qiang came up to her and nodded. "If you take Suri, she might be helpful in finding Michael. Does she have a good nose?"

"Are you kidding," laughed Lois. "I registered her in a program to train as a cancer-sniffing dog. There was a pilot study, and she passed the initial screening test here at the U." Suri's tail wagged as if she knew Lois was talking about her. "Okay, then."

"Let's get you ready," said Cong.

Qiang pulled up the maps for the hospital and the anatomy building. The three looked at them and Qiang showed Lois the intersection that collapsed and the remaining tunnels that connected to the hospital. Lois kept staring and pointed to the screen with the anatomy building blueprints.

Qiang leaned in to speak. "Look at this building closely. Now find the diagrams for each floor. Now, see that the Anatomy building has an extra floor because the lower tunnel starts with 2. The older nomenclature for buildings was to use B and SB for Sub-basement. As they converted this blueprint, they changed the levels as on an elevator. The first level was a sub-basement."

"So that's the tunnel that Michael used? It exists, but how did he find it?" said Lois. "Let's prepare some food for Bai and Hung in case we run into them. I'll grab my backpack and put a few medical supplies in it." Lois looked up at the screen and saw Clark carrying Karey and leading the others.

"They have a ways to go, but I suspect they should be back within the hour," said Cong.

They all got busy and Qiang prepared a download on a device that Lois could use to reference the blueprints. The double door opened and Bai came through first, followed by Hung. Lois shrieked and hugged both of them. They are quite the pair, thought Lois. Bai with his now tattered floral shirt and linen pants and Hung in his beautifully printed green camouflage shirt. She stood back and scanned their faces. They look different, Lois thought. Like they aged a lot since they left. It must be their eyes, she thought.

They prepared something to eat. Food was simple, crackers and peanut butter, but nourishing. Suri ate the dry dog food that Hung found in a storage room. They all sat quietly for a while.

"How many people are in the tunnels?" asked Cong.

"I'm estimating five hundred and forty-five," said Hung.

"That sounds like a well-defined estimate," said Cong. "I guess photographic memories are hard to control."

"Not a lot of significant injuries," said Hung. "There are groups forming. They blocked anyone from leaving the tunnels to go outside and become exposed to radiation."

Lois stated, "More than one tunnel collapsed, right? I wonder if Michael was in a tunnel? If you don't find him, that is the only conclusion we can make, right?"

"Yes, I suppose," said Hung. "I'm disappointed in him. We spent all of this effort locating him and he takes off."

"That's why I will look for him. We have a plan and think there is a sub-tunnel in the anatomy building that links to the hospital and somehow hooks up to the main tunnels you've been walking. Have you seen any access spots that you could not explain?" Lois wanted to move quickly.

Hung shook his head. "We should be able to find it, if it exists. We can get new batteries for the walkie-talkies and communicate what we find."

"When Clark gets back, there will be a lot to do. The rest of you can fill Marcella in about seeing Michael firsthand. I think that Hung, myself and Suri can easily move unobstructed, checking out different areas. Have you recorded any areas with high levels of radiation? Are you up to going again, Hung?"

"I should be okay," said Hung. "And I've not recorded any significant readings in the tunnels so far."

Lois got up and placed her plate on the counter and said goodbye. She took Suri's leash, and Hung got up to join her. He grabbed three bottles of water and dropped them in his backpack.

Lois was relieved to leave the room. They had a plan, and she was moving things forward. No one seemed to doubt her abilities. As long as she felt their support, she could move forward. Now to find Michael.

As they approached the locked double door entrance, Hung unlocked the long chain that draped through the handles of each door. The chain dropped, making a huge noise, and they left it unlocked behind them. Still no one had found this area. I wonder why, she thought?

As they turned toward a longer tunnel, she started to see people either walking the hallway or sitting along the wall. It was a strange feeling for Lois. What was their future staying here? Was someone going to rescue these people? Quite a few individuals did not look healthy. Anyone in a wheelchair sat quietly. As they walked, Suri was sniffing and people were reaching out to her and smiling. Suri knew she was on a mission and did not stop.

Hung explained to Lois how the tunnels were laid out and how they systematically combed each tunnel for Michael. They looked at the map of the five tunnels crossing the point where they stood. Lois took the anatomy building overlay, and it became obvious which two tunnels moved in an eastern and southern direction.

They walked the first tunnel and Lois' device showed that they were going straight east. They went to the end of that tunnel and the tunnel stopped. Checking each door with an exit sign, they all contained stairs that went up. They walked the second tunnel, and the story was the same. This was the tunnel where most people stayed. Each door had someone posted in front, not allowing anyone to go up. They talked to the person guarding the entrance who did not know about any sub-tunnels. They walked a second time slowly, looking for any sign, and at the end of the second tunnel, Suri stopped and barked. There was one woman, dressed in white pants and a navy blazer, sitting against the wall, head tied with a beautiful royal blue paisley scarf, matching her crystal blue eyes. Suri's bark echoed loudly, and people stopped to stare. This poor woman smiled and put her hand on Suri to calm her down. Lois felt queasy, knowing that Suri was just doing the job she trained her for. They lingered and Lois asked her if she needed anything and she said water. Lois looked around and saw a janitor's closet and walked in to find a deep basin with a large faucet. There was a cart that held a carboy, empty of water and a few cups. She filled three cups and gave them to the woman.

Lois paused for a moment and went back to the janitor's closet. She stared at the cart. Didn't Bai or Hung say Michael was passing out water? She went back and got Suri and Hung to follow her and closed the door. Suri was wagging her tail and sniffing around until she started to scratch the floor where a round manhole cover was flush with the floor. Lois turned on the light hanging from the ceiling, opened the manhole and felt a cool breeze of stale air hit her face.

"Well, this must be it. It looks just like the way we got here from the alumni building," said Lois. They both used their flashlights to shine down into the unknown depths. "I guess this could be the route that Michael took. How the hell are we going to get Suri down these rungs? We don't have the ropes the other closet had," she said.

"Not a problem," said Hung. "If you shine your flashlight, I'll get her down." He picked her up with such ease and climbed down with one hand and his feet barely touching the rungs. "I used to be in gymnastics," he shouted up to Lois, grinning. Hung was incredibly strong and he was quite proud of his accomplishment.

Lois followed and the three of them stood, looking both ways and catching the significance of where they were. There was debris everywhere. The building was shifting and each time plaster hit the floor, the collective sound literally resonated through Lois' body. She needed to distract herself.

Lois flashed the headlamp onto a brass plaque "I wonder, how long is this tunnel? It says here the building was built in the early 1903. No wonder some of it collapsed. Well, it looks like my compass is showing the

Anatomy building would be in that direction." They carefully navigated around the debris while Suri trotted on top and they soon saw more signs of debris and cracked walls. They ceiling was made of old plaster materials mixed with sharp, almost glass-like shards.

"What are we doing, Hung?" said Lois. "If Michael went this way, he didn't get very far. This stuff looks dangerous." She picked up a piece of the ceiling and ran her fingers across it. "It's sharp as a razor. I wonder why they used such dangerous materials?"

"Maybe that's why the tunnel was closed off," said Hung.

Suri suddenly pulled on her leash and Lois released her hands letting her go. This is extremely hazardous, she thought. Dogs have a major artery that could be severed against the soft tissue of their legs.

"Suri," she called. Then she heard her bark repeatedly just like when she came up to squirrels. They cautiously moved closer as the ceiling dropped more plaster and raised more dust. Strange behavior for Suri, thought Lois. "Suri, come here," she repeated, but her barking increased in frequency as they approached. A feeling of dread was taking Lois by surprise. What's there?

As their headlamps fixated forward, it appeared Suri was fast approaching a body lying in blood. All she could see was blood surrounding both sides of this man's right suit leg. It stained his thin pants red. The blood pool had coagulated with a skimmed surface and it was clear that this man had passed.

Hung took the man's pulse to confirm and Lois was quietly bringing her thoughts together. Wasn't this the day when nothing goes right? This could be Michael and he was dead. What a catastrophe! He went down here, completely on his own. God knows why he thought he would find Marcella here. If he had only waited. They stood quietly, but the sounds of this unstable building were distracting. Hung took the man's wallet out of his pants and showed it to Lois. It said Michael D. Kraken, III. He was born September 11, 1962. Suri sat down and started to softly whine.

"Lois, let's head back. This tunnel isn't safe or maybe the whole building will collapse." That was enough encouragement for Lois to turn and head back to the ladder.

"I'm afraid Suri might get hurt with these sharp pieces of ceiling."

"I'll just pick her up, then. Let's hurry."

Hung went first, showing no distress at carrying Suri. Once they got to the closet exit, Hung carried her up the rungs. Lois climbed up, feeling thankful that they were out. What a horrific death. She then remembered the walkie talkie they left behind.

They replaced the cover and just sat there for a moment, in stunned silence.

"Michael was almost a fictional character for me. Now he's dead. I'm feeling rather numb. That is the first dead body I have ever seen. I really want to get back and find out how Clark is doing. We can bring this news back with us and plan our next move. Telling Marcella her husband turned into a crazy lunatic, looking for her, and killed himself unnecessarily trying, will not be easy." As they stood up, the building shifted again.

"Let's get out of here!" said Hung. He grabbed Suri's leash, and they opened the door. The tunnel started to look unstable. They took off running while the noise increased. It almost felt like they were in an airport, feeling the vibrations of planes taking off and landing. They did not look back but caused others to run in the same direction. Finally, after reaching the center of the tunnel system, everyone slowed down. As the crowd started to exchange experiences and naively speculate, Lois looked back and saw the woman in the blue scarf being helped by a young male intern. Lois decided that would be her sign that there were good things ahead. Hung led the way. Most people were walking in the opposite direction toward the center to find out what was going on as they pressed against the crowd.

They carefully paced themselves and eventually came upon the empty hallway to the Physics building. Lois wondered how long it would be until the masses started moving in this direction.

They came upon the double doors, went through quickly and locked the two doors together as before. Lois was getting excited. Would Clark be there? Could she finally have him with her in safety?

Retracing their steps, they finally pulled open the doors to find Clark speaking to a tall, thin women in a white lab coat. Lou and Cong were in the room, but Qiang and Bai were missing. Clark had a strange look that combined tired and excited which aged his baby face ten years. As he looked at Lois, they ran toward each other and hugged.

"Sis, you could have been killed. The anatomy building is collapsing."

"How did you know? Hey, we forgot to use the walkie talkie. We started to run, and it never occurred to us to use it."

"Dr. Anthony told us. He was just here. Look. He left this fifty-pound bag of seeds for us to take to the Seed Bank," said Cong. "He's headed back to the hospital in one of our suits to help out."

"Why the change of tune?" said Lois.

"We told him he couldn't go to the Seed Bank and that he had to leave. He was not happy, but Dr. Brown was very persuasive," said Cong. "I use the word persuasive in air quotes." He smiled at this last comment, which told Lois there was a lot to that story.

"Hi." Marcella shook Lois' hand and Hung's. "We can quit talking about Dr. Anthony. The word pompous a-hole was created exclusively for that man. I'm not sure how he gets away with it, but he does. I'm sure he can be useful at the hospital. I would like to be miles away from him with Michael soon. Now, for your news. Where's Michael?" She was wearing small beady glasses that only covered her eyes and not her face. Lois noticed that she had a strong correction, which looked like small pieces of a magnifying glass resting between her eyes. This made her look intelligent, smart, and sensible. She had probably not touched her hair since this morning as the soft bun on the top of her head was unraveling off onto her shoulders. She cast a very striking figure. Lois took a breath in and let it out slowly, collecting her thoughts. Marcella's face dropped with this small gesture, knowing the meaning right away.

"He's dead?" she shouted. "He's dead?" She now looked like a teapot ready to boil. Lois took her hands and showed her to a chair.

"Listen to me, Marcella. We found him in a partially collapsed tunnel that he must have thought led to the hospital. He severed an artery and bled out onto the floor. We had to run out of the tunnel as it showed signs of collapsing. I'm very sorry. I think we did the best we could. It was Suri who found him." Hung handed her Michael's wallet.

She looked at the wallet and then sat straight up. "His body? Where is his body? I can't believe we were so close to each other. I had no clue. I was treating patients when I could have been looking for Michael. One minute, I assumed he was dead and then I found out he was alive and now he is dead again."

Bai sat next to Marcella and handed her a cup of tea. Lois stared, wondering if Marcella could handle the cup as it was shaking in her hand, but she was an emotional pro. She sipped it and seemed deep in thought. From time to time, she asked for more details about Michael, which Bai patiently went over with her. Lois felt sorry that they could not provide her with the comfort of having a private moment. There was no privacy here. Just as Lois was walking over to Clark to catch up with him, the lights started to flicker.

"What's that?" said Lois.

"Yes, this is a new development. Bai and Qiang are working on the back-up generator. Things are more unstable. We're working on another exit plan. I'm ready to connect with the Seed Bank in about ten minutes."

Lois looked at Clark and started to recognize the signs of another issue surfacing.

LUMING - 43

Troy was competent and Luming realized that he was doing better without him. Troy did not show a lot of emotion and was wantonly looking at the computer as Luming asked two friendly questions. He tried to maintain a conversation, but casual conversation without a specific purpose made Troy twitch. It turned out Troy was on to something. He was scanning satellite networks and was picking up more noise than usual. This was significant to Troy in advancing their ability to communicate with the satellites. Luming was out of place here. Troy stirred up a strong feeling in him to do something worthy. I've got to do something, he thought. He walked back to the library and found Brother still reading in the deep purple brocade chair while Sharme was in the corner, in front of a computer. Sharme's head raised as he entered the room.

"Luming, how are you doing? How is Dan doing? I'm researching heart conditions and we might have tinctures that would be safe for him to take and calm his condition while we wait for western medical help. He told me he wasn't receptive to homeopathy yet. I'm okay with that and hope we can get Marcella here soon. Maybe she'll be open to alternative medicine approaches. Balancing his chi, well, acupuncture is a must." Luming nodded.

Sharme looked into the other room. "As you probably concluded, Troy is a genius regarding electronics. I've always had a hard time getting him to join large groups. Dealing with more than two people is impossible for him to handle. He finds that human interaction disrupts his equilibrium. If I were to summarize, and I'm not talking out of school as he's heard this before, he's a loner. He has a hard time speaking about his feelings, and since he does not reveal them to others, he does not receive the benefit of receiving the warm connections that can be gained or felt from others. People then leave him alone, which begins the cycle of isolation. He was not always like that. His father left us when he was ten. That was when he started to withdraw from social interaction. Not armed with an education in child rearing, I let him, to coin a phrase, do his thing. While I blossomed with the new freedom of uncompromised independence, he withdrew and read books, lots of books. The library told me he checked out each book in the library at least once. With this important assignment," and she nodded toward the other room, "...I've already seen signs that he is opening up to others. I can see how much he likes being with you."

Luming smiled and was refreshed at Sharme's openness and decided not to share his reaction to working with Troy. He might have been opening up, but Luming did not experience that. Sharme's beautiful shawl of a dark indigo was softly folded around her body. The clear crystals hanging from her ears, bracelets of Lapis Lazuli, and the single bird hanging from a thin-chained necklace, all reminded him of Wu, a wise woman from his village. She was older than Sharme, but always presented herself to others with wisdom and clear thinking. Sharme was all of that, but hearing her express her insecurity about motherhood was still refreshing to him. Wu would never share her vulnerabilities with anyone.

"What is that around your neck?" asked Luming.

"It's a Sparrow Hawk, my totem."

"I always wondered about totems. How did you find your totem?" he asked.

"Luming, it came to me when I was very young. I've always known it and it's possible my parents knew it before I did." She smiled at him. She had such a youthful personality; he hadn't questioned her age until now. If Troy was in his twenties, how old was she? She could be in her sixties or she could be forty-ish. "Let's check and see how the group is doing."

"What group?" he asked.

"Well," she paused, "Bill, Trudy and the others. Come along. Truthfully, Troy does not need you and he probably would be happy to be alone right now." She got up and Luming followed. As he left, he touched Brother on the shoulder. He absently waved back to Luming.

They walked toward Tunnel 3 where the manhole cover was, which reminded Luming of the last time he went there with the cook, Karyn. Sharme opened the large cover and slipped into the dark space, moving down the rungs with the agility of a teenager. Her shawl was floating around her and the crystals from her ears seemed to catch light from some unknown source. She looked like a mystical figure to him as he stared down. A little intimidated by her strength and flexibility, he started down cautiously, carefully finding each rung as he descended. The sound of animated voices became louder, and the laughter was inviting. I wonder what's going on, he thought.

Sharme was waiting for him and her eyes were now sparkling as light flashes bounced off the walls of this large cavernous space. He noticed a familiar rock-and-roll song playing at the other end of the room. That space was lit to reveal concrete walls, smooth gray surfaces and a honeycomb structure with people moving around.

They walked toward the action. "This is our living space," said Sharme. "We are all going to share this space for sleeping and living. We built pre-formed walls to separate each room for privacy, like the cubicles currently used in offices. For tonight, we just need to clean the surfaces the best we can and find enough futons, cushions or stacked yoga mats to sleep on. Let's check it out."

The larger, older man, Bill, came up. "Hey, Sharme, Luming. Besides prepping for sleep tonight, we are also working on changing this space long term. Take a look," said Bill, as he pointed to a blueprint on the long table.

Trudy was sitting at the computer and smiled briefly as she looked up.

"We are famished," said Bill. "I've been passing around small bits of beef jerky I had in my office. Would you like some?" He handed it to Luming which he accepted, but Sharme gestured no interest and said, "I'm fasting."

Bill looked at the far corner with a man standing outside a door labeled, Restroom. "McLane, what do you need?"

"We're gonna need paper and towels over here," McLane shouted. "I think they're in the pantry."

"Got it," he shouted back. "We also need lights. I'll see if I can find them. Anyone else need anything while I'm up there?"

"Check on the status of dinner," asked Francine. "Frank and I are famished. Thanks for doing this, Bill."

After Bill left, Luming studied what they were doing. Each space was divided strong, wooden-like green poles, anchored on the floor in hexagonal rubber molds. As they finished lashing each pole together, they draped the space in wild colored fabric, sculpting the room into a large honeycomb structure. Several pots of Spider plants, Philodendrons and Cactus were scattered around. Lamps were located around the room with an extensive array of extension cords being taped to the floor by Lincoln.

"This is just a first stab at what we need now," said Sharme. "We clustered groups like Dan, Lizzy and Betty together with you and Brother next to them. Chris and Dorothy were placed on the opposite side."

"That is so cool," said Luming. "How considerate."

"I'm glad you like it," said Trudy still typing away at her computer. "Scar gave us the task and we've been organizing the project ever since. I've always appreciated her fortitude, but I had no idea how competent Scar would be in a crisis. She's hands off in how things get done." She hesitated when Sharme coughed and then said, "Well, most of the time." They made eye contact with each other and laughed. Trudy turned toward a large stack of long poles. "We are using hemp stalks as our major construction material. It is amazing in its versatility as we use it for lashing as well. If you look over in the corner, Frank is building half a dozen dressing rooms from the same materials. Hemp is sturdy and if protected from moisture, will last a long time. Eventually, we will process fabric, toilet paper, plates and writing paper from hemp. Amazing."

"Wow," said Luming. "Who thought of that?"

Trudy smiled. "I'm not taking credit for that. That was all Frank. He was our production guy and has a creative mind, especially under pressure. He can make things by the mile or by the inch. I would be understating if I said we are extremely lucky that he made it here." Luming already knew that Trudy had a way of speaking that was half-condescending and half-unintelligible. He smiled back at her, recognizing that he did not need to understand anything about the dynamics between Seed Members. He already knew Frank and Trudy were both very talented.

"You all have worked together before. You know each other's strengths and weaknesses," said Luming. "My corporate job was all about the team and I found that once a group worked out their interpersonal differences in an earlier project, we could accomplish anything, collectively. We let differences lead us to better solutions but the slate was always cleaned. Of course, management took advantage of that and requested that projects be done at an impossible pace. No one seemed to mind though; as long as we were passionate about the task and were willing to jump through hoops."

"Doers are good to have around," said Sharme. "Of course, we all get caught in the cycle of feeding the fire. I used to ask, to what end does all of this work amount to? Catastrophe has changed that. Now we are in a situation that you have to be a doer, thinker, and planner in order for everyone to survive. A human experiment is being hatched as we speak. Death is around the corner."

Luming was reminded of the Buddhist practice of using death to be present and guide your life, marana-sati. He learned from this practice that very few things standup when you shine the light of death on them. If you are near death, conflict becomes trivial.

"You know, Sharme. I don't need a paycheck to motivate me to work. I think I would work just as hard, but now things that I love doing," said Luming.

"That's right, Luming!" said Sharme. "Ideally, there's no reason why we all can't do what we are good at. At least, we should find out if that will work for us. As we become a close group, we'll be able to find each person's personal energy and skills. I want to know what makes someone smile and what brings them to tears. Just think what could happen if everyone could follow their own personal dreams. An artist like Constantine, would pick up his brushes each day and paint our walls, or assemble mosaics into a pleasing portrait."

Luming nodded. He almost felt like he was high. This was the first time since the attack that his heart felt light instead of heavy. Could he replace his anxiety with something that felt good? Sharme made him feel warm, and her gentle, quiet presence was calming. How could he even explain this feeling of acceptance? I wonder what it is I'm good at and what I like to do?

Trudy stopped what she was doing and looked up. They made eye contact. Trudy got up and walked over to them.

"Sorry, I probably appear rude. As I was listening to you two, I was feeling so disconnected. Here I am, so typical of me, planning and researching and missing the whole point. Sometimes, I feel so alone, even sitting here surrounded by friends. I'm afraid I'm only capable of speaking my mind and I might have sounded rude and insensitive in the past. It is kind of a defense mechanism I have, Luming. I'm really a nice person and I just get carried away with fairness and justice issues. Since I declared my identity as a black lesbian feminist, I've never felt like I was a part of anything until I joined the Seed Bank. This has always been my home. Everyone here knows me. They know my MO and my heart. Given a chance, Luming, we will learn about each other and how to get along."

"You are lucky to be able to speak about it. I had friends in China that were desperate to hide their sexual preference. They told me ugly stories about living in China when the penalty for homosexuality was death. So I'm cool, Trudy, and thank you for letting me know."

She hugged him and sat down back in her spot.

"Let's get back," said Sharme and she led Luming back toward the entrance.

"Are there other ways to get here?" asked Luming.

"Yes, of course. There are three ways, but you might as well discover them in due course. Leave it a mystery that you will solve eventually. Let's go check on Troy."

As they walked back, Luming was feeling better. It's strange how one can go in and out of feeling comfortable. This was a completely new situation, tragic and yet comforting. He was thinking that he was no longer a complete stranger, people recognized him and used his name. It was small things that made him feel good.

Now he just had to perform in a way that would justify this attention. Could he step up? Could he find a few things that allowed him to shine and earn respect from this large group? He did it before in a corporation under a very different kind of stress. This was more self-imposed and definitely more challenging as there was no place to hide. He would have to pay attention to his motives, his opinions and his actions. As long as he operated truthfully, he felt he could defend himself in any circumstance.

They walked in as Troy was waving to them.

"Here he is, Lois. He just walked in through the door and I just waved at him," said Troy. Troy mouthed, "It's Lois." That was obvious to Luming, but he thought it was interesting that Troy was so nervous about talking directly to her. He might have a form of Asperger's, thought Luming. They were often well read, smart, literal, but socially awkward. He thought of asking Sharme about that sometime.

Luming grabbed the headset. "Lois, fill us in. Do you have Michael and Marcella? Were you able to connect with Flying Hawk?"

"Just a minute," said Lois. "We're getting a communication from Flying Hawk right now."

Word must have gotten around as the whole Seed Bank team started to filter into the Hub. Bill bounced in with McLane and Francine. Frank and Lincoln, followed by Trudy, who even cracked a tight smile as if resisting any news until it was certifiably good. Chris, Dorothy and Scar were the last to arrive.

Dorothy mouthed the words to everyone. "He's doing fine. He's sleeping."

Chris added, "I left Betty behind to watch over Dan. He's stable and not sweating anymore. Let's see if we can get a doctor here, stat!"

The room was still. Each breath measured with all attention on Luming as he took over the exchange from Troy. They were hearing Lois talk to Flying Hawk, but nothing was distinguishable. People started to move around. It worried Luming, wondering how long this call would last.

"I'm back," she said. "We have news from Hawk. We have news from us as well. First, Dr. Marcella Brown is here. She has a few instructions to make Dan comfortable and stable. I don't know how to say this." The line went quiet. This was bad news for sure, thought Luming. "Let me say this," another pause on the line. "Michael, her husband, Michael, died in a collapsed tunnel. He died looking for her. We are all shocked and sad, but Marcella wants to help, and we just completed arrangements to meet with Hawk and Jane, they're still using the helicopter." There was stillness in the room. This was unexpected.

"Hi, Marcella here." She spoke clearly and slowly with about ten things to do and observe. She was concerned when she heard he had numbness in his hand. Dorothy asked if he should take his nitroglycerin tablets.

"Give him three baby aspirin every four hours to lower the risk of blood clots. Keep him warm in blankets, but not hot and sweaty. Have him take nitroglycerin when he feels the need. He'll know." They exchanged more details, and she was effective at providing valuable information in a calm and reassuring way.

"I'm so sorry, Dr. Brown, for your loss," said Dorothy. "Thank you for putting yourself in danger to come here."

"Yes, there are a lot of reasons to come and help, including keeping myself busy. Michael would not want me to sit around." Her voice cracked with that last statement and Lois' got back on the phone. "Cong wants to say a few words."

"Greetings, everyone. Cong here. We are very lucky to have Marcella with us. She's amazing. So let's make arrangements for us to find you. Hawk and Jane have had quite a journey, but we have not spent a lot of time sharing the details. Our priority is to get Marcella to the Seed Bank quickly. She's ready and is coming with her medical supplies and some that we retrieved from a pharmacy."

Scar stepped up to the microphone. "Scar here. Dr. Brown, we are all sorry for your loss and grateful to you helping us with Dan." She also spent a moment to collect her thoughts. "We'll have you enter in from the back of the parking lot. That way, we can manage contamination in our most remote part of the SB. We'll open the doors when we hear you coming." Troy had a map of the city open and Scar was looking at it closely. "I think the best thing is for us to provide latitude and longitude settings for you. That should work, right?"

"Yes, we've downloaded several maps of your area. Hawk said he can easily carry four passengers. I'd like Lois to travel with Marcella from here. Would that be okay? That way, she can help bridge the status of our supplies and fill you in on our needs," said Cong. "Is that okay, Lois?" There was a long pause and Cong said, "She's nodding. One more thing. We're bringing you a drone kit that was developed for a local robotic race we competed in last fall. We're hoping that ..." and the line was cut.

There was tangible excitement in the room. It was balanced with the news about Michael but obviously this presented a new project and opportunity to enhance their ability to bring in someone from outside.

"A few things before we break," said Scar. "They will wear protective suits and respirators. We need to walk them through a procedure that controls contamination. We need a Geiger counter to measure the radiation once they complete the last step. This is our newest challenge but will be an ongoing concern. Anyone entering the facility will have to follow it. We are unspoiled so far and we have to contain particles that have been exposed to radiation. Luming, go back to Dan and Betty and tell them the news. What else?" Scar now looked tired, thought Luming. While having people arrive safely, it was a lot to take in. "I'm going up to portal 9," she said.

She walked out and Luming grabbed Brother who was sitting in the corner and did not look that enthusiastic himself.

"Are you okay?" asked Luming.

"I'm okay. I've been reading about the psychology of survival. I think there is a need for relationship building. It is well documented that this is an absolute necessary survival skill required for long-term success. I've found Lao Tzu's Tao Te Ching in the library. Luming, you must have read it. We need to talk about this message. I've thought about it, but not sure it applies to us."

"Sure, my family studied the Dao. I would love to hear your interpretation," said Luming. Luming was on the edge of remembering where he was and who he was with when he first heard the Tao. His father had a large book on a podium and often read to him from that.

"Thanks, Luming. Let's go check on Dan," and they left the room.

DAN - 44

Dan was feeling much better after Betty served him tea. It relaxed him in a way that he had not experienced before. Maybe they gave him Ocha-O. It tasted slightly more earthy than normal tea, but not being a tea drinker, he wasn't sure. The soft cushions of the bed he lay on provided a warm feeling to his back as he relaxed. This place was almost Bedouin with tapestries hanging from the wall, large candles positioned randomly on wall sconces and soft repetitive drumbeats coming from speakers around the room. Each candle cast an overlapping shadow on the wall that enhanced certain figures on the tapestries. The combined effect revealed a story that marched across the room, detailing a journey from a stream, through a swamp to a wooded area and ending on a mountain that repeated the cycle back to the stream. He could not take his eyes off the walls and he was at ease with just laying here.

After the initial shock of having a heart attack, all of these people left him alone with Betty and Lizzy. He started to memorize the names of the new people he met. The efforts everyone was making to ensure he was okay finally passed, and they just had to wait for Marcella to arrive. Once he realized he had the freedom to just relax and not be busy, he started a breathing ritual that Brother taught him. The room was perfect for Lizzy. She could walk around cause no harm. She had to navigate between pillows and what looked like hard cushions used in meditation. When she fell, she quickly got up and continued to explore the room. Betty said she found a small room just outside the chapel that Scar told them to use if she wanted to sleep. Lizzy was a trooper. She was good with different people and loved to play. Deep down, his deepest worry was that she was orphaned. Where's Susan right now? Was she safe? These thoughts stressed him to where he was back breathing and looking at the walls.

He thought he was the oldest person here, but now he was not sure. A brief encounter with Sharme made him rethink that assumption. It made no difference; he was used to being the old one. People here pulled together when needed and then split apart into small group projects or just disappeared. While waiting for the helicopter, he sensed that the arrival of Marcella, Lois, Jane, and Hawk was not just about a medical emergency. This helicopter meant transportation. It meant that they could extend their reach beyond these tunnels.

He was excited about Jane being here. That would be amazing. Comparing her to Scar, he saw many differences, but also similarities. They were both practicing survivalists in their own way. Dan did not know too much about Jane's obsession, but he suspected that if she was en route to the Seed Bank in a helicopter, she was prepared for anything. Jane was part of Dan's previous life, the life they left behind. Of all the people that deserved a chance of survival, it would be Jane. It was not just an obsession. She practiced what she preached. She was a caring and conscious human being that always stuck to her principles, which was not always a strategy for success in corporate America. And it wasn't that corporate America was corrupt. It was just not human. The corporation itself was treated as if it was a human being, requiring constant feeding with a very sensitive diet of continuously changing requirements. Food that would burn the soul out of your body and make you do things to others that were unkind at best and fatal at worst. Yes, over the years, Dan knew of two suicide attempts. Knowing the circumstances taught him how corporate life could invade your life-force. No, he could not swallow the Kool-Aid, but he did his fair share of not always taking a stand when he should have. There was a list of "Things I'm Not Proud Of." A "Proud of" list follows that and one thing on that list was Jane. She had it all and could be assertive against bullies and still be authentic to her nature. She would be a great addition to their emerging enclave.

Just thinking of Jane being here raised his hopes for the future. He was painfully aware that new people brought opportunities, but also more voices and possibly more tension. Or maybe not. This was a new society, based on the ashes of the old one. Dan wondered what they could do to make this one better.

Dan looked up as Brother and Luming entered the room. Brother's appearance was always soothing to Dan. Here was a man who was content all the time. He asked questions like, "Does one need to stop yearning for the past to grasp the future? Is this a better existence?" The existence we are building will be built on buried bodies. They better do a good job and pay attention conflict when it arrives.

"Hey, Dan. How are you doing? Is everything okay?" asked Luming.

"I'm fine. Karyn stopped by and told us that there were a lot of baby things located somewhere in the SB. Wondering if you would check that out?"

"I'll go with you, Luming," said Betty. "I think I have a good idea where they're located."

"Sure, that's fine. Scar specifically asked how you were doing?"

"Yeah, Karyn filled me in about the call. I'm fine and just chilling in this room. They rightly called it, The Serenity Room."

Luming left with Betty, who talked about a time when she took care of her niece's baby. Her voice faded out as they walked away.

"Dan," Brother whispered. "I'm going to sit with you for a while. I have been going over and over the message we received from the Lao Tzu from the Tao de Ching. I finally found the passage it fits, number 67. How are you feeling?"

He wished people would quite asking him about this condition. "Brother, I've heard of the Dao. I would be interested in hearing what you have to say. So many things have happened in the last forty-eight hours. This is the first time I could really sit with what happened to us. Ironically, at such a tragic time like this, I have a strange sense of peace within myself and hope for the future. I don't know when I've felt this way. This chapel is very soothing, with the candlelight flickering and the soft warm color of the fabrics."

Brother smiled. "I see you have had a cup of Ocha. I have also had this tea and experienced a deeper focus about spiritual things. They say Ocha-O has a different effect on people, but almost always slows things down. I've been thinking about my purpose in this new situation. Many people are fired up to do things and to help. These people are very mindful of what they are doing and are working hard to create and collaborate for the greater good. These people are different from ordinary ones and I just can't put my finger on it. Maybe you can help me with this?"

"Sure. I'm not busy." He laughed.

Brother sat down on a small round pillow, crossed his legs, and took a few long breaths. He opened his eyes and looked at Dan. "It's best if you stay relaxed against the pillow. Let me know if you get tired of me talking. When I heard the broadcast referencing Lao Tzu, I became very excited as my parents took the Dao seriously. Now I'm trying to piece together the message that is still being broadcasted."

"Who was this Lao Tzu guy? I think I ran across something about him."

"Lao Tzu authored the Tao Te Ching and was a Chinese philosopher from 500 BC. He wrote this small book that has been used over centuries as a guide to living. This poem of eighty-one chapters is directed around a path for living by ways of not doing rather than doing. Simplicity, Patience and Compassion come from the sixty-seventh poem. I'm always surprised at how powerful these ancient texts are that explain the modern issues we are experiencing. As we fill our lives with daily survival actions, I wonder what it would look like if we introduced the concept of not doing. A Buddhist term for acceptance. People come to me all the time to ask how they can disconnect from the world. I think there seems to be a natural yearning for not doing with an inability to practice such a skill. There is always something we need to do. It is a form of distraction. In reading these texts, I'm surprised to find that more primitive human beings had the same problem. Too much mindless doing. Buddha lived in India 400 BC and had the same observation that the busy mind created suffering and a distraction from suffering is doing.

"I know this sounds like rambling, but I'm trying to understand the Chinese philosophy from which Lao Tzu came from. I am a Buddhist priest and my training is different. If I think about the basic premise around western thought, it is around reasoning, beliefs and desires. We build our thought processes around making things. Chinese concepts are more social than psychological. Lao Tzu introduces his philosophy starting in the dark, reaching for the light. He often references opposites, light and dark, win and lose, seen and not seen as social precepts. Where western thinking analyzes what looks good and what looks bad, determining what is right or wrong, we are in a hamster wheel of constantly judging one against the other, leading to an unlimited amount of dissatisfaction. Lao Tzu suggests we rise above the language of opposites to find the way that is not based on judgements. The mere act of judgement takes us to a no-win place. Anything positive in our lives provides a fleeting satisfaction and usually returns to the hamster wheel of negative thoughts. Buddhism solves this kind of suffering through the concept of being present and mindful. If one is always present, the negative and the positive go away and you just experience what is here right now."

"Brother, it sounds like you are the person that could potentially unlock the message. How could an ancient text from sixth century BC be communicated in connection to a nuclear event?"

"Somewhere there is an answer. We trust our government to know even the smallest actions of nuclear armament. Any group able to escape the eyes and ears of US surveillance is powerful."

Dan sat up. "You're right, Brother. I was thinking of our early warnings of a catastrophic effect coming from China. These emails were translated into a warning that we had a hard time understanding. But when we finally deciphered the message, it was clear. The learning of a catastrophic event with little time to react meant very few people were properly warned. Once we sit down with the Five Guys, we'll probably be able to understand it better. What's the government doing now?" Dan sat in silence for a while. "You know, I'm interested in the message, Simplicity, Patience, Compassion. What are you thinking?"

"It's probably too strange to voice broadly, but I wanted to run it by you."

"No problem here. I'm not going anywhere."

"Well, it's interesting that you are sitting here, not doing anything. Just sipping some tea and feeling it relax your body and your mind. The Dao teaches that opposites such as violence and peace are bound together. Debilitating war, war that could destroy the world and bring it back to more primitive states, is the very thing that could create a new harmony. Because of the tension of fighting, we find fighting begets more fighting. Alternatively, we could have years of peaceful existence rising from the bodies of dead humans if we recognize that violence and peace are bed fellows. A Lazarus Effect."

"Okay, I'm kind of following you," said Dan. "I get the dilemma that violence flies in the face of peace, but sometimes the ends are justified by the means. I'm a little tired. I think I'll lay back a little. Can you hand me that large pillow over there?"

Brother got up and handed the pillow. "Yes, that's a perfect summary of war. The ends justify the means. What if a group placed nuclear bombs around the world, not to dominate the world and win power over the future, but to dismantle the infrastructure to start over in a new way that would destroy a percentage of humanity but save the planet? Take down not only political power but also technology power and rebuild it in a way that calls for less doing. Are we willing to not only learn the lessons of our past, but to not-do something about it by practicing not-doing."

"Okay, Brother, you got me there. I'm not exactly sure what that means, but aren't human beings wired to advance, to move ahead to do better than previous generations?"

"Yes, you're probably right. The Wu Wei of being that was taught by Sun Tzu is understanding how much of our behavior is simply tied to the social constructs of opposites. If something looks good to you, then something else will be bad because of that. Once your so-called society is tied to certain social constructs, you are limited to naming them and acting on them. You will never be able to break the cycle."

Dan pushed himself up again, away from the pillow, but was still feeling a little tired from that small amount of exertion. "I guess what you are saying, Brother, is we have an opportunity right here to take part as a small society, using our own rules. I wonder what would happen if we created changes around simplicity and compassion."

"Yes, and the paradox is there are no rules. Finding the natural path will be the challenge. If we allow people to follow their path and give them a chance to explore what their own personal way is, independent of others, would that bring a more nurturing, sustainable healthy life? Once rules are in place, you are now caught up in the winding and unwinding of judgement, the right way and hours of mind-time devoted to creating lines that can't be crossed."

"From what I know of the people here, I think it's worthy of exploration, especially if it is a better way of being together socially. Who knows, they may practice something like this already. Something you said earlier has made me think a little about a conversation I had with my friend, Shin, living in Hong Kong. He was talking about a radical group protesting GMOs outside his factory. They protested, were reprimanded and never heard from again. Shin said they went underground. He also mentioned that he could hide his research underground in a series of caves in the mountains in China and I'm wondering if the source of these nuclear bombs could come from someplace similar. A place where no one would be looking. I wish I knew more about nuclear surveillance."

"That is an interesting theory, Dan. It might help us understand what will happen next. Or we just take our own step and find a way of moving forward."

"What would make me feel better is to know who survived. My friends, family, and what government still is in place. Secondly, I want to create a healthy learning environment for Lizzy and the rest of us. I imagine we will spend a lot of time making sure we have a future of subsistence living here and are reasonably protected, but I also want to see what we can do to share what we have in abundance, maybe by creating an old-fashioned barter system. What we have going for ourselves is protection from radiation and any aggression."

"Dan, it looks like we will have to continue our deeper discussion. Soon, the helicopter will be arriving. I'm sure Marcella will want to check on you first thing."

"Yeah, I suppose so. I'm feeling good, but it's probably better to stay here and wait." Dan lay back against the large cushion and closed his eyes. He was now completely exhausted and wanted to store energy for the meeting with Lois and Jane together. He was excited at that exchange, since both women did not know each other, and he smiled at how that would go.

JANE - 45

They were in the air for over ten minutes. Nothing looked familiar. Jane watched as they first flew over a large suburb, burned in blocks of gray and black. She realized that the shade of black represented what was burned, which helped her get a handle on their location. As they came up to a large building footprint, Jane wondered if it was a Wal-Mart. There were no signs of life anywhere. The parked cars gave it away. Thank God, she thought, my car was not parked outside. One day, I might reclaim it. Interesting how the future planning was popping up in her head. Feeling optimistic while flying over death, so complete, it pulverized everything in its path.

Hawk was flying low as they came up to a very familiar sight. "That was the center of the bomb that hit the corporate campus," Hawk said as he pointed past the direction of the cluster of buildings she used to call work. "I'd estimate bombs landed two miles to the north, across the duck pond. Over there is where I picked you and Jake up." Hawk then turned his body around and pointed. "That's where we're headed. We'll be even closer to a ground zero situation. I dropped off Michael at the university football stadium. Vast desolate areas surrounded the stadium, left by similar bombs. If you can believe it, that area looked even worse. Why did this happen? Those words from the broadcast could provide some answers."

Jane thought about what Chris picked up. The broadcast of three words: Simplicity, Patience, Compassion. She wondered how the hell this fit in? Would she call this a holocaust? The Greek definition of holos is whole and kaustos meaning burnt offering. The message sounded peaceful. She knew Lao Tzu teachings were about opposites.

"Wait, I can see two more blast points, one farther west and one south of here. That would make four blast points relatively close together. There was no question some power wanted to annihilate everything. What a mystery," said Jane. She was sad, thinking of the people who perished.

The helicopter flew along with an occasional sputter, resulting in a dive, followed by a lift in the hot air gusts. Hawk seemed nonplussed, but Jane prayed that everything would be fine. Jane thought Dr. Blue would get a kick out of her praying. She was not one to leave her future in the hands of fate, but she now realized the future needed a lot of help. Where was Dr. Blue's farm? She needed access to a database containing her personal information. How could she find that?

Their trip now involved going to the university, finding Marcella and dropping her off at the Seed Bank. Jane was desperate to see Dan and get Marcella there to treat him. She hoped he was okay. What about healthcare? They all had to think about how to survive without formal healthcare and encourage doctors like Marcella to stay close. Jane had her storage of pharmaceutical drugs and she even had an infusion pump with two back-up batteries. Sometimes planning was opportunistic. She had the pump but had no idea how to use it. Would Marcella need it? Dr. Blue would help too. She would have many ways to help humans cope with desolate feelings of helplessness. I have to find her. She must survive.

What was the survival timeframe? she asked herself. How long will they be without civilized medicine? How deep a cut was made into civilized standards? What are the future possibilities? She realized her contingency planning was strong so far, but now many solutions required others. What treatments did she have for Dan's heart condition? She could do nothing for him except provide typical cardiovascular drugs. She had beta blockers, ace inhibitors, calcium inhibitors, and a diuretic. What was the proper dosage? Maybe the Seed Bank had a pharmacy.

They continued to fly over the jagged building tops that were rendered undistinguishable. Hawk knew the way, but Jane continued to check for key milestone markers that would help track their progress. As they flew over the capital, Jane felt sad at the gold statue of pioneers crossing the Great Plains, pulling their sole possessions in a covered wagon. Was that made of pure gold or was it bronze? Once we complete this mission, with any luck, I'll be home to really start planning our future. That thought excited her and she smiled a little.

It was 3:00 PM. They were not going to get back after getting to the Seed Bank. Hawk did not want to chance finding their way back in the dark. As they got closer to the university, they started to use the freeway as a marker. The first sign of being close to the university was a large lake, blackened with soot, sitting in the middle of campus. The football stadium was a mile away.

"Hawk, it looks like we're close."

"Yep." He pointed out toward the north. As they moved closer, he said, "There's the stadium. I can still see my imprint." The helicopter started to descend as Hawk expertly brought it down onto the field and quickly turned off the blades. They looked at each other as the rotors slowed down. Jane was not enthusiastic about walking in the black soot again, but she knew she needed to do this. It was important for her to contribute, and it made sense for Hawk to stay with the helicopter.

"I don't see them coming out, do you?"

"Nope. This is exactly where I let Michael off. You can still see his tracks to the door over there. I told the Five Guys to look for his marks."

"Gotcha. Didn't Michael take suits with him?"

"Yep, but we don't know where he left them."

"I'll bring two additional suits and two respirators just in case Marcella and Lois can't find the suits. What's our capacity, anyway?" Jane could feel tension rise with each question. Making a mistake at this point could be shattering. The respirator had not left Jane's face since they left her home. It was getting sweaty and loose, so she tightened up the strap. Hawk shrugged with no answer to her questions. He was a smart guy, she thought. He knew she was nervous. "I'll find them. We'll work it out," she said. Hawk handed her the suits, packaged in transparent plastic sheets. She carefully jumped onto the ground, spreading waves of sticky black ash everywhere. She waved at Hawk and then looked toward the half-moon shaped entrance to the stadium. Isn't that where football players came out from their locker room during a game?

This was a perfect place to land. This open space was once a grassy football field surrounded by bleachers. The concrete enclosures were all that was left of the stadium. Hopefully, the tunnels below were intact. As she walked, she realized she would soon be filled with black sticky soot. This was much worse than what they walked through on their trek to her home. Finally, she got to the same entrance Michael took. She walked through the opening and through a dark tunnel that opened up into a large concrete hallway. One Chinese guy, not much over five feet, dressed in a brown corduroy jacket with elbow patches, jet black hair smoothed down around his head and a red/blue ascot, covering his neck, reached out to her.

"You must be Jane," he shouted. "I'm Cong. You're a mess. We've got extra suits so you can leave that one behind if you wish."

"We're in a hurry, right? What about Marcella? Is she ready? And Lois?"

"They are not here yet. They should be here soon. Sorry, but you will have to wait here unless you want to take off your suit."

Jane was disappointed. She wanted to get going. How can she update Hawk about the status? She was heating up in the suit and the respirator was annoying her. She would love to take off her suit, but that would add a lot of time to getting away quickly. She could take her respirator off. It was a Blackwell 6078, the best in class mask.

LOIS - 46

If they hadn't left when they did, they probably would have been crushed below the physics building. Everyone started to throw things together. The Five Guys filled bags light enough to carry, leaving behind computers, screens, even sensor equipment. Marcella contacted Max, her son, who was safely tucked away in a computer fortress across the river. Max assured them he could provide any equipment they needed, but only if they could cross the river. Marcella's mood was lifted from this conversation. Lois was grateful for that.

Just as they were gathering the bags to head for the stadium, cracks began to spread unevenly, across the old, gray cement walls. Suddenly, a tremor shook the building. Dreadful sounds followed. As Cong screamed, "Move out now," it was impossible for Lois to take a step. Bai noticed and came over to her and said, "Lois, help Marcella!" Lois nodded, looked up and saw Marcella sitting with her head down, sobbing. What happened to her mood? As she ran toward Marcella, she looked directly at Lois. She got out of her chair, wiped her eyes, and they fell into a hug. She needed to get her to move. She didn't expect this strong accomplished woman to fall apart during a crisis.

Lois walked Marcella toward Cong and he gently reached for her hand. Lois looked for Suri, only to realize she was attached to her leg. She saw Clark pull on Karey's arm to move. Bai, Cong, Hung, Lou, and Qiang had a quick consult and Cong opened up a drawer to remove an emerald carved dragon in a long bottle. It needed no explanation, thought Lois. It was beautiful and definitely worth saving.

As they rushed out of the room, vibrations came from the floor, making running difficult. Suddenly, plaster pieces dropped from the widening cracks onto the floor.

Lois looked back and saw the lights flicker, followed by a moment of darkness before the generator kicked in. Lois experienced her body sweating from every pore; she was now soaked in fear. Cong shouted, "Run, run!" As they ran down the hallway, a strange orange light showed them the way. They could hear the sounds of another building collapse from the direction of the hospital. Were all the tunnels collapsing this time?

They were now running down the first floor of the building next to the physics building. According to Cong, that would lead to another tunnel below. Strange, she never realized that the northern tunnels did not link up to the southern ones. That was a nice surprise. Clark was running first, encouraging Karey to keep up. They were all tight behind him, not leaving anyone behind. Qiang ran last, carrying the large bag of seeds on his shoulder. I wonder what is happening with Hawk. Will this affect their rescue? Let's hope the stadium is still standing.

As they ran, Lois was crushed by others joining them, moving away from the crumbling buildings. She realized these students were not coming from the hospital or the anatomy building. She wondered where they came from. But they could not stop and ask as they needed to get to the stadium and wait for Hawk. She started to count again. Hawk said the helicopter could only carry four people. Marcella and she would make four. Clark would not leave Karey, so he could not ride in the first group. She was not leaving Suri behind. She would just have to sit on her lap. Cong wanted her on this first trip to update the Seed Bank of what happened here. He believed in her. This was a great feeling and his support would propel her to be her very best. The circumstances have changed dramatically. Now, they all needed to leave. If they could talk Hawk into returning, they could do it. Could Hawk handle five people and complete their transfer in two more trips? Lois struggled with the thought of depending on Hawk for their survival. This was it. They all might find a better situation ahead of them. I wonder what the Seed Bank would think of that? They did invite them.

They saw a sign pointing to the stadium. "We're below the stadium now," shouted Cong. "We need to go upstairs, but be careful. We need to find the entrance that Michael used. I'm not sure how this crowd will react to the helicopter." Marcella was standing close to Cong and talking to him a lot. He was nodding in agreement.

Once on the main floor, they found more clusters of students. Lois wondered if they came from some auditorium. They were trying not to draw attention. Far more people were here than any tunnel they used before. Was that the sound of a helicopter was landing? This will be tricky, thought Lois.

The first entrance they came to was a concrete tunnel that eventually opened out into the stadium. It was dangerous and would expose anyone to radiation if they went too far. Someone had to go out and find Michael's tracks. That entrance would be the pickup point.

Lois had an idea. "Michael probably left tracks once he entered the stadium building. We need to check all four entrances to the playing field for signs of him."

"Great idea, Lois," said Clark, beaming at her. All nine of them followed Cong to the right and slowly walked past students, checking out each entrance. After passing the second entrance, they knew the next entrance was the right one, unless he did not leave any signs. As they approached the third entrance, it was obvious that this was the one he took. The black, sooty footmarks went directly into the football locker room.

Cong opened the locker where his suit hung. Everyone stared and Marcella looked at it stoically and shook her head. Lois opened the adjacent locker and found two large hockey bags with full protective gear in them.

Now all they had to do was wait at the entrance to the stadium. Would Jane or Hawk come through this wide concrete tunnel? Not sure of next steps, they just listened to the sound of helicopter blades coming closer.

Lois walked around and checked out the crowd, collecting information as the students petted Suri. There was a lot of speculation that the Physics building collapsed after the Anatomy building came down. Tunnels were not safe, and she was shocked to hear how close they were to being buried. Even now, the fear still rested in her bones.

They moved forward a hundred feet past the entrance and there were fewer people. Now the helicopter sound was strong and created a harmonic vibration in the building. How stable are these concrete structures surrounding the stadium? she thought. I wonder if Hawk is bringing suits with him?

She needed to stay connected with Clark. How long ago was it when Clark got off the train with Suri? Clark looked strong, alive and helping everyone. His attention to Karey's needs was sweet. She still did not look too well, wincing in pain from her injury. Lois was still not sure what happened to her.

"Clark, can you help me a minute?" Lois walked back into the locker room and Clark followed. Suri laid down at her feet.

"Sis, you know I have to stay behind. I wish I could go with you, but this looks like a very safe place."

"Yes, I'm comfortable with you here, but you have to promise to come on the next flight. Now, I need your help with something. I want to take Suri with me." Suri started to wag her tail.

"Whoa, that's a tall bill. Would the others would agree with that?"

"We'll cross that bridge if we can first figure this out. Clark, what do you think? Do you have any ideas? We need to find a way to get Suri into a suit and respirator."

"My experience with black sludge is it sticks to everything. You saw our suits. They're covered." He spent a while looking down, and then he smiled. "You know, I have an idea," and he quickly left the locker room. Lois sat down on a wooden bench. There was hope, she thought. She felt the silence of the room. It was the first time she was alone. So much happened. Did she have the energy to do what's needed to survive? Surviving was now a new normal. I wonder what will ultimately happen to us?

The sound of the helicopter rotors was slowing. Lois pushed herself up and left the locker room. People were reacting to this new development. She imagined that it provided hope of emergency medical treatment or a way to leave. She joined her group but did not see Clark. As they waited, Cong suggested they find a barrier, something to rope off the entrance. They all went in various directions and Hung found two heavy pillars with a rope. They all joined in to string the rope and set it up with Hung standing next to it with his imposing appearance. The helicopter finally slowed to a stop. Landed! Students continued to congregate, waiting for something to happen. Lois slumped to the ground and lay against the wall. They crowd was expecting someone to come out of the tunnel. Lois overheard someone say, "People are coming to provide food and medicine."

Lois was listening deeply for any sound of Clark. She looked up to find him standing beside her and said, "Lois, come." He reached down for her to get up and follow him.

"Clark, what did you find?" She ran after him as they pushed past the growing crowd. They ran almost halfway around the stadium where Clark opened a door labeled, "Landscaping."

It was a room, not a closet, and had all kinds of gardening implements. Buried in the back of the room was a small John Deer tractor and grass cart. "What do you think?"

"I think you are a genius. Marcella and I can take the tractor, holding Suri in our laps! The cart can handle extra supplies. This is amazing, Clark. We can fit Suri with a protective suit that covers her fur from contamination from the other suits." She hugged him tightly. "I am so proud of you."

Before she could cry, Clark got the tractor fired up and backed it up. Lois jumped on and Clark lifted Suri onto her lap. They rounded the corner, moving through the crowd until they reached the entrance where the suited Jane continued to stand with her respirator in her hand, speaking to Cong.

Clark drove up towards the crowd and the group parted. Clark inched forward until they were a few feet away from Cong, Marcella and Jane. "Hi, I'm Jane. Cong and Marcella have just been filling me in on who's taking this trip." Lois lifted Suri and put her down.

"So glad to finally meet you Jane. This is my family, Clark and Suri." Clark waved and Suri clung to Lois' side. "We're in a hurry, right? Marcella, we're ready to suit up?"

"Yes, we are. Let's get to the lockers," said Marcella.

"How about this John Deer? Isn't she fantastic? I thought we would take her to the helicopter."

"I love that idea," said Marcella.

"That would work, Lois...and also limit contamination," said Cong.

Jane nodded and smiled a little.

"Yes, that's the idea. Clark found it in a landscaping room. There's no end to what you can do once you put your mind to it." Lois was easing into what she wanted to say. She wondered how Jane would respond. She seemed cautious as if knowing there was more to the story. Well, here goes nothing. "Jane, I want to bring Suri on this trip. We'll have some good protective clothing and she will disturb no one. She won't be walking in the black sludge and we can lift her into the helicopter, if there's room." Lois stopped talking. She had to appear confident and strong for Jane to agree to such a thing. Her face showed how calmly she processed information. Cong just stood there, looking at her, quietly supporting Lois' proposal.

"I'm not sure about this. While she seems just fine now, she might get agitated in the helicopter. It's loud and shaky. Lois, I'm not sure how to respond. I'm wondering if the Seed Bank would approve taking on a dog."

Marcella stepped forward, looking quiet and thoughtful. "I'm wondering if I could give her a mild sedative to calm her down. We do this all the time with Max's German Shepard. She hates to be in a car. Suri is around the same size and I carry injections in my bag."

Lois stammered a little. She could not conceive of drugging Suri even as she knew she would be fine. However, putting others at risk if she was wrong too. Should she stay back with Suri and let someone else go?

As if reading her mind, Cong said "That sounds like a reasonable solution, Marcella. I'm not surprised at Lois wanting to do this. She has been very devoted to Suri, and she is like a family member. Marcella might not know this, but it was Suri who found Michael's body. She's just a dog but her extraordinary actions toward others tells me she is more than just a dog. I'm finding some decisions are not linear and practical."

"We should hurry up before it gets dark," said Jane. "I understand what you said, Cong but I'm not sure if I can make this call."

"Jane, I know the Seed Bank wants me to treat Dan for a cardiovascular event. So, to help you advance your decision to take Suri, I will not make this trip to the Seed Bank for Dan unless Suri joins me. She has talents way beyond anyone's comprehension, besides being integral in finding my husband."

Jane nodded, looking thoughtful. "This is crazy. You've got to appreciate how dangerous it is out there. Any dog can get freaked out and hurt herself and potentially others." Marcella was anchored in her stance and did not stop looking at Jane. Jane took a breath and smiled. "Okay, well then, I guess that leaves us with the question, how are we going to make this happen?"

"Marcella will drive and I will carry Suri on my lap. We need to protect Suri, but we have two extra suits that Michael left behind. We'll use one for Suri and bring an extra one that the Seed Bank can have."

"I will administer the sedative now. She'll be ready to go by the time we get back from changing into our suits." Marcella grabbed her medicine bag and found exactly what she was looking for. She pulled the skin up from Suri's neck, who seemed fine after the shot.

Lois and Marcella headed back toward the lockers to put on the suits Michael left behind. Lois was grateful for Jane's calm presence, Marcella's quick thinking, and her own steadfastness. In fact, she was believing that all the women here possessed special characteristics. Did the crisis bring this out or were they always amazing?

As Lois opened the locker, she turned to Marcella. "Thank you for what you did."

Marcella smiled and said she meant every word. She said she was having a hard time and welcomed this distraction.

The bathroom was huge. After changing, the two of them found an XXL sweatshirt for Suri to wear underneath the suit. In case the suit did not provide one hundred percent protection, this sweatshirt could add a little extra. The three of them walked out toward the entrance, attracting lots of attention, two women and a dog in suits of white. Suri was slowing down.

Clark came up once he saw them and picked Suri. Qiang, Lou, Hung, Bai and Cong were all talking to Jane. Clark said he let the crowd know what was going on as they observed and did not show the agitation they previously showed. I wonder what he told them, thought Lois. Yes, Clark, the irresistible showman.

"You better go," said Cong.

"Ready?" said Jane. They nodded, and each placed their respirators on. Marcella turned the key, and the tractor started. Lois hopped on and Clark handed Suri to her. He fitted the respirator around Suri's head.

Someone shouted from the crowd. "Really, you're taking a dog on a helicopter. We have sick people here. You could take them someplace that would heal them." Another voice said, "What about us? Why take a dog?" Two more students seemed upset and pushed their way out of the crowd toward the tractor. The braided ropes stopped them and Cong stood strong.

Marcella took off immediately, navigating the barrier. There was no reason to hesitate. She handled the tractor brilliantly. It was like driving through slushy snow. Halfway to the helicopter, they saw Hawk pop his head out the door and waved. Jane, sitting on the cart, waved back. Lois looked around the stadium, which had an eerie quality. Lois was breathing hard into the mask, smelling large doses of a petroleum. She felt her stomach lurch into her throat, knowing she was going to vomit soon.

LUMING - 47

The tunnel was filled with people. Once the sound of a helicopter was felt across the whole Seed Bank, everyone ran toward Portal Number 8. Brother went up to Luming and Scar and told them Dan was doing fine in the Serenity Room. Betty was staying with him. That statement amused Luming as he realized he was now part of a group that had rooms called Serenity. Being in the middle of a catastrophic event and having access to an underground room called Serenity made everything seem like a dream. It gave him such confidence in being with like-minded people who shared a lot of what he stood for. For now, the group came first, but if they survived this, he could see individual freedom being important. He had to respect the group as each decision made affected the whole, but he knew it would be hard for him personally to give up his independence. How different this was from his whole life's experience. His small village was so filled with suspicion and jealousy, there was no room for the individual. That was communism and communism did not work.

Luming noticed that Scar looked at him with curiosity. He already felt he knew her enough to understand the look. More than once, she asked him what he was thinking. She looked tired. How long had they been awake? He looked at his watch. It was 4:20 PM. They arrived at the Seed Bank at 11:10 AM. If that was Thursday, it must be Friday? We've been up thirty-three hours. Bodies keep moving and minds keep working, but maybe the essence of life or the soul slowly burns out with time.

Everything was ready. The portal had a new chamber of thick clear plastic touching the floor that was attached to a set of hooks, hanging in a circle like a shower curtain. When the portal opened, people would climb down the rungs and step down, surrounded by clear plastic. That will be interesting. The entrance team, Trudy, Frank and McLane, were planning on helping each individual follow the strict protocol of entry as they instructed them about what to do. It should not be a problem, since Hawk and Jane were as knowledgeable about contamination as they were. Once an established protocol was worked out, Marcella would come down first. That sequence was hotly debated as getting Marcella to Dan was the main priority. An informal consensus dictated that contamination was of critical importance. No one person decided, but this one emerged out of weighing all the factors.

The plan was to come down the portal, one at a time, while the others stayed in the helicopter. Once they reached the floor of the tunnel, they would be instructed to move into another plastic enclosure, take off their respirators and hang them up on hooks. As they took off their suits, they would step outside that room and into the final chamber where there was a Geiger counter to measure residual contamination. Then they could walk outside the last chamber and into the common tunnel space. This design was a complete collaborative effort. Everyone brainstormed, with Mina and Karyn organizing the last chamber complete with the Geiger counter. They also had water, fruit and toast for the visitors laid out for them to eat, since they might not have had food for a while. It was impressive to Luming that they were all consummate leaders and followers. Once an action was identified, all pulled toward the goal. Everything was based on trust and individual strengths.

As the now louder sound of helicopter blades started to vibrate through the tunnel, Luming could understand fully what was happening. Seeing Lois again would be great! Meeting Hawk and Jane and learning what it was like outside the enclave would fill this vacuum of speculation that everyone was creating in their minds. They must have had a heart-breaking journey, being the only ones who saw the full extent of destruction. Suddenly a red light started to flash all along the tunnel and probably everywhere throughout. He understood once lockdown occurred, anyone trying to obtain entry would be considered an invader. He read that in booklet he found in the library.

Scar pressed a large button against the wall and the red lights stopped flashing. All eyes looked through the plastic as the portal door opened in slow motion as the hydraulic mechanism pushed the door fully open. Black ash fell like snow coming off pine trees in the dead of winter. A pile started to form on the floor and the plastic clouded up as the ash adhered to the plastic from static electricity.

"At least the debris is contained," said Scar, voicing everyone's disappointment that they could not see through the black.

"Hi, everyone. This is Jane and I'm looking down into your portal. I can see we have created quite a mess of ash build-up, but it also looks like you were prepared for us. We have Lois, Marcella and Hawk sitting in the helicopter and one surprise guest I will tell you about once I'm down."

"Scar here," Scar shouted loudly. "Hope everyone's okay. I suggest that you come down one at a time. We worked on a procedure for you to take off your protective suit without contaminating the tunnels."

"Let me go first and then we'll talk," said Jane. No one could see, but they could hear each step that Jane was taking and when she reached the bottom.

"Look around until you see the area with double plastic. Slide through that, start at the top. Take off your respirator first and then your suit. Look for hooks to hang things. The hooks are placed toward the exit of this room. Step into the final room as you take off the legs of the suit and hook it on a rack behind you."

"You've thought of everything. Oh," she exclaimed as she looked around at everyone staring at her once she removed her suit.

Luming could see Jane was very slight of figure and had a similar body to Scar's. In fact, they almost looked like sisters, except that Jane was taller with longer legs. Her agility was impressive as she managed to pull off her suit and step into the room on one foot without grabbing support. He was pretty sure his stocky body could not do this in such a graceful way. She was quick, did not need additional prompting on how to enter the last room nor how to use a Geiger counter. She cleared at a reasonable level. Luming wondered what would happen if she didn't pass. Someone must have a plan for that! Jane had been with Hawk, flying around, so Luming was encouraged that if she was clear, the rest of them would pass.

Jane stepped out of the last chamber and said, "I cannot tell you how amazing this is, an underground sanctuary. With so little information, it's been hard to imagine anyone surviving what we've been seeing. Complete annihilation everywhere. We weren't sure we were going to find the portal and were hoping it was unobstructed. Being in the middle of a large parking lot had the advantage of not a lot of debris falling on top of the portal." She sighed and started to cry but stopped. "This is lovely," as she pointed to the table of food. "You must be Scar and you must be Luming," and she started to go around and introduce herself to everyone individually. Suddenly, a knock could be heard from the portal. "Oh yeah, we decided to descend every twenty minutes." She looked at her watch and nodded. "Marcella is next."

The first chamber now looked grey and with areas caked with gooey black tar. The plastic was sagging slightly under the weight. Luming saw that Scar also noticed this. They could not afford having this collapse. As Marcella descended, they were all brainstorming a solution and Jane suggested that they reinforce what they already had. Frank left for additional hooks.

"Once Marcella is down, I'll bring her to Dan," said Luming. Everyone nodded and Luming noted his voice being clear and decisive. I guess confidence emerges when things quickly go wrong and one needs to act.

As Dr. Marcella descended, she moved into the undressing chamber effortlessly. Being a surgeon, Luming thought she would not have problems. Just after her feet touched the ground, she started to unzip her suit and her hair got caught in the zipper. A few loose strands of auburn hair became tangled in the mechanism. She struggled and finally was able to get herself free. Stepping into the second chamber was a disaster as she had to walk around the chamber to get the whole suit off to hang up. She tried to step into the final room and eventually, Frank had to talk her through each step. She set off the Geiger counter immediately, but they were able to isolate the contamination to her shoes. After removing her shoes, she was fine and finally stepped out. She was sweating and exhausted. A chair was quickly provided and she took water and a towel to cool down.

She was here and that's what counted.

"Lois is coming next in ten minutes," said Jane as she walked back and forth with concern. "We have a dog with us." She looked around. "I repeat, we have a dog with us."

"That would be Lois' dog, Suri, right?" said Luming. Luming understood the implication that everyone was thinking and he wanted to find a way to soften the blow. Nothing came to mind.

"Our plan is for Hawk to bring her down if the Seed Bank agrees to allow her to enter. She is wearing two layers of protective suits and a hockey sweatshirt wrapped around her body. She was subdued by Marcella who gave her a strong sedative, so she is not moving, it's like she's in a coma. She is a very disciplined dog and the group benefited from her significantly. She found Michael's dead body, for example. Alternatively, if the Seed Bank does not support her being here, Hawk will stay in the helicopter and Lois will leave with Suri and Hawk once we have sorted out communications and future plans."

Scar looked carefully looked around. This surely upset her and the members' equilibrium. A dog. How could they cope with a dog? The group seemed too stunned to comment, unusual, thought Luming. Scar read the group's response and acted.

"We have a no-dog policy. This will not be possible. Sorry, guys. We've already had challenging things to work out. How can we contain her sufficiently to not contaminate the SB plan for survival?

Was that a collective sigh from the group standing behind him? He wasn't sure of the implication of what Scar actually said. The chamber was being worked on by Frank who added massive amounts of duct tape which provided additional attachment points from water pipes on the ceiling.

Luming was torn. He knew he needed to take Marcella back to Dan, but he wanted to be here to greet Lois and help with the Suri issue. He heard her descend, but walked up to Marcella and she got up, ready to move.

"I'll check on Dan," she said simply.

"Hi, I'm Luming." She waved good-bye to the group and followed him down the tunnel. "Oh my," said Marcella as she looked around. "I had no idea."

They walked briskly until they got to Dan who was laying in the Serenity Room, surrounded by tapestry and pillows. The room was lit solely by candles and Luming realized why this was called a serenity room.

Betty was playing with Lizzy inside the circle. Betty was showing her how to play ball with another person.

"Hi, Dan. My name is Dr. Brown. How are you feeling right now?" She bent down and immediately took a stethoscope and a blood pressure cuff from her bag. "Can we find some light here?"

"There's a flashlight in the corner, doctor. I'm afraid this is the one room without electricity," said Dan.

"Oh great," said Marcella. "Let's take your blood pressure, Dan."

Luming grabbed the flashlight and held it while Marcella got through the basic vital signs. Dan was sitting up and not saying a word, passively letting the doctor do what she came to do.

"Everything seems normal, Dan. Do you know what your blood pressure usually is?" Dan started to relay a few bits of information about the tea they served him and Luming was relaxing into a sense that this was either a false alarm or Dan recovered quickly. "The tincture you are taking may have had a positive effect on your vitals. Everything seems normal, so let's continue on without taking any more tea and see what happens. I've had colleagues who studied the effect of THC on heart conditions and they so far have reported slight improvements in both systolic and diastolic. If you have atherosclerosis or clogged arteries, this will not help. Surgical intervention would be required if that is the prognosis. Let's keep you here for a while, stay hydrated and I will monitor your vitals over the next twenty-four hours. Hopefully, this was an episodic event triggered by a panic attack of sorts. You have had a challenging forty-eight hours, have you not? I recommend rest. This looks like a good place for that! Betty, are you going to stay here with Dan?"

"Yes, I'll be here taking care of Lizzy until her nap." Betty stood up. "Thank you for coming. I'm glad that things have stabilized for Dan. He's been through a lot. You need to hear our story sometime of how we got here. We were minutes away from being decimated. Lizzy, Dan and I made it though. I still wonder if my students made it. It makes me sad." She hesitated and looked directly at Marcella. "Oh, yes, of course, I forgot. I'm very sorry for your loss. You have also experienced strife and loss. Please know we are very appreciative of the sacrifice you took even getting here."

She smiled back at Betty in a little too plastic way that physicians often use to hide information, Luming thought. We are lucky to have a doctor for Dan and for anyone else that will need care.

"Your granddaughter is adorable Dan," she said. They continued to talk about Lizzy and Luming announced he was getting back to the portal.

As Luming walked back by himself, he felt satisfied. So many things were resolved; communication with the Five Guys, transportation, and of course, connecting with Lois and learning about her attachment to Suri. As he turned the corner toward the portal, Lois was outside the chamber and all eyes were on Hawk with a large blob in his arms. Hawk landed with a heavy thud and the biggest splash of ash floating upward. The plastic was showing a lot of stress. As promised, it looked like Suri was alive, but barely awake. As Hawk set her down, her legs initially splayed. She reacted to this and continued to try to stand. Lois was shouting through the plastic with encouraging words.

By this time, Frank had taken charge of coaching each individual through the process. The plastic was barely holding. Frank was already designing another containment area in case this one collapsed. Someone already mentioned that they would close off this tunnel because of exposure.

Hawk had the least flexible body. Taking off his suit in this small space would be a challenge. It was obvious that someone had to help Suri out of her suit before Hawk could remove his. Someone had to enter the second chamber to move Suri to safety.

Luming saw Scar suiting up and popping on a respirator before entering the first chamber. She got onto her knees and, with gloved hands, grabbed Suri's head to move her toward the second chamber. Suri was slowly waking up and seemed disturbed. Lois continued to soothe her with affectionate phrases. Gently but firmly, Scar started with her respirator, and moved down onto her front paws. Then Suri wanted out of the suit bad enough to walk out of it into the second chamber.

Everyone took another collective sigh. The rest went rather smoothly. To be safe, Scar took off Suri's hockey sweatshirt and she bounced into the last chamber and shook herself off. Everyone clapped. Geiger counter showed a low enough response that allowed her to bolt outside into the arms of Lois, who buried her head in her fur. She got up again and then scouted the whole group, sniffing and receiving pats on the head. Luming was again impressed by the unusual sequence of events. He felt so much affection for Scar.

The attention went back to Hawk, apparently having some difficulty. Luming watched his large, strong physique move into the second chamber. As he removed his suit, standing on one foot without a problem, and pivoting around to grab his belt and backpack that were stashed inside the suit, he looked weathered. Standing firmly in the third chamber, he started the process of radiation detection. Hawk did not pass the Geiger counter test. Scar made several suggestions for him until they realized that his belt and backpack were the major contributors of contamination.

Luming went up to Lois and reached for her hand to squeeze. "I'm sorry I was not here when you got here. I'm so glad you are safe. How are you doing?"

"Well, we just experienced a view of devastation that makes pictures of Hiroshima look like the fourth of July. Hawk and Jane are the heroes here. I just found out about the no-dog policy. Now what? I'm grateful to be safe here but what can I do?"

Jane came up to Lois, looking concerned. "Lois, I know how this looks but the Seed Bank is a very well-organized group. I've also been told they are flexible and this is not the last word. Have some patience and we'll work on this together."

Luming noticed Lois' face lighten up. "Thanks Jane. I will work on patience. I'm so glad to be out of that suit! It was built for slimmer women like you. My sweat was accumulating inside and I was having a hard time getting out of it." Luming was relieved to hear someone speak about something as ordinary as discomfort. Lois had that sense of the ordinary about her. He remembered his conversation with Scar, when she revealed part of her past and the womanline she was part of. He wanted to hear more about that and realized that Scar grew up in a unique and interesting culture. There will always be areas that couples cannot fathom the other's experience, and with that thought, he realized he was saying the word couple to himself. Was it sacrosanct to be thinking about a relationship? That moment was cut short when he heard Hawk say, "Yeah, that makes sense. My exposure has probably been the highest of anyone here and this backpack has been with me from the beginning. Are you sure you want me here?" he laughed.

"Hawk, I'm Scar. Good to meet you. Let's take another measurement to be safe. Then you are good to go."

"Nice to meet you and nice to meet ya'll." His genuine smile warmed the room as he looked over the group staring at him.

Lois turned to Luming. "I'm wondering, we're probably going to have to work out a lot of stuff between our groups. Luming, our place collapsed and Clark, my brother, his girlfriend and the Five Guys are all behind at the stadium, waiting for us to pick them up. We have to stay the night, but tomorrow, we'll go back for them. What am I going to do with Suri? We need--"

"It's all right, Lois." Luming squeezed her hand. "We have room and there are plans being worked out to include everyone. The new challenge is how to manage a dog. As you probably guessed, this is a highly sophisticated facility and I'm confident that no one will kick you and Suri out! Scar can be very direct and it takes a while to get used to her."

Jane nodded with what Luming was saying. "Eventually, I need to also get back to my home, once we have finished these transports. We left Jake behind and he is not aware that the Five Guys are now homeless. They were going to stay in contact with Jake and give him updates but we had to move so quickly, we lost all communication with him."

Luming was feeling like they needed to change the conversation and he knew what to do. "Let me give you a tour, Lois. I'm sure we will eventually get to everything. Are the Five Guys and Clark going to be okay overnight?"

"Yes, I'm pretty sure. It looked like at least five buildings collapsed, including the Physics building, but the stadium was still intact."

"I know something about that," said Jane as she started to walk with them. "Stadiums are one of the most stable buildings as they are completely made of concrete. The bleachers are not above the tunnels where everyone is hanging out now. As we flew out of there, I thought it looked stable. We have no choice at this point. We'll be ready to go back tomorrow, first thing."

"Let's get everyone working on this. I'm sure we can come up with solutions," said Luming.

Luming caught Scar's eye and she said, "Maybe a shower would feel good. Luming, can you show Lois and Jane around? There are drawers down there someplace with spare clothes. Someone down there will help you. Hawk has a question about his fuel line. We'll catch up to you later." She lightly touched Luming which he noticed and headed back to the hub.

"Okay then, follow me." Lois and Jane all turned toward him, looking ready and Suri pushed her legs up to support her. Luming led the way and felt pretty good about answering questions. He could tell even Jane, who asked general questions like water supply, generators, solar capability, was satisfied with his answers. She was speechless when she saw the plant room. Seeds were obviously her passion.

"I will come back here for sure. This is fascinating." Suri pulled Lois into the room and relieved herself. No one said a word.

Luming then took them to the Serenity Room to see Dan. He was asleep, but Marcella stepped out of the room to greet them. She was also interested in taking a shower. Betty motioned for her to go and the four of them continued down the hall.

The showers were in the living quarters. Luming stopped and looked at a map which showed two other entrances to the lower level. They did not require going down a set of rungs. As they easily moved down a wide staircase, the place was cool and quiet. He could see a lot of progress was made in setting up sleeping cubicles. They found separate men and women's bathing areas. He found stacks of towels, soap, shampoo, everything, even razors. Like a hotel, he thought, except these commodities would eventually run out. He walked back and shouted into the locker room, "Let me try and find someone to help us with clothes," he said.

"No need, Luming," said Lois. "Look inside this trunk." She had opened it up and there were neat stacks of pants and t-shirts. They found some Docker looking pants and a long sleeve, mock turtleneck. Wow, he thought, this is great. He stepped into his side and took the best shower of his life.

LOIS - 48

Taking a shower, with Suri no less, was nothing short of amazing. Washing Suri and having her shake off the water gave her the chills. As she finished her shower, she realized Suri took off. She quickly got out and ran around the corner to find Marcell and Jane giving her water and patting her on the back. Completely fine.

"Lois, do you want me to help you figure out how to, you know, do her business here?" asked Jane.

"Sounds interesting. I'm going to leave you two and get back to Dan. I will see you later," and Marcella left.

"It seems obvious she was comfortable in the Plant Room. They probably have a need for nitrogen and manure. Knowing that Suri probably had to go soon, Jane and Lois ran down the tunnel, past the Serenity Room, the Kitchen and into the Grow Room.

Suri pulled on her leash and Lois let her go. She ran to the back of the room, behind two enormous marijuana plants, and did her business. She scratched behind her, lifted her leg on another plant and trotted back as if the world was okay again. After Lois went back to clean up, she realized Jane was engaged in talking to a tall man from the Seed Bank. She walked up to listen.

"So, Bill, you're a grower. What does that mean?" asked Jane.

"I'm responsible for selecting certain hybrids that are compatible with GMO seeds. The combination of the plant and genetics are responsible for the success of the plant in various conditions. I've mastered several hybrids for these rooms and conditions. Knowing your background Jane, I would assume you have some interesting hybrids already selected for our seeds, which will make my job that much easier. We can swap plants and scale up production in a short time."

"I've been working with Dr. Shin's seeds for a few years," she said. "Nothing like this scale, but you would be surprised how easy it is to stack plants if you prepare layers of shelves within a finite space."

"Yep, we also do that with our pot plants. In fact, we were able to double our yield, using an alternating stacking system," said Bill.

"I hadn't thought of it that way," said Jane. "Are you going to continue to grow pot?"

"Well, that is a hotly debated topic right now. It can be a valuable source of paper, clothing, construction material, and its full medicinal value is significant, but not proven. It is also a kind of nutrition of the soul, but not shared by everyone. The SB houses a lot of seeds, including hops. I can see us brewing beer one day. But first things first, we need to start with basic nutritional needs."

He turned to Lois. "Hi, I'm Bill. I saw your dog, Suri, making a contribution. I think it's fantastic that she's here. We'll work something out. Eventually, we will put everything to good use."

Thank god, thought Lois and she smiled. Lois suggested they get back to Dan and Bill recommended they stop by the kitchen to introduce themselves.

They stopped where Chris, Mina, Karyn and Dorothy were working on preparing food. It was embarrassing to Lois that her stomach was making strong noises until she realized that was happening to Jane as well.

Chris came up and said, "Hi, I'm Chris and this is Dorothy. Jane, so nice to meet you. I think we have a mutual friend."

"That must be the Dr. Shin. I always suspected he was involved with your group, but he was always discrete about what he was up to. Dan and Shin also share a long-time history. He first brought up issues he was having with strange emails coming from Chinese and Dan came to be to help out. That led to the Five Guy's involvement."

"Too bad Anthony screwed it all up."

"He was a complete," she rolled her eyes, "asshole to us. We're grateful not to have to deal with him anymore. When our room started to crumble, we ran for the stadium. Have not seen him since."

"Lois, it's okay," said Dorothy. "Dr. Anthony's scheme went terribly wrong because he only thought of himself. Shin worked with Anthony to scale-up seeds. These seeds hold a significant promise for our future. As you know, this plant will be key to our long-term survival and will not make us dependent on animal protein. Dr. Shin was a visionary for saving the planet. He recently became aware of this group that was planning a catastrophic bombing event. Once he recognized the threat, he contacted me in Finland to come over, get the seeds from Anthony at whatever price and transport them to the Seed Bank within this very precise timeframe."

"What about Anthony's story about growing plants together without the sun? Is it true that was an actual thing? Was it true that Anthony had access to those seeds?" asked Lois.

"Actually, that is all true. We have those specific seeds and I suspect Jane does as well. Thank God you're here, Jane. Dr. Shin was reluctant to release them to anyone he did not trust, which included Dr. Anthony. I recall he was quite angry about how he handled GMO seeds in the past. He would never trust them to Anthony. The downside is we have not scaled them up and between all of us, we have no more than fifty seeds. I saw Shin's video using night vision technology. It showed two soybean plants cut off from light, completely in the dark, and growing robustly. It was amazing, but we need more information about growing them before we start. We cannot afford to start growing without knowing if they have special nutritional needs. We're still trying to connect with Shin."

"I'm amazed at all of the experts needed to support plants. I never thought about it. It's global winter that you're concerned about, right? While we have proper lighting here, what happens when we can no long mass produce crops to feed the world?" Lois paused. "Let me know if I can help. I can write algorithms about anything."

"We'll talk later," said Jane. "I have some ideas."

Lois looked all around, at the mural and the beautiful table already set for fifteen. She wanted to see Dan and they departed with farewells. The Serenity Room sign was handwritten in flowy characters on the door. Lois directed Suri to lie down and knocked lightly. Marcella was taking Dan's blood pressure and talking quietly. Betty was watching Lizzy crawl around the pillows, joyously pounding them with her hands while trying to stand.

Once Dan saw Lois and Jane, he said," I should get up," and started to push himself up, but Lois came over before he got very far and plunked herself on a pillow, facing him. Jane stood at the door. Dan looked relaxed, but his face was a little red and puffy.

"Well, you've got color to your face," said Lois. She looked over at Marcella who seemed absorbed in taking multiple readings every few minutes. She looked up and smiled.

"I think he is fine for now. Of course, we want to run tests to see if this was a heart attack, but for now, I advised Dan to rest and relax. This is perfect room for recovering, better than any hospital bed. I wish I knew about these rooms before. So many people would benefit."

"She's adorable," said Lois as she watched Lizzy tumble around with the pillows.

"Well, I've been waiting to talk with you, Lois," said Marcella. "You do look familiar. And you, Jane, Dan was just catching me up on your various hobbies. Looks like you are brilliant beyond your years."

Jane smiled. "I'm wondering how I can find a friend's address. Actually, she is my therapist, but also a dear friend. I know it sounds crazy, but I would like to find her farm and see if she is still alive."

"There is an incredible library here and file storage of a lot of things we would typically search for on Google. I wonder if they would have the information you are looking for," said Dan.

"Sounds interesting. I'm going to check that out." Jane headed for the door and waved goodbye.

"Lois, I want to hear what happened to you. Did you ever connect with Martha? I knew she was leaving for vacation and I'm trying to place where she might be. How many survivors did you see from the helicopter? We've been here underground, completely safe, but wondering what is going on."

"Dan, you need to rest more." said Marcella.

"Naw, I'd be more stressed, not hearing Lois' story."

Betty poured Lois some tea and said, "Please be aware, this tea may give you a slight head buzz. It is called Ocha-O."

Lois laughed. "I know Ocha-O. How do you think I got by as an undergrad? You don't know how lucky you are to have a stash of this. The only bad thing is it makes me want to eat, but it looks like we are going to eat very soon."

The quiet room continued to soothe everyone. Marcella finally stopped taking measurements and sat back against a large pillow. Dan and Lois shared their experiences so far and Lizzy found multiple ways to throw herself onto pillows. Lois felt some peace for the first time since she left home.

The quiet room continue by sending everyone. Marcella finally stopped taking medications and sitting around the room. How that and Lois shared their experience so far and Lazy Land sunlight ways to form their dyou pillow. It is felt some power for them the thing is she left hour

DAN - 49

As Dan looked down the long table, he noticed that everyone put a little personality in what they were wearing. There were sequins, glitter, and colors from bright yellow to Saxon blue. Luxurious fabrics including Sharme's taupe-colored suede jacket with a turquoise lariat. The braids around her head were woven with pastel-colored ribbons, matching her rose quartz necklace. Hawk wore his well-worn leather vest that Dan noted as fitting his muscular body perfectly. After a long series of showers and radiation checks, he was still able to wear the '60s vest he came with. Someone gave him a chambray shirt that complemented his outfit perfectly. To Dan's left sat Lois, who wore a pale lavender tunic and a necklace of purple with blue sparkling stones. Luming had contrasting color combinations of leathers woven in intricate designs, and a jade necklace with golden seashells woven into the leather band. Dan was told that almost everyone had a hand in creating outfits to lighten their spirits, wearing celebratory clothing and resulting in a lot of fun, putting things together. The results were an eclectic composition of color, texture and harmony. Dan and Marcella missed all of the fun as he was still resting. Marcella, thankfully, finally declared that he probably did not have a heart attack, but she wanted to make sure that he had a chance to stabilize with his blood pressure meds. Scar and Jane were working on a long-term supply of meds for him, comparing what was stored in their respective pharmacies. Betty was also suggesting yoga for him that was proven in clinical studies to lower blood pressure. Marcella was not aware of this, but said, "It couldn't hurt." He still wore his plaid shirt and jeans and she was still in the simple navy-blue suit she wore to the hospital that morning. After some debate between Marcella, Betty and Sharme, they agreed to allow him to partake in Ocha-O again, only if he wanted to. Marcella knew the research on THC and Betty and Sharme had the experience. Dan felt only a mild effect anyway. He was deeply relaxed but was not tired or sleepy. He was getting a different insight into Ocha use and how it was practiced and dispensed. The surprising part was the importance everyone had that nothing was forced, no one was judged, and everyone felt safe.

This was a community respecting differences with a willingness to come together around solving problems using their collective mission as a touchstone. He read that somewhere. What was the mission before? Had it changed? Was there still tension around Suri? No one said anything out loud about Suri.

Lois' face was alive as she also looked down the table, twenty settings in total. Dan felt a suspenseful tone as if no one knew exactly what was going to happen, except maybe Scar. If secrets were going to be revealed or decisions made, no one was talking. They weren't just going to eat, thought Dan. We are celebrating being alive, as if the burden of being a survivor was lifted. This occasion was festive with grieving set aside. That would come another day. Every individual at the table represented a milestone in a journey that required courage and innovative perspectives. Conversation was weaving along the table with laughter and tears in abundance. They could finally relax and enjoy this moment of coming together over much-needed nutrition. Dan was happy they waited for the helicopter before eating, a mere six-hour delay. Marcella put him on IV fluids initially, which surprisingly took the edge off his hunger.

He spoke to Lois at length. They talked about her relationship with the Five Guys and her concerns about Clark and Karey making it here safely. A second trip could spell disaster. It was hard for her to relax, knowing the seven of them were still suffering in that environment. She thought once they started to create a future out of this catastrophe, the Five Guys would be essential to any type of problem solving. Tomorrow, Hawk and Jane would pick them up in one trip. Hawk had a plan for that and reassured her the over capacity would be okay. She hoped the football stadium would provide safe shelter overnight. She was also uncertain about what her fate was at the Seed Bank, knowing Suri was complicating things. Dan was positive that things would work out for her. Lois was the kind of person that expressed her concerns, a healthy attribute but he was never sure if he could listen to her all through dinner.

As Dan silently observed the long oval room, with a fresco on the wall of sea-blue and turquoise, he wondered at the significance of the painted scene. Wasn't there a volcano that erupted in Greece and similar wall paintings were discovered thousands of years later? He wondered if the effect of Ocha-O had not quite worn off. He was feeling the room, not just sitting in it. Betty leaned over Jane to tell him that this community would stay together only by holding up their collective head, hands and heart. He was never sure what she was saying but it felt like the description of how a family works. Of course, it was different also. The structure that the SBers created could only help. Lizzy would know nothing else. And then, he spiraled down his thinking to Brenda. Where was she? Was she safe? Could he find her? He could not push away the sadness. It was still too fresh. Would that feeling of guilt go away? Should they let it disappear? This was a bunker, well supplied, but a bunker nevertheless. Were they safe from intrusion? Dan thought about how modern-day living used to mean you had multiple layers of security and now that all disappeared, replaced by a fragile existence, based on planning on the part of a family group.

Jane, sitting to his right, practically straddling the corner of the table, nudged him, smiling as if she read his mind. She was wearing a very tight-fitting pair of jeans, showing off her slim figure of youthful agility. The only embellishment she wore was a lavender scarf around her neck. She was still traveling with her backpack and briefcase that were set against the wall behind them. She told him how she passed radiation testing because of the fitted covers she used anytime she went outside. Everyone was very impressed by her level of preparedness, down to battery chargers for multiple devices which made Troy happy as he left his Gameboy charger at home that day. Jane started talking to Lois, across Dan, about her place and the dog they found. They wondered if there was some way they could protect Blue from radiation exposure and let her live outside. She didn't think they would be able to fully clean her from radiated particles. At least, they could try using the multiple radiation monitors she had set aside for this day.

Jane described her home as underground, facing a large gorge that might not be affected by radiation fall-out due to the protection of old oak trees, amur maples and big cottonwoods planted along the ridge surrounding the valley. This was all new to Dan. He never thought about where she lived. Lois was asking questions and the conversation turned toward Lois' skills with sewing machines and how she sewed clothes for herself.

"I don't know why you couldn't sew here, Lois," said Mina from across the table. "Karyn and I sew all of the time."

"That's great!" said Lois.

"I wasn't working and stayed here at the Seed Bank, doing trimming shifts during harvest. For entertainment, I brought my machine to sew on and left it behind when I finally moved."

"I have a sewing machine which I have never used. Got it from an old Lutheran grandmother. I'm not even sure how to thread the sucker," said Jane. She seemed to be enjoying the conversation.

Dan, surrounded by sewing information exchanges, looked down at Brother who was also surrounded by conversation and seemed to be listening deeply, but not generating any conversation of his own. To Brother's left was Hawk and to his right was Marcella. Bill was sitting to the right of Scar and sitting next to McLane; the two of them seemed almost inseparable. Hawk was speaking in an animated way and Chris and Dorothy on his left were laughing at his antics. Dan suspected that Brother was fine with this situation, giving him additional time to observe and feel the energy coming from the table. Dan suddenly had a vision or strong feeling of energy coming out of everyone's heads; cool colors blending with warm ones swirling above the table. Dan's next thought was maybe the Ocha-O he took hours ago made him feel strange things like energy and colors mixing. He laughed at this. Betty was still allowing Lizzy to shove Cheerios into her mouth one by one. Lizzy looked at Dan and he made a funny face. She suddenly threw a Cheerio right at him. Betty, seeing this happen, looked over to Dan, smiled and went back into a deep conversation with Sharme, leaning in front of Mina. They were nodding a lot, as if they were old friends catching up. Maybe they knew each other, thought Dan. He couldn't remember.

Dan was getting anxious about eating but was told about the tea ceremony had to come first. Once they received a blessing from Brother, the meal would be served. Dan thought about having a beer instead of tea. He then realized going forward, beer would be a tough commodity. He would have to grow hops to make it or find a way to adapt to drinking Ocha. Everything was complicated. Was beer a need or a want? Wine, beer, scotch and now Ocha, ranked according to potency, was a list of possible relaxing beverages. He looked forward to experimenting and maybe finding alternative sources of relaxation. The Ocha he took felt something like having a couple of beers. Brother mentioned daily morning meditations he would be offering. Not something of his choosing, but it was here and he could try it out. They all needed to look at this world, this underground world, a little differently. They were preparing for a long siege below the surface until the radiation MSVs, 1,000 sieverts, dropped to less than 100, safe levels. He could not imagine better accommodations. What was surfacing from the ashes of complete destruction was a forced, but new perspective on how to live. Dan realized his past life would never have changed him this dramatically. This will not be anything like retirement. In this new life, he would be dedicating his actions toward a community that would need the gifts and energy from all of its participants. Could participating in a thriving community underground be better? He would desperately miss his independence, but an opportunity to help others live and not just survive, is a fascinating challenge for all of them. His most important goal was still Lizzy.

The strangest thing he witnessed so far was how this community was ready for this tragedy. They planned for it in a thousand different ways. In order to secure Lizzy's future, he would have to change, accommodate, put her first before himself. They were extremely lucky to be here, and he was grateful.

Suddenly, Scar stood up at the other end of the table and said, "Welcome, everyone." She looked very small in comparison to the large table. She made eye contact with everyone individually with soft brown eyes, taking her time, flipping her braids behind her back. Her power was in focused, caring energy, thought Dan.

"We are leaving our past lives behind and creating new ones." Dan noticed that Brother disappeared while Scar was speaking. "We want to acknowledge this moment in time with our traditional tea ceremony that Brother, Mina and Karyn will create on behalf of this new community." Scar then sat down. That was it. That was her speech? thought Dan.

Karyn and Mina left through the double doors into the kitchen. Brother came out and went around the table, placing a large, white bar in front of each individual. "Please eat your cakes," he said. "Compliments of Karyn." As everyone was chewing, individuals sometimes said mundane things like, "I love the soft elastic texture," or "I love the flavor, is that cardamom?" Dan knew the etiquette and realized that they were was adhering to it closely. How unfortunate for him, since he botched it last time he did it. The first thing that Dan noticed was how quiet the room was, to the point he could hear a kind of low hum coming from the speakers. "I hear humming sounds."

"Oh, those are Tibetan healing sounds. It's a mixture of Tibetan gongs, bowls and chimes," said Lois. "Interesting that you are just noticing that now, Dan. It's been on the whole time we've been sitting."

Dan was impressed with Lois' awareness of her surroundings. Judgement seemed to have left Dan's head and he experienced what he felt in the Serenity Room. Amazing to think that this room was buzzing ten minutes ago with conversation and now it was almost quiet, but for the soft sounds coming from the speakers.

The second step of the ceremony seemed challenging for a large group. Mina and Karyn returned from the kitchen, pushing two carts. Mina announced the tea ceremony and added, "For our newest visitors that are unfamiliar with our special brand," she said as she looked around," we have our Ocha teas. Ocha-O is the weakest tea, especially for visitors and first timers. This tea is a combination of Peppermint-Pine and Serenity^R. Ocha-O is refreshing and relaxing, much like swimming in a warm pool that connects to a waterfall. Ocha-B is our medium strength tea, having a higher THC level equal in Indica and Sativa that combines black cherry and rum flavoring, reminding me of a Black Forest Cake. This tea balances relaxation, intuition and cerebral stimulation, and is a fan favorite. The strongest tea, Ocha-T, is cerebral, ninety percent Sativa, giving an energizing lift to the mind and creativity. By the way, for our tea-totalers, there is a delicious Ocha," she laughed. "It's always something new and today it is white tea and mango, from the top of a mountain in China."

Mina and Karyn started serving on each side of the table. Bill selected the first cup that had soft shades of brown with a large white spot on the side. Karyn used her air pot of hot water to wash the cup and pour it out into a glass pitcher. Dan could not hear what tea he asked for. Does it matter? he thought. Karyn continued down along the wall, while Mina started with Scar. Scar turned to Luming on her left and then had a short dialogue before Luming selected his tea cup and tea selection.

Lois was smiling. Jane looked skeptical. Lois leaned over Dan to Jane and said, "Dan already tried Ocha-O."

"What was it like?" she asked him.

"Well, I just had a frightening episode with a racing heart. I started to sip the Ocha-O, while sitting in the Serenity Room, and it calmed me down. Marcella has given me permission to partake. I'm not sure what I'm going to do," said Dan. "I think still feel the very mild effects from six hours ago. I haven't lost my mind yet."

Karyn continued around the table with McLane, then Lincoln and Frank. Dan had not even met Lincoln until Sharme mentioned he was in quality assurance. He seemed unusually silent. Karyn did not ask but prepared a cup which Frank received with a bow. Karyn selected a teacup that was all white with an indigo blue line that separated the cup in half and Frank smiled once he realized that was the cup Karyn selected for him. After he tasted the tea, he bowed again slightly toward Karyn. Then he smelled the tea, took a sip and swished it in his mouth as if he was an advanced wine taster. Francine and Trudy both nodded to Karyn, who seemed to know what they liked. Dan could not tell what Ocha was being poured but was no longer remotely curious. She nodded and moved on to Trudy. Karyn selected a soft blue cup, like a summer sky with a hint of green on one side and she placed the cup with the green facing Trudy. Trudy commented on how beautiful the cup was as she held it in her hands and then took a sip and placed it with the green leaf turned out toward the others. That was when Dan remembered the part of the traditional tea ceremony. The cup was turned outward so one could share the beauty of the cup with others. It was a very charming adaption for the use in this Ocha ritual.

"I remember the time we were in a park, and Karyn brought us all teacups in a wicker basket," said Frank.

"I remember that as well," said Trudy. "The sky was blue against the green trees of mid-summer."

"Yes, the smell of warm air mixed with pine trees was so nice," said Karyn. "Lois, you know your way with Ocha. What is your preference?"

"I see you also have Flowering Tea blossoms steeping. I will have some of that mixed with Ocha-O."

"Perfect choice." Karyn reached over for the clear glass teapot in the center of the table that had a flower floating in the middle. She poured tea into a pale blue cup with splashes of yellow on one side. Again, after she carefully measured the Ocha-O tea in the cup with the blossom tea, she placed the cup in front of Lois with a bow and said, "Namaste."

When she said namaste, Brother said, "Namaste means, I bow to the divine in you." He bowed, saying, "Namaste," and then the whole table of twenty-one bowed, repeating the word and some repeated the blessing a second time. Dan thought that was funny and tried to hold back from laughing. He was unsuccessful and laughed out loud. A little embarrassed, he could feel the heat rise behind his ears. Bill was the first to laugh and then everyone joined Bill. All looking at Dan. This moment reinforced that this group did not take themselves so seriously. They could laugh.

Lois took a sip, placed her cup down and turned the yellow part outward for everyone to see the beautiful delicate flower painted on that side of the cup.

"Dan, I have several options for you. There is a delicious chamomile mixed with tropical mango and papaya if you don't want Ocha-O."

"This all sounds great, but I'd do anything to have a beer right now."

Nonplussed, Karyn reached down like a flight attendant and opened one cold, home-brewed beer and poured it into a tall black mug with white crooked streaks across the top. This put a big smile across Dan's face. "This cup is Raku, Dan. It is one of my favorites. Constantine brought it back from Japan many years ago and it is used only for very special occasions, of which this is one." Dan sat up a little straighter and accepted the cup with a bow, strangely feeling natural doing it, completely ignoring the dagger-eyes Marcella was sending to him.

Jane blurted, "I'll have plain tea, if you've got it. I know chamomile has calming qualities."

Karyn smiled and nodded. She reached for one of three cups left and selected a beautiful cup in indigo and white. "This is a very rare cup as the indigo color is very hard to formulate in pottery, Jane. A potter from Korea visited us once and gave this to me as a gift for our collection."

Jane accepted the teacup with both hands. She looked at it for a long time before she took a sip. She bowed deeply to Karyn, saying, "May you continue to bring us to this peaceful place in our hearts, Karyn."

Mina was working the other side of the table, but Dan did not pay attention. After Luming, she skipped Marcella and Brother who waved for her to skip them. She then served Hawk, Dorothy, Chris and Troy. Once she served Sharme, sitting next to Betty and Lizzy, she prepared the last tea. Jane was trying to talk to McLane across the table and he was straining to hear her. As Dan looked down at the whole table, the room mysteriously got quiet and the soft music changed from quiet Tibetan drumming to a Bach prelude. Someone mentioned it was their favorite Bach. The whole table sat in silence, like listening to a concert. Karyn, Mina and Brother got up and collected the tea pots and the cups. Once everyone was seated, Dan noticed Brother's white shirt was smudged with the dirt he picked up throughout the day. He looked thin and weathered, but he had a smile that radiated down the table. Whatever this ceremony meant, he thought, the ceremony gave everyone a collective feeling of peace with small moments spent with each individual. He wondered about Marcella and Brother not partaking in the ceremony, but no one seemed to notice.

Trudy stood up and said, "Thank you, Brother and Karyn and Mina. This was a profound act of community that I have not experienced outside of the membership of the Seed Bank. I appreciated that we all found our way to share in our tradition."

"Yes, Trudy, I agree," said Scar. "I suggest we do not linger anymore, and we eat. We can follow the meal with a short council meeting of the Seed Bank members." A few good-hearted groans were heard around the table, but most were looking at the door that was going to open with the food.

Later, Dan looked at his watch. How could one hour and a half have passed? Were they eating steadily for that long? As each dish came out of the kitchen, it was passed around the table. Each serving dish was spotless before it reached Mina to bring back to the kitchen. No food wasted. The meal started with apricot glazed turkey, squash with marshmallows, mashed potatoes and green beans. This feeling of community and abundance would make this a thanksgiving meal, a memory that would be called up many times. They needed to start with a reminder of what was important. This was a way of saying goodbye to the past. This amount of food might be a week's worth of food, something they will adjust to. But wasn't this a simple celebration of life, thought Dan. It was a generous gesture on behalf of the Seed Bank and one which made him feel like he was a part of this community. In general, establishing a ritual around abundance was smart thought Dan.

Lois mentioned from time to time that she wanted to save something for Suri who was left in a large caged-in area, near her sleeping cubicle. Suri had a bed and initially seemed anxious, but later settled down to sleep in a nice comfy bed that Troy found for her. Lois was not going to join the group at all, but Jane talked her into coming. Jane also found a plastic container from her backpack so she could quietly set aside food for Suri. Frankly, Dan thought people were getting kind of agitated over Lois' fixation over her dog, but he couldn't prove it. The tension of an individual making demands over the good of the group will always create issues. Dan admired Lois for standing up for herself but recognized that she needed to show other sides of her personality that would be valuable to this group.

Over the course of the dinner, Dan got the impression that Jane and Lois were getting along. Was it possible for Lois to join Jane at her home, taking Suri with her? They were very different people, Lois being less focused than Jane. Jane complimented Lois on her divergent thinking. Shortly after Lois shared that she was just completing a PhD in algorithmic analysis of natural patterns. Suddenly they were speaking fast, leaning in front of him and Dan tuned them out, while he focused on eating.

When all of the serving dishes were removed, Scar stood up. "This was an amazing experience. We need to thank the cooks and everyone involved in Ocha production." She clapped and everyone stood up to clap. Lizzy liked the clapping and she tried to stand up and clap, but she lost her balance and fell back into the chair. She started crying. Everyone laughed until she wouldn't stop crying and Betty took her outside the room. Arrangements were made for everyone to wash their own dishes and silverware in the sink in the kitchen. A line formed and Scar said original Seed Bank members were meeting in fifteen minutes in the Serenity Room. She left after that.

Dan walked up to Betty. "How are you doing? I'll take Lizzy for a while." She smiled and they chatted about the amazing dinner.

"What do you think is going on?" asked Betty.

"I think the SBs are a highly sophisticated organization. They are ritualistic about many things. They must resolve a few things around bringing in new people, the no-dog rule and who knows what else. They must anticipate that The Five Guys, Clark, Karey are arriving tomorrow. I think Suri is a big issue."

"It sounds bureaucratic but you're right. They have to resolve their internal issues as a group before they can officially extend an invitation to the rest of us. I sense they are very democratic and also want to flesh out any concerns before they do anything," said Betty. She did not seem surprised.

"We obviously have many things to offer. I'm sure they would want Marcella to stay," said Dan. "I look forward to the result. It will be great to feel some closure."

As the members started to filter out after cleaning their dishes, Dan, Luming, Brother, Betty, Jane, and Lois were left. Hawk and Marcella were in a deep discussion in the corner. There were eight of them remaining, plus Lizzy.

What gave Dan some peace was, as an outside group, they never felt unwelcome. It seemed like their needs were already taken care of and helpful actions by the outsiders were received with a generous heart. How can this be? Dan wondered. On the other hand, neither Brother nor Luming felt any concern. In fact, they seemed to be nicely integrating into the group. As he looked at the two of them laughing over something, he knew they were not worried about the Members. Lois and Jane had not let up on their conversation and when he heard Jane describe again her house and the open landscape around her, he was sure she was talking Lois into coming to her home. They were both intelligent, kind and caring, with Jane being a person that initiated ideas from her head and Lois seemed to react from her heart. Dan had an idea and walked over to Brother.

"Brother, what are the chakras again?"

Brother took a moment to consider the question. "It would help me to understand your question. To put it bluntly, why are you asking?"

"Right. I know there are chakras that involve the head, the heart and the gut. Aren't people oriented around these regions? Don't the chakras impact what you do and think and feel?"

"Yes, Dan. Where do you think you operate?"

"I'm not sure."

"My observation of you is you love to mediate and bring people together. You must have loved observing the interactions at that table. It must have given you a great deal of energy and comfort."

"Wow, you are right about that. I keep seeing people's strengths and weaknesses and how they are going to combine as we move forward."

"This is a time of great sorrow. We need to respect our feelings and not ignore the great tragedy above us. Eventually, we may be calling these tunnels home for some and a prison by others. There will be a great sorting of who we become."

"I never thought about that. What do you think---?" asked Dan.

At that moment, Scar came in, smiling. "We are so sorry to do this to you, but we needed to make some changes in our Seed Bank policy, a horrible bureaucratic thing, but necessary. It was done simply and quickly. Please come in and we will explain."

The nine of them followed her into the Serenity Room. Dan felt a flow of energy when he entered. Everyone jumped up from their cushions, they were smiling and welcomed everyone with a hug or a squeeze of hands.

A large circle was formed so all twenty-one were surrounding the now familiar centerpiece made of infinity circles and random semi-precious stones. Lizzy got down to crawl around on the pillows while Betty watched. Candles were placed around the elevated centerpiece with light bouncing off the walls. Dan could not get over the relaxed feelings of peace he felt.

"Welcome, everyone. We just passed a unanimous vote to officially invite Betty, Brother, Dan, Elizabeth, Hawk, Jane, Lois, Luming, Marcella and Suri to be members of the Seed Bank. Yes, Suri too. You do not have to respond right now. We have a summary of rights you have as a member for your review. Basically, your obligations are to support and serve our higher purpose in any way you feel you can. Staying here, as with any other member, is optional, but our location cannot be disclosed. This contract is a life-long commitment that you will sign. We can all help you in the next few days to understand this. We'll also be making the same offer to the others, including the Five Guys, Clark and Karey."

Dan looked at Lois' face. She looked relieved. That's perfect, he thought. While it was hard on Lois, he appreciated that they followed a tough process of discernment and came out with a satisfactory answer. Authentic groups are supposed to work this way. No one can anticipate every scenario and flexibility in law or policy is essential.

Scar looked very calm as she surveyed the group. "You might have many questions, but we are all tired. We would like to close our evening with a reading and go to bed. Brother, can you help us with that? We've all been through a lot and already worked hard to get to this point. What an incredible experience. Brother, what can you share that will make everyone sleep tonight?"

"Yes, well, what comes to mind is the full Lao Tzu poem we are hearing. It's sure to put you to sleep." Brother adjusted his pillow and spoke just loudly enough for his voice to bounce around the room.

I have three treasures,
Which I hold dear:
The first is compassion,
The second is frugality
And the third is refraining from being ahead of the world.

Compassionate, therefore courageous;
Frugal, therefore abundant;
Refraining from being ahead of the world,
Therefore, serving as the head of all servants.

Nowadays people abandon compassion to seek courage;
Abandon frugality to seek abundance;
Abandon the back to seek the front–
That is a dead end.

For compassion
Brings victory in battle
And solidarity in defense.
Whoever heaven sets out to rescue,
Compassion comes to protect.

"Various interpretations are presented here. The world honors daring, exalts ostentation and emphasizes progress. What Lao Tzu treasures is patience, frugality and humility, all of which the world considers useless.

"Compassion means to embrace all creatures without reservation. Austerity means not to exhaust what one already has. Reluctance to excel means to drift through the world without opposing others.

"Through compassion, we learn to be soft. When we are soft, we can overcome the hardest thing in the world. Thus we can be valiant. Through austerity, we learn when to stop. When we know when to stop, we are always content.

"Compassion is the chief of the three treasures. They who attack or defend with compassion, meet no opposition.

"The Chinese character for compassion is composed of two parts. The top, zi, means this and the bottom, xin, means heart. This means a way of feeling compassion for others from one's own heart. Lao Tzu feels humanity has the capacity to feel for our enemies and bring any conflict to an early and peaceful end." Brother sat down.

"Thank you, Brother, let's retire. May your dreams be sweet and peaceful," Scar said to close the meeting.

Individuals slowly got up and wandered out of the room quietly. Marcella walked over to Dan and asked him to sit while she took his blood pressure. He thought about himself and saw Betty who was waiting for him, holding Lizzy. Scar and Luming came up to Dan.

"Do you want to stay here tonight instead of in the living space?" asked Scar. "You won't have to get up and move to the lower level."

Marcella piped in, "Staying here sounds great and I'll stay here as well."

"Sounds like a plan," said Dan.

Everyone helped pitch in to create two sleeping areas. Betty took Lizzy back so she would not wake Dan if she woke up hungry. People were slowly leaving the room. The sound of waves came out of the speakers, at the lowest level. It must have been that long dialogue of Brother's monotone voice that slowed things down. He wished he could care about the esoteric stuff, but right now, he could not see the relevance. He closed his eyes without thinking of anything but the pillow underneath his head.

JANE - 50

Jane agonized over the helicopter trip all night, worrying if it would hold everyone in one trip and return home. Something happened as they could not speak to Jake. Would Jake assume the worst? Why was the satellite link messed up? There was something not right, something foreboding, as if they were running out of luck. Were the Five Guys still at the football field? She got up early to find Hawk standing, deep in thought, under the portal door opening. Everyone else was still sleeping from the late dinner. I wonder what Hawk was thinking? Did he want to return to her home as much as she did? They didn't have time to discuss anything beyond this next step

The plan was slightly over capacity to what the helicopter specs said, but Hawk assured everyone it would be okay. Nothing challenged Jane more than uncertainty and not knowing what conditions to expect. The breakdown in communications left everyone a little nervous, but hoping it was a minor issue. They were prepared for general safety, with improved protective clothing provided by the Seed Bank and fresh respirator filters. They were safeguarded from most exposure issues, but for a crash. But why did she have a feeling that there was a danger they missed somehow? Maybe it was those dogs they saw. Why did they only see dogs?

It was 7.8 miles between the Seed Bank and the stadium. Jane was hopeful that once the Five Guys came, they could use what they learned about satellite communication and help the Seed Bank advance their set-up. Jane frequently stated how important it was to have communication established once they returned home. No one really knew what would happen next, but everyone was concerned. Having a group supporting her was different. The Seed Bank had an unlimited capacity to solve problems with their stored resources and expertise in so many areas of science. This was not a group starting a fledgling effort at survival; they had been planning for some event, like this, even longer than she had.

"I want to go soon, Jane," stated Hawk.

"Of course, Hawk, I want to go as well, but we can't exactly sneak off."

After a long wait, they finally left at 8:30 AM. Troy, Scar, Lois, Chris, Dorothy and Luming were there for the send-off. Jane and Hawk suited up, received a box of food and additional treats stuffed in plastic bags. Nothing was more poignant than Lois saying, "Be safe and bring them back." She then walked out of the room.

The travel back to the university was an uncomfortable reminder of the truth that they momentarily forgot about. Nothing moved and there were no signs of the wild dogs. Things had not changed, but this reality looked more unstable than before. Fires blazing, fueled by broken gas lines, that had a life of their own. Some buildings must have recently collapsed, producing more debris aftermath flying in the air. It's been three days, and nothing changed. After what seemed like a very long time, they landed in the same spot in the middle of the stadium. Jane jumped off and started the John Deere, first time. She thought, great sign. Hawk handed her the supplies from the Seed Bank and she slowly ran the tractor toward the same entrance. Once she got inside, she saw a line of people standing outside of the ropes she left behind. The sound of the helicopter must have raised a lot of awareness. This group felt active and interested, but not agitated. They were waiting to see what was going on, seeking help. She wondered what the Five Guys said to them to lower the anxiety level.

Cong was prepared and knew just what to do. "Back away. She's contaminated. Please back away," he shouted.

The crowd obeyed and Jane was able to take him aside and talk through the plan; taking all seven at once. Cong was very impressed with the thought that Hawk was comfortable bringing all of them together. It made sense if the numbers were correct. He estimated each individual was around 100 pounds, except for Clark, who was tall, slim but still 180 pounds. Karey might have been less than 100. Cong looked so out of place, still dressed in corduroy pants, a vest and an ascot. Finally, he shook his head. "Take Karey and Clark. We have a few boxes of communication equipment for you that can be used to talk between us three-way, so we are not dependent on satellite communications. With these two experimental drones," as he pointed to two large boxes, "we can also pass light materials between us. The range is ten miles. That's the latest Phantom technology that Qiang procured just a week ago."

"What?" she said.

"We're staying behind. It makes sense and we're needed here. Once we get ourselves established in this new area we found, we can be far more effective. The university resources we have will be very useful to you and to the Seed Bank. There are several remaining supercomputers that can be formatted to establish a base operation for anything, but first for communications. We've already connected with Max, who is a valuable asset for us. He called, using the Ham Radio just after we set it up. He is in a different location, closer to the river, but claims it might be a great place to establish home base. We think we can find a tunnel in that direction and find a way to cross the river. That's what we would like to do, while staying connected with you and the Seed Bank. Tapping into this supercomputer and access to research labs would be a really big plus for everyone. Ours went down when the last tunnels collapsed in the physics building."

She was holding seven suits and respirators tightly, not processing the information quick enough. What did this mean? Was it a smart thing to do? She might never get back here.

Clark moved in on the conversation as Jane stood there, speechless. "Hey, Jane. Are these our suits? They look boss. So much better than the ones we used to get to the hospital."

Jane understood the wisdom of the Five Guys. Almost everything that they needed came from either the university or the Seed Bank. It was a perfect three-legged stool. The university was clearly their domain. That's how some things work, she thought, and then smiled at the realization about her own choices. Dr. Blue was the first person to make her aware of when she was making an intuitive choice and not a logical one. Making a choice and supporting it with logic and data, never worked. She needed to find Dr. Blue. Maybe this supercomputer could help.

The Five Guys stood together, what a sight, thought Jane. Cong was in the middle, with Hung to his right in military camouflage and Bai in a long flowing shirt and cotton pants. To his left was Qiang in beige pants, hiking boots and a plaid shirt and Lou with Dockers, like a Dad from the suburbs. "This is a cobbled-together communication system for you to take home, Jane," said Cong. "It should work perfectly, it's just not the latest in design. Sometimes, the older versions rely less on circuit boards and work better, longer." Jane loved the idea and felt they now had a solid chance at long-term communications. They needed to keep moving, but she was trying to process this change.

"Are you planning on growing plants?" she asked. Cong nodded. "Well, take these then," she said as she handed him a bag from her Tool Box. "I have more at home, but we need to scale up production as fast as we can." They all smiled as she presented the bag to Cong. "And here are the growing conditions." Bigger smiles came across their faces.

"Jane, we are grateful."

The first to jump into action was Clark. "We have to move all of this equipment. What if we load it onto the cart, take it to the helicopter and I come back alone? We'll leave the tractor here and I'll walk to the helicopter." Jane nodded, recognizing the wisdom and generosity in Clark's words. After unloading the supplies Jane brought, they stacked multiple boxes onto the cart. After all of the last-minute pieces of information were exchanged, Jane, Karey and Clark said goodbye and hopped on the tractor. Hawk was sad about the news. Clark returned the tractor and walked back in a well-worn path. His suit was not that black.

During their trip back to the Seed Bank, they noticed dogs running below, passing in and out of collapsed buildings. As Hawk flew closer to them, the dogs jumped up to charge the suspended helicopter, then ran in circles and snapped their teeth. Their mouths were foaming white and then Clark shouted, "It looks like they have rabies!" That comment was powerful, thought Jane. Why would animals have rabies now?

During the trip back to the Seed Bank without the Five Guys, a nagging idea came to Jane. They were facing another decontamination step if they were going to go back into the Seed Bank. Had Lois decided to come with them? With the Seed Bank accepting Suri, she might no longer be interested. They talked about it as a possibility and Jane made her a formal invitation, but was she ready? She seemed pretty close to Clark.

They were anxious about getting home, so the turnaround at the Seed Bank needed to be brief. While Hawk and Jane wanted to say goodbye, the decontamination procedure would take too long. They needed to get back. She needed to find out Lois' decision right away.

LOIS - 51

Everyone was moving slowly towards their respective living spaces. Lois and Suri were sitting on her futon, alone for the first time. She needed a break from people and just sat in her little bedroom. It was a cubicle, mattress and a small table with a light. She could not get over all of the planning that took place before they arrived at the Seed Bank. There had to be a reason that the Seed Bank was prepared for a long-time siege. She heard many rumors about the Seed Bank, it had a mythic status around it. There were many stories of an old, underground marijuana-growing operation. All of the stories were collections of conflicted details. Most of them had them located outside the city, never in the middle. One story put them in connecting limestone caves near the river and one rumor had them connected underground in a city block.

At least that rumor was not too far from the truth. Unless you were looking for it, its tunnels and carefully thought out access points and a lock-tight trust system, made it impossible to find. A warehouse district was a perfect place for such a facility. Luming walked her back to this space, describing the stacks, how they managed to find them and the seconds they had before the bombing started. There was a level of sophistication way beyond Lois' imagination. Luming had matured, as far as she could tell. He was assertive and supportive with everyone. He had what seemed like an attraction to Scar and she thought Scar liked him as well. What a time to have a romantic relationship, she thought. Well, one can't always choose your moments. She was happy for Luming and thought he might complement Scar's tense personality.

Lois woke up to Suri whining to "go out." She got up and they walked to the Grow Room. As she walked back, she ran into Chris who was headed to the portal. Hawk and Jane were leaving. The goodbyes were brief and they departed quickly. After the helicopter left, they were invited to have breakfast, courtesy of Chris and Dorothy, another pairing. Lois was tired and said she was going back to rest for a while. Lois' long conversation last evening with Jane triggered unspoken insecurities about staying here with Suri. Jane was sympathetic and spent some time describing the dog that followed them, who she called Blue. She wanted to get back to make sure he was okay and could find food and water. Jane would not be satisfied until she saw him, among the other things she left behind.

"Why don't you come back with us?" said Jane. "Once we get everyone back here on the last trip, you let us know if you want to join us. You have some time to think about it."

"Wow, what an amazing offer. I'd have to stay here with Clark, of course. Who knows what he is going through? Otherwise, I would love to go and give Suri a better place to live. Even though the Seed Bank made a magnanimous gesture to allow her to stay, I'm pretty sure they would not be disappointed if she left. Clark is getting closer to Karey and both would have to join me so that would be two more. Can you handle three more people and a dog?"

"There is a lot of consider, Lois. My first thought is about the Seed Bank. They might be very interested in having Clark and Karey stay. There is more room here than I've got and my place would get pretty crowded with six people and a dog. I would say no to adding Clark and Karey. Please think about joining us, Lois. This is, of course, a lot to consider. I know you and Suri will fit in, but you have to trust me about that." Imagine being a person that insisted on taking her dog with her, everywhere. What kind of person is she? Does she fit in anywhere? Jane's place sounded like a quiet sanctuary and maybe it was a better fit for her. Maybe it was time to let go of things.

Lois woke up to Dan and Betty in the cubicle next to her. She got up and rounded the corner.

"Hey, just letting you know I was here and taking some downtime."

"Lois, we missed you at breakfast," said Betty. "We had a riveting conversation about solar panel lighting and battery comparisons. Luming is quite the expert in that area. Hey, do you need to be alone? Are you okay?"

"Yeah, sure." She leaned against the cubicle wall and tears started to form.

"Oh honey," said Betty as she gave her a warm hug. "You're dealing with a lot now, I understand. You probably won't be content until Clark gets back, right? It won't be long."

"Jane is an interesting woman," said Dan. "In all of our mentoring hours, I never suspected she was so advanced in her survival capabilities and the extent of her preparation is beyond comprehension. When Hawk described her home to me, I was dumbstruck. A tank? Really?"

"Now I did not hear anything about a tank. How cool is that! I was just thinking about her and wondering if Suri and I would work out there. Jane and I talked about it. She was serious, but I'm not sure what to do. I have to make a decision pretty quick."

"Not a bad idea, Lois," said Betty. "Maybe Jane's bothered about long-term living without another female companion." She laughed and said, "Sorry, that sounds kind of crude. I don't know what I was saying. It is an interesting opportunity for you and Suri. That's for sure."

"You're safe here, Lois, and you have approval to keep Suri," said Dan. "I'm not sure if it is a good idea to go out again and risk your life. Who knows what will happen on that last trip?

"Well, there are many points of view to consider." Lois suddenly felt a little better and went back to the small cubicle space. She looked at this mattress filled with marijuana leaves and the wall built with canvas and hemp. This was fine for her. She could think about how to personalize her space here. She thought about joining Jane. Betty's comment about Jane balancing her relationship with two men. She wondered about that. Would that be any different than staying at the Seed Bank? It seemed like she would complement Jane's skills and fill some gaps. It was an intriguing opportunity. What was this tank all about? On that thought, Lois drifted into sleep again.

An announcement woke Lois up. Luming's voice over the loudspeaker said the helicopter landed safely. Lois jumped up, having slept for an unknown amount of time. Dan and Betty had vanished and she was slightly disoriented. Suri had warmed her with her body. All the comfort she ever needed. The two of them made their way to the Stack 9. The same crowd was waiting. Clark's feet started to climb down. Lois felt a thrill as he descended, smiling big and waving to everyone surrounding him through the transparent plastic.

"The Five Guys are staying behind. There is a lot of information to convey and an experimental drone to drop off. Karey is safe and ready to disembark. Where is Lois? I have a special message."

"Here," she shouted. "You're all right?"

"Yes, I'm fine. So, sis, Jane wanted to know if you and Suri are going to go to Jane's home. If you are, you need to get ready. Are you ready?"

Everyone looked at Lois. Lois walked up to the plastic barrier to get closer to Clark. "I'm torn, but first, I want to know if you are okay with that."

"Of course I am. It's not like we will never see each other again. There are multiple modes of travel, a tank, to name one. Now we have a communication unit provided by the Five Guys that makes a three-way conversation between them, the Seed Bank and Jane's pod. Sis, there isn't much time as they want to leave right away. I'm happy for you, but I will miss you terribly. Now, I'll go back, get Karey, and let them know of your decision. What's your decision?"

Lois was still feeling a little relaxed from her nap. Yes, yes, of course, she thought. This is the right option for many reasons. There won't be any time to spend with Clark, but he's doing fine. He's doing better than he ever has. She felt all eyes on her. "Yes," came out of her mouth. "Yes, and please thank Jane for the invitation. I've got to get Suri ready!"

Scar came over to Lois. "We'll help you," and Lois felt a warmth she never had before from Scar. She continued to stand by Lois as they watched Karey descend down the rungs. Clark let Karey pass into the second chamber as Hawk started to hand him boxes. As the stack of boxes grew, Clark had less space to stand. Each box was carefully documented, several labeled communication equipment and one big unlabeled box was brought down by rope. They would all have to be decontaminated. Everyone looked on with excitement, even Troy cracked a smile.

"Let's get you ready," said Scar to Lois. "Bill, can you help get Suri ready for the trip? We need to figure out how to move the boxes before Suri and Lois ascend." Scar and Lois left to go back and get Lois' things.

"I want to apologize for my initial abruptness toward you and Suri. I hope you will forgive me for not providing the appropriate welcome. There is no excuse for my rudeness." Scar looked down.

"Scar, you are the best. I had no appreciation for what was going on here and I can't believe what you are doing for everyone. There is hardly a need to apologize. You were following protocol and the final vote last evening meant a lot to me. I think we're good." She brought her arms around Scar's slim shoulders and gave her a strong hug.

Scar smiled and said, "Well, let's see what we can provide you for your new home. I wonder what Jane needs? Oh, I have an idea! Get yourself ready and I'll meet you at the port." Scar swiftly departed.

Lois and Suri were both suited. Clark had just come out of the chamber. "Let's talk every day. You be safe," and she touched Clark's gloved hand.

"You be safe," he said. "You know what it's like out there. Please let us know when you get there. By homing pigeon, if you need to." He smiled at her and they both understood what this meant. They were like twins, communicating silently, understanding each other without speaking.

Dorothy and Chris entered the room with a large sack. "We grabbed seeds, ones to complement what Jane has already. There are about two hundred and fifty species in this bag. We know you will use them appropriately. We'd be happy to help with information on planting once we have communications set up. Some seeds are for much later and some can be planted right away. We put a few potato tubers in here and even a few dahlias. You might even enjoy the orange-striated cosmos we picked out for you.

They were ready. Lois hugged each individual and was amazingly calm. Marcella had already given the dose of sedative to Suri, so she was sleeping on a small mattress that the Seed Bank wanted to give her for her trip. Clark and Karey came up for the final goodbye. Lois was still calm. It felt like the right decision. She knew Clark was going to be safe and that was all she could ask for. Dan and Betty were aware of the need for speed and kept the goodbye casual. The rest of the group waved goodbye as Hawk descended down the rungs.

Hawk made three trips up the rungs to bring the seeds and bags that Lois was bringing. It seemed like everyone was adding something to a mysterious bag for Lois. Lois slowly led Suri through the two barriers and then Hawk lifted her with his strong arms. Once he was up, she grabbed the mattress, then the first rung and looked up. There was Jane's smiling face looking down and welcoming her. She felt great.

Once Lois was in the helicopter, she handed them the mattress which fit perfectly in the back. Suri was shivering slightly in the corner, but quiet. Once they lifted off the ground, Lois peeked out the window and realized that nothing changed. She just sat back with Suri to make sure she stayed quiet and she did not have to look out. Jane and Hawk were in conversation.

She must have fallen asleep as she woke up to Hawk's loud voice say, "We're landing, Lois," said Hawk.

"There's Blue," said Jane. "Wow, has she changed! Her mouth is foaming white, like the other dogs we saw." Lois could hear him bark. "Is that Jake in the window? There." Hawk was leaning forward. "Blue's not right in the head, Hawk. I think that's what Jake is signaling. Can we land and still avoid him?"

Hawk took out his gun. "I think we need to do this, Jane."

"Hawk, really!" gasped Jane.

"Jane, I'm sorry. I really am. I think we need to do this. Our lives are in danger of Blue coming up and biting us. We can't take a chance."

"If Blue attacks, you can shoot. Otherwise, let's handle this once we know more."

"Deal," said Hawk. He carefully opened the door. Lois was watching through the door and saw the dog jumping up toward his leg. The dog was growling with dripping foam coming out of his mouth. Hawk pulled his leg back, carefully adjusted his gun and shot twice.

Suri jumped off her mattress onto Lois' lap. Her back legs poked into Lois stomach and she kept churning her legs back and forth. Lois could not settle her down right away. Suri had probably never heard a gun before.

Jane didn't speak. Lois asked, "Did you kill him? Is he dead?"

"Yes, I'm pretty sure he's dead. "Hawk looked back at Jane. "I'm really sorry."

"Hawk, I understand. Let's just get out of here." Lois surprised herself at how calm she felt. Jane was still quiet but looked like she was getting things ready to disembark. They slowly left the helicopter.

"Let me grab Suri and bring her in first," said Hawk. "That way, we don't have to worry and she will be safe with Jake."

As if just coming out of shock, Jane said, "We'll have to start decontamination, Lois. I hope you are okay."

"Yes, I am. I'm grateful to know that dog will not be tearing us apart. I'm grateful to the two of you and your quick thinking." Lois started to unwind her body, realizing how cramped she was and wanting to stretch out. This was the beginning of her great adventure. What a poignant way to start.

EPILOGUE

Jane was sitting in her favorite spot. The luxury of sipping tea was a pleasure reserved only for early mornings. The rest of the day would be filled. She felt the plants growing around her. The smell of green, yes, green was a smell for her that brought her the most pleasure. The glorious vapor that plants released and the moisture it left on her skin made these morning moments divine. Sun rays were starting to show through the sky lights, so appreciated, after the years of darkness. These were signs of a promising Spring. This was a true Spring after nine years of dark gray days and totally black nights with rare glimpses of stars or moon. Somehow, nine years of struggle seemed to get in the way of a perfect reflective moment. She was always comparing now to what happened before, how long it took to get to where they are and not knowing what each year's challenges would be like. That was okay, she remembered Dr. Blues' comment. They were no longer living a modern life, filled with every need being met. She used to meditate to be present, to calm her mind and feel better about herself. Now being present was a necessity to be alert to imminent danger and overall challenging circumstances. This was why these few unencumbered relaxing moments were so important.

They all discovered that everyone had some kind of mental challenges. Everyone was different, which was also a valuable teaching tool, noted by Dr. Blue as she coached everyone on how to name their challenge. "You're halfway there, if you can name it." She was so popular that Jane rarely had time to talk to her and had only brief periods when they were together.

Jane never thought about what a happy life would look like for her. Something started in the middle of this catastrophic event that changed her outlook on happiness forever. She and Hawk worked closely during their many hours together. They clicked functionally, with ease. It was not long after they returned from Dr. Blue's rescue that they surprised each other by expressing feelings of love. Initially, their lovemaking would compete with fatigue at the end of the day. However, the newness and passion still survived even now, despite daily energy drains. They both loved work and did everything together.

Jane was reminded of the famous meal she experienced before heading to pick up Clark and Karey. How they sat together, drinking Ocha, feeling some hope for the future and forming lasting bonds with each other. It was as if relationships were as important as survival itself. She thought of those moments of being together like a family. Her crystal-clear memory of everything that happened over those three days made it seem like yesterday.

Community was then and still is the Seed Bank's specialty. With Scar's non-leader leadership style, it worked, balancing issues with flexible structure, but always facing challenges as they arose. Hiding from difficult situations was an extravagance they could not afford and they sorted everything out carefully. They could not make mistakes. The Seed Bank formed a small society that was capable of sustaining itself and serving the larger community. The events from those days reset everything. Their embryonic stage of existing together, in close quarters, and creating something that had never been done before was exceptional. All members contributed in parallel, as Trudy would define it.

Once the Five Guys connected with their contacts in China, a month after Jane and Hawk returned home, they learned that not only did nuclear bombs land in hundreds of major cities around the world, but each bomb was followed by more bombs containing a silent killer–bombs filled with a fatal virus that affected the nervous system through skin contact or inhalation. It killed quickly, in roughly ten hours. The university scientists finally isolated the virus and determined is was a new, fast acting strain. Exposure to these biological bombs without protective gear was fatal. This prevented anyone from going outside unprotected. Most infected mammals died, but the small percentage that lived were altered, reflected in the dogs they saw with foaming mouths. They lived, demonstrating aggressive, violent behavior. Blue was infected and resisted the virus, leading to her aggressive behavior. This also made it impossible to have meat from livestock or pets outdoors. The only animals that could be raised were now indoors. Thankfully, Jane's chicken coop was protected and survived the fatal virus, providing eggs, chicks and an occasional stew. Until they had a crop of their magic soybeans, chicken and eggs were their only source of protein.

The immediate altruistic action was to warn people of the danger of exposure to the air and, later, a plan was developed to grow plants for survivors. The Seed Bank and the Five Guys, with Max's help, achieved most of these goals. The virus was the fast kill and radiation contamination was the slow killer. No one went outside without protection and they maintained strict protocol for re-entry from the beginning.

Suri gave a bark and slowly lifted her head to Jane, as if she was also thinking of Blue. Suri was a survivor but getting to the end of her life. She had trouble going up and down stairs and was generally in arthritic pain that she suffered through stoically. Jane looked out the window and saw a deer walking at the bottom of the gorge. These deer were somehow protected from radiation and virus. They showed no signs of aggressive behavior. The deeper part of the gorge, surrounded by trees, provided a filter against contamination. At least, that was the going theory which they were going to test very soon. Even as an old dog, Suri always provided a sensitivity they lacked. She alerted them of any animal or human outside of their home. Her hearing was limited, but whatever she used to sense invasive species was as sharp as the first day she came here.

The communication network, credited to the Five Guys, was able to advance their understanding of the virus, utilizing the university's labs, and make recommendations about the risk of exposing any skin to the outside environment. After they returned to Jane, Hawk returned to pick them and take them to Max's laboratory where they thrived intellectually. If Max had hesitated, all of them would have been exposed to the virus.

Looking back on the nine years, the accomplishments of the Seed Bank would fill libraries. Their bravery to keep challenging the norm, the insightful problem-solving and the relationships they developed were staggering. The relationship the Five Guys had with Max, Marcella's oldest son, was critical to advancing their knowledge of the outside world. Marcella was very proud and said Michael would have loved seeing him blossom, but she rarely saw her son.

Max's help was monumental in locating Dr. Blue. It took several attempts, but they finally got to her farm and found her barely alive, having suffered a minor stroke. After taking her back to the Seed Bank and getting her under Marcella's expert care, she made progress each day and her strength and determination made a difference to everyone she encountered. Dan had an idea of putting Lizzy and Dr. Blue together, which created amazing results. For even a mild case of stroke, like Dr. Blue's, she still had to go back to forming basic words and sentence structures with her mouth. Therefore, Lizzy was the perfect participant in her therapy sessions. After a year of care, Dr. Blue was back and a very important contributor to the general health of each member of the community. Jane was thankful for her and could not imagine such extreme survival conditions without her wisdom and practical nature. She was the one who asked Dan to organize sports teams, where everyone participated. They tried a lot of different things, but the one sport that lasted in the Seed Bank was ping pong.

Annual gatherings with the Seed Bank were celebrations, but well-choreographed to eliminate any danger involving exposure. These gatherings were exchanges of seeds, supplies, batteries, and an amazing number of things that were important, like sewing machine thread and needles. Dr. Blue was able to get back to her home to retrieve a large inventory of thread she used in making quilts. Quilts, thought Jane, who would have thought that was her hobby? At these annual gatherings, they also chose to celebrate weddings, births and a memorial around T zero with plenty of Ocha to go around. No surprise to anyone that there was the marriage of Luming and Scar. They already had a girl, Jade, with another on the way. Marriage was not Scar's thing, but Luming must have gently persuaded her that it was a good idea and they called it a union. They started to keep personal journals of their relationship history which no one was able to read, but Jane guessed it was full of insights and learnings they were finding as a couple. When she heard Scar was pregnant again, she realized Marcella was a busy gynecologist as well as a cardiologist. While not married, Dan and Betty formed a tight bond, establishing themselves as Elizabeth's official guardians. Most of the time, Lizzy was the bright bulb, the lifeline that kept everyone optimistic and hopeful. Lizzy grew into a red-haired beauty, not quite ten years old. She was so smart, curious and annoying that she kept Francine, Trudy and McLane busy, setting up problems for her to solve just to keep her quiet. While there were few survivors in Washington, D.C, Dan never gave up looking for Brenda. He monitored a frequency dedicated to finding survivors.

Clark and Karey did not waste time, nor did they mind populating their world. Karey was having her fourth child soon and Clark was a very attentive father. Jane could tell that Lois missed being there for Clark but she took great delight in the kind of man he had become.

Jane observed many moments between Lois and Jake and was delighted in how they formed a close friendship long before they became lovers. Unlike Jane and Hawk, who simmered and quickly became 'lover-friends', as Hawk named their relationship, Jake and Lois were slow to become a couple. Jake obviously admired Lois' technical skills and how she used algorithms and language to help decipher the many strange messages they received from China. All three groups were working on the messages being broadcasted from China, but it was Lois that ultimately cracked the code. It was probably the thousands of hours taking on the task of following each pattern and seeking what was behind the messages that formed their relationship.

Qiang continued to work on a larger scale and he found out the real message from the Lao Tzu poem. Poem number 67 was dissected in hundreds of ways and fortunately, the Seed Bank saved twenty-one different versions in their massive virtual library. The connection between

Poem number 67 and blowing up the world was determined to be this Chinese group called Yamagata. Their mission was to save the world. It did not make sense to anyone that these carefully placed bombs, strategically focused on massive destruction of modern civilization, was a way to save the world. However, if one looked more closely, the world they were saving was not humankind, but the world itself. A massive shutdown, under any means, even nuclear, stopped the slow, uncontrollable destruction of the planet. Everyone was then shoved into a survival mode that focused on real needs rather than superficial ones, one step at a time.

Beijing and Shanghai also experienced heavy nuclear bombs and the deadly follow-up virus, taking their population back two thousand years. There were underground enclaves that survived and who communicated with Qiang. Someone in the Chinese government, outside of the cities, found the group that set up all of the bombs and annihilated the whole mountain. No records were retrieved; at least that was what the authorities stated. The statement the government communicated was they apologized, but they were equally affected and would not take responsibility for actions against humanity. The bombing attacks changed the world climate, pushing continents into deep nuclear winter and offsetting any effect from global warming. The most successful small groups were underground, but very few had the magic seeds they needed in order to have nutrients necessary for healthy, long-term survival. With great collective ingenuity, the initial seeds were immediately germinated by the Seed Bank and food was handed off to the Five Guys via the drone until they got their growing operation running. The Seed Bank and university were producing crops twice a year, using the hydroponic methods developed by the Seed Bank and artificial lights. These seeds were disseminated to those they could reach. Dr. Shin, who also survived, was producing the life-giving seeds and providing growth kits that could be taken and used in distant locations.

The buildings where Jane and Jake worked met a tragic ending. The building finally collapsed, crushing the tunnels below it. The tunnels that were not under the buildings were sealed off, encasing those survivors in a tomb of unprecedented tragedy. Jane was helpless to save anyone there since spending time outside would have endangered all of their lives. The Seed Bank was protected from collapse since it survived the initial bombing and did not have the weight of a building above it to crush it. Most of the university tunnels collapsed, but about one hundred survivors were able to stay alive at the football stadium.

So, our circles are tight and small, thought Jane. Nine years was a long time with constant changes in weather, mostly from bad to worse. But now, they were getting a bit warmer and sunlight stayed longer each year. Nuclear winter slowly annihilated the virus that was causing so many deaths of individuals venturing out without the knowledge of the consequences.

"Hey, a penny for your thoughts," Lois said as she entered the sanctuary. "Isn't that the sun out there? When was that last time we actually experienced a sun ray in the morning like this?"

"Well, we had one about ten days ago. This reminds me that I need to start aligning the lights with the actual daylight hours for the season," said Jane. "Why are you up this early?"

"I don't know. I guess I was working on a problem. Just troubled with a population model I set up a few years ago. There was something I missed but could never figure it out and I woke up, problem solved! I was so excited, I couldn't sleep. Have you seen the boys?"

"I saw them playing video games in the family room this morning. There were signs that they made their own breakfast. Lois, your boys are so interesting. I'm finally getting a chance to witness how boys grow up to become competitive and aggressive. Tray was pushing Neven so hard that Neven got really mad, probably madder than I ever saw him get."

"Oh, great. If my boys are growing up to be assholes, Jane, I'll never forgive myself. You've always been interested in their growth. Are you sorry you didn't have kids?"

"Not really. I never had brothers and it is interesting to me that I have some of the same interests your boys have. That explains a lot about me," and she laughed. "At least it explains why I can't cook and hate to clean."

"What's up this morning?"

"I'm making a gift. I'm knitting a scarf for Dr. Blue."

"Let me see," and Lois reached over. "Where did you get this blue thread color?"

"Trudy and Bill planted a few hybrids of Indigo and gave me the seeds. I've had a plant over in the corner and processed it last week. I took an old sweater and dyed it and now it is ready to be knit into something. Hope I can get it done by the time we get together. I would like to surprise Dr. Blue with this. Just knitting and purling. A stockinet pattern is what it's called."

"Jane, that is pretty cool. I'm sure she'll love it, especially since you are doing something out of your comfort zone."

"She's an inspiration to all of us, Lois. Sharme maintains the information Dr. Blue shared with the Seed Bank about survivor's guilt was invaluable. There's a physical manifestation from survivor's guilt. Without the body scan work, where she leads others in a meditation that honed in on where the deeper feelings resided, they would not have been able to accomplish all that they did."

"That's so interesting, Jane. I had no idea. Our annual visits to the Seed Bank are not long enough to know how everyone is doing."

Jane smiled. "You spend a lot of your time with Luming, Lois. What a special friendship that has been for you."

"Yes," as Lois turned to look at Jane rather than out onto the greenhouse plants. "I like to think that our relationship fills something that Scar, or Jake, for that matter, can't provide. We all need to have someone that can listen to us and it is not always the person you are closest to. Dr. Blue was very helpful in noticing this and helping me sort out my feelings and relationships."

"I'm making breakfast. How about French Tofu Toast?" Jake said as he walked in the sanctuary. "That reminds me, we need to make up our seed list for the gathering. If our testing is validated, this will be the first year we can garden outside and I want to make sure we can get a field planted of wheat. There's a sourdough starter I want to make as well. Imagine, an active culture of yeast for baking bread!"

"Stop that. I'm getting hungry," and Lois leaned over to peck Jake on the cheek. "Are you coming, Jane?"

"You two go ahead. Hawk and I are preparing to fast for a few days. It's best if we do not hang out with you two initially," and Jane smiled.

"You two and your fasting," said Jake. "We'll see you later."

Jane shifted her position in her chair and started her breathing meditation once they left. She cleared her busy mind and felt the freedom she was now enjoying. The absence of the business of doing, thinking and creating was what she needed. Once she felt centered, she went into a deeper place. A soft lip on her neck brought her into the room and she smiled over at Hawk who was already sitting next to her. I wonder if I was sleeping instead of meditating, thought Jane. She had no awareness of Hawk entering the room. He sat for a while in his breathing posture. She loved his long torso and straight black hair. Jane was amazed at how they stumbled on meditating together. They did everything fast. Initially, Jane was working every conceivable hour of the day and some of the night. Hawk became concerned about her, but there was so much to do and to think about. He ran across a shelf in her library of meditation books that Dr. Blue gave her over the years, barely read, of course. Hawk read them, every one. He approached her with an idea of doing this together and the rest came slowly, but with an impact that helped her anxiety about taking care of every detail. What a pain she must have been to be around. They found the peace that both of them craved and found that all of the scientific, creative work their lives required them to do was even better with the added benefit of having more patience. Meditation literally saved her life. The path they chose brought their relationship past the physical. She was definitely blessed and forever grateful to Dr. Blue for giving her such a gift.

THE END

ACKNOWLEDGMENTS

"The best way out is always through."
-Robert Frost

April 4, 2020.
This is a unique time. Ironically, we are involved in a global, catastrophic period of history. A heartbreaking phase involving social distancing and isolation. Health care workers, pharmaceutical innovations, and medical devices are providing life support and hope. The Government is assisting individuals and companies with financial funds. Lastly, our masters of mindfulness are spreading their practices in digital presentations, like Zoom, to lessen fear and anxiety.

This book was in my head for a decade. R.E.M.'s song, The End of The World As We Know, was sung at high volume on the commute to work. Now relieved of the burden of releasing the story into this world, I have mixed feelings. Is this an opportune time to be publishing Apocalyptic Fiction? I'll hang on the thought that hopefully it will be engaging, refreshing, and intriguing.

I want to thank Kathie Giorgio, Kathleen Eull, Deb Byers, Jody Semchuck, Jane Iwan, Anna Maria Paleocrassas, Summer Hanford, David King, Suzanne Weinstein, All Writer's Workplace & Workshop Annual Retreat, The Cocos, Geneen Hogan, The Women's Leadership Community, Mindful Self Compassion, Making Friends with Yourself, and last but not least Jon Nornberg. These contributors provided insight, editing and enthusiasm about all aspects of the writing process and feedback as they read hundreds of pages about five interesting characters.

ABOUT THE AUTHOR

Sharon K. Grosh is the author of *Lazarus Rising*, an apocalyptic fiction inspired by her reading John Hersey's *Hiroshima* at a young age.

A textile artist as well as an author, Sharon creates sumi-e paintings, Indigo-Shibori fabric wall hangings, and teaches Mindful Self-Compassion to teens in and around Afton, Minnesota, where she lives. She is a member of the Art Retreat Tamarindo and AllWriters' Workplace and Workshop. *Lazarus Rising* is her first novel.

NOTE FROM THE AUTHOR

Word-of-mouth is crucial for any author to succeed. If you enjoyed *Lazarus Rising*, please leave a review online—anywhere you are able. Even if it's just a sentence or two. It would make all the difference and would be very much appreciated.

Thanks!
Sharon

Thank you so much for checking out one of our **Dystopian Sci-Fi** novels.

If you enjoy our book, please check out our recommended title
for your next great read!

Shadow City by Anna Mocikat

"*SHADOW CITY* is full of adventure, thrills, and twists and turns. The
characters are fully realized and the swift pace keeps the story moving
along, so readers will likely find themselves turning pages in rapid
succession."
–IndieReader

View other Black Rose Writing titles at
www.blackrosewriting.com/books and use promo code
PRINT to receive a **20% discount** when purchasing.